ACTION PAYOFF

Marc Dean had a beautiful sex-bomb of a playmate picked up in an orgiastic night of carnival in Rio.

Marc Dean had a crew of fighting men under him hand-picked from all over the globe.

Marc Dean had a mission that was worth all the money he was being paid if he succeeded—and worth his life if he failed.

Marc Dean had the kind of action he lusted for—and the kind of enemy he would have fought for free. . . .

THE SECRET OF SAN FELIPE

THE MERCENARY #2

PAPERBACK TRADE INN
145 E. 14 Mile Rd.
Clawson, MI 48017
(248) 307-0226

SIGNET Books You'll Enjoy

- ☐ **TRIPLE** by Ken Follett. (#E9447—$3.50)
- ☐ **EYE OF THE NEEDLE** by Ken Follett. (#E9550—$3.50)
- ☐ **THE REVENANT** by Brana Lobel. (#E9451—$2.25)*
- ☐ **THE BLACK HORDE** by Richard Lewis. (#E9454—$1.75)
- ☐ **A FEAST FOR SPIDERS** by Kenneth L. Evans. (#J9484—$1.95)*
- ☐ **THE DARK** by James Herbert. (#E9403—$2.95)
- ☐ **THE DEATH MECHANIC** by A. D. Hutter. (#J9410—$1.95)*
- ☐ **THE MAGNATE** by Jack Mayfield. (#E9411—$2.25)*
- ☐ **THE SURROGATE** by Nick Sharman. (#E9293—$2.50)*
- ☐ **THE SCOURGE** by Nick Sharman. (#E9114—$2.25)*
- ☐ **INTENSIVE FEAR** by Nick Christian. (#E9341—$2.25)*
- ☐ **AUCTION!** by Tom Murphy. (#E9478—$2.95)
- ☐ **ELISE** by Sara Reavin. (#E9483—$2.95)
- ☐ **HAWK OF MAY** by Gillian Bradshaw. (#E9765—$2.75)*
- ☐ **GAMEMAKER** by David Cohter. (#E9766—$2.50)*
- ☐ **CUBAN DEATH-LIFT** (3rd in the MacMorgan series) by Randy Striker. (#J9768—$1.95)*

* Price slightly higher in Canada

Buy them at your local bookstore or use this convenient coupon for ordering.

THE NEW AMERICAN LIBRARY, INC.,
P.O. Box 999, Bergenfield, New Jersey 07621

Please send me the SIGNET BOOKS I have checked above. I am enclosing
$_____ (please add 50¢ to this order to cover postage and handling).
Send check or money order—no cash or C.O.D.'s. Prices and numbers are
subject to change without notice.

Name _____

Address _____

City_____ State_____ Zip Code_____

Allow 4-6 weeks for delivery.
This offer is subject to withdrawal without notice.

THE SECRET OF SAN FELIPE

#2

PETER BUCK

A SIGNET BOOK
NEW AMERICAN LIBRARY
TIMES MIRROR

PUBLISHER'S NOTE

This novel is a work of fiction. Names, characters, places, and incidents are either the product of the author's imagination or are used fictitiously, and any resemblance to actual persons, living or dead, events, or locales is entirely coincidental.

NAL BOOKS ARE AVAILABLE AT QUANTITY DISCOUNTS WHEN USED TO PROMOTE PRODUCTS OR SERVICES. FOR INFORMATION PLEASE WRITE TO PREMIUM MARKETING DIVISION, THE NEW AMERICAN LIBRARY, INC., 1633 BROADWAY, NEW YORK, NEW YORK 10019.

Copyright © 1981 by The New American Library, Inc.

All rights reserved

The first chapter of this book appeared in Thirteen for the Kill, the first volume of this series.

SIGNET TRADEMARK REG. U.S. PAT. OFF. AND FOREIGN COUNTRIES
REGISTERED TRADEMARK—MARCA REGISTRADA
HECHO EN CHICAGO, U.S.A.

SIGNET, SIGNET CLASSICS, MENTOR, PLUME, MERIDIAN AND NAL BOOKS are published by The New American Library, Inc., 1633 Broadway, New York, New York 10019

First Printing, July, 1981

1 2 3 4 5 6 7 8 9

PRINTED IN THE UNITED STATES OF AMERICA

For the late Stan Sefton,
who knew South America
before the corruption.

Prologue

In the background of [guerrilla] wars are the mercenaries. Not all are white, but most are. Many come from former colonies or southern Africa, but some are freebooters. . . . Some are attracted by promises of high pay, but few receive it. Others simply cannot adjust to a normal life after service in their own countries' armies. . . . Their military standard varies from the solid professionalism of the ex-regular to the erratic behavior of the young man with a liking for guns. Their performance in the field depends on their equipment and the quality of the opposition.
—William Fowler

The island batteries began firing when the leading assault craft was still half a mile offshore. The attackers, crouched behind steel gunwales in their netted and camouflaged combat gear, saw flame belching from the gun muzzles reflected on low cloud an instant before the first shellbursts fountained from the dark water. Then the tropical predawn blackness was split in a hundred places as all hell broke loose around the tiny port and along the cliffs on either side of the inlet.

It wasn't a very big raid—three World War II infantry landing craft, each carrying twenty men, and a remodeled, converted LVT-6, modified to take a Saladin armored car and a Büssing-NAG truck laden with arms and explosives. The mother ship from which they had been disembarked, an old Florida automobile ferry, lay hove-to safely out of range of the guns.

The defense wasn't all that strong, either: it just seemed alarmingly powerful after the dark silence of a moonless Caribbean night. In fact, according to intelligence reports smuggled out of the island, the port commander had at his disposal four Oerlikons; two 75mm tank guns; a dozen 105mm mortars; a quantity of heavy machine guns, bazookas, and 40mm cannon; and two self-propelled Ontos vehicles, each firing six 106mm recoilless rifles. "No radar, thank Christ, no sensors, and no computerized fields of fire!" the leader of the expedition said to the helmsman as the LVT plowed at eight knots through the swell. "I guess the bossman can't afford as much ironmongery as he would like to defend this neck of the woods."

The same wide-disk caterpillars that could rattle the tracked landing vehicle up to 20 mph on dry land also propelled it through the water, and it was the phosphorescence from the froth churned up by these rather than the whine of the 250-horsepower diesels in the stern that had alerted the islanders to the attack.

The night was alive with orange, scarlet, and crimson flashes crisscrossed by multicolored streams of tracer as the three LCI's, moving at more than twice the speed of the heavy transporter, forged ahead toward the port. The roar and thwack of 75's, the hammering of the Oerlikons, and the sharp stutter of automatic fire mingled with the sound of the invaders' weapons to compete with the shells exploding among the raiding vessels.

The men in the LCI's were mercenaries—Puerto Ricans, Cubans, expatriates from Nicaragua, Venezuela, and the former British West Indies, officered by a small group of Americans and Europeans. Their mission was neither to take the town nor to establish any kind of bridgehead, but simply to ensure the safe landing of the two vehicles in the LVT ... and make sure that they were able to drive off into the interior unmolested.

They were armed with the latest Russian Kalashnikov AKM automatic rifles, Skorpion machine pistols from Czechoslovakia, Soviet RPG-7 rocket launchers, and a variety of mortars and grenades. But the weapons stacked to the canvas roof of the 4½-ton ex-Wehrmacht Büssing truck were all manufactured in the United States or at the FN arsenal near Liège, in Belgium. Destined for rebels whom certain powers wished to help but dared not openly support, they would be unloaded as soon as the convoy reached the mountains in the center of the island and dispersed among the guerrilla bands hiding there. It was the devout hope of the international businessmen who had, with government encouragement, financed the operation that these groups, spearheaded by the Saladin armored car, would eventually march on the capital and oust the dictator who was threatening to sequester the profitable mines in the interior.

"The idea is to make them think it's some kind of invasion raid," the spokesman for the business interests had told them. "Tie down the whole port defense until the two vehicles have gotten clear—then you can withdraw your men as if the attack had been beaten off." The native islanders crewing the truck and the armored car, he said, were familiar with dirt roads and trails that could lead them to the rebel headquarters without the risk of any interference from the dictator's patrols.

"The 75's are located on top of the bluff—one on either side of the creek mouth," the commander of the expedition had said at the final briefing. "The two mobile Ontos batteries—again one on either side—can maneuver between there and the port at head of the inlet. It's about three hundred yards in. The rest of the hardware is deployed around the basin."

A huge African who was in charge of the leading LCI said, "You mean we have to run a three-hundred gauntlet, Cap? Being shot at by 75's and a dozen 106mm pom-poms before we can get ashore?"

"Yeah. But we got the two best mortar teams in the islands aboard the LVT," the leader replied. He was a tall, muscular American with pale hair and blue eyes. "You got your RPG-7's on each of the landing craft. Between us, we concentrate all our firepower on the run-in on just *one* side of the creek. That way, if we knock out the two sets of guns there, we can sail on in the lee of the other bluff, knowing that our craft will be too close inshore to be touched: they'll be in dead water, safely below the traverse of the batteries above."

"Okay, Cap—but those Ontos bastards are tough weapons. Six 106mm barrels firing at once—that packs some punch!"

"Sure. But they're easy targets on direct aim: there's a hell of a back-blast visible from those eight-foot barrels . . . and one hit puts the whole half-dozen out of action."

The actual assault proved the commander right. In the sky, star shells wrapped red and green octopus arms around the dark as the flotilla approached the two small headlands framing the inlet. Soon the explosions from mortars and rocket launchers added vivid orange flashes to the twinkling points of fire along the right-hand clifftop. Then a parachute flare dissolved the night to silver the roofs of the port.

At once one of the mortars in the bows of the LVT scored a direct hit on the Ontos vehicle. Detonating rounds etched firecracker patterns against the dark bulk of the island as the stricken battery flared into oblivion. Soon afterward—perhaps because the streams of lead hosed shoreward from the LCI's had killed the crew—the 75mm gun on the right headland ceased firing.

The expedition leader barked instructions into the microphone of a hand-held radio. The three landing craft wheeled through a forty-five-degree turn and headed for the opposite bluff. Two of them made it, but the third, a fraction slow answering to the helm, blew up in a spectacular eruption of flame and steam, victim of a concerted attack from the remaining Ontos and 75.

Sailing through the tower of white water still falling

back into the sea, the cumbersome LVT was caught in a hail of crossfire from the clifftop and the port. Steel-jacketed slugs thrashed the upperworks; antitank grenades burst harmlessly against her heavily armored sides. "Mazzari!" the leader shouted into his mouthpiece. "Run ashore as soon as that goddamn bluff's low enough to scale. Send half your men to silence that shit on the headland. The rest can work their way inland and join Neilsen's team on the west of the basin."

"Willco!" the big African's voice crackled in the receiver.

Below the white-painted houses surrounding the basin, a dozen fishing boats rocked in the wash of the landing craft. Men from the second LCI waded ashore between them, firing submachine guns from the hip. Beneath the barnacle-encrusted piers of a wooden jetty, half of Mazzari's men stole behind the hulls of private powerboats to link up with them. But the main objective—the reason this small port had been chosen rather than another—was a stone slipway slanting down into the water from a boatbuilder's yard at one side of the basin.

Two hundred yards away, the LVT maneuvered through 180 degrees in the center of the creek and then backed up toward the paved slope, its caterpillars churning.

The port area was now becoming an inferno. Flames from a tarred shack set alight by a grenade flickered redly on the underside of a pall of smoke hanging over the town. In the fiery light, invaders scrambled up banks of rubble spilling into the water where the RPG-7's rockets had breached the quay. They charged along the jetty, blasting the strongpoints from which Oerlikon and machine-gun volleys were sweeping the dock. Grenades and mortar shells exploding in the narrow lanes leading to the port punctuated the incessant rattle of small-arms fire. Voices shouted, boots clattered on cobbles, soldiers screamed and died. The oily surface of the harbor was strewn with planks and splintered spars, its crimson reflections pockmarked by the heads of survivors swimming away from the sunken assault craft.

As the parachute flare guttered and died, allowing darkness to settle again over the sea, the caterpillars of the LVT grounded on the submerged portion of the slipway. Steel links skidded on the weed-slimed surface, bit through to the stone, and slowly hauled the big amphibian out of the water.

Fierce hand-to-hand fighting had broken out on the headland, but the crew manning the remaining 75 managed to swing the gun around and fire two shots inland before they were overwhelmed by Mazzari's men. Their aim was good.

The first round burst high up on the LVT's side, buckling the plates and reducing the mortar platform to a tangle of steel sliding with fragments of human flesh and brain. The second blew off the port caterpillar track and sheared a drive shaft.

It was no longer important. The target had been reached. With a rattle of chains, the ramp at the stern of the vessel slammed down, and the truck, followed by the Saladin armored car, roared out onto the slipway. Two minutes later, screened by a line of smoke canisters launched from the Saladin, they were on a tarmac highway heading at 45 mph for the intersection where a dirt road led to the mountains.

As they passed through the outskirts of the tiny port, the gunner in the six-wheeled Saladin's turret blasted two of his 75mm shells into a blockhouse from which Oerlikons were firing. The rest of the vehicle's forty-three-round magazine was too valuable to the rebel cause to waste. Beneath the canvas top of the German truck there were crates of Armalite rifles, MP40 machine pistols, Belgian-made Uzi submachine guns, and a quantity of bazookas and mortar tubes. In addition to grenades, cases of plastic explosive and antipersonnel mines, the truck carried more than one hundred thousand rounds of 7.62, 5.56, and 9mm ammunition in magazines and belts.

The assault group's instructions had been to keep the port defenses tied down for a quarter of an hour after the convoy had left. In that time, the rebel islanders had told them, they could be in the foothills beyond any possibility of pursuit.

Promptly fifteen minutes after the LVT's ramp had grounded, the commander blew a whistle and then shouted instructions into his radio. With the helmsman and the remaining member of his crew, he quit the stricken amphibian, leaping from the slipway into the water and wading to Neilsen's assault craft among the fishing boats.

Dodging behind bollards and stacks of lobster pots, crouching in the shelter of an upturned dory, Neilsen's men fell back toward the jetty, firing as they retreated. Five houses were burning, the streets around the harbor were littered with rubble, and the quay was strewn with dead.

The two halves of Mazzari's team had joined up and reembarked in the second LCI. As soon as the wounded, under cover of the high dockside, had been loaded into Neilsen's craft, the ramps were raised and the two vessels backed out into the creek and headed for the open sea.

Out of the seventy-odd mercenaries who took part in the raid, seventeen were killed or missing, a further thirteen were wounded, and three were taken prisoner. ("Any sense, and those poor bastards'll bite on their cyanide capsules," one of the survivors said sourly as they climbed back aboard the mother ship. " 'Less they wanna be gagged wtih their own balls and then strangled with their guts!")

On the way back to Florida, the go-between who had arranged the assault with the expedition leader paid out the end money in cash, with an agreed bonus to go to the dependents of those killed. "Where to now?" the leader asked Mazzari as the big African buttoned the wad of bills into his breast pocket.

Mazzari grinned. His thick lips puckered and he whistled the first few bars of "Kingston Market."

"Jamaica?"

"There's a torch singer in Montego Bay," Mazzari said. He shook his head. "Oh, *brother!*" And then: "What about you, Cap?"

"I feel like music too," the American replied. "Singing and dancing. You know. I figured on heading for Brazil and staying in Rio awhile."

The Destroyers

> *It is interesting and disturbing to note the attacks on such organizations as the CIA, the FBI, and Special Branch by left-wing writers, for these are the bodies which organizations who would take over a country have most cause to fear. Hence if such official bodies can be considered undemocratic . . . then the task of those who would destroy freedom is that much easier.*
> —Toby Wrigley

1

A blond who was slightly overweight sat next to the slender brunette at the wheel of the red convertible. White teeth gleamed in tanned faces as the car swept past Miguel da Silva on his mule and then braked for the first of the hairpins leading down the mountainside to the main road and to Rio de Janeiro.

The old man turned and watched it out of sight around a shoulder of the sun-baked rock face. Plenty of young people drove up here at weekends, but it was unusual to see two girls alone in a car. He listened to the squeal of tires and the rising bellow of the exhaust as the convertible accelerated away from the corner; then he transferred his gaze to the brush-covered scree which dropped away to his right. Presently the car reappeared on a loop of road far below him, its coachwork winking in the bright light as it arrowed down toward the last of the curves.

Sixty feet below the parapet guarding the bend, the broad highway leading to the capital bisected the valley. And just beyond the curve, hidden from the girls in the low sports car but clearly visible to Miguel da Silva, there was an ancient truck laden with fruit blocking the roadway. Evidently the driver had found himself on the wrong route; he was now laboriously turning his decrepit vehicle before he returned to the highway.

The convertible entered the hairpin too fast. Da Silva saw its brake lights blaze red as the brunette stamped on the pedal. The car slewed sideways, was expertly corrected, and snaked out of the bend . . . to find the way almost completely obstructed by the truck. Again the twin lights glowed, and then the girl, realizing that she could never stop in time, swung the wheel over in a desperate attempt to squeeze through between the tailgate of the truck and the parapet.

But the convertible, already partly out of control, lurched sideways again and slammed into the low wall.

Horror-struck, da Silva saw it burst through the parapet, rise into the air, and then plunge out of sight onto the steep slope linking the mountain road with the highway below. As the truck driver leaped from his cab to run to the edge, a cloud of dust mushroomed up over the shattered wall. It seemed to the old man that seconds passed before the sound of the impact floated up to him through the heat.

"Will they live?" the police captain asked the hospital intern.

The young doctor raised white-coated shoulders in a professional shrug. "Barring unforeseen complications," he said. "It was fortunate for them that it was an open car. They were both flung out before it landed upside down on the rock."

"And their injuries?"

"Multiple contusions and extensive laceration in each case. The one who was driving broke both legs against the wheel as she came out. But the other, the blond, is really worse off: there were boulders among the scrub where she landed." The intern permitted himself a nonprofessional grin. "Well covered, that one is: a delicious body! Even so, she collected a cracked skull, a fractured pelvis, and several broken ribs. It will be some months before she can bear the weight of a man again."

The policeman frowned. He did not like to think of his cases as human beings; they were numbers on a dossier. "They are still unconscious, both of them?" he said primly.

"And likely to remain so for some time. It was nearly half an hour before the ambulance got to them, and the sun is fierce at that time in the afternoon."

"All afternoon, this time of the year," the captain said. He sighed, flicking a speck of dust from the sleeve of his olive-green uniform. "I suppose we had better go through the motions. I'll have to make a report, get in touch with relatives, and so on. Shall we have a look at their effects?"

The intern nodded and led the way to an anteroom at the far end of the rubber-tiled hospital corridor. A highway patrolman sprang to attention and saluted as the two men entered. Behind him, the sounds of suburban traffic filtered through green shutters and closed out the dusk.

"Ah, Garcia," the policeman said, returning the salute. "What have we discovered about these unfortunate ladies?"

The man looked uncomfortable. "Captain," he said, "I am very sorry, but there is nothing, nothing at all."

"Nothing? But their names, surely? Their addresses?"

Garcia shook his head slowly. "Nothing," he repeated. "No driver's license, no insurance certificate, no passports, no papers at all. I think they are Americans, but so far I have been unable to make any positive identification."

"You have tried the embassy, of course?"

"Naturally. Nobody is missing."

The captain stared in disbelief. "That is very curious," he said at last. "Let us see if perhaps their clothes . . ."

He moved across the room to a table on which were two purses and their contents, a pair of shattered sunglasses, shoes, several tourist maps, an entertainment guide to Rio, and two piles of bloodstained clothing.

"I am afraid we had to cut the garments quite a bit . . . to get them off, you see," the young doctor began apologetically.

"It does not matter," the policeman said. He picked up the ripped material gingerly and examined each item—brightly colored blouses, underclothes, a skirt, what had once been a pair of white trousers. Finally he dropped the last one back on the table and turned to the doctor. "The man is right," he said. "This is very odd: not one of these things has a name tag on it; even the labels and the makers' names have been removed."

"It is the same with the purses, Captain," the patrolman interrupted. "See—cigarettes, lighters, money, lipsticks and compacts, keys, suntan oil, Kleenex . . . but no letters, no papers of any kind."

"Evidently," the captain said, "these are ladies who wished to remain incognito. But we have our duty to perform; we must force ourselves to be sufficiently ungallant as to unmask them." He stretched his lips in what was meant to be a smile. "There will, after all, be relatives who must be informed."

Garcia dutifully returned the smile. "Yes, Captain," he said.

"No doubt the laboratory could trace them eventually through these clothes and the shoes, but for an ordinary road accident, it hardly seems . . ." The captain paused. He said, "What about this accident, by the way? How did it happen? What do the witnesses say?"

"There were witnesses in three different cars on the highway. But all they saw was, so to speak, the second part of the accident. They saw the convertible bounce down the bank after it had broken through the parapet of the road above."

"Were there no witnesses up there?"

"We have found none."

"But what caused the accident? *Why* did the car break through the parapet?"

"We could find no reason for that either, sir. There were two skid marks just after the hairpin, about a hundred and fifty yards from the breach in the wall—as though someone had braked hard there. But of course they could have been made by some other car: those are dangerous curves if you do not know the road."

"Quite," the captain said dryly. "So, other than the broken wall, there are no marks at all where the car left the road?"

"No, Captain. None at all."

"This begins to get very puzzling. What about the car itself, then?"

"It was an Alfa Romeo 2000; a beautiful car," Garcia said enviously. "It is completely wrecked, beyond any hope of repair."

"Yes, yes," the captain prompted gently. "No doubt. But what I meant . . . What is its registration number, Garcia? Where does it come from? What was there inside it of interest?"

The patrolman shook his head. "Another blank, I am afraid. There was a Japanese transistor radio, an aerosol for cleaning the windshield, a pair of string gloves in the cubbyhole, brandy in a flask that was smashed inside a door pocket. No papers."

"And the owner's name?"

"The car was rented, Captain. Locally registered and hired from a garage two blocks inland from Copacabana."

"Ah. Perhaps the hire company can give us a line on the person who rented it?"

"Yes, sir. Gomes is over there now, making inquiries."

But the rental company was unable to reveal the name either of the driver or of her companion. The papers had been signed on behalf of an organization.

"S-I-S-T-E-R-S?" the police captain read out slowly in his office the next morning. "What the devil does that stand for? Is it some kind of a religious organization?"

"Not exactly. It is a *yanqui* welfare foundation," the patrolman called Gomes said. "It means . . ." He consulted a piece of paper in his hand. "It means Sanders International—Southern Territories Emergency Resettlement Service."

"My God! What a mouthful! I have never heard of this organization, frankly. What are they doing here? Do they have an office in the city?"

"We have no idea what they were doing, but from the descriptions, these two were the ones who booked the car all right. Sanders International is a trust: a millionaire of that name left money so that a worldwide charitable institution could be formed. This particular branch concentrates mainly on South America—doing good works where they are needed, looking after earthquake survivors, helping famine victims, that kind of thing."

"We have neither earthquakes nor famines in Rio."

"No, sir. We don't have a SISTERS office, either."

"Perhaps it is just as well." The captain eased his collar away from his neck with a damp finger. It was stuffy in his office; there was not enough window space. "Did anyone think to check out the mileage on the car's trip recorder against the mileage logged by the garage when it was rented?"

Gomes' plump cheeks bunched in a self-congratulatory smile. "Yes, Captain. I got the figures from the clerk at the garage and went to look at the wreck early this morning. It had covered well over a thousand miles since it was hired three days ago."

"Ha! If they had no passports, they could not have crossed a frontier. Let us, therefore, take a look . . ."

The captain rose from his desk, removed his jacket and draped it over the back of his chair, picked up an outsize pair of wooden dividers, and walked to a wall map. The ceiling fan in that corner of the room stirred the hot, heavy air and detached a tendril of hair from his carefully groomed head as he applied the points of the dividers to the scale. "Yes," he said a moment later. "As I thought. . . . They could have been to Porto Alegre, Bahia, or Brasilia. Or, for that matter, done many small trips locally. But get in touch with our people in those cities and ask if *they* have any mission or bureau run by this foreign charity."

"Yes, sir."

The officer sat down at his desk again. He took a small hand mirror from a drawer and studied his face. Above the thin mustache, there were hollows in his cheeks, and the sallow skin below his eyes was pouched and puffy. He was already overworked: there had been a series of burglaries with violence among the luxury villas in his subdivision, and his superiors were pressing for results. Now he was burdened with this extra mystery. If only, he thought, the *yanqui* girls had written off their car farther away from the city, or waited until the weather was less oppressive...

He loosened his tie and patted his forehead with a white handkerchief. "I am not happy with this affair of the witnesses," he said, combing his hair into place and putting the mirror back in its drawer. "Surely somebody must have seen what happened? It is a busy road, and after all, *something* must have caused the car to break through that wall! Put out a message on the radio. You know: an accident occurred... a red sports car left the road... two foreign women gravely injured... will anyone who saw the accident please contact... The old routine."

"Very well, Captain."

"And, Gomes, you had better take Garcia and go back to the hospital. If these girls are still unconscious, ask permission to fingerprint them. Wire the prints to Washington. In the matter of identification, we might save ourselves a lot of trouble that way."

2

The room was small and its one window faced the slender monolith of the United Nations Building across New York's East River. A short, spare, gray man with shell glasses and a military bearing sat behind a big desk with his back to the window, staring at four pieces of paper that he had taken from his In tray. Two of them were onionskin carbon flimsies, one was a short newspaper cutting pasted onto a sheet of A4 bond, and the last was a leaf torn from a calendar memo pad on which a single word was scrawled in pencil.

The man—he was the regional director in charge of an outpost of the Central Intelligence Agency—moved the papers around on the polished teak desktop and read them again. Finally he shrugged and flipped down the switch of an intercom. "Okay," he said, "you can send him in now."

There was a perfunctory knock on the door. Hugh Quinnel

strode into the room—tall, lanky, sallow-faced; a mournful-looking individual with pale eyes separated by a prominent blade of a nose. "You wanted to see me, sir?"

"Yes," the gray man said. "I want you to read these four pieces of paper. Sit down and take a look." He flicked the press cutting and the two carbons across the desk as Quinnel took a chair. After a quick glance at the director, he began to read.

The cutting was from that morning's edition of one of the New York dailies. It was clipped from an inside page, below the fold, and was headed "SISTERS IN SMASHUP." The story read:

Rio de Janeiro, Wednesday—*Two young women, believed to be American citizens, were seriously injured in an auto accident near the Brazilian ex-capital yesterday when their sports car crashed through the retaining wall bordering a mountain road and fell to the highway below. They are thought to be members of a Sanders International (SISTERS) welfare team. Every effort is being made to establish the identity of the two women, neither of whom had regained consciousness early today.*

One of the carbons was a copy of a letter from the SISTERS headquarters in the East Fifties to the Rio police. It was signed Caroline Bowling and stated succinctly that the service had no teams presently operating in Rio, Porto Alegre, Brasilia, or indeed anyplace in Brazil. The other was a copy of a cable to the same address from the FBI. It read:

160780/1118 YOUR 150780/1622 PRINTS IDENTIFY AAA CHARMIAN WEISENBURGER TWENTY-NINE CONVICTED LOS ANGELES 1975 FELONY 1977 1978 VICE BBB BERNADETTE ANCARINI TWENTY-THREE CONVICTED BERKELEY 1977 VICE PRESENTLY WANTED FRAUD CHARGES NEVADA STOP AIRMAILED DETAILS FOLLOW PLEASE DETAIN BBB AND ADVISE.

Quinnel placed the papers carefully back on the desk and raised inquiring eyebrows at his superior. "And the fourth, sir?"

The director spun the memo sheet around so that he could read it. The penciled scrawl read: *"Quinnel?"*

Quinnel scratched his head. He looked more like an overgrown schoolboy than a field operative working for the world's most powerful intelligence agency. The cuffs of his gray flannel pants terminated at ankle height, bony wrists protruded from the short sleeves of his tweed jacket, and there was an unruly tuft of hair sprouting fanwise from the back of his scalp. "Don't quite get the message," he said. "So two call girls wreck an auto in Rio. The newshounds figure them for SISTERS, but they ain't. So what has this to do with us—or with me?"

"The balance of probabilities has to do with us," the director said. "You state the problem too simply. The newspaper cutting was one of the minor pieces of trivia that come my way. I should never have given it a second thought if I hadn't run into Mrs. Bowling this morning. She happened to mention this odd query from the Rio police. Then, as a matter of routine, I was looking through the courtesy copies sent to me by the FBI and I noticed the cable. Taken together, the three things—"

" 'Kay. But I still don't. . . ."

"You don't think it's curious? Two American citizens, both with police records, pass themselves off in a friendly foreign country as members of an eminently respectable trust based in New York—you don't find that strange?"

"Sure it's strange. If they were doing that. But were they in fact? Maybe the papers got it wrong."

"I have been in touch with Rio by radio," the director said. "There's no doubt about it: the car was hired and all the documents they produced were on official SISTERS paper. Yet *in* the car itself they appear to have gone to a great deal of trouble to remove any reference to the organization or to their own identity. There were no papers, no licenses, no insurance certificates, no letters among their effects. Even their clothes had all the tabs removed."

"Yeah. Kind of screwball," Quinnel admitted. He spoke in short, staccato bursts, discarding pronouns, conjunctions, and auxiliary verbs right and left. "Doesn't add up. Can't see any sense in it."

"One would think that anyone sailing under the wrong flag, as it were, would keep it flying especially bravely," the director said. "To foster the illusion. Of course, there may be nothing more to it than a simple case of intended fraud or false pretenses. They may just have been setting up some kind of confidence trick. On the other hand . . ." He paused.

Quinnel said nothing. He waited patiently, his forearms

16

resting on his splayed knees, the fingers of his large hands interlaced.

"You're relieving Ruggiero on Latin-American Station Three, aren't you?" the director said.

Quinnel nodded. "Off tonight."

"Exactly. I may be out on a limb, but I've got a hunch ... Well, let's say I figure it might be worth our while to have you run down to Rio and nose around a couple of days."

" 'Kay. What do you want me to check out? What should I do?"

"Be discreet, above all. You know how careful we have to be these days. The agency's become the whole goddamn world's whipping boy." The director's even voice was tinged with anger. "Every damned thing we do is wrong: if an operation succeeds, we're fascists; if it fails, we're incompetent bunglers! With the Congress of Pan-American States and the OAS conference coming up, we have to walk more delicately than ever, avoid treading on Brazilian toes at all costs. You can imagine what the Latin-American press would make of it if we were rumbled and it turned out there was nothing in this thing!"

Quinnel nodded again. "Hundred percent undercover, then. I can't go officially to the Rio police?"

"Absolutely not. What's your cover?"

"Lawyer. There are still loose ends from United Fruit, and points to settle in the railroad-compensation case." Like most field executives, Quinnel actually carried out the work associated with his cover identity: he was in fact a graduate of Harvard Law School.

"That should fit in quite well," the director said.

"Sure. Present myself to the hospital—the police too, if necessary—as an attorney acting for these dames. Find out anything I can from them. And then ... ?"

"If it turns out to be merely a police matter, we'll hand the facts over to the proper authorities. If not, if there's something more sinister involved, we may have to state our case and ask for Brazilian cooperation. In any case, keep me filled in through Rio Station."

"I'll be there tomorrow morning," Quinnel said.

During the lunch hour, soon after Quinnel had collected his cover documents and travel vouchers, one of the girls from the CIA switchboard left the row of derelict brownstones fronting the headquarters and went to a drugstore. After she had eaten, she went to a phone booth in back of the store and dialed a number. She spoke rapidly and concisely for half a minute and then returned to her seat for coffee.

The fat man who had taken the call replaced the receiver on its cradle in an apartment not far from Wall Street. He sat for a few moments drumming ringed fingers on a Sheraton occasional table. Then he reached for the instrument again.

"Hallo, operator?" he said. "Give me long distance, international. I want to make a person-to-person call—a subscriber named McCaffery in Rio de Janeiro."

Palm trees lined the private road leading to the hospital and shaded the green verandas that surrounded the low white building. From the steps rising to the visitors' entrance a bright crescent of sand and surf marking the distant waterfront was visible between two soaring apartment blocks farther down the hill. Away to the right, above a colony of flat-roofed villas, the Sugarloaf humped itself into the hot sky at the seaward end of the wooded mountain chain encircling the city.

Quinnel braked the rented Toyota to a halt on the graveled circle. He strode up the steps and pushed through the swing doors into the reception lobby. Quinnel rarely sweated, but now his oatmeal-colored shantung suit clung uncomfortably to his shoulders and thighs. After the long flight and a sleepless night in a hotel room, he was finding the unaccustomed heat trying.

A large pendant fan revolved slowly in the shadowy entrance hall. Beneath it, a uniformed police officer was talking to the dark girl at the reception desk. Under her starched cap, the girl flashed a professionally inquiring smile at the CIA man. Quinnel placed his briefcase on the desk and leaned forward. "Forster," he said. "From New York. Attorney delegated to represent two patients here: Miss Weisenburger and Miss Ancarini, the Americans injured in the auto accident. Are they conscious yet? May I see them?"

The police officer had swung around and was staring curiously at Quinnel. His sallow, mustached face was creased with fatigue. As the receptionist was about to speak, he interrupted. "Captain Oliveira at your service, Counsellor," he said, holding out his hand. "Clearly, you have not heard."

"Heard?" Quinnel repeated, shaking the hand. "Heard what?"

"Both the ladies are dead, *senhor*," the girl said.

"Dead? Both of them? I thought . . . ?"

"Yes, they were improving, both of them, though it is true that neither had recovered consciousness. But then something . . . happened." The girl glanced at Oliveira.

"Regrettably—most regrettably—there seems to have been someone with an interest in seeing that they never did recover consciousness," the policeman supplied.

"You mean they were killed? Murdered?" Quinnel was shaken.

"Unfortunately. We might very well have believed that they had succumbed to their injuries, were it not that the intruder left open a window that should have been closed. But once we had become suspicious, we asked the postmortem pathologist to—how do you say?—keep the open eye."

"And he found . . . ?"

"He found that, beyond all doubt, they had been killed by that simplest of all methods: the air bubble injected straight into a vein by means of a hypodermic syringe."

"Don't wish to be a nuisance, Captain," Quinnel said later in Oliveira's office. "And as a lawyer, of course, I have no right to question you, but purely as a matter of interest, do you have any idea why these girls were killed? Or who did it?"

"None, Senhor Forster. At the same time—purely as a matter of interest, of course—I am curious to know how these unfortunate ladies managed to instruct an attorney to come all the way from New York to represent them, when in fact they had never recovered consciousness after the accident. An accident they presumably never knew had occurred." The policeman's stare was expressionless.

Quinnel smiled. "My bad Portuguese. Expressed myself poorly," he lied. "I said I was *delegated* to represent them. I was not, of course, instructed by the victims. Be impossible, as you say. No, I was briefed by Sanders International, the SISTERS people they pretended to belong to. Directors want to know what the hell goes on. Naturally. I hoped to find out by questioning the girls." He slumped back in his chair, elbows outthrust, apparently exhausted by such a long speech.

Oliveira said, "So. The brief, then, was what you call a watching brief?"

"Got it. Anything you can tell me, therefore, will be a great help."

"There is very little," the policeman said tiredly. "The car was rented on behalf of the organization and they gave, at the time, no names. It was paid for in advance and the papers and indemnities they produced seemed to be in order."

"Was the accident itself . . . engineered?"

"We think not. At that point, there were no direct witnesses—only drivers on the lower road who saw the vehicle tumble down the slope. But after putting out a radio message, we pulled in a trucker who seems to have been the unwitting cause of the affair. He had taken the wrong road and was making an illegal turn just before a sharp curve. The sports car hit the wall and went over, attempting to avoid him."

"Didn't come forward at the time?"

"No. He drove away because he was frightened he would be blamed."

"Then it looks . . . You have not found out where these women were based? Where the car was coming from?"

"Not yet, *senhor*. It is a big country, with many states. We shall certainly find out in time."

"Sure you will. In time." Quinnel cleared his throat. "But it looks like they may have been killed to delay any inquiries."

"Yes," Oliveira said with a sigh. "I am afraid it does."

One of the phones on his desk was ringing. He picked it up and barked something into the mouthpiece. For a moment he listened, and then, *"Madre de Dios!"* he said in a low voice. Still holding the receiver against his chest, he stared at Quinnel. "The truck driver," he said blankly. "Found on a garbage tip outside the city with his throat cut. . . ."

From a suburban villa on the outskirts of Rio, Quinnel had the station head call up his regional director that evening on the radio. "Your hunch paid off," he said. "Something smells. Somebody trying to stall off any investigation, killing the witnesses."

"What do you suggest?"

"American nationals," Quinnel said. "Figure we should investigate. Tricky, though, if the agency's not to be involved: my cover's under suspicion already."

"The agency must on no account be involved. On no account."

"What I thought. How'd you feel about subcontracting?"

"Subcontracting?"

"Use a free-lance. Nothing rubs off on us if it turns sour on him. Pay him to play gumshoe and ferret out the facts."

"You have somebody in mind, of course?"

"Sure I do. Ex-army man, hero of the Tet offensive, working for himself now. Mercenary, if you like, but he's the right guy."

"You can rely on this man? He's discreet? Efficient?"

"The best." A touch of enthusiasm colored Quinnel's clipped delivery. "We were buddies in Vietnam. His heart's in the right place—behind a chestful of medals!" He paused and then said, "I mention it because he happens to be in town, at loose-ends, and I ran into him today. Fellow by the name of Marc Dean."

The Wolf in the Heart

All men who feel any power of joy in battle know what it is like when the wolf rises in the heart.

—Theodore Roosevelt

3

Marcus Matthew Dean had spent all of his thirty-six years under military influences of one kind or another. His father, a country doctor, had lied about his age to become an aviator in World War I. In the second global conflict, Dean Senior had been attached to the USAAF as a medic. The boy, youngest of three children, was born on June 6, 1944, the date of the biggest amphibious military operation in history. Already the proud holder of a pilot's license at age eighteen, he was an enthusiastic ROTC member at Yale, signing on for two years as an infantry lieutenant as soon as he graduated. Twice decorated for bravery and initiative in Vietnam, he found civilian life too tame for his restless spirit and, in 1970 and 1971, broadened his experience of guerrilla activity with the Peace Corps in Central Africa. Later, Marc Dean returned to Vietnam as head of a "pacification" program sponsored by AID. He had worked for some years as an international arms salesman before he decided, in 1975, to put his military skills up for hire. Successful operations in Angola, Katanga, Morocco, and the Middle East followed. But Dean's interests were by no means exclusively martial, and it was with a pleasant sense of anticipation that he agreed to Quinnel's suggestion that he should act (to use his own private evaluation) as the CIA's "messenger boy." He would have been as surprised as anyone if he had been told then that this apparently simple detective assignment would turn into a full-scale guerrilla operation.

At the start, it was no more than a question of legwork. "Low profile," Quinnel had instructed. "Leave you to fix your own cover. Mine seems to be blown already: called in by the embassy this A.M. and warned off. Seems that certain high Brazilian officials have let it be known that 'they do not wish the matter pursued.'" Quinnel gave a snort of laughter at the end of the pompous quote. "They should know the agency better than that. Anyway, I'm off to Venezuela. You need me, want to check out anything, don't go near the embassy. Call me through the Rio Station contact I gave you."

"If the local heavies want the thing squashed," Dean said, "it figures that something more than a con trick is involved. I'll be in touch."

He found the site of the wreck without any trouble. Newspaper reports enabled him to identify the section of highway, and once he was there, the evidence was only too plain. The brushwood was still scarred and flattened where the salvage-department cranes had penetrated to drag away the remains of the Alfa Romeo; above, a trail of stones fanned out from the breached wall of the side road that curved up around the flank of the mountain.

Dean took the minor road and parked the Toyota he had inherited from Quinnel a hundred yards below the fatal hairpin. He walked slowly up to the shattered parapet—a tall, muscular figure with pale hair and piercing blue eyes.

There was nothing much to see. Just the gap in the stonework and the remains of chalk marks made by police investigators on the scorching macadam. Nearer the curve, where the foliage of mountain scrub shimmered in the heat haze rising from the roadway, four black skid marks angled across the surface. Clearly the car had been out of alignment, drifting partially sideways when the driver had braked. She must have taken the bend too fast, seen the truck, clamped on the anchors when she had already lost the back end, and then released them and tried to get through, Dean thought to himself.

He strolled to the far side of the bend and crouched down until his head was at a level corresponding to the eyeline of a sports-car driver. He had not been mistaken: the road beyond the hairpin was invisible.

There was not much traffic. An ancient bus full of black women in bright headscarves rattled down toward the highway in low gear; an electric-blue Mustang hissed past on its way up into the mountains. He walked slowly back to his rented car, fanning his face with a newspaper. By the Toyota, an old man with a wide-brimmed straw hat and a blanket over one shoulder had halted his mule. Dean greeted him politely.

"A good day to you, *senhor*," the old man replied. "And a good route." He looked at the sky. "It is indeed a good day for those who travel prudently. But no day is good for those who would arrive before their time . . . for example the *yan*-

qui ladies you have been investigating whose haste brought them only to disaster."

"You saw the accident?"

"Naturally. I am always on this road at this time."

"But . . . you did not come forward in answer to the police radio message?"

"The *senhor* will forgive me—but he is perhaps of the police himself?"

"No, no. My name is . . . ah . . . Forster. I am an attorney," Dean said, hastily borrowing the CIA man's cover as well as his car. "I am trying to find out what caused the accident. I represent the ladies."

"So. A lawyer. Miguel da Silva at your service," the old man said courteously, holding out a seamed hand. "As to the matter of the police, when you reach my age you learn that it is wisest to avoid any unnecessary contact with them. I have seen many different police forces, and today's friend may be tomorrow's enemy. Also," he added, "I do not possess a radio."

"But you did see the accident," Dean pursued, shaking the hand. "Why do you think it happened?"

"They were going too fast. There was a truck. But then, they always went too fast. Man is not intended for such speeds."

"Always? You had seen the girls before?"

"Indeed, *senhor*. Those or others like them. In different cars. Perhaps three times each month, perhaps five. It could not be more frequently, because they lived so far away."

"You know where they came from?" Dean asked in astonishment.

"*Si, senhor*. From far, from very far away, as I have said."

"Do you know the name of the place?"

"That I cannot tell you. But it was very far. Many hundreds—perhaps thousands—of kilometers. Beyond the mountains, across the plain, beyond the great forest, beyond Belo Horizonte, beyond Goiânia even, somewhere in the hills of the interior behind the new city that men say rises like white towers into the sky."

"You mean Brasilia?"

"I believe that is the name," Miguel da Silva admitted graciously.

"But . . . how in hell—you will forgive me, Senhor da Silva?—how can you possibly know this?"

"Simply," the old man said. He extended an arm toward the tree-covered crests thrusting into the aching blue of the sky. On the road somewhere above, an automobile windshield flashed fiercely in the sun. "Below the pass, Pedro Diaz keeps a small shack where he sells refreshing drinks and trinkets for the tourists who stop to admire the view. Each afternoon, I pause to bid him good day and to drink a little wine with him. He knows the *yanqui* ladies well. On two occasions I myself have heard one of them make a telephone call from there, and I understand some American, although I do not speak it very well."

"You heard what they said? You remember the exchange they called?"

"I cannot recall the name. But on each occasion it seemed that the operator was unaware of it. The lady telephoning insisted, and said, yes, that was the correct name; it was a small place in the mountains, beyond that city, where they make a new lake."

"Beyond Brasilia—a small place in the mountains where an artificial lake, probably a dam, is being built," Dean repeated thoughtfully. "You have been more than helpful, *senhor*. I cannot thank you enough."

"It is nothing, *senhor*."

"One final question. If you could see both the car *and* the truck, you must have been farther up the hillside. Did you see anything else, anything at all, that might have had something to do with the accident? Was there anybody else around, near the scene of the wreck?"

"No, there was nothing. Just the car and the truck. If there had been anything, I should have seen it."

"Thank you again," Dean said. He went back to the Toyota, turned, and headed for the highway and for Rio.

"God go with you," the old man called as he urged his mule to resume its laborious climb.

Farther up the hill, the driver of the blue Mustang put away his field glasses and opened the trunk of the car. He propped up the lid of a small shortwave transmitter-receiver and maneuvered its switches and dials. Then he held a single can to one ear and spoke quietly into a hand microphone.

"McCaffery," he said. "Quinnel went to the hospital again with Oliveira, the police captain. He stayed some time in Oliveira's office, called in at the embassy, and then headed for the airport, where he handed the heap over to this other guy—a big blond guy, about six feet and one-eighty, looks kinda tough. This other guy calls on the hire company and a coupla newspaper offices, then he drives out to the place where the dames left the road. . . . He just spent fifteen minutes gumshoeing around and yakking to some peasant on a mule who hands him some kind of story. Now he's on his way back to town. You better tell Schultz to pick him up at the next intersection: he saw me pass while he was on the road. . . . Yeah, a red Toyota. . . . What's that? . . . Oh, him. Sure I will. I'll look after it right away."

He swung the Mustang around and went carefully back down the hill. After the third hairpin, he saw Miguel da Silva jogging slowly toward him on the mule.

The man called McCaffery drove a few yards past him and braked. He got out of the car and called, "Hey, you! Old man!"

The mule continued its upward plod. Da Silva did not turn his head. Swearing, the driver of the Mustang dropped his cigarette to the ground, swiveled his heel on the butt, and shouted again, "Hey, old man! Are you deaf?"

This time da Silva turned his head. He spoke without checking the pace of the mule. "Are you addressing me, *senhor*?"

"Of course I'm addressing you, you old fool," McCaffery snapped in his bad Portuguese. "Do you see anyone else around?"

The old man reined in the beast and sat waiting patiently while McCaffery strode up to him. "What do you want with me, *senhor*?" he asked.

"First, I want to teach you to speak when you're spoken to, peasant. Get off that mule."

Da Silva sat silent and regarded him impassively.

"I said get off!" McCaffery shouted. He bit his lip, then raised his right forearm across his chest and struck the old man viciously, backhanded, on the face. Da Silva's broad-brimmed hat fell to the ground. His leathery cheek had flushed a dull red with the blow. Yet still he stared unwinkingly at his aggressor.

McCaffery hit him again: a wicked right to the solar plexus. The old man gave a choking grunt, folded forward over the neck of the mule, and slid to the roadway.

The driver of the Mustang drew back his foot. He was wearing tan-and-white shoes with pointed toecaps. He kicked the old man three times, once on the side of the head and twice in the kidneys. After a while, da Silva rolled slowly over and tried to sit up, supporting himself on gnarled hands. He spit blood into the dust. "Why . . . why do you do this . . . to me, *senhor*?" he croaked. A thin thread of scarlet still ran from one side of his bruised mouth.

McCaffery made no reply. Measuring his distance carefully, he drew back his foot for the fourth time. He caught the old man full on the chin with the iron-tipped heel. This time, da Silva did not get up.

The rasping of a cicada in a tree across the road shivered the silence as McCaffery straightened his necktie, smoothed down the front of his white jacket, and looked cautiously around. The stretch of road between the hairpins lay empty in the sun. Neither human beings nor vehicles were visible among the succession of wooded undulations rising into the hot blue sky. The mule stood motionless in a patch of shade cast by a stunted oak, its head hanging low.

Bending down, McCaffery seized the unconscious figure of Miguel da Silva by the shoulders and hauled it into the roadway not too far from the spots of blood that were already congealing darkly in the dust of the shoulder.

After a final look up and down, he lit a cigarette, walked quickly to the Mustang, and backed it a hundred yards up the road. Then, steering carefully, he accelerated down toward the body sprawled on the blacktop.

4

After the red earth of the coffee country and the alternating woods and escarpments of Minas Gerais state, the plateau on which Brasilia is built seemed almost indecently bare. Marc Dean leaned his forehead against the cool double glass and scanned the bleak terrain sliding past below the 727's wing. Threads of silver splashed the ravines, and away off to the northeast, a wide river coiled itself between trees. But there was nothing he could see that suggested in any way the building of a new dam or an artificial lake.

The smart young corporation lawyer in the government office, his Bahia university degree framed on the peeled-sycamore wall behind his desk, was equally discouraging.

"I cannot imagine, Senhor Forster, how you came to be so

misinformed," he said with a frown. "Every hydroelectric project connected with Brasilia was completed before the city was inhabited. Naturally. If there were some supplementary scheme under consideration—and especially if construction had actually started—you may be sure that we should know about it. As for the options you mention . . ." He shrugged, staring at Dean as if he found such naiveté hard to credit. "This is a new town, barely twenty years old. There is still very little building other than the normal civic and municipal developments."

"There might not be—forgive my saying this—there might not perhaps be a certain amount of what we call wheeling and dealing going on behind the scenes? Projects that are kept secret because too many people would want to jump on the bandwagon if the plans leaked out?"

"Physically," the lawyer said, "there is no place for undercover intrigues to go. Not in Brasilia."

"I see." Dean was apologetic. "I should explain that I was not of course sent to Brazil only to investigate these options—if they exist. I happened to hear of them in a roundabout way when I was negotiating an entirely different deal in Rio, and I figured that maybe . . . well, maybe it might be worth looking into the matter."

"Quite." The lawyer cleared his throat. "Now, you must forgive me, but . . . are you sure you have come to the right city?"

Dean grinned suddenly, looking all at once very young. "No," he said frankly, "to tell the truth, I'm not, and that's the hell of it!"

"In that case . . ." The young man looked slightly bewildered.

"I heard of it from an old man, a peasant—and it was I who suggested Brasilia, thinking from his description that this must be the city he was describing. You know, white towers rising into the sky, the whole ultramodern bit. But of course he may have agreed just to be polite: the courtesy of your country folk can be exhausting!"

The young lawyer smiled. He steepled his fingers. "Of course," he murmured after a moment's thought, "the description would fit the plans of Getuliana equally well."

"Getuliana?"

"Another of our bright new cities, named after our late president, Getulio Vargas. Scheduled population half a million, mostly to be employed in light industry; red carpet to be unrolled at the beginning of 1983. I shouldn't wonder if there weren't some hydroelectric schemes tied in there."

"Where exactly is this place?"

"Beyond the Serra das Divisões, about two hundred and twenty miles from here. It's wild country on the fringe of the Mato Grosso, west of Goiás."

"And you think...?"

"That there might be a dam? Really, I wouldn't know. The site is below the Serra do Roncador, between the Rio Grande and the Rio das Mortes, both of which flow north into the Araguaia, so it is certainly a possibility. You would have to inform yourself at the Goiás state river catchment authority, in Goiânia. Or better still, while you are here, why not ask Menezes?"

"Menezes?"

"Umberto Ladeira de Menezes, the head of International Construction—Intacon—pulled off the deal to build the entire city center. If there are options around, he'll know where and what they are. And he'll know whether it's worth your while chasing them up."

There was a blond girl in the elevator whose face was somehow familiar. Dean turned his back. He could not see a certain type of blond without reopening the wound. It was more than two years now since Samantha had divorced him, and he wanted her as much as ever.

He could not bring himself to regard the separation as final: it was a bad dream, a nightmare; it hadn't really happened. Each time—as the law allowed—that he visited Samantha in their Massachusetts cottage in order to see his young son, Patrick, he became once more convinced that she too remained in love. Each time, his way of life came between them, and any possibility of reconciliation vanished. "Mental cruelty isn't joking!" Samantha stormed once. "I refuse, I absolutely refuse, to have my son—"

"Our son."

"I refuse to have our son grow up in the company of a man whose profession is killing and violence."

"He doesn't come out of it too badly in terms of a stable economic background," Dean said mildly. "I can't see that he lacks anything much."

"He lacks a father, for one thing. He needs a home—"

"Who started divorce proceedings?"

"Exactly because you're *un*stable yourself. A child needs a *settled* life. And if you're talking about stable backgrounds, you could have been just as stable financially working for my father. Why you threw up that job for a . . . for a salesman's job in the death business I'll never know!"

Dean sighed. "Vice-president in an electronics corporation isn't my idea of an exciting life, that's all," he said. "And as for killing as a profession, your father was an army colonel, wasn't he? Where do you think all that rocketry installation he makes goes? Into space ships taking tourists to the moon?"

"Oh, Matt," she said. "If it was only that . . ." Samantha always used Dean's middle name. As a man born under the sign of Gemini, her husband displayed to an exaggerated degree the twin but opposing facets characterizing the sign; he was capable of analyzing seventeenth-century poetry or playing Vivaldi on the harpsichord with the same enthusiasm that he devoted to the precise location of an explosive charge or the enfilading of an enemy position in jungle terrain. It was this polarity in his nature that had at first attracted her to him—and it was the restlessness and inability to "settle down" that lay behind it which finally drove them apart. Samantha affected to believe that the Marcus in his name corresponded with his adventurous, militaristic side, while the Matthew symbolized the softer intellectual she loved.

Unfortunately, although Dean could reconcile the two in himself, she was never able to accept as part of her own life the throat-tightening thirst for excitement he was unable to do without.

But however much the two of them tried to shield him, almost all of their serious quarrels broke out over the boy. Once, lying bronzed and naked on a secluded shore, Samantha had cut short an amorous advance because Dean had taught Patrick to make castles—rather than houses—in the sand. Another time, she turned on her heel and walked out on him in a department store because he wanted to buy the boy a box of lead soldiers rather than a painting set as a birthday gift.

Dean shook his head. It all seemed very far away now, under the hot sun and high blue sky of Brasilia. He went into the steel-and-glass polygon housing the three floors occupied by Menezes' Intacon corporation. Judging by the indicator board in the lobby, his influence extended through most of the other fifteen floors as well. Rising silently in the elevator, Dean passed the Ladeira Investment Trust, ULM Electronics, Umberto Engineering, the Menezes Mining Company, M & M Quantity Surveyors, MeneBraz Realtors, and Menezes-Fleischman, Architects. The president of all these companies was sitting behind a teak desk staring at the wall when Dean was ushered into his office by a pretty black secretary—a big, gray man with empty eyes.

"You wished to see me about some aspect of the building of Getuliana, Senhor . . . ah . . . Forster?" he rumbled, glancing at the card Dean had been given by Quinnel.

"Not precisely, Dom Umberto. At least, not the city itself. My interest centers rather"—Dean risked a long shot—"on the dam."

"So! The San Felipe project!"

"Exactly. The San Felipe project."

"But I cannot see what interest that can have for an American, Counsellor. Especially an American lawyer."

"I had been told—perhaps wrongly—that there might be land options negotiable on the fringes of the site, in areas cleared but not inundated. The corporation I represent would be interested in such options . . . either for development or simply for the mineral rights."

A door shut softly behind a dividing screen of potted plants. A tall, thin man in a white suit sauntered across the deep pile carpet. "Oh, sorry, Menezes," he said casually. "I didn't realize you were occupied." But he made no attempt to leave, dropping into a tan leather armchair shaped like half a golf ball and staring at Dean with unabashed curiosity.

"It's all right, Fleischman," Menezes said. "This gentleman has been sent here under a misapprehension. He seems to think there are land options available in connection with San Felipe!" He chuckled throatily.

"Options?" The thin man sat upright, his tanned, skull-like face a mask of incredulity. "At San Felipe? But where the devil . . ? If you are serious, may I ask where you got that idea?"

"In Rio," Dean said calmly.

The two men exchanged glances over the desk. "I am afraid I do not understand," the contractor said finally. "There never have been any options available in connection with this project. The whole thing is what you Americans call a package deal. Dr. Fleischman here conceived the idea of building the city and opening up this barren area, persuaded the government to give him the go-ahead, raised the necessary finance in Europe and elsewhere, and negotiated the contracting deal with me. My companies are responsible for everything—land clearance, drainage, electrical installations, construction, everything. The San Felipe dam is simply a means of providing power for the city, that is all."

"One would be interested to learn just who gave you the idea that there were options available," the man in the white suit pursued. "We are more than adequately financed. We do not want your American dollars here: you cannot buy your way in everywhere, you know."

"That was neither my intention nor that of the corporation I represent." Dean kept his temper with an effort: the man's tone had been little short of insulting. "It was just, as I have explained, that I heard of the possibility and considered it—foolishly, as it turns out—worth exploring."

"Yes, but heard it from *whom*?" Fleischman insisted. "There has been very little publicity, mainly because the whole project *is* being handled by one concern, and I am astonished to find that it's a talking point in Rio at all."

"I heard it from a woman," Dean said, deciding to trail a line in deep waters. "A woman who works for the SISTERS . . . at San Felipe."

Again the two businessmen exchanged glances. "Ah, the welfare ladies," Menezes said after a moment. "Yes, of course. They are engaged in . . . er . . . resettling the natives displaced by the new lake. Although that part of the Mato Grosso plateau is relatively bare, a big reservoir such as the one formed by the San Felipe dam is bound to drown a number of villages and farms in the valley it floods. The SISTERS have been most helpful in explaining to the country folk how they will benefit, and smoothing out the task of rehousing them elsewhere."

"Also, it seems, setting up an unofficial agency for the disposal of our land," Fleischman remarked dryly.

"I think you exaggerate, *senhor*," Dean said. "The lady did not specifically offer land for sale or state that options were available. She merely mentioned the area of operations and said in passing that she guessed there must be a lot of money to be made by anyone who could get in on the ground floor. As getting in on the ground floor happens to be my business, I figured it was worth following up, that's all."

"How very curious," Fleischman drawled. He rose abruptly to his feet, his elegant suit, creaseless and immaculate, bright in the shadowed office. "There are many ladies of this organization at San Felipe. I don't suppose you recall the name of the one you talked to?"

"At the moment," Dean said, looking him in the eye, "I'm afraid it escapes me."

"I see." Fleischman walked to one of the wide windows and stood looking out over the new city. "Permit me, then, to save you wasting any more of your time. You may take it from me that the dam, which has inundated a valley carrying a tributary of the Rio das Mortes, lies in a stretch of country that is wild and inaccessible. The rocks, in the main, are ancient porphyries, of no value for mining, building, or any other work. Apart from San Felipe do Caiapo itself—a village of three or four hundred people only—there are no centers of population nearer than the unfinished town. Nor are there likely to be, since there are very few roads. Nor will there be any question of land or mineral options."

"Since you use the services of the SISTERS, you must nevertheless be prepared at least in some degree to work with Americans," Dean said. "The trust is wholly American-financed, you know."

"That is scarcely a parallel. They provide a service we need; by contributing to their trust, we, in effect, are paying them—which is some way removed from accepting money from those wishing to share our future profits."

"Admittedly. Even so, as a businessman—"

"Good day, Senhor . . . Forster," Menezes said firmly.

And that was that. Dean decided to leave without argument. He had found out more than he dared hope for: there was a dam; he knew now where it was; he knew there was a team of SISTERS—or at least a team claiming to be SISTERS—and this was undoubtedly where the murdered girls had come from. The people working on the project were from the same stable as those building the new town. And it seemed certain beyond all doubt that they wanted to keep their activities secret.

Why?

What was there about the construction of a new town in Brazil—even if graft had been involved in the dispensation of contracts—that was so special? Why should convicted whores be masquerading as members of a charitable organization? Above all, why should two of them, along with the witnesses to a banal automobile accident, have been murdered? What secrets could they have revealed if they had been allowed to live—and were those secrets connected with the mysterious dam?

There was only one way to get a lead, Dean thought: go to the place and see what he could find out.

Between slender, modernistic pillars supporting the giant canopies designed to protect the inhabitants of Brasilia from the sun, he threaded his way across the city. Within the plane-shaped overall design of the place, squares, gardens, parking lots, shadowed pedestrian precincts and the geometric forms of buildings merged into a homogeneous whole that was as stimulating as it was right. Here was the city of the future. Yet somehow the very perfection of the concept rendered it sterile: it had sprung into being straight off the drawing board, without the time to develop organically from older, more traditional failures. Perhaps because of this, Dean saw with relief that the rent-a-car headquarters came from a different mold, being an unholy mixture of adobe and corrugated iron, a series of long walls topped with improvised roofs linked by French-truss girders. The office was a wooden shack shoveled into a corner behind a double row of Chevrolets. To Dean it all looked like home.

He pushed through the rickety door and flipped a silver coin at the young Latin equivalent of a New York radio-cab dispenser who sat behind the scarred counter. "I want to rent an auto," he said, "as of now."

"Okay, bud," the dispenser drawled, rolling a toothpick from one side of his mouth to the other. "Where you wanna go then?"

"Does it matter?" Dean asked, surprised both by the question and by the fact that it was expressed in archaic Hollywood English.

"Well, sure it matters, pal. Like, if you was to wanna drive to Januaria, or Claros, or Rio Branco in Bahia state, then I'd give you a Chevy, see. It's a long ways there, first off, and then again, it's a comfortable heap and the roads ain't too bad. Same thing if you was crazy enough to wanna go to the railhead at Pirapora. But if you just had a mind to mosey around here, maybe go up to Palma, down to Carvalhas, why, I'd fix you something smaller, cheaper on the gas. A Volvo, maybe, or a Fiat, 'cause it's like flat up here an' you got no call for the power. On the other hand, if you was headin' for Leopoldina or Goiânia or any of those places, you'd be better off with a jeep. Those mountain roads are rugged, man."

"I want to go to Getuliana!"

"Getuliana!"

"Sure. If that's okay by you . . . buster."

"Jesus! What you wanna do that for?"

"I'd like to see it, that's all. Anything wrong with that?"

"Only that it ain't there," the boy said. He removed the toothpick from his mouth and stabbed it in Dean's direction to emphasize his words. "There's nothin' to *see*. . . . You go to the public library here, you can see the *plans*. . . . Look around this dump an' you can see the way it's *goin'* to be. . . . But out at the site you won't see nothin'. It's like this place, but less so, if you take my meaning."

"Even so, I'd like to take a run out there and have a look-see. I'm interested in town planning."

"Oh, sure. Me too. But an interest can turn into an *obsession*. . . . Look, lemme tell you about a great trip you can take down the valley—"

"Thanks, but it has to be Getuliana. I'm being paid for it."

"Yeah. Well, if you're sure," the youth said doubtfully. "I guess you better take the Lada, then. Iron Curtain buggy. She ain't pretty, she ain't specially fast, she's not what you call *comfortable*, but she's tough, man. Real tough. And she'll do you your hundred kilometers on nine, maybe ten liters of gas . . . even, so help me, on the roads around Getuliana!"

"Okay," Dean said. "I'll take the Lada. Maybe you could help me work out a route, huh? You have maps here?"

"Maps we got, bud. The road system in Bahia state. The road system in Minas Gerais. The trunk routes of Rio. Street maps of Belo Horizonte. Brazil's river system. Tributaries of the Amazon. How to make the best of our railroad network. A tourist guide to Brasilia—lots of those, in all colors, with electricity and drainage diagrams added. But a map that shows you how to get from here to Getuliana. . ." He shook his head. "Man, that's a drag."

"Do you know the way yourself?" Dean asked. "You've been there?"

"Sure. Coupla times. But I ain't no chauffeur."

"Okay. I just meant that maybe you could kind of show me the general way on that big wall map you have there." He gestured toward a six-foot plaster relief that dominated one wall of the office.

"If that's all you want, no sweat." The boy shambled to his feet. "You head west across the plateau here, see . . . practically desert all the way. Then you gotta get through the Pireneos—that's this ridge here—and cross the Divisões. After that, watch out."

"Hostile natives?"

The dispenser looked at Dean suspiciously. "This is a modern country, bud," he said. "You have to watch out for the *roads*. Now, you'll see signs directing you to the grand new turnpike for Leopoldina and Getuliana—"

"And the road's not built yet?"

"Oh, the *road's* there—only they haven't put in the bridges where it crosses the ravines, see . . . here . . . and here . . .

and here. You have to take the old road, but only as far as this junction here. There's a big old church right on the intersection; you can't miss it. When you get there, forget the signs, turn off that road, and head southwest."

"No bridges on the old road either?"

"There *were* bridges, sure. Only they got kinda washed away in the rainy season and nobody got around to fixin' them yet. . . . Look, you'd best make for Goiás from there. It's farther south, but the road's much better. Then you can strike north again along this valley, cross the saddle here, and come down on Getuliana from the other side, through San Felipe—you'll recognize that because there's a big new dam there."

Dean made a few notes and completed the necessary insurance and financial details before the boy led him out to a bright red Lada Niva—a kind of cut-and-shut estate wagon that looked like a tall, outsize jeep. "Like I say, she's tough," the boy said. "And she's got plenty of ground clearance in there. But if it rains, you wanna watch out for that back end, man . . . like especially when they're minin' that bauxite stuff."

"Thanks," Dean said, pressing another coin into his hand. "I guess maybe you get them pretty late down here, huh?"

"How's that?"

"The movies. They're on late release here. I mean, you ought to know this. *Waterfront* was a long time ago. Brando's out now. Not way out, man; right out. Not the in thing at all."

"He's not?"

"Definitely not. The in thing today is to be all British. Frightfully proper, what! Clipped voice and school English; high collar with a necktie. Buttoned down. Buttoned right down, the whole scene."

"You're kiddin'!"

"Absolutely not, dear lad. Hadn't you noticed *my* collar?"

Dean was still grinning as he swung the Lada onto the main highway to the west outside the city limits. Allowing for detours, he had more than two hundred and fifty miles of rough country to cross. Since it was already past noon, he would be wiser not to press for too much: he would stop for the night at Goiás and prospect San Felipe and the dam tomorrow.

The road plunged across the empty countryside in wide sweeps, now smooth and hard-packed, now pitted, rough, and covered with a layer of white dust. Once through the jagged rock defile breaching the first ridge, it ran gradually downhill and the spiny plants of the desert were overlaid by a denser vegetation. Soon the car was bowling through the middle of a forest, shaded from the fiery sun by a palisade of tall trees. Green parakeets swooped and soared across the road in flocks, and an occasional pair of toucans flapped heavily away into the undergrowth.

Traffic was light. In an hour, Dean saw only three cars, a jeep, the inevitable rattletrap bus, and a convoy of trucks loaded with something in steel drums. For a time he could see in his driving mirror that there was a blue Mustang keeping pace with him, but the convertible pulled into a gas station at one of the more populous villages and he didn't see it again.

The forest receded, was replaced by ragged bush country, and finally gave way to a plain of tufted grasses bounded by hills, violet with distance, to the west. Halfway across the plain was the fork, with the church, just as the boy had said, between the two roads. Ignoring the signposts, Dean turned left onto a dirt road and soon found himself in an arid region gashed with dried-up watercourses. The track appeared to be quarried from bedrock: dust billowed into the air and penetrated the Lada in choking clouds; both fabric and metal became too hot to touch in the shadeless glare of the sun.

Several times Dean had to drive across *mataburros*—the primitive country bridges comprising two steel beams spanning a gap, with a series of planks laid crosswise to form the roadway. Once, finding himself stranded on one of these high above a desolate gorge, he had to stop the car, get out, collect an armful of planks from behind, and lay them down again in front of the wheels to fill a space in the swaying structure before he could go on. Another time he missed a turnoff and found himself, according to a signpost, on the way back to Brasilia. It was after dark before he finally made Goiás.

The following morning—he had retired early after a dinner of *feijao*, eggs and roast meat, washed down with a mixture of coffee and *pinga*—he went out into the town determined to put a few questions to the locals.

It was another hot day, the sun blazing from a dark blue sky between drifts of white cloud. Goiás was pleasant, a survival from an earlier age. There was a river, a square with green turf and a bandstand overlooked by a peeling building much like a Venetian *palazzo*, and a 1930's cinema with a ornate facade. There were narrow cobbled streets warping the rules of perspective. And above the jumbled roofs with their curved tiles, wooded hills surmounted by a wild rock escarpment pierced the sky.

Against the blinding white walls of the houses, men in straw hats tipped back their chairs and drowsed. From inside, occasionally, the age-old profile of an Indian woman gleamed against the shadows.

Dean threaded his way through a market, enjoying the spicy odors in the shade beneath the awnings, and crossed a square loud with the clatter of small boys on ponies. On the far side, over the ever-present babble of the river, he heard a low murmur of men's voices from a window below street level. He went down half a dozen steps, pushed open a wrought-iron gate, and found himself in a *bodega*.

It was moist and cool in there after the glare of the sun, and the low-pitched conversation blended well with the woody smells of barrel and cask. Dean ran his eyes over the double row of labeled spigots behind the counter as he approached the bartender. "I'll take a *sercial*," he said, "provided it's chilled but not too cold."

Although he spoke Portuguese well enough, it was some time before Dean was able to break down the countryman's mistrust of strangers and take part in the general conversation. Finally, however, as he started his third glass of the dry, clean-tasting Madeira, he found himself sitting with three men at a heavy, polished table, talking of local trade. One of the men was a wholesaler of groceries and dry goods.

"I guess you'll find a big difference, now they're building the new city," Dean suggested. "More clients will mean bigger stock orders, larger stocks will need more important premises, and so on?"

The man gave a short laugh. "Getuliana?" he said. "The new city? *When* they build it—*if* they build it—I may have to think about such things. For the moment that is just fantasy."

"They will never build it," a fat fruit farmer said sadly.

"If you ask me," put in the third man, a pharmacist with drooping mustaches, "they never intended to build the place. It is just a way for businessmen to chisel subsidies out of the government."

"It is not completed, then?" Dean asked innocently.

"Getuliana completed?" the pharmacist exploded. "That would be the day, *senhor*! The site is flattened and streets are marked out. They say some power cables and drains are down. But not one stone has been laid on another."

"Even the machines have departed," the farmer said.

"There are a couple of bulldozers left, a handful of trucks, and one crane, I believe."

"Window dressing!" the wholesaler snorted. "To make the people think that work proceeds. In fact only the dispensation of money proceeds—while the contractors and their lawyers disport themselves at Copacabana and São Paulo and Bahia. Maybe even in Brasilia."

"But I thought the new dam . . . One had heard . . ."

"Ah, the San Felipe project! That is a different matter. For some reason, they have gotten a move on there. They have—"

"That is just what I mean," the pharmacist interrupted. "Not a house is built in the so-called city, yet already the hydroelectric scheme is completed: thousands of hectares of land drowned, thousands of people made homeless, and nowhere for the electricity to go! This is town planning?"

"You are right, Pedro, it is madness."

"I do not agree," the farmer said. "If—I say if—the city is ever to be built, surely it is prudent to have the power ready beforehand? Then they can use it in the actual building."

"No, no, no: you miss the point—"

"One must consider the dispossessed peasants—"

"The land—"

"I thought"—Dean in turn interrupted—"I thought those displaced from their homes and land by the new reservoir had been resettled with the aid of this American charity organization."

"Resettled? Unsettled, more likely," the wholesaler said. "Those women, I suppose you mean? The ones in uniforms?"

"Er . . . yes. But . . ."

"This is a Catholic country, *senhor*. Admittedly most of the people resettled were either Caraja Indians or country blacks who worship at their own Candomblé. Even so, the susceptibilities of the population as a whole must be considered."

"You cloak the truth with words, Alvaro," a man from a nearby table interrupted. He turned to Dean. "The fact of the matter is that these women behave in a manner likely to offend anyone, anywhere."

"Really?" Dean was intrigued. "I'm afraid I do not understand. The trust—the SISTERS it is called—is highly respectable. All the girls are carefully vetted. Whenever they are posted abroad, they have to live in special hostels and observe a rigid set of rules. The way they behave, I mean. And yet you say . . ."

"There is indeed a hostel," the farmer said. "But how it is

used! I do not know about rules, but the women act in a manner more suited to *uma casa das putas*."

"Drunken singing far into the night," the man at the next table said. "Indecent behavior with the men from the site. Unseemly dress. Reckless driving on the roads. Rudeness. You name it."

"But this is quite astonishing—" Dean began.

"It astonished us too, *senhor*. You will not take the criticism personally as an American, I hope, but San Felipe do Caiapo is a very small village."

"I understand. Perhaps the women will go away when the dam is completed, and leave the villagers in peace."

"Perhaps. But it is already finished, I believe."

"You do not know for sure? Is it not a remarkable thing, a sight that people drive out to see, this artificial lake?" Dean inquired.

The pharmacist laughed. "The road from Goiás to Leopoldina is reputed to be the worst in all Brazil," he said. "Halfway along it, there turns off the road to San Felipe— and this makes the Leopoldina road seem like a turnpike! From here to the dam is more than fifty miles—and over the second half of the journey it is not possible to average more than seven or eight miles per hour."

"Also," the farmer added, "those building the dam and the power station below it actively discourage visitors, it seems. Besides, it is high up between the bare hills and the forest, and the road, such as it is, runs below."

"But surely there must be many trucks, convoys of trucks, taking materials to the site?" Dean asked.

"Not through Goiás. We see a few. Mainly haulers from the coast carrying Brazilian goods from Volta Redonda: oil and chemicals, that sort of thing. Others bring supplies south from the river at Leopoldina, where it is offloaded from boats. But the bulk of it is flown in to the strip at Getuliana."

"I see," Dean said. "Gentlemen, your glasses are empty. Allow me . . ." And then, later: "Well, there is certainly one place, after our conversation, that you will *not* find me visiting while I am here!"

It was nevertheless toward the road leading to Leopoldina and San Felipe that he headed the Lada as soon as he could decently leave. After he had gone, a thin man wearing tan-and-white shoes with pointed toecaps walked to a pay phone in back of the *bodega* and put through a call to Brasilia.

The clouds had vanished and the staring blue of the sky was unbroken save for the shapes of vultures soaring over the gables as Dean left Goiás. He draped his jacket over a hanger in the rear part of the car, loosened his collar, rolled up his sleeves, and prepared himself for a long, difficult and intensely hot journey.

It was nearly ten o'clock at night when he returned. As soon as the dusty Lada turned the last bend and came in sight of the scattered lights of the town below, he pulled off the road and cut the motor. There was a canvas rucksack on the passenger seat. From this he took a small but powerful portable transceiver. He got out of the car, pulled out the extensible aerial, and operated the tuners. When he heard an answer to his call sign on the wavelength he was using, he thumbed a button on the side of the instrument and spoke softly into the microphone grille.

"Hallo, Recife?" he said. "Is that Ramirez at Recife? . . . This is Forster for Quinnel. Are you receiving me loud and clear?" When a faint voice had answered in the affirmative, he continued, "Look, I'm no detective—this isn't my bag at all—but there's something screwball going on here. Something that smells. I need guidance before I go any farther. Tell him that. And here's a message I want you to transmit. You know the routine. It'll read kind of crazy because you have to send it in clear. You get that? It has to go in clear for political reasons. . . . Okay. Message begins. Following are certs and probables for Brazilian Hit Parade. . . ."

Half an hour later, he ran the Lada in under the eaves of the huge barn that acted as garage for the inn where he was staying. Hardly a light showed in the shuttered streets. He stumbled across the yard, cursed as he barked his shin on the fender of a convertible parked by the back door, and climbed to his room.

Once there, he checked the personal signposts he had left to tip him off in case of a search. Of the five cigarettes in the pack carelessly thrown on the night table, three still had the brand names on the paper facing downward. The corner of the folded map on the bureau still coincided with the angle of a letter V in the title of a book below it. He poured himself a glass of water from the carafe and opened his grip. Balanced on an electric razor inside was a small pile of coins. The top one should be a 1937 Spanish peseta with the first numeral of the date pointing at the top-left-hand corner of the valise. It was.

He took another drink of water and gave a small sigh of relief. He wasn't expecting burglars, but it was always good to be sure. Drinking again, he began to undress. It sure was one hell of a close night. He moved to open the window.

He was staring straight at the ceiling. For a moment he couldn't think why, and then he realized that he was lying on his back on the floor. He had no recollection of having fallen. Very odd.

He got up, shaking his head, and reached for the glass of water. At least some of it was left, and he was thirsty as hell.

The floor spun away to his left and the bed moved in and hit him on the shoulder. He opened his mouth, but no sound came out of it. The religious pictures on the wall advanced and receded giddily.

He frowned; then suddenly, in a blinding moment of clarity, he understood. Of course, whoever it was hadn't troubled to search the room or turn over his baggage. Why bother when you can drug a man's drinking water on a hot night—and then search to your heart's content without arousing his . . . Without arousing his what? . . . It was too dark to remember.

Desperately Dean struggled to a sitting position. You jerk, a voice screamed into his dwindling consciousness. What a prick to be caught by such a trick!

He clawed at the bed, but his fingers seemed swollen and shapeless. The covers whirled away into the stars as the night sky burst though the wall. Dimly he sensed the presence of people, of figures moving in a mist.

And then something exploded with a soft, almost caressing flare in his head, and he began to fall. . . .

5

Icy rain lanced across the East River and rattled on the window of the CIA office facing the United Nations Building. Outside the shabby block hiding the intelligence complex from a curious world, people turned up the collars of their raincoats and hurried to get in off the glistening street. A young man wrestled with an umbrella that had blown inside out on the sidewalk by the entrance. Quinnel, taking the steps two at a time, scarcely gave him a glance.

In his office, the regional director faced a woman across the immensity of his desk. She was short and red-faced. She wore no makeup, and she was dressed in a green military-style uniform topped by a black hat with a gold-starred cockade. Apart from the low humming of the air conditioning, there was silence in the room.

At length the woman gave a short sigh of exasperation and shrugged her plump shoulders. "Very well, Alec, if you *insist* on playing by the book of rules, I guess I'll have to accept it. But I think you're being unnecessarily obstructive. As commandant of the SISTERS, surely I have a right to—"

"Caroline! Please!" Alexander Mackenzie interrupted. "There are no 'rights' in this matter. And, believe me, I'm not being overscrupulous, whatever you think."

"I didn't say that. I said obstructive. And I think—"

"You meant that. But the point is simply this: we happen to have come across a case where, in another country, certain women have been posing as members of your organization. The . . . ah . . . circumstances in which the case came to light aroused our interest, so we are making a routine investigation. Because the women are in fact not members of your team, you are naturally interested too. You want to know why. But that does not give you the right to demand information about the case as a whole, or to be made a party to confidential reports from my operatives. Indeed, I'm astonished that you should ask."

"Oh, Alec, don't be so stuffy! You know perfectly well what I mean. I simply want you to wise me up; I want to know what it's all about. That's all."

"If I knew," Mackenzie said, "I couldn't tell you. I don't have the right to. If it's any help, the fact that these women chose *your* organization as a cover seems to be coincidental."

"Okay. But what I'd like to know—"

"I promise you that the case we are investigating has nothing to do with you. Nothing whatever."

"Since you have interrupted me three times in the past two minutes, I gather that's as much as you're prepared to say," Caroline Bowling remarked with asperity. "But I'll tell you frankly: I shan't let the matter rest there. We do have friends in the Pentagon, you know."

Mackenzie rose to his feet. He was smiling good-naturedly. "By all means," he said. "Pull all the strings you can. And if you come across anything interesting in *your* investigations, let me know, won't you?"

Quinnel came into the room as soon as she had gone. "If you ask me, there's something pretty strange going on down there," he said. "Think we should send in a squad of heavies to find out the score?"

"Be your age," Mackenzie said irritably. "You know we can't do that. That's one hell of a sensitive area. We're still being blamed for Pinochet in Chile. The Dominican and Bolivian—"

"Not what I meant," Quinnel cut in. "Too risky, as you say. No—let this guy Dean go in with one of his mercenary units. No skin off our nose then, if he fouls up."

"You mean. . . ?"

Quinnel plucked a handkerchief from the short sleeve of his jacket and blew his nose. "I mean there's this group has finagled the concession to open up an area. The town isn't started, but the dam's complete—and they won't let anyone in to have a look. They're prepared to kill if they even think someone could be questioned about the dump. All this, plus the whores—it adds up to something mighty suspicious, I'd say. I figure we ought to go on in there and take that look." Quinnel subsided into a chair, all elbows and knees.

"You're suggesting that this man Dean—?" Mackenzie began.

"Find out what the hell there is to hide. Permission to send in Dean with three, four of his mercenaries—blast their way in and report on what they find, right?"

"I suppose so. Provided the agency is not in any way—"

"Not a chance. Man's reliable. I told you."

"So you did," Mackenzie said. "The only thing is, if you want him to lead a squad of mercenaries . . . well, he too seems to have vanished."

"What!" For once Quinnel showed his astonishment.

"We received a radio message through Recife—just the way you arranged with him—the evening of the day before yesterday. Since then, not a word. That's why I asked you to return."

"Maybe he found himself on a promising trail. Couldn't find time to get through again," Quinnel offered.

"Unlikely," said Mackenzie. "We were expecting him to call back. At his suggestion, too. He told our man in Recife to listen at the same time the next day, to make sure he didn't miss out on Dean's transmission, as it could be important."

"Yeah. Don't sound too good. And he *is* a reliable guy."

"I'm afraid something may have happened to him. After all, he's not a professional operative in our sense, and these people sound ruthless. If only he'd been a little more explicit in his message . . ."

"I told him not to send anything in code or cipher," Quinnel said. "Explained we couldn't risk offending the Brazilians by sending secret messages out of their country when they didn't know officially that we were there. Never know when a regular station might be monitored. But you say this message. . . ?"

"Oh, it's in clear all right," Mackenzie said. "But it has to be . . . interpreted. Here. Take a look." He picked a flimsy from his in-tray and handed it across the desk. Quinnel read:

FOLLOWING ARE CERTS AND PROBABLES BRAZILIAN HIT PARADE STOP CERTS LADY IS A TRAMP REPEAT TRAMP REPEAT TRAMP STOP DAM YANKEES STOP UP THE LAZY RIVER STOP I'M GOING FISHING STOP PROBABLES STARS FELL ON ALABAMA STOP OUT OF NOWHERE STOP UNCLE TOM'S CABIN STOP HERNANDO'S HIDEAWAY STOP TOMORROW WHO'S AFRAID OF BIG BAD WOLF ENDS EXDEAN.

"Hmm." Quinnel knitted his brows, caressing his bladelike nose with a finger and thumb. "I guess putting it in the form of a popular-song listing is no more than an excuse—for getting together a series of unusual images, I mean?"

Mackenzie nodded. "That's what I think."

"We got eight songs: four certs and four probables. You figure them for facts and guesses?"

The regional director nodded again.

Quinnel said, " 'Kay. Now, why the repeats in the first entry? I don't get that."

"Simply, I think, to make the title plural," Mackenzie said. "Several ladies. In other words he confirms that there are phony SISTERS there, none of them—as my mother used to say—any better than she should be."

"Right. Then he tells us he's going to investigate some place. Going fishing. That's obvious. But the lazy river? I'm damned if I . . . Oh!" Quinnel paused and looked at Mackenzie. "I see the 'Damn' of 'Damn Yankees' is spelled wrong. Would that be deliberate?"

"Certainly. Recife said he was insistent on treble-checking all the spelling."

"Then the river could be lazy because it's dammed. So he's

telling us that he's chasing after these dames someplace where there's a dam, right?"

"Could be. Now, the second half. Stars fell on Alabama out of nowhere—that's an alarming image, don't you think?"

Quinnel gave one of his rare snorts of laughter. "Sounds like a sequel to the Cuban missile crisis," he said.

Mackenzie looked at him. "It's just possible that you may not be joking," he said soberly.

Quinnel sat up very straight, his eyebrows climbing his forehead. "Come again?"

Reaching into a desk drawer, Mackenzie took out a buff folder with the word "Secret" printed across the top-right-hand corner in red. He removed a single sheet of paper, cleared his throat, and read aloud: " 'Top Secret FYI. Not to be cross-indexed in any file. No copies to be made. Station Three Latin reports Brazilian concern at disappearance of two NIKE ground-to-ground missile transporters from army proving range near Ituiutaba, in Minas Gerais state. The trucks, together with rocket-propulsion units (but not, repeat not, warheads), are thought to have been hijacked, as their crews have disappeared. One report, so far unconfirmed, states that they were seen by a witness on the road leading to Goiás. All reference to the loss has been censored in Brazilian press, radio, and television newscasts. Pass on to Pentagon, but do not, repeat not, file any information, speculation, reports, even unconfirmed rumors this subject.' "

Quinnel whistled. "You think. . . ?"

"I don't know what to think," Mackenzie said. "Is it just a coincidence that the theft of these nuclear-missile transporters, the location of the phony SISTERS, the place where your man Dean sent his message—and where presumably he disappeared—all center on Goiás? Or is it too much of a coincidence?"

"You want me to go down there and check it out?"

"No." Mackenzie was definite. "No way. You've already been seen in Rio; in connection with this case, at that. The ambassador has received the strongest intimation that the Brazilian authorities want us to lay off the SISTERS deal. If there's a mystery, they want to handle it themselves."

"Or cover it up?"

"Or cover it up. It's their country. If it turns out there is a nuclear angle too, or even the hint of a nuclear angle, they'll be even more cagey. The situation will be even more delicate and we'd be even less welcome. No"—Mackenzie shook his head—"it's out of the question for *us* to investigate. All the same, any possibility of a nuclear angle makes it imperative that we *know*." He replaced the paper, closed the folder, and shut it back in the drawer.

"Tell you what," Quinnel said after a moment's thought. "Why don't we send in another free-lance . . . to look for Dean? Then, when he finds him, Dean can wise him up, and they can continue the operation together."

"You have somebody in mind? Somebody discreet and reliable enough to stay undercover and still come up with the goods?"

"Yeah. Dean's own number-two. He knows the way the guy works; he'll be the most likely to succeed, backtracking him. I happen to know where he is. Could even reach him today."

"If Dean's still alive. Would this man agree to do it?"

"Oh, sure. If the money's right. He's a black guy, too, which can't be bad in Brazil." Quinnel gave a wintry smile. "Touch of local color."

"What's his name?"

"Mazzari. Edmond Mazzari. Used to be a sergeant in the Congolese Army. When there *was* a Congolese Army. Tough guy, but straight as they come. Funny thing, though"—Quinnel laughed again, a short barking sound, as if to prove the point—"the guy's about as big and as black as Muhammad Ali, but he's got one hell of a dude accent! It seems he went to school in England or something."

"Yes. Well . . ." Mackenzie looked at the cable again. "If Dean told you nobody can get to see this dam; if you think that's the best thing to do . . ."

"That's what I said."

"Right. But we still haven't worked out 'Uncle Tom's Cabin' and 'Hernando's Hideaway,' whatever they mean."

"Black people? South-American Indians? Someplace where whoever runs this deal shacks up?" Quinnel suggested. "These are guesses, not facts, remember. For my money, they don't make sense until somebody's in the field, out where the action is."

"You're probably right," Mackenzie said. "But we're still left with the Big Bad Wolf."

Quinnel blew his nose again. "Don't like that. Wouldn't have thought of this if it hadn't been for those NIKE transporters—but Big Bad Wolf means BBW to me."

"BBW?"

"There's an association of ex-Nazis, war criminals, and younger, ultra-right-wing businessmen spread through Paraguay, Argentina, and some of the other Latin countries that go for that kind of shit. My German ain't that good, but they call themselves the Bandenkrieg, Bruderschaft Werkstatt, something like that. BBW, see. It means like a workshop for brotherhood in guerrilla warfare. Cozy."

"Of course," Mackenzie said slowly. "We even have a file on them. The head nut's a guy called Fleischman—son of one of the Auschwitz doctors who escaped to South America. And they have this badge, don't they: a flag, an emblem. . . ?"

"Wolf's head with a swastika around its neck. Right." Quinnel stuffed the handkerchief back into his sleeve. "I guess the 'tomorrow' in that signal indicates that Dean meant to follow up with more details?"

Mackenzie nodded. "This latter-day Nazi American Bund, this BBW thing—our evaluation was that it was all pretty small-time stuff. I mean like Little Bad Wolf. Saturday-night beer blasts with the Horst Wessel song and an occasional fascist slogan daubed on a synagogue wall. But if it's tied up with murder and nuclear hijacks . . . and if it's spread to Brazil . . ."

"And if at least some of the powers-that-be in Brazil are trying to keep the connection under wraps . . . ?"

"You better call this man Mazzari right away," Mackenzie said.

Outside in the street, the rain had stopped and a hundred sections of gutter dripping above the brownstones played an obbligato to the mournful swish of tires on the wet macadam. But there were still very few people about. The young man with the wrecked umbrella—he had finally thrown it into a trash can—had little difficulty following Quinnel back to his hotel and then out to the airport.

6

The stars were unusually large and unnaturally bright. Each time the wind blew cool against his skin, they advanced and receded, swinging left or right as the bed creaked.

Spread-eagled, he lay watching them for a long time, wondering when the pain in his head would go away. Some of the less brilliant stars moved in pairs among the brighter ones. A long way behind and below him, a jet plane droned across the ...

Behind and *below* him? If he was lying on his back?

Dean twisted his head and looked over his shoulder. He saw more stars, smaller and more orderly this time, with the tiny red navigation light of the jet gliding through the dark.

There was harsh and uneven pressure against his chest. Something flat and cold rasped against his cheek, and when he turned his head back, his ear was scratched. He moved his hands, feeling for the covers, and they swam in space.

How could there be stars above *and* below? How could he ...?

With the return of consciousness he was able to orient his body: he was not in a bed; he was not lying on his back.

He was facedownward and those brighter stars were beneath him. ...

The coldness against his cheek, the sharpness scratching his ear, the pressure on his chest? Exploring, he found with numb surprise the answer: a leaf, a twig, the branches of a tree.

Those were no bedsprings he had heard creaking; the boughs of the tree were moving in the wind.

What was he doing facedownward in a tree at night ... and if he was looking down, what were the lights he saw beneath it? Shifting his position, he shivered, and realized that he was naked. The flesh of his chest and thighs and belly smarted where the rough bark had lacerated them. How tall was the tree *and what were those lights?*

Behind the pain in his head, blurred images formed and faded. An airplane, modernistic buildings, rough roads, and the wall of a dam. There had been a radio message; he had stopped at night above the town . . . and suddenly image and memory coincided; all at once he recalled the pattern and he *knew*. The bright stars below were the lights of Goiás, with automobiles traversing the streets.

And the tree?

The height of the tree was academic, because there was nothing between the branches and the lights but space. He looked painfully over his shoulder again and saw the real stars above blacked out by an irregular mass bulked against the night.

This was no tree growing tamely out of the ground: he was lodged in the branches of something that grew out of the bluff that towered above the city. . . .

Dean struggled to remember—the empty streets, the darkened hotel yard, the routine check in the airless heat of his room.

The Mickey Finn!

Then it all came back. He remembered the blue convertible parked near the hotel door. They would have come in earlier and then slipped up to his room to doctor the water carafe, taking him away in the car after the drug had worked and his gear had been searched.

And after that?

They must have stripped him and thrown him over the cliff. It was the only logical explanation. If his fall had not providentially been broken by this tree, he would be lying dead among the rocks on the fringe of the forest below.

But why? Simply to rid themselves of a stranger who was asking too many questions? That seemed rather extreme . . . even if they had discovered the transceiver hidden in the Lada. After all, he still had no idea who "they" were.

Unless, of course, they had been onto him before he came to Goiás . . . unless it was a more big-time operation than he had thought, and the operators had somehow been tipped off to the reasons behind his inquiries.

Dean supposed that was possible. Right now, he had more important things to think about. Like how far up or down the bluff his tree was growing, and whether he had any chance of getting out alive.

So far as he could remember, the bluff was several

hundred feet high. Below it, the forest sloped steeply to the outskirts of town. But the lifesaving branches would hardly be near the bottom of the cliff, or he would have broken bones landing among them. He guessed he must have plunged in before he reached his terminal velocity—and that would be . . . how many feet? He couldn't remember. He was only aware of wind whistling in the void beneath him, of the black mass of rock above. He didn't even know if the bluff was sheer or pitted with fissures and crags; it was too dark to see, and when he attempted to ease himself back along the trunk toward the rock face, the tree swayed alarmingly and a small shower of earth and stones dislodged from its roots pattered into the abyss.

Dry-mouthed with apprehension, Dean realized that he would have to cling on until daylight, trying not to move and hoping that the wind would not rise. It was his only chance: only then would he be able to judge the best way of reaching the cliff . . . and see whether he had a chance in hell of climbing it.

And if not? He put the thought from his mind. His predicament was too horrifying to take unless he could believe there might be a way out. But how long would he have to wait? Was it even the same night? Cautiously he crooked his elbow to check the time and the date on his Rolex. The wrist was bare. They had even taken that. A naked foreigner dead at the foot of a cliff . . . Who was going to connect that with a lawyer who had taken a plane from Rio to Brasilia—how long ago?

Dean steeled himself to ignore the peril. To occupy his mind until the dawn finally came, he recapped the events of the fateful day preceding his coded radio message to Recife.

San Felipe do Caiapo was a collection of shacks, some wood, some adobe and thatch, dispersed around a rutted open space that did service as central square, market, sports ground, and local park. There was an inn, a mud-walled church, a bridge that swayed over the river on wires, and a garage. Flanked by a single rusted gasoline pump, the garage was an open shed surrounded by an assortment of decrepit vehicles that looked as if they had just managed to stagger as far as San Felipe when they were new and had never been able to raise enough horsepower to leave.

Dean had driven through not long after noon, when most of the population were seated outside their houses, tipping their chairs back against the walls to take advantage of the shade beneath projecting eaves. There were, however, several groups of hostile-looking men gesticulating along a boardwalk linking the buildings on one side of the square. Most of them stopped talking to stare sullenly at the Lada as Dean bumped across the open space, scattering chickens, dogs, and mules. He edged the car warily over the bridge on the far side of the village. A rapid current frothed and swirled between shingle banks below.

Beyond the buildings, the road twisted through a belt of acacia forest, breasted a rise, and dropped down to the river again, where it joined a wider macadam highway running almost due north and south. Dean took the northerly direction and headed for Getuliana.

Soon the valley widened, the hills on either side became lower, and the river looped away across an alluvial plain in a series of oxbows. Within a few miles he caught sight of the new city. Or rather the place where the new city was destined to be.

The road clung to higher ground at one side of the wide valley, and the excavations—a couple of miles off in the center of the plain—were spread out before him like a map. The drinkers in the Goiás *bodega* had been right: hundreds of acres had indeed been cleared, bulldozed into squares and rectangles and crescents, segmented by radial boulevards converging on a central space, laterally divided by broad avenues. But apart from the temporary huts erected by contractors, there wasn't a building in sight. A cloud of dust above the yellowish earth hung over a single bulldozer working near a pair of idle cranes in a corner of the vast site. But the only other activity Dean could see was a mile away to the north, where the antlike maneuvers of a fleet of trucks and several dozen men spread out from a pair of heavy-bellied transport planes drawn up at one end of a wide landing strip.

The distant puttering of the bulldozer was submerged by a heavier, deeper rumble. For a moment Dean sought the source of the noise. Then he saw a moving dust cloud to his right. A column of artics was winding its way along a dirt road leading from the site to the highway. In a few minutes the trailer trucks roared past, heading for San Felipe and the valley where Dean believed the dam to be. All of them were covered, and each carried a man in some kind of uniform riding shotgun beside the driver. It was unbearably hot in the glaring sunlight at the side of the road. On an impulse, Dean swung the wheel of the Lada over and followed them.

Three or four miles past the intersection where the road

for San Felipe twisted up among the trees, the valley narrowed and the sides became steep and rocky. Soon Dean was driving along a serpentine defile above whose thickly wooded lower slopes great cliffs reared skyward. Then abruptly the gorge divided. The road forked too, one branch following a cracked and peeling sign that pointed to "Aguacalinda . . . Santa Maria da Conceicao . . . Goiás," the other leading to a concrete gatehouse behind wire-mesh gates on steel frames. Half a mile beyond the gatehouse, the great bulk of the dam was visible around a bend in the gorge.

Dean had no means of knowing how wide the reservoir might be in the drowned valley behind the barrage, but the dam itself was one of the highest he had ever seen. From the curved lip spanning the gorge high up against the blue wedge of sky, the great curtain of reinforced concrete plunged downward in three stages like a frozen wave. At each level, multiple arches housing the sluices linked blockhouses from which giant-bore pipes dropped to the hydroelectric generating station below. And around the power station an ancillary web of transformer housings, masts, insulators, and steel pylons had been neatly spun. Towering between the age-old rock faces of that desolate valley, the dam was a testament to the ingenuity of man, a beautiful piece of engineering.

The only man in sight, however, was less ingenious than menacing. He came out of the gatehouse as Dean drove up the approach road and braked by the gates. He was dressed in the same khaki-and-black uniform worn by the guards Dean had seen riding in the trucks, and he was cradling a German MP40 submachine gun in his arms.

"What do you want?" he called over the top of the gates. His voice was not friendly.

"This is the San Felipe dam, isn't it?" Dean called, putting his head out of the Lada's window. "The Menezes-Fleischman project?"

The guard continued to stare at him, saying nothing.

"I am a construction engineer . . . in Brazil on a short visit to survey progress in hydroelectric works, bridging, and so on. They tell me the barrage here is particularly interesting, and I wonder—"

"This is private property," the man said. "On your way."

"Most dams are on private property, but that does not mean that a polite request—"

"I said beat it!" the guard snapped, his sullen face scowling. "We don't like snoopers around here. Like I said, it's private, see. Now, get out."

"But how can I get to see the artificial lake that—"

"No way, buster. You can't. You can either fuck off back to San Felipe or go on to Aguacalinda and Goiás—if you like driving over bare rock. Either way, you won't see no goddamn lake because she ain't overlooked by any road: she's too high up in the hills and the rocks is too steep around her." The guard spit into the dust at his feet. "There's a third choice. You hang around here one more fuckin' minute and I call out the site police and have you towed off of our property. They ain't gentle, neither."

"Well, for Chrissake!" protested Dean, feigning outrage. "I'm not on your property anyway: I'm still outside the gates."

"You're on Intacon property the moment you quit that turnoff. Now, are you gettin' the hell outta here, or do I have to . . ." The man raised his weapon threateningly.

Dean knew that the machine pistol fired 9mm Parabellum ammunition at a rate of five-hundred rounds a minute—and he was unarmed. Hoping that he had displayed the right amount of indignation to pass for a visitor consumed merely by professional curiosity, he turned the Lada and drove on toward Aguacalinda. There was nothing else he could do.

The smooth blacktop he had been following ever since he left the site of the new city now deteriorated: the macadam was worn and potholed, with occasional stretches of earth and gravel between the metaled sections. Judging from the multiplicity of tire marks in the dust, the road nevertheless appeared to carry fairly heavy traffic. Perhaps the convoy he was following was one of many. But where could they be going? Such few buildings as he saw were mainly peasant shacks or the dwellings of subsistence farmers who scratched a living from the stony soil, and these were strung out along one hillside, far from the road and without even a trail wide enough for a vehicle leading to them. So the traffic must either be heading all the way south for Goiás and the next state (which seemed unlikely) or to some other place farther up the valley.

This, Dean thought, was equally improbable: both the dam and Getuliana were in the other direction; the higher parts of the valley—according to the maps, which were admittedly imprecise—were bare of any large-scale habitation before Aguacalinda . . . which was some way on the other side of the pass at the head of the gorge and was in any case even smaller than San Felipe.

Could Menezes, Fleischman, and their colleagues be engaged on some other project that nobody knew about—and if so, where?

On the far side from the peasant huts, the road was flanked by a ten-foot-high wire-mesh fence which had enclosed the Intacon property ever since the gatehouse where Dean had stopped. Behind it, trees had been felled and the bare ground rose steeply to the rocky ridge forming one wall of the canyon. If the maps were right, the drowned valley was on the far side of this ridge, for it appeared to run almost parallel with the one he was in.

When the fence curved up the hillside to pass over the rim of a disused quarry, Dean pulled the Lada off the road behind a grove of bamboo shielding the old workings and got out to investigate.

Parting the canes, he peered through the broad leaves and saw, as he had expected, that alarm wires were threaded along the barbed top of the fence. Every hundred yards there were notices, with white lettering on a red ground warning:

DANGER! This is private property. Keep off. Warning is given to trespassers that the ground beyond the fence is patrolled by armed guards and by dogs.

Menezes and his co-contractors certainly liked to keep their work under wraps! Dean thought wryly. He crossed the road and began to climb the far slope. Here the trees grew densely, and for the first quarter of an hour, pushing his way in the damp heat through thickets of acacia and birch and chestnut underlaid with a secondary growth of brier and creeper, it was tough going. Then he came out onto a stretch of rough porphyritic scree punctuated by clumps of broom where it was easier to pick his way. Finally he stopped where the scree met the vertical cliffs lining the gorge.

But the surly guard had been right. Even from here he could see nothing of the artificial lake beyond the far mountainside; behind the opposite rock face, the barren ground rose again and cut off his view before it dropped to the next valley.

Dean was panting. His bush shirt, dark with sweat, was plastered to his body. He scrambled back down to the road and drove on.

From time to time guards were visible on the far side of the fence, and once he saw a dog handler with two Dobermans on a chain leash. After another three miles in the sultry heat, he observed that the fence had divided, the inner section passing up the hillside and around a sizable property bordering the road and the lower portion continuing as far as another pair of gates. This time the gates were open, but there was a concrete guardhouse with two sentries standing by the doorway just inside. Beyond, a driveway led toward a small wood at the foot of the bluff. Tall cypress hedges bordered one side of the drive, and behind them was a long, low two-story house with a shingled roof and wooden balconies, a group of outbuildings, and a pool beneath palms planted around green lawns. It could have been a country club or a summer camp in the Adirondacks if it hadn't been for the surrounding terrain.

And the killer dogs and the guards on the far side of the fence.

It was in any case an unexpectedly luxurious property to find among the poor cabins scattered along the other side of the valley. Beyond it, the wire continued toward the head of the steepening gorge. Dean had driven another mile, and the road was beginning to zigzag up toward the pass when he realized that the evidence of heavy traffic was no longer visible: the dusty spaces between the potholes were now bare of tire marks.

He turned and drove back, pulling the Lada off the road again and running it behind a stand of holm oaks so that it was hidden from any passersby. Once more he forced his way up the slope to the rock face and scanned the valley below through field glasses.

The property was visible behind a belt of woods. What was it—an estancia? a hacienda? No, surely that was Spanish. It certainly wasn't a farm: there were a number of people about—some of them women in the green SISTERS uniform—but no animals. There were several station wagons and a few sedans parked between the house and the barns. Among them was a bright blue Mustang. Could it have been the convertible in the hotel yard at Goiás? There was no way of telling. He swung the binoculars back and focused on the gateway. The powerful Zeiss lenses showed up the beaten earth of the entrance—*and the unmistakable traces, the tread marks of many wide, heavy-duty tires that proved where the convoy he had been following had left the road.*

But if all those trucks had turned in at the estancia, where were they now? They couldn't have been more than a few minutes ahead of him . . . and there wasn't one to be seen anywhere on the property!

The outbuildings were extensive, but certainly not big

enough to accommodate a convoy of thirty-ton artics as large as the one he had seen leaving Getuliana. Dean lowered the glasses. There had still been trucks loading material from the transport planes when he had turned to follow the first convoy. Maybe if he waited, they would show up here too, and he could see for himself where they went.

But first he must find a better viewpoint. From where he stood, the foot of the bluff was masked by woodland and he couldn't see the termination of the driveway. It didn't look as though there was room there for a large collection of trucks. Nevertheless...

He began working his way back to the car. He had covered about half the distance when he emerged from a screen of bushes to find himself in a clearing above the road. A man was standing there—a poorly dressed Indian staring flint-faced across the valley at the estancia. "Nice place," Dean said conversationally.

The Indian swung around and stared at him. He was wearing an old fringed frontier jacket and one of the dark, high-crowned felt hats favored by village Indians all the way from Mexico to Tierra del Fuego.

"I mean, like it's a surprise, finding a big place like that right out here near the Mato Grosso," Dean burbled, playing the naive Yankee tourist. "All the others are so small."

"Nice place sure," the Indian said bitterly, "if you have money."

"It belongs to rich people? From the city?"

"Surprise, also, for the folks who live here," said the man, who appeared to favor a delayed-action response to questions. "People with house or farm that is take away and put beneath a lake. Very nice."

"Did you have a house that they put beneath the lake?"

"Rich people down there all right. But richness is not all."

Dean looked suitably encouraging and said nothing.

"A farm," the Indian said. "Was a small place, but I like it. Over there." He waved an arm at the far side of the gorge. "Now it is underwater and I am give small, poor house here with stony ground and some money. But money cannot give me back thirty years' work on that farm, and my father before. Now I am not even allowed to walk past and look down into lake where it was!"

"But I thought the ladies—the foreign ladies down there in green—had been sent here to . . . to make easier all the problems affecting those who were forced to move because of the dam."

"Ladies!" the man burst out. "Ladies? Our women are not allowed to behave like that in private, and certainly not in public. It is a disgrace . . . drunken singing and shouts and unseemly acts. Why should these foreign women be permitted to mock our customs in this way? It is a disgrace," he said again.

"I understand," Dean said. "Do *all* the women down there behave in this way?"

But the Indian suddenly bit his lower lip, an expression that was both guarded and watchful closing like a shutter over his features. "I say too much," he muttered. "It is not permitted. It is forbidden to speak of these matters."

"Why?"

"The gods will be angry and spoil our crops."

"Who says so? Who says you must not speak?"

"The *caboclo*. It is instruction."

"*Caboclo?*"

"The old one. The mouthpiece of the spirits. Pai Hernando told me so. Through the *caboclo* he talks with the spirits."

Dean knew something of the voodoolike spiritist cults to which a large proportion of the poorer folk belonged in Brazil. Between his Peace Corps and AID service he had taken an extra course studying the Afro-Indian-Catholic religious syncretism that had produced them, while studying for a master's degree in political science at USC. "Who is Pai Hernando?" he asked now with increasing interest.

"The father-of-saint at the Candomblé down there."

"That place is a Candomblé headquarters?" Dean was astonished. Members of that cult customarily met in very modest quarters.

"Not whole place," the Indian said. "There is a Candomblé *tenda*, a hut, behind the big house."

"And the name of the father-of-saint is Hernando? And he speaks with the spirits through a guide, a *caboclo*?" Dean was frowning.

"A black man, Pai Hernando, yes," the Indian said.

There was still a puzzled and thoughtful expression on Dean's face when he returned to the Lada, drove nearer the estancia, and found another vantage point, a little lower down, from which he could see the whole of the property. There was something here that didn't stack up, though for the moment he was unable to pinpoint what it was that disturbed faint echoes of alarm at the back of his mind.

His bewilderment—and his concern—increased when he

trained his glasses on a flag hanging limp in the heat from a pole in back of the barn.

Soon afterward the second convoy arrived from Getuliana—ten flatbed trucks this time, each with two armed men perched on the running boards beside the I-C Intacon monograms stenciled on the doors.

It was when he saw what they carried—and where they went once they were inside the estancia gates—that Dean decided to hurry back to Goiás and contact Recife on his radio.

The sky was lightening in the east. Through the leafy branches of the tree that had saved his life, Dean saw the landscape far below take shape; like a photographic print assembling its images beneath the fluid in a hypo bath, roofs, streets, walls, towers, and a swell of country beyond the valley slowly emerged from the dark. Warily he turned and looked at the cliff. At once the blood drained away from the upper part of his body and the dread sensation of vertigo clawed his guts.

The tree was only a sapling; the trunk was bent under Dean's 180 pounds. It projected almost horizontally from an imperfection in the rock face, and the tangle of roots above was already pulling away from the ancient limestone. The lip of the escarpment was about forty feet higher up. Dean was lodged in the lower branches of the tree, ten feet out from the cliff . . . and below him there was nothing but the wind, until the foot of the bluff curved out in a scatter of boulders to meet the forest five hundred feet lower down.

He shifted his weight cautiously toward the bole of the sapling. The forty-foot stretch of rock was weathered and cracked, eroded by millennia of storms and frost; it was just possible that an agile man in tip-top physical condition might climb to the top without the aid of crampons and picks, although it would be tough as hell on bare feet. In any case there was nothing else to do. Nobody was going to notice a naked man in a tree from the town far below; there was no one to hear him call; no helicopter would arrive to pluck him into the sky. Still facing outward, he edged back until he was sitting astride the trunk. The branches swayed and tossed alarmingly with every move he made.

Carefully he turned, swinging a leg out and over to reverse his position. The trunk sagged, and then suddenly canted downward. Facing the cliff now, Dean saw a whole matted section of roots and earth and rotted stone detach itself from the cliff face. Once more pebbles and fragments of humus showered down into the void.

He gritted his teeth. If he didn't get clear of the damned tree in the next few seconds, his weight could drag it free and it would drop down the cliff face, taking him with it. If he tried to hurry, on the other hand, he could dislodge it even sooner: with each tiny shift in his position, almost with every heartbeat, more root fibers pulled away and the sapling sank fractionally lower.

It wasn't just the cool dawn air and the effect of exposure that dried Dean's mouth that morning and turned his skin clammy. Willing himself not to look down into the chasm, he was aware of the blood thudding in his ears as he inched toward the cliff.

He was almost within reach of it, no more than an arm's length away, when a fragment of limestone the size of his head fell out of the center of the root mass and dropped. With a rending, tearing noise, the tree folded down against the face of the bluff as forcefully as the tailgate of a truck.

Dean plunged forward as he felt it drop beneath him, outstretched fingers grabbing wildly for a projection in the rock. His left hand closed on the lip of a crevice. It crumbled away under his weight. His right struck a tiny ledge, slipped off it, grasped a boss lower down, and held. His nude body swung against the limestone, grazing a kneecap with a shock that numbed his leg. Below, there was a diminuendo of rattles and thumps as the displaced material bounced off the face of the bluff.

He was hanging by one hand, shoulder muscles on fire, his undamaged leg cycling in search of a foothold. He found a gnarled root still attached to the pocket of earth in which the tree had grown, and this gave him the purchase to push upward far enough to find a second handhold. But the thrust severed the last remaining fibers attaching the sapling to the rock, and it plummeted down.

Five hundred feet up the face of the escarpment, Dean was spread-eagled against the stone like a fly on a wall. When the small rumbling noises of the earth and rockfall had died away, there was no sound but the thin whistle of wind probing the crevices and teasing out occasional clumps of coarse grass that somehow managed to survive in fissures scarring the limestone. With a sudden pang of nostalgia he heard again the dune grasses rustle in October gales on the seaward side of Cape Cod, behind the cottage where his divorced wife, Samantha, lived with their son, Patrick.

He put the thought from him. The sun appeared above a belt of cloud over the eastern horizon, gilding the roofs of the town below. The pale sky darkened until it was deep blue between the wisps of cumulus sailing into view over the rim of the bluff. A little to his right, Dean saw wild campions nodding pink heads in the breeze. There were campions too among the sea lavender and goldenrod that strewed the paths he explored with Samantha, an arm encircling her pliant waist as the blond head rested on his shoulder. Savagely, as though he was rupturing all links with the past, he gouged the plant away from the ledge on which it was growing and used that as a foothold to lever himself a few feet higher.

The ascent was a nightmare. As a physical-fitness freak, Dean possessed abnormal stamina. The strain therefore was less due to the mechanical difficulties of the climb—there were, after all, crevices and projections in the weathered rock—than the traumatic knowledge that a false move, a single glance at the heart-stopping depths yawning beneath him, would mean instant death. His grazed knee was bleeding. His fingernails split. The soles of his feet soon became raw. Once, making a difficult traverse along a two-inch ledge, he was obliged to stop for nearly ten minutes while an agonizing cramp in his toes eased off.

("Easy, son; easy does it!" he had called out to five-year-old Patrick, marooned on a rock by the incoming tide. "We'll fetch the boat and have you off there in five minutes. Just don't panic, that's all. In Vietnam it was the soldiers who didn't panic that came home." And then Samantha cried, "Oh, Matt! Why *do* you have to poison the child's mind always with stories of violence and war?")

Gradually, with infinite patience and a supreme effort of will, Dean coaxed his tortured muscles to deal with his own rock; inch by inch he reduced the distance between himself and the clifftop. He had a little less than seven times his own height to climb. At that time, on that morning, he would have preferred the south-col approach to Everest or the north face of the Eiger.

He was within three yards of the top when he encountered an intrusion distorting the convoluted limestone strata—a bland, unscalable curve of stone as smooth as though it had been polished.

He looked to right and left: there was no ledge on which he could traverse, no projection he could use to bypass the intrusion. Some distance away, rough scrub grew on a slant of cliff that was less than vertical, but it was far beyond his reach. He could go neither up nor sideways, and he dared not even look down. . . .

Then he saw, against the upper curve of the smooth boss, a dried-up tangle of some herb: was it a variety of thyme? sariette? serpolet? He wasn't sure. But he was certain of one thing. The plant was just out of his reach—but if he could grasp the withered stalks, and if they were firmly enough rooted and strong enough to bear his weight, he could pull himself up to a position where he could cant one leg over the edge of the cliff and drag himself to safety.

If he could grasp the stalks.

If they were firmly enough rooted.

If they were strong enough.

There was no way he could check it out. The only way he could reach the herb was to project himself upward, to make that tiny two-inch leap that would bring his fingers into contact with the stalks. And if he failed to hold on, if the herb pulled out of the rock or the stem snapped, he would drop back to the ledge on which he was standing, and the impetus of his fall would topple him from that precarious foothold as surely as if he had pushed himself away from the cliff. No, if he was going to try it at all, it would have to be for real, or . . .

Or what?

The breeze was freshening. The cumulus had built up into a thunderhead that obscured the sun. There was nothing else he could do.

The plant looked parched and fragile, but Dean remembered the wild herbs growing on the hills of Provence, and how he had once tried (unsuccessfully) with all his strength to uproot a small bush of rosemary from the *garrigue* of the Basses Alpes. The plant might appear to be frail, but the roots generally penetrated far into the cracks and fissures of the bedrock. He decided to try his luck.

For a chilling hundredth of a second as he made his small upward leap, he was in midair, unsupported over a five-hundred-foot drop. Then his outstretched hands clenched on the rough, spiny gray-green foliage of the herb and he was hanging just below the lip of the bluff. Sweat broke out on his forehead as he flexed his biceps and slowly drew himself up until his face was level with the minute aromatic leaves. He panted, maintaining the pose like a gymnast, and then slowly, slowly, as the tough little plant held, he brought up a knee, an ankle, a heel, to rest on the lifesaving edge.

Half a minute later he was lying facedown in the rough

grass of the clifftop, sobbing for breath while his body relaxed after the ordeal.

Five minutes after that he pushed through a bamboo thicket and found himself on a dirt road skirting a field of corn. On a patch of soft ground by a gap in the cane screen, he saw the tire marks of the car that must have brought him here. But as he limped, still naked, unsteadily away, his mind was occupied not with the would-be assassins but with a curious and desolate sense of regret that he had been forced to uproot and wrench from their home a clump of rose-colored campions.

Something Rotten in the State of Goiás

War is a continuation of politics by other means.
—Karl von Clausewitz

The soldier . . . is a weapon used by political leaders. But, whether he be infantryman or general, he is an individual who can perform feats of great valor while stricken with justifiable fear.

—Ray Bonds

7

Edmond Mazzari took the press cutting from the police captain's desk. It was quite short, from an inside page of a Rio daily. He read:

> DEATH STRIKES TWICE AT FATAL CURVE
> The body of Miguel da Silva, 73, retired fruit farmer of Carvalho de Freitas, was discovered yesterday afternoon on a mountain road outside the city at the very place where two American women were involved three days ago in a fatal accident when their sports car left the highway. The old man, who traversed the route every day, is thought to have dismounted from his mule for some reason and suffered at the hands of a hit-and-run driver.

"It was published the day after your friend was here," Captain Oliveira said. "I . . . ah . . . I happen to know . . . that is to say, well, it seemed so strange that a lawyer should come all this way . . . in short, one of my men, shall we say, kept an eye on Senhor Forster while he was in Rio. And he visited the scene of the accidents not long before the old man was killed."

"You're not suggesting . . . ?"

"No, no. Do not mistake me. It is possible, however, that Senhor Forster spoke to da Silva: it is not a populated area, and my man was obliged to stay some distance away in order not to be noticed. He could not observe every move your friend made while he was there. It is even possible that da Silva witnessed the first accident but did not come forward to say so. The peasant mentality, you understand . . ." Oliveira's shoulders heaved in Latin resignation.

"But you think he might have talked to my friend?" Mazzari shifted in his chair. He was a very big man, and very dark, the kind of man who made all furniture look frail, yet moved himself with a catlike grace and agility.

"It is possible," Oliveira said again. "If he did—if the old man had seen something untoward and repeated it—there is also the possibility that his death was not accidental. Certainly those who killed the *yanqui* ladies seemed determined that all questions should remain unanswered: there is, after all, the case of the truck driver, too."

"The newspaper stories didn't say that the girls in the hospital had been murdered, did they?"

Oliveira smiled tiredly. "In this country," he said, "there are always certain things that the public are not required to know."

"With a spot of luck, then, the killers may not realize that we're as clued up as we are." Mazzari's British sojourn at Oxford University had lent him an accent—and a turn of phrase—that was in bizarre contrast to his looks.

"That is so," the police captain agreed.

"But you have no information on my friend's movements after he'd been rabbiting with this old chap? If they did meet, that is."

"We know that he went straight back and checked out of his hotel," Oliveira said carefully. "And that he took the next plane for Brasilia. After that he was no longer in our jurisdiction."

"You didn't check with your opposite numbers there?"

"There is a great deal of crime in this city, *senhor*," Oliveira said. "Surveillance of your friend was entirely unofficial—a hunch, as you say—and we had no reason whatever to make a request to the federal authorities. Also, we are much too busy to waste time going through such formalities unless it is absolutely imperative."

Mazzari sighed. "Nevertheless, it's pretty clear from the evidence that he might well have gone there because of something the old fellow told him, don't you think?"

"Perhaps."

"I suppose I'd better toddle along there myself and have a look-see," Mazzari said.

Mazzari decided to try the car-rental agencies in Brasilia after he had discovered that no Senhor Forster (or Senhor Dean) had checked in to any of the city's main hotels, and nobody of that (or those) names had made any kind of reservation at travel agencies, bus station, or airport. It wasn't until the fourth attempt that he found anyone who could recall a "Mr. Forster." But in this case, the youth behind the shabby counter remembered at once. "Why, goodness me, yes," he exclaimed, his dark face lighting up at the memory. "It was a couple of days ago. Actually, he hired the old bus personally from me. Nice chap, really top-hole."

"He was going to have a look at some dam, was he?" Mazzari asked, remembering the enigmatic cable that had been shown him by that equally mysterious CIA man, Quinnel.

"San Felipe, yes. It's in the back of the beyond, near Getuliana. Except that Getuliana doesn't exist. In fact, he asked me to help him work out the jolly old route. I fancy he planned to spend the night at Goiás."

"Goiás. I see. Well, that makes sense all right," Mazzari said, thinking of Dean's message again. "Now, tell me, old chap: has the bally car been returned?"

"Oh, rather. Absolutely. Chap handed it back this A.M. Not a scratch."

"A chap? Not the Mr. Forster who rented it?"

"Well, no. As a matter of fact, it was a different bloke. Just handed it in, paid out the extra cash, and hooked it, you know."

Mazzari leaned forward across the desk. His huge hands reached out and closed gently over the lapels of the boy's tweed suit. "You wouldn't by any chance be sending me up, would you?" he asked in a quiet voice. "Because if I thought you were. . ."

The boy looked frightened. "Sending . . . ? I don't quite . . . ?"

"Taking the mickey." The grasp on the lapels tightened fractionally.

"Good Lord, no!" Now the boy looked shocked. "Why ever should I do a thing like that? I mean, what makes you think . . . ?"

"You're not going to tell me that's your normal way of expressing yourself, of talking!"

Behind his counter, the clerk flushed. "Not to say a hundred percent normal. But I mean to say, one has to go with it, doesn't one?"

"Does one?"

"Absolutely. I mean, I was still on a kind of Brando kick. Can you imagine! To tell you the truth, it was your friend Forster who wised me up . . . that is to say, who gave me the gen . . . on British being the in thing now. After all, it stands to reason, doesn't it, what with David Niven and the Rolling Stones and all?"

Mazzari let go of the boy and straightened up. He was smiling. "You need a refresher course," he said. "Anyway, this other bloke handed in the car, and you haven't seen your man since?"

"Who? Forster? No. Not a hide nor a jolly old hair. But—"

"But you have seen the other man?" Mazzari asked quickly.

"Not to say since, old bean. Before. I've seen him around, you know. Cove by the name of McCaffery. Hardly the type one would expect your friend to—"

"Does he live here?"

"In Brasilia? Who does, old chap, who does? No, I fancy he's a backwoodsman. Usually drives a blue Mustang registered in Minas Gerais. To be honest, I rather thought he was a foreigner employed on the construction site or something of that sort."

"You've been very helpful," Mazzari said. "Here, take this—and I'd like to hire a car myself for a few days. Any chance at all of getting the same one that Forster had?"

"Oh, I say, thanks awfully," the boy enthused. "Most decent of you. . . . But the Lada? Not to say the actual one. One just like it—another Niva. But you can't very well have Forster's. The girl's already taken that."

"The girl?"

"Smashing bird, old boy. What a piece of crumpet! About an hour ago. Asked all the same questions you asked—and off she drove."

Mazzari was astonished. The information he had been given by the man Quinnel, who had met him at the airport when his plane landed from Kingston, Jamaica, had made no mention of any girl who might be backtracking on Dean too. He had simply been told that Dean was investigating something that looked as if it might turn out to be sinister, when he had apparently disappeared—and would Mazzari for Christ's sake please find him quickly because the CIA wanted to know what he had discovered. Could this girl be another of the lowlife SISTERS impostors . . . and, if so, why would she be tracking Dean if the people she worked for had engineered his disappearance? Mazzari didn't know enough about the case to hazard a guess. But knowing that she was ahead of him—and not knowing which side she was on—added a completely new dimension to his search, a factor that had him obscurely worried and actively irritated. "Don't you find that collar uncomfortable in this weather?" he asked sourly as he followed the boy out into the garage where the cars were kept.

"No, sir," said the boy. "Not if it's the thing to do. And let me say it's been a real pleasure talking to you: it proves that this chap Forster wasn't pulling my leg."

Mazzari had driven through the subtropical forest and traversed the bush beyond when he saw the covered truck pulled up at an intersection by an ancient church. The driver and his mate were trying to drag somebody out from among the crates and packing cases in back. A hobo stealing a ride, Mazzari assumed when the man had finally been thrown to the ground—a tall unshaven man clothed in filthy, tattered rags. The two truckers got back into their cab, still shouting insults, and drove away. Mazzari slowed, passing the hobo, checking that the man had not been injured when he was manhandled from the truck. He was scrambling up from the verge shoulder agilely enough, and the big Congolese sergeant lifted his foot from the brake pedal to the accelerator, intending to press on. The hobo had in any case been going in the opposite direction. Abruptly, as he drew level, Mazzari stamped on the brake once more, and the Lada slewed sideways across the road with squealing tires, shuddering to a halt thirty yards farther on.

The man in the dirty rags was Marc Dean.

"What the *hell* are you doing *here*?" Mazzari shouted when he had backed up the Lada.

"I guess that's my line," Dean replied as soon as he had gotten over his own amazement.

"Looking for you, old chap. Why on earth are you got up like some dirty old tramp?"

"Waiting for Godot," Dean said. "What would you do if you found yourself naked on a clifftop with no money and no papers?"

Mazzari stared at him.

"They'd shoved me over the cliff while I was out for the count," Dean explained. "Luckily there was a tree . . . but a guy can't just walk into town in the altogether. Especially without any papers."

Mazzari went on staring. He said nothing.

"Straight into the local jail for Jesus knows how long—if the news ever did get to an embassy or a consulate so that I could be identified and released. I figured the first thing to do was to get covered up. There's a vacant lot outside Goiás where they dump the municipal garbage and then burn it. I kept to the woods until I got there, and then I found these rags. Aren't you going to ask me up into your nice clean automobile?"

"My dear chap!" Mazzari was at once contrite. "Most remiss of me. Do jump in, of course. There's a change of clobber in my bag. I can even let you have a battery-operated razor." He paused and then added, "I think I'll turn the old bus around and head back while you're changing, just the same. There's a bloke named Quinnel wants to hear from you."

"You know Quinnel?" Dean asked as he climbed into the back of the car and began stripping off the rags.

"He's why I'm here, old lad," Mazzari said.

"Great. I was thinking of making it back to Goiás, maybe trying to contact some consular guy so that I could become a person again. Then I saw this truck on the way to Brasilia and figured it might be better to make tracks that way: this deal's getting too important to handle on my own, and I need advice before I go any further." He smiled and clapped Mazzari on the shoulder. "Just as well, for me, that the goddamn truckers got wise and threw me out!"

While Dean freshened up, shaved, changed, and then scrambled into the passenger seat next to Mazzari, the two men filled each other in on what they knew of the case and what had happened so far. "You don't have a radio, I guess?" Dean asked when the exchange was over.

Mazzari shook his head. "It was all too much of a rush, old boy. But Quinnel gave me an address in a Rio suburb where some local field agent can put us in contact with Recife."

"That'll have to do, then," said Dean. "Because, like I say, we have to have a second opinion on this thing."

"Recife, Recife . . . do you know, I haven't the faintest idea where the bloody place actually is," Mazzari admitted, grinning.

"It's the capital of Pernambuco state, below Rio Grande do Norte and Paraíba—a port at the eastern limit of the bulge on the right-hand side of the continent. I guess that's why our intelligence friends keep a station there: nothing to interrupt direct radio beamed at Langley, Virginia."

Dean stood six feet in his socks and he was muscular with it, but Mazzari's clothes hung on him like a scarecrow. They had to smuggle him in through the rear door of a small hotel not to attract too much attention when they reached Brasilia. It was too late to buy fresh clothes that night, and the reception clerk booked them onto the early plane for Rio, which left before the stores opened. They took a cab out to the airport, leaving the hall porter to return the Lada to the rental company.

It was some time after they landed that Dean emerged from the Rio airport boutiques, resplendent in a Pucci flowered shirt, a Pierre Cardin foulard, soft black leather pants, and lizardskin shoes by Gucci. "Let's hope to Christ that the agency has an unlimited budget on this assignment," he murmured to Mazzari, "or else I'm going to be in debt to your American Express account for the rest of my life!"

"You'll be lucky if you don't land up in jail for soliciting, you gorgeous thing!" Mazzari said.

The address furnished by Quinnel was an unpretentious villa screened from a suburban street by a cypress hedge. There was a small Fiat in the carport, and the modest television aerial gave no hint of the wealth of electronic communications equipment beneath the roof.

The local CIA operative was called Mendoza. An amateur of *la haute cuisine*, he regaled Mazzari and Dean with a seemingly endless succession of terrines, farcies, quenelles, boudins, and even a *canard au sang* in the time between the original radio alert to Recife and Quinnel's arrival at the villa the following morning.

"Getting out of hand," the agent said after he had heard their stories. "Can't go any further now until we've checked this thing out with the local talent."

The local talent presented itself at the villa at precisely eleven o'clock: a short, tubby man with a head shaped like an egg, with sleek, dark hair; and a saturnine olive-skinned giant sporting a bushy mustache and a mouthful of gold teeth. "Senhor Gonçalves and Professor Rodrigo Manuel de Soares," Quinnel introduced them as they installed themselves around a polished walnut table in Mendoza's front room. Dean was unable to rid himself of the impression that they were a burlesque act about to leap to the table and go into a song-and-dance routine at any moment. "Don't call us; we'll call you," he was on the point of saying when Quinnel revealed that the two men were in fact very highly placed officials of the administration in Rio—and that although they were not actual members of the government, they wielded a great deal of power in Brazil. "Trouble is," he concluded, "that, as these guys will tell you, there's two different factions within the ruling junta right now. And while the more regular party—to which these gentlemen belong—wouldn't want to know about this fascist BBW routine, the other party could easily be all for it. And they'd certainly want to squash any attempt to expose anything." Quinnel gave a crooked smile. "There's a hell of a lot of loot floating around that's available for—shall we say?—persuasion."

"Perhaps," Gonçalves, the egghead, suggested, "our friends would be generous enough to repeat for our benefit what they have already reported to you?"

Dean glanced at Quinnel, who nodded. "I'll make a brief recap first, gentlemen," Dean said. "Right. Two girls, apparently members of the SISTERS organization, rent an auto and wreck it. Inquiries show that they are in fact B-girls, but they are murdered, along with any witnesses to the accident, before they can be questioned. Later investigation shows that a whole lot more girls, with equally bad reputations, are employed as phony SISTERS, mainly to resettle Indians dispossessed when a valley is flooded to make the reservoir behind the San Felipe dam."

He paused and cleared his throat. "It seems these dames are also required to offer more . . . uh . . . personal services to guys working on a big construction project. This is no less than the new city of Getuliana, and the dam has been built to supply power to it. But although the dam and the power station are completed, no building work has begun on the city. Just the same, the government has advanced huge subsidies to the contractors, who have also raised capital in Europe. All forty of the subcontractors are in fact connected with Intacon—the International Construction Corporation—which is run by a neofascist organization with the initials BBW.

"Question: why not use genuine SISTERS, since this kind of resettlement is exactly their bag? Answer: because something smells; nothing about this deal is on the level. Witness the killing of anyone who could talk about it, and the attempted murder of myself."

"You are saying, *senhor*, that this organization will go to any lengths to block investigation of its activities?" the professor queried. His high tenor sounded as though it had been roughed up getting past his gold teeth. Gonçalves' voice was deep and throaty. He said, "So much, I imagine, you found out before you got to San Felipe. What discoveries did you make on the spot?"

"For one thing," Dean replied, "I found that the lengths they would go to included armed guards, killer dogs, and electrified fences. The property around the dam is about as easy to get into as Fort Knox!"

"Intacon acquired an enormous tract of land," de Soares said. "The reservoir alone is nearly twenty miles long."

"Sure. But you try to get in to see it. I was still aiming to do just that when I happened on the clincher."

"The . . . clincher?" Gonçalves sounded puzzled.

"Yeah. The proof that these guys are pulling some kind of a fast one. Very fast indeed, according to what I saw later," Dean said. "Some way out of Getuliana, beyond the dam, there's an estancia that seems it might be the HQ of the outfit. The convoy of heavy trucks from the airstrip went there and turned in the gates, but by the time I arrived a few minutes later, the whole damned lot had disappeared. Not a sign of them anywhere. So I figured I'd wait for another convoy to show."

Once more Dean paused. "Number one," he resumed slowly, "these were all flatbeds, so I could dig the freight they carried. Among it were parts of the two missing NIKE propulsion units. Number two, in back of the property there's this bluff rises straight from the yard. It's half-hidden by trees, but I could see a tunnel, with a double line of lights in the roof. That's why I could see no sign of the first convoy: the whole goddamn bunch had driven through into the heart of the mountain!"

There was silence around the table for a little while after he had finished speaking. Then Quinnel said, "Don't like it. Secret fortress apparently underground, with a nuclear angle. Don't like it at all. Thing is: what the hell do we do next?" He turned toward the professor.

"Those of us who like to think of ourselves as liberal," de Soares announced in his high voice, "do not serve under the present government because we believe in its policies, but because by staying at our posts we hope to ameliorate some of their more noxious effects. We are, however, considerably outnumbered by the hard-line junta men. No official notification of the facts you have just summarized would, I can tell you, be acted upon. Like those of our neighbors, the administration prefers to turn a blind eye to the upsurge of fascism on our continent."

"It should perhaps be added," said Gonçalves, "that any overt action on Brazilian territory by the Central Intelligence Agency would raise such a storm of manufactured protest that diplomatic relations might well be broken off."

Quinnel rubbed one side of his bladelike nose. "Just the

same, we have to know what the hell goes on. I mean, with nuclear—"

"Exactly," Gonçalves cut in smoothly. "If, therefore, we could perhaps persuade these gentlemen, who have no nationalistic affiliations . . . ?"

"We're professionals," Dean said. "We don't need persuading; we need signed contracts, cash on the line, and bank-certified checks for the balance, to be collected when the job's done."

"Just so. Would five thousand dollars interest you?"

"No," Dean said flatly.

"Each. In cash, with no receipt required."

"Look," Dean said, "this is a dangerous business; you're hiring skills that it's taken a good many years and a hell of a lot of risk to acquire. Don't expect to buy that kind of thing cheap. What you want will cost money."

"It can be made available." Gonçalves was unperturbed. "The BBW are not the only people to have contacts with capital. We want the best. Had you agreed to work for such a small sum, I would in fact have hesitated to employ you."

"What exactly had you in mind, Senhor Dean?" de Soares asked.

"Ten thousand each. Plus expenses. And that only buys you a preliminary investigation. If you wanted a follow-through, that would come expensive."

"For instance?"

"I would probably need to form a squad. Five or six men. For each of them, a thousand in advance and a thousand a day as long as the operation lasts. Two thousand a day each for Mazzari and me. No advance. Then you'd have to pay the guys' air fares from wherever they are—and ours to go find them and sign them up."

"Anywhere served by PanAir do Brasil, we can guarantee you free travel," Gonçalves said. "For other places, very well, we pay the fares. Tourist class."

"First class for Mazzari and me."

The Brazilian inclined his head. "As you wish."

"Then you have to think of arms. People in my profession don't keep stocks. They use fresh ones each time, according to the kind of job. Here we'd need machine pistols, grenades, bazookas, perhaps a couple of armed personnel carriers. Either that or choppers for an air drop."

"There would be no difficulty paying for those," Gonçalves said. "I assume you yourself would handle the order and dispatch? . . . Just so. . . . But I would not want any weapons used that could point at an interested party, any country that might have a political interest, however indirect, in South America. Arms manufactured in the United States, Russia, Britain, Czechoslovakia, or China are therefore contraindicated."

"Would you say that Belgium or Israel had designs on the Latin countries?" Dean countered with a lopsided smile.

Professor de Soares had been totting up figures on the back of an envelope. "So," he said, "assuming the operation required your preliminary investigation and one week's work by a squad that you organized, the global cost should be somewhere between one hundred and twenty and one hundred and fifty thousand dollars?"

"Check. But I can't promise to complete it in a week—not until I've been out there again to see what the score is."

"Understood." De Soares glanced at Gonçalves, who nodded his heavy head. "I think we are agreed, then. Those terms are acceptable to us. Let us now attend to the more important details."

"I guess the briefing is kind of simple," Dean said. "Go on in there and find out what these bastards are cooking up, huh?"

"Depending on your findings," Gonçalves said softly, "there may be a more specific goal: find out what they are doing... and stop them."

Quinnel had not spoken for some time. He asked now, "What kind of country do you have around there?"

"Pretty barren," Dean said. "There are belts of woodland, but most of it's bare. I figure the only way to find out what you want to know is to gate-crash—blast our way into that tunnel with a couple of armored vehicles, and then blast our way out again once we've found out what's on the other side. But before I start anything like that, I'd like to go back with Mazzari and make a more detailed recce. It's just possible there may be an easier way in."

De Soares said, "The country on this side of the dam, as you say, is barren. But San Felipe is on the edge of the Serra do Roncador. The far side of your drowned valley should be subtropical forest, almost jungle. You're practically in the Mato Grosso there, after all."

"You mean...?"

"I mean that if you started from the other side of San Felipe, cross-country, and went through the forest on foot, you might be able to work your way nearer to the lake without alerting them. It's still Intacon property, the far side of the reservoir, but at least there you could see without being seen."

"Good point, sir. Although it wouldn't do us a frightful lot of good with regard to the tunnel, would it?" Mazzari spoke for the first time since they had sat down.

"No," Dean said. "But it might give us a better chance of getting *into* the place. Then, if we could maybe cross the lake, we could try to get to the bottom of all this tunnel routine from the inside."

Quinnel was sitting with his legs splayed out and one bony arm flung over the back of his chair. Now he drew up his knees and rose to his feet. "Don't suppose you really want me in on this," he said. "Better if I don't know, in fact. Interested party, interfering Yankees, and all that. Tell me one thing, though: Professor, if our Nazi friends are up to the wrong kind of funny business, and Dean here smashes them, will your government make a song and dance about it when the dust has settled?"

"About an unknown band of unidentifiable 'terrorists' making some kind of raid in a wild part of the interior? Not on your life, as you Americans say. They dare not—without admitting that they were allowing a different kind of terrorist to hatch . . . whatever plans they are hatching . . . on Brazilian territory. In any case, Gonçalves and my other colleagues are strong enough to . . . er . . . show them the error of such a course of action."

Quinnel nodded. "What I wanted to know," he said. "It's just that I'd hate to recommend an old friend for a job and then find I'd left him in the shit." He turned to Mendoza. "What say you and me go on out to the kitchen and brew up some of that crazy local coffee?"

"There's a lot to arrange and a lot of questions to ask," Dean said when they had gone. "Obviously I can't risk any direct contact with you gentlemen from now on. Justice must be done, but you mustn't be seen to be connected with it! But there's one question I'd like to ask before we get down to the problems of communication and finance and arms supply and suchlike."

"Ask any questions you like, Senhor Dean," de Soares said.

"It's just this: if we decide on a frontal assault of this fortress or whatever it is, there'll be armored vehicles and a certain amount of sophisticated weaponry about. But it's not as though we were planning one of those in-and-out raids on a stretch of uninhabited coast: this dam is almost a thousand miles inland. Can you assure us that we'll be able to get the stuff there without being hindered, questioned, jailed, or having it confiscated by customs men?"

Gonçalves smiled. "A fair proportion of the army is on our side," he said. "They think the wrong colonels got to the top, and there is always jealousy. I can guarantee, not only that the relevant authorities will be looking in another direction, but that the transport of your material itself can be arranged as part of an army maneuver."

"By Jove," Mazzari exclaimed, "this should be one of the smoothest jobs we've ever done! A piece of cake, don't you know . . . with jam on it!"

He was never more mistaken in his life.

8

It was so hot in San Felipe do Caiapo that the wires supporting the ramshackle bridge across the river looked as though they might melt in the sun. Dean and Mazzari sat under a faded parasol that had once advertised Bacardi in a patio at the back of the inn. They were wearing lightweight jeans and bush shirts. A dispirited rooster pecked at the beaten earth floor, and lizards lay motionless in the fierce light that shimmered off the flaking walls.

"What puzzles me, old son, is why you want to sit here and broadcast the fact that there are bloody foreigners around," Mazzari said. "Frankly, I'd have thought that the nocturnal flit and the stealthy tiptoe into the forest would have been more the thing."

"Question of priorities," Dean replied. "I take the point: less chance of discovery, therefore less chance of disaster, if we do it in secret. But there's another side to it. I noticed when I drove through that most of the folks here looked as if they were mad at something or somebody. Kind of, you know, sullen. Clearly, foreigners are neither welcome nor popular here."

"Yes, that's exactly what I—"

"Especially," Dean interrupted, "foreigners working for Intacon. The guy I talked to who'd lost his farm was typical. Our fascist friends, you see, aren't bringing work to San Felipe. So far as I could see, they just import heavies—the kind of guys that look as though they busted out of San Quentin in the fifties! So apart from lousing up the district, they don't even bring any cash to spend here. Even the girls go off to Rio or Bahia or Brasilia in their automobiles. Foreigners who *don't* work for the organization, therefore, and show themselves maybe half-sympathetic, are likely to get an earful. All the San Felipe grudges ventilated in front of your friendly local docs, Mazzari and Dean!"

"And among all this unsavory material, you fancy there may be some tidbits we could nibble, some info we could use?"

"Right." Dean nodded toward the doorway of the inn. At the far end of a corridor they could see a section of sun-baked street. The once-weekly bus to Aguacalinda and Goiás had just arrived and there were Indians in striped blankets, black laborers in blue coveralls and wide-brimmed straw hats, swarthy villagers, and the usual crowd of barefoot children crowding around the passengers as they disembarked, manhandling the packages and crates handed down from the roof by the driver. "Those people know this country," he said. "They were brought up here, played kids' games here, probably roamed the valleys before Intacon fenced them in and flooded the people out. Don't tell me that some of them won't know shortcuts and trails and vantage points the interlopers never even thought of!"

"All right, I won't," Mazzari said equably. "Does this mean that we shall have to pass the night in this delectable showcase of Brazilian culinary art?"

"I'm afraid so," Dean said. "But the *feijao* is not too bad . . . just so long as you have the local equivalent of tequila to wash it down!"

But although they each consumed a fair quantity of the local equivalent of tequila that evening, both at the inn and in a shabby *bodega* across the street, the loquacious drinkers with grudges to air simply did not show. Trying to start up conversations together and separately, they met with reactions varying from surly indifference to excessive (but meaningless) courtesy—and in neither case were the few comments made on Intacon, the dam, or the unfinished city anything but evasive. Even when Mazzari went off on his own, thinking that perhaps a man of color might be more likely to win confidence—and confidences—among the non-Portuguese population, he fared no better. "Something is scaring these people," Dean said when at last they went back to the inn. "After all, I could be wrong about the grudges, but it's kind of screwy that they won't talk about the projects at *all*. They're mostly simple folk. I'd lay my money that it's something to do with that goddamn Candomblé the Indian told me about."

His hunch was to be confirmed the following morning.

Once more they were sitting in the patio; the sun was as hot as ever and the lizards didn't seem to have moved since the day before. The waitress who brought their lukewarm Madeira was a black girl whose flesh bulged in increasing convexities from chin to thigh. She appeared also to be working as receptionist, chambermaid, and hall porter, for they kept seeing her busy about different tasks through different windows of the inn that gave onto the patio. "You may have to wait," she said when Dean went into the tiled hallway to order a second round. "The *padrone* has driven to Goiás today to fetch supplies, and I am all alone here with everything to do."

"It doesn't matter," Dean said. "We're not in a hurry. But since there is nobody else here, you must be overworked. At the same time, there is nobody to see if you sit down for five minutes and take a rest that you have well earned. Why do you not write down a supplementary round on my account, bring out whatever you would like to drink, and join us? You must be in need of refreshment on a day like this."

For a moment she stared at him. Then, without any further comment, she vanished into the kitchen. A few minutes later she wobbled across the courtyard with their two drinks and a glass of orange juice on a tray. She pulled up one of the rusted iron chairs and sat down at their table. "They say that you try to trick men into saying things against the *yanqui* company that builds the dam," she announced.

"So much for the dimwit peasantry!" said Mazzari.

"It is not a *yanqui* company," Dean said. "And the girls who work there are not what they say they are. You used the word *padrone*. I think perhaps you do not come from this country yourself?"

"I was born in Chile," she said. "But my parents they leave when the Presidente Allende is betrayed by the Americans. We are living some years in Bolivia. But I myself leave a year ago when there is again a *revoluçion*. I do not like this kind of life with always violence."

"Do you think this country is any better?"

"Perhaps not. But here, a long way in the country, we are far from those thing."

"Perhaps not as far as you think. . . . What is your name?"

"Escolastica."

"Well, listen, Escolastica: we are not sent by the Americans, but we think there are bad men working with this company, men who will not only exploit the country people but may also bring back the violence from which you have escaped."

"It would not surprise me," the woman said.

"If they plan to do this, we shall try to stop them—but first we must find out about these plans, and for this we must get inside the property that surrounds the new lake."

She shook her head. "That is not possible. There are big dogs, men with guns—"

"We know about that. All the way from the powerhouse to the estancia and beyond. But what about the other side of the lake? The side where the forest begins. Do the trees come right down to the water? Do they have the same fence, the same guards?"

"There is another estancia on the far side," Escolastica said.

"Another . . . ? But I thought there were no roads in that direction."

"There are none. But it was completed just before the *arroyo* was flooded, and now you can reach it only by boat. It is where the most important of the company stay."

"That is very interesting," Mazzari said. "But you say it is completely impossible to reach the place from this side of the lake? There are no footpaths, no trails through the jungle, nothing?"

"I believe there is a path that leads there from the place where they make electricity, but it is inside the fence. And, yes, they say the guards go there, too."

"There is no way of approaching this second estancia from above?" Dean asked. "Not along the lake, but from the ridge on the far side, down through the forest?"

She held her thick lower lip for a moment between finger and thumb. "There is a track," she said at last. "There used to be a track. By a water mill on the road to this Getuliana. Perhaps it is overgrown by now. It led through the forest to Santa Maria da Regenceraçao."

"Which is what? A village? A church?"

"A shrine. It was used by the old ones. There is a bare place on top of the hill from which they used to signal to the men of Aguacalinda."

"Something like smoke signals?" Mazzari asked.

"I do not know."

"Why do you say it may be overgrown?" Dean asked. "Do the people not use the path anymore?"

Escolastica glanced around the courtyard. The rooster had persuaded two bedraggled hens to join it, but otherwise the place was empty. "It is wiser not to talk of these things," she said, just as the Indian had said to Dean some days before.

"What things? Why must you not talk?"

"That evil shall not fall upon the village."

"Evil *will* fall upon the village, if we are not able to stop these bad men," Mazzari said. "People like you must help us, by giving what information you can."

Her eyes flicked rapidly up to meet his, then slid away. She rotated the stem of her glass between the finger and thumb of one hand, saying nothing.

"This is to do with the Candomblé, isn't it?" Dean asked on an impulse. "The spirits have forbidden you to discuss certain things."

"I know nothing of such matters," she said evasively.

"Has it not occurred to you that the spirits are acting in the interests of the foreigners who build the dam? Do you never ask yourself why these spirits—?"

"You must not say such things!" protested Escolastica. Clearly she was scared.

"This path through the forest—there has been a taboo put on it, hasn't there, a *coisa feita*?"

"I tell you I know nothing . . ." she began, half rising from her chair. "Anyway, it is all superstition. . . . I do not believe—"

"Escolastica!" Mazzari reached out and gripped her wrist, forcing her gently back into her seat. "One cannot *will* things out of existence simply by pretending they are not there. That is the way of the ostrich. I can see that you are afraid—afraid of the violence that may come, on the one hand; afraid that the spirits may harm you, on the other. But the way to combat the unknown is to face it, not to run away. Because once you *have* faced it, it is no longer unknown and therefore less frightening. Also, you have run away twice already. Is it not time to stand fast and take a positive action?"

She was staring at her fat hands, dipping a finger in the ring of moisture left on the table by her glass, tracing a watery line from there to the edge of the table. "Perhaps," she said.

"We are, after all, only asking you to answer some questions," Dean said persuasively. "To tell us something you know already."

"We are not asking you to *do* anything: it is simply to find out about the countryside," Mazzari coaxed.

"In any case, nobody has seen us talking; nobody here will know what you have said—or that you have said anything at all."

"Besides, if you are able to help us stop these men continuing the violence, the good spirits must surely be pleased, and you will yourself have one thing less to fear," said Mazzari.

"There are only two things we want to know," Dean said. "About the path through the forest, and about the Candomblé itself and this Pai Hernando."

The woman hesitated. She was still sitting with lowered eyes. A bar of sunlight slashing a segment of the round table had already evaporated the trail of moisture. Finally she sighed. "Very well," she said dully. "From the shrine, you can look down on the second estancia and the place of the boats. There is a steel electricity post on the other side of the road from the mill, and the path begins about one hundred meters from there, where a giant walnut tree stands on the edge of the forest. ..."

The trail was overgrown, all right. A quick-growing mixture of manioc and cane had been planted on the fringe of the wooded region, and if they had not been told about the walnut tree, Dean and Mazzari would never have found their way to what remained of the path. Casting about behind the thicket—which had evidently been cultivated with the sole purpose of masking the entrance—they eventually came across a stretch of undergrowth that was a little less tangled than the rest, and beyond this was clearly the remnants of a forest trail. Fifty yards in among the soaring trunks of cedars and chestnuts and royal palms, the beaten earth track was crisscrossed with a kind of frame made from interlaced branches, and beneath this was a curious collection of items: bloodstained white feathers in a small earthenware pot, a glass of some amber liquid, yellow *farofa* meal, a pair of goat's horns, and a cigar balanced on a box of matches.

Dean whistled softly. "A *coisa feita*," he said. "No wonder the village people don't want to come here anymore!"

"What was that again?" Mazzari said.

"An *encosto*, a kind of spell. What you see is an offering to the Exú Tranca-Rua—a demon who does any dirty work required by Oxóssi, the god of the forest."

"Is that what they call a *despacho*?" Mazzari nodded at the strange collection.

"Yeah. It's supposed to be stuff that the Exú likes, a sort of bribe, I guess. That's probably some kind of liquor in the glass. Tranca-Rua is also known as the road-blocker; that's why he's been invoked here, to make a *caminho fechado*, a closed path. No believer in spiritism would dare go farther along the trail after he saw this."

"Why the hell not? What's to stop him?"

"The fact that he believes some ill would befall him or his family if he defies the Exú's warning," Dean said soberly.

"Well, I'm damned if I know . . ." Mazzari shook his head. "It's all beyond me."

"Of course it's beyond you, you ignorant limey," Dean said playfully. "The basis of all this is African!"

Mazzari said, "Now pull the other one!"

"Fact. All those gods in the Brazilian cults are derived from Yoruba deities that crossed the ocean with the slaves. I'll explain it to you next time we have half a day to spare!" Dean walked around the magic offering in its twiggy shelter and began to hack with his machete at a complex of thorny bushes barring their way. As he swung and slashed, he sang to himself:

Sarava Meu Pai, vou me benzer,
Vou pedir ao Pai de Santo,
Para quebrar o teu encanto,
Para me proteger.

"What's that supposed to be? An entry for the Downbeat award?" Mazzari asked.

Dean grinned. "It's an old samba: it won first prize at the Mardi Gras carnival in Rio fifteen years ago. But the words mean: Hail, Father, I'm going to bless myself by asking the priest to break your charm and protect me."

"You don't mean you believe in all that mumbo jumbo?" Mazzari was scandalized.

Dean smiled again. "It never does any harm to make sure," he said lightly.

The trail twisted now in between banyans, broad-leaved bananas, uadua hardwoods, and teak; dense curtains of liana hung from branches splayed far above their heads; the undergrowth grew head-high in spiny clumps. The air, heavy and humid and strangely silent when they entered the forest, had become damper and more oppressive as the ground began slanting upward, loud with the humming of anopheles mosquitoes and piums, occasionally shrill with the chatter of monkeys. It was quite unbearably hot.

Dean and Mazzari—no longer posing as lawyers in search of land options—had let it be assumed in the village that they were naturalists of some kind; botanists, ecologists, ornithologists, it did not matter so long as their interest in the Intacon project was seen to be minimal, no more than the curiosity of travelers denied the right to enter certain areas they wished to study. Only to the woman Escolastica had they admitted openly an anti-Intacon position. They had therefore arrived from Brasilia in a jeep (provided secretly by army friends of Gonçalves) loaded with lightweight camping gear, cameras, specimen boxes, and a quantity of rations. Once they located the entrance to the jungle trail, the jeep had been hidden in a stand of trees several hundred yards away on the opposite side of the Getuliana highway, and they had taken only the essentials on their expedition. By far the most important of these were the machetes, for the disused trail frequently lost itself in thickets of impenetrable thorn bushes equipped with black spikes almost a foot long, or shallow depressions where the ever-present creeper had woven an impassable barrier between branch and root. Hacking their way through one of these, they came out suddenly on a hillside glade bright with magnolias and fenced in by sachapelma—giant Brazilian tubers related to the potato, with prickly ten-foot stalks and huge leaves like some demon variety of rhubarb.

Beyond this obstacle, the path, climbing more steeply now, was clearer. The high, thin thrumming of mosquitoes, hornets, and other insects in the damp heat below the distant roof of trees was punctuated every now and then by the grunting of peccaries, the screams of startled birds, and the occasional slither of an armadillo through the undergrowth. Once a black-and-white tapir wandered across the path fifty yards ahead of them, and they were accompanied all the time by the cries of a band of cinnamon-colored monkeys that seemed to have followed them all the way from the edge of the forest.

One of the most distressing and discouraging aspects of a climb in jungle country is that the traveler never knows how much farther he has to go before a crest is reached: the forest floor rises inexorably beneath the impenetrable blanket of vegetation, and no skyline ever comes into view. Dean and

Mazzari had been struggling upward for more than three hours when they paused for rest and refreshment. Mazzari was sitting at one side of an open space split by a gully gouged from the soft earth by a stream overhung with mosses. He was dabbing blood from the wasplike stings of pium flies that had been attacking his arms and neck. Dean had crossed the stream with the compass and was staring moodily uphill (it was the fourth time they had been mistakenly convinced that the spine of the ridge was at hand). Just beyond him, sunlight fell through the branches of garumo and balsa trees, dappling the leaf mold with shifting patches of light and dark.

Sunlight and something else. There was movement in the shade, a quick, darting motion of paler color, a threshing of the dark, a sudden dry slither among the broad leaves.

Dean cried out, and the shout was choked in his chest.

On the far side of the glade Mazzari started to his feet. A traga-vendao, one of the jungle varieties of anaconda that can attain more than thirty feet in length, had dropped from a tree and wrapped two of its coils around Dean. Half of his body was covered by the twin two-foot-thick loops of green, black, and brown. Mazzari raced across the open space and leaped the gully, drawing his gun from the concealed holster each of them wore under his bush shirt. The huge snake's tail was whipping between the trunks of two trees.

They were carrying 9mm Beretta Model 92 automatics—heavy-caliber, fifteen-round pistols that weighed only a pound and a half and were less than six inches long. Mazzari slammed back the slide as he landed on the far side of the stream and aimed at the snake's head.

"No!" Dean called in a strangled shout. "Convulsions . . . tighten coils if you . . . kill it." His arms were imprisoned and the slowly contracting reptilian loops were forcing the breath from his lungs. He could hear his own ribs creak. *"Tail . . ."* he panted. "You mustn't let . . . anchorage . . ." His voice died away as the anaconda started squeezing the life from his body.

Mazzari caught on at once. Like most boa constrictors, the traga-vendao—forest Indians call it the antelope crusher—kills its prey by crushing it to death and then swallowing the remains whole. The jaw hinges are elaborate and the mouth opens cavernously wide, so that in the case of a bullock or deer, the whole animal is ingested except for the horns, which continue to project from the anaconda's mouth until its gastric juices have dissolved away the body. It is not, however, venomous, and before the powerful coils can do their work, the tail end must lock around a tree trunk or something similar in order to provide anchorage for the fatal constrictions. Mazzari dropped his gun and hurled himself at the nearest tree. It was a thick-boled uadua: the snake's tail had just curved around the trunk and was sliding farther to improve its grip before the final contractions that would reduce Marc Dean to a bloody pulp.

The big Congolese sergeant seized the tip where it had narrowed to a diameter of not more than nine inches, hauling it with all his strength away from the tree. Abruptly the long snake body uncoiled; the tail flicked viciously, sending Mazzari spinning across the glade to crash into another tree trunk and slide to the ground. He sprang to his feet and ran back. The momentary slackening of tension had enabled Dean to free one arm. Mazzari picked up the pistol and thrust it into his hand. "Vertebrae . . . when I get . . . tail away," Mazzari gasped.

Dean nodded. His face was deathly white. No force that he could command could withstand the relentless tightening of those steely hoops of muscle that threatened to squeeze him as flat as a used orange.

The anaconda had wrapped its tail around the uadua again. Mazzari could see the muscular contractions begin to ripple along the segmented back. Dean cried out as the coils contracted once more.

Mazzari grasped the boa constrictor's rear end where it was thicker this time—about six feet from the tip, where the second length began to loop around the tree. He folded his arms around the cool, dry, scaly envelope of skin, braced one foot against the rough bark, and heaved.

The dark snake flesh within reacted like a tempered spring. Mazzari felt the incredible force of the reptile drawing him toward the tree as he exerted every ounce of energy that he possessed, trying to haul it away, toward his own chest.

The cords in his neck stood out like hawsers. Knotted muscles in forearms, biceps, and the calf of the leg braced against the tree gleamed ebony in the diffused light. A heavy sweat started from his brow and splashed down onto his bush shirt. Beyond Dean, the snake's flat head had turned, black reptilian eyes staring incuriously at the struggle waged around its own farther end. For an eternity the man and the jungle creature remained locked in combat, unmoving in their battle for supremacy. Mazzari's breathing grew hoarse and deep. His shirt darkened across the shoulders.

Then, almost imperceptibly, the pendulum began to swing in the human's direction; the tiny gap between snakeskin and uadua bark widened; the distance between Mazzari's chest and the steel-hard armful of sinew and tissue that he held narrowed. He was prying one of the coils away from the tree.

Abruptly he released his grip, ducked underneath, slammed his back against the trunk, and shoved outward with both hands and a foot. As suddenly, the anaconda decided to change its tactics—perhaps to lock itself around another tree, where there would be no interference with its contractions. The tension slackened and the tail whipped around and away from the uadua. At the same moment, Mazzari shouted: *"Shoot!"*

Semiconscious from the suffocating pressure on his lungs and abdomen, Dean sighted the Beretta with a shaking hand. Aiming for a spinal undulation just behind the snake's head, he pulled the trigger.

The whiplash detonation of the shot was lost in a maelstrom of action. The anaconda jerked, straightened, convulsed in a whirling knot of interlocking loops, threshing among the forest trees with a ferocious hissing noise as loud as the escape valve on a steam engine. Mazzari leaped for the far side of the tree. Dean, mercifully thrown clear by the first convulsion, fired again and again at the writhing coils. When at last the traga-vendao lay still among the broken branches and the palm fronds that it had brought down in its death agony, he tottered to the edge of the clearing, fell to his knees, and vomited into the undergrowth.

Half an hour later, they walked out into a larger clearing and saw the bright blue of the artificial lake glittering beneath them.

They were just below the crest of the ridge, on a slant of land about a hundred yards across, studded with clumps of paramo and pasto grass. What the woman at San Felipe had called the shrine stood on the far side of the glade. It was an old *jivaria* or *finca* whose wooden walls had rotted and from which the palm roof had long ago blown away. Behind it, a plantation of yucca had run wild.

Below the open space, forest trees ran down to the water's edge, where Dean's field glasses picked up the gleam of Intacon's ubiquitous steel fence. Half a mile away to their left, the blue water stopped at the lip of the dam. On the right, the reservoir curved out of sight around a bend in the drowned valley. The far shore appeared to be bare rock, but on their side of the lake, in extensive grounds hacked out of the forest, was the second estancia they had been told about. It was an extraordinary sight in that desolate region.

An imposing white mansion in the colonial style, with a pillared and pedimented facade and outbuildings discreetly masked by a line of cedars, stood at the end of a driveway leading to a jetty. Dean could see formal gardens, greenhouses, even orange groves, bathed in the dusty late-afternoon sunlight on either side of the driveway. But the field glasses revealed no approach road on the landward side. Neither, although a number of people were visible in the grounds, was there any sign of a boat tied up at the jetty. Guards in pairs patrolled the fence. Men and women were lying on a sundeck around a heart-shaped pool. Gardeners leaned over flowerbeds where automatic sprinklers spiraled a mist of rainbow drops onto the lawns. "But it doesn't make sense," Dean muttered to himself. "How the hell do those guys and dames *get* there?" He raised the binoculars and swept the far shore of the lake. From the dam to the curve in the valley, there was no breakwater, no quay or road, no indication that any craft ever put out from or sailed to the bleak rock shoreline. "There's something screwy here," he said aloud. "Those people have to come from *some*where!"

"Choppers, maybe?" Mazzari offered.

Dean shook his head. "It's possible, of course—but unlikely. There has to be quite a shuttle service operating to keep that place going. And I guess we'd have heard tell in the village if the sky was full of goddam helicopters all the time."

He stared through the field glasses for a few more minutes and then shoved them back in their leather case with an irritable gesture. "I'm going on over that fence and see what gives," he announced.

Mazzari looked at him. "It must be the sun," he said. "Chaps who aren't used to equatorial—"

"I'm serious. I even figured out a way to get over the other side, give you a chance to make use of your West African woodcraft!"

"May the gods gaze kindly on thine all-powerful ju-ju, O great white chief," said Mazzari.

Dean punched him on the shoulder and led the way down toward the line of forest trees. Within a half-hour they were staring out at the fence across a fifty-yard strip of land from which all trees and undergrowth had been cleared. Waiting patiently, they discovered that the guards, working singly again here, passed every fifteen minutes, each man covering and recovering a beat of around half a mile. This meant that the intersection of two beats, after the two men had exchanged a word and then marched off in opposite directions, would be free of surveillance for almost thirty minutes. Dean chose a place where the fence ran along the top of a low bluff overhanging the lake, leaving only a narrow footpath between the wire and the drop.

"And just how did you propose to lob yourself over here?" Mazzari inquired. "Pole-vaulting?"

Dean grinned. "In ancient times," he said, "the men of your country had a neat way of executing their enemies. They bent the tips of four palm trees to the ground, pegged them in that position, and then lashed the victim's limbs, one to the tip of each tree. When the pegs were cut away, the trees sprang upright, dividing the condemned man into four equal parts, which were distributed over the countryside. I *propose*, as you say, to use an amended version of that technique."

Mazzari shook his head. "You left me behind," he said.

Dean explained. There were young palm saplings at the edge of the cleared ground. Choosing the one nearest the fence, Mazzari reached as high up as he could and locked his hands around the trunk. Then, using all of his strength, he pulled the trunk toward him, walking slowly backward so that his grip moved farther up the bole. When the upper part of the trunk was being held down horizontally, he gasped, "If you think . . . the jolly old snake . . . was difficult . . . just try to deal with the tension . . . of this bugger!"

Dean was stripping off most of his clothes, stuffing everything but his shorts into the lightweight camping packs they carried. When he was naked except for a pair of Y-fronts, he ran to lend his weight to that of the African. Together, sinews cracking with the effort, they dragged the sapling down until it was bowed into a U-shaped hoop, with the fronded tip touching the ground. Both of them were shining with sweat. "Can you hold it long enough?" Dean panted.

"Do my best. It's . . . other three that are going to be . . . difficult!"

Dean laughed. "That's my boy. Now, listen, Edmond: when I've gone, take the packs, work your way back to the highway just inside the fringe of the forest, and make camp a couple of hundred yards off the road. You should hit it somewhere near the power station. I'll join you there after dark. Okay?"

"If you don't go soon, I'll hit the other side of the blasted lake," Mazzari groaned.

"Steady. A few more seconds." Cautiously Dean released his hold on the palm trunk. Mazzari stiffened and his muscles swelled still farther. Now only his brute strength held the tip of the tree to the ground. Dean swung a leg over and straddled the tip, his head toward the roots. He wrapped his arms and legs around the thin bole and called, *"Now!"*

Mazzari let go of the tree and sprang back.

Quite slowly at first, and then with increasing speed, the palm sprang upright, quivering like a knife-thrower's blade in wood.

When the tip reached the zenith of its arc, Dean flung his arms and legs wide . . . and was catapulted headlong over the cleared ground, across the wire fence, and beyond the footpath crowning the bluff. As he began to lose height, he closed his legs, joined his fingertips above his head, and dived into the lake twenty feet below with scarcely a splash.

The water was icy: the cold hit him with a shock that almost stopped his heart the instant he plunged beneath the surface. The lake must be exceptionally deep, he thought dazedly, arrowing up through the numbing blackness toward light and air. He headed for the shore, and then, when he was sheltered by the bluff from any watchers on the footpath, he swam in the direction of the dam with an effortless crawl that left hardly a ripple on the water.

Even for a man of Dean's physical condition it was an ordeal. Twice, when the bluff had subsided to a bank no more than four or five feet high, he saw patrolling guards and was forced to swim underwater for long periods, never knowing when his mouth appeared momentarily above the surface to drag in air whether he risked attracting a burst of fire from a machine pistol. When the bluff disappeared and the shoreline sloped straight into shallow water, he was obliged to strike out toward the center of the lake to minimize the chances of detection. And all the time the freezing cold penetrated to the marrow of his bones and sapped his energy with every stroke.

He was a hundred yards from the dam when a strengthening current warned him that if he didn't make for the shore, the undertow caused by water flowing through the sluices could prove too strong for him and sweep his body inexorably toward the slanting concrete lip. He glanced in the direction of the forest. There were pebbles and stretches of coarse sand interspersed with driftwood at the water's edge. The guard whose beat ended at the dam had his back turned, on the way to the rendezvous with his companion. Facedownward at the lakeside, Dean allowed himself to drift slowly in until his knees grounded on the shingle. He looked up. The fence was twenty feet away, the trees some distance beyond. Between him and the nearest buttress at the outer edge of the *barrage* was about thirty yards of bare, stony ground. And around the buttress there was a thicket of sachapelma and wild cassava.

He crawled slowly from the water and lay flat while the moisture ran in runnels from his muscular frame. The sun had vanished behind the ridge on the far side of the reservoir and a cool wind now heralded the approaching dusk. With a final look around, Dean rose to his feet and sprinted for the bushes.

On the far side of the uncomfortable, spiny thicket, he looked down the original steep hillside to the complex installations surrounding the power station far below. To his surprise, he could see no workers among the forest of steel girders and insulators beneath the high-tension wires, nor were any guards visible on the blacktop leading to the gates.

There was, however, one nearer at hand. "Raise 'em high, buster, if you don't wanna be drilled in the spine," a harsh voice growled behind Dean.

The mercenary leader froze. And then, slowly raising his hands to shoulder height, he half-turned and saw a big man in the uniform of an Intacon guard emerging from among the huge sachapelma leaves. The MP40 resting in his capable hands was trained on Dean's naked back. It was the same hood who had stopped him at the gate before.

"Jesus," the guard said. "You again? Well, don't give me no shit this time about fuckin' engineers or whatever the hell you said you was. This time we go straight to the boss an' you'll see what we do with motherfuckin' snoopers around here."

Dean said nothing. Caught inside the perimeter fence wearing nothing but a pair of wet shorts, he could hardly pretend that he'd lost his way or was looking for a place to picnic.

"Get goin', snooper," the guard snarled. "Out along the dam . . . and watch your goddamn step. You try any funny business, an' you're down in the water." He chuckled throatily. "We keep them piranha fish in there, like to discourage strangers!"

Dean's blood froze. He had never thought, in the excitement of adventure, of the deadly little South American killer fish. He knew—thankful that he had not suffered the pium bites that had enraged Mazzari—that the slightest spot of blood, the tiniest opening or cut in the skin, could attract a shoal of razor-toothed piranha that was capable of reducing a living human being to a clean-picked skeleton in less than three minutes. Shuddering at the thought of the terrible death he had escaped, he walked out along the curving concrete causeway surmounting the dam.

Hints of thyme, rosemary, and wet earth floated on the moist sunset breeze. Behind them, the rustling of dry grasses where the *barrage* met the hillside faded as the dusk thickened and the wind stirred the water into wavelets that slapped at the dam. Somewhere ahead, the gathering darkness trembled where the outlet flows from invisible sluices roared down the sloping face of the dam in their gigantic pipes.

The mean-faced guard was close behind Dean—so close that gusts of beery breath mingled with halitosis soured the herbal scents of the oncoming night, and the cold ring of the gun muzzle bored into his spine the moment he slackened his pace. The guard was tough, all right, but he was no expert, or he would have known that a man with a machine pistol jammed into his back has a better chance of escape than one menaced from several feet away.

Reaction time faced with an unexpected move was the deciding factor. At the right moment, with a sweep of his arm, Dean could probably knock the barrel of the MP40 aside before the guard pulled the trigger. But he couldn't whip around and seize the gun quick enough to stop the man firing, and even a single shot would certainly bring more guards at the double. If he was really being taken to some guardhouse, it might therefore be better to wait and take his chance there.

Except that, judging by the ruthlessness they had already displayed, his chance of getting away alive seemed slim—especially when they realized he was the man they had tried to kill in Goiás.

There was a possibility, too, that Bad-breath had no intention of going to any guardhouse and intended simply to beat him and then push him into the water for the benefit of the fishes. From his point of view that might save a heap of trouble.

Dean shivered at the thought, weighing the possibilities. Maybe after all he should attempt . . . ?

Suddenly theory was obliged to give way to practice. They had arrived at a small observation platform surrounded by a guardrail, and from this steps zigzagged down the sloping concrete face into the darkness below. "Down there, quick," the guard snarled. "Get smart and I'll drop you six hundred feet with a slug in your ass."

This, Dean thought, is the moment. His pulses quickened as the adrenaline flowed. It was the kind of situation on which he thrived—the sudden challenge, a lightning decision; action, for better or worse.

He turned and went down two steps, grasping the iron stanchion at the end of the rail as if to steady himself when his raised hand was low enough to touch it. Then, in a single smooth continuous movement, using the stanchion as a pivot, he prolonged the turn, ducking swiftly under the rail and swinging out onto the steep slant of concrete.

Flame stabbed the dark as the machine pistol spat a hail of lead into space. Dean felt the wind of the slugs ripping past his head. But before the detonations of that first burst had died away, he had completed his turn, grabbing the guard's legs and pulling his feet from under him. The guard fell to the iron deck of the observation platform. Before he could fire again, Dean had leaped back up and seized the barrel and stock of the man's gun. For a moment, face to face, they wrestled for possession of the weapon. Then, instead of trying to snatch it away, Dean slammed the machine pistol with all his force *toward* the guard. Since the man was already heaving it in that direction himself, it struck him on the face and chest with stunning force, breaking his nose and momentarily blinding him with tears.

He cried out in pain, threshing on the iron platform. Dean tried to take the gun, but the guard's convulsive movements knocked it from his grasp to go spinning and clattering down the face of the dam. From far below, half a dozen more shots sprayed skyward as some obstruction jarred the trigger mechanism.

Dean scrambled back onto the lip of the dam. It was man against man now—but he was unarmed and practically naked, while the guard had a blackjack hanging from his belt and wore heavy-duty boots. From Dean's point of view, therefore, space to move in was vital.

Although he scorned the ritualized techniques of judo, kung-fu, and karate, he was a master of unarmed combat, tremendously strong but knowing precisely where and when to strike most effectively with the least effort to himself. He crouched now in a wrestler's stance, arms held low and wide, waiting for the attack. Swearing vindictively, the guard unclipped the cosh and sprang forward. It was still twilight up here above the lake, and Dean watched the eyes that glittered with such malevolence in the bloodied mask of the man's face, alert to duck, sway, dash in a quick, shrewd blow, and then dance away again, as the opportunity presented itself.

In actuality, none of this expertise was necessary. The guard hurled himself at Dean. The blackjack whistled through the air. Dean dropped sideways, straight as a felled tree, thrusting out a foot to knock one of the man's ankles against the other. He felt a glancing blow on his arm, and then the guard had stumbled, tripped, and fallen over the lip of the dam into the water.

Somewhere along the lakeshore, a voice shouted something unintelligible. The guard surfaced, blood still spraying from his broken nose . . . and then, with a dreadful scream, he sank again. The water boiled with movement. Dean stared, horrified, as a skeletal hand, the bones already shining whitely in the dusk, clutched air above the crimsoned wavelets. Then that too vanished, and he was alone.

He crouched down on the observation platform. He could hear voices and running footsteps now from each side of the lake. Here and there, the beams of flashlights lanced the dark. Yet there wasn't a sound from the powerhouse or the alley below, where the concentration of guards might be expected to be strongest, nor did there appear to be anyone patrolling the causeway itself. It seemed almost as if the owners of the mysterious lake were more concerned to keep people away from the reservoir than from the dam forming it, or the hydroelectric plant below.

Frowning, Dean bent double and moved farther out along the causeway. If there was nothing to see, the approaching guards might with luck assume that both sentry and prisoner had fallen victim to the killer fish. If they did look further, the stairway would be the obvious place to start—and he had no wish to be caught halfway down in the spotlight beams and shot like a dog. In any case, he wanted to have a closer look at this power station that wasn't considered worth guarding.

When he was immediately above the modernistic cube of the main building—the guards had almost reached the two ends of the causeway—Dean lowered himself from the lip to another observation platform, swung from the guardrail to a buttress, slid down fifteen feet of rough concrete in the dark, and finally found with his feet the curved surface of one of the huge-bore pipes leading the water below.

The great iron tube dropped down the face of the dam at

an angle of more than forty-five degrees. Dean climbed astride it and began lowering himself slowly and carefully, while the footsteps, the voices, and the lights came together, separated, and eventually dispersed in the blackness above.

Forty minutes later, half-deafened by the tumult of falling water which had battered his ears from inside the conduit, he thankfully unstraddled the pipe, wiped the grazed palms of his hands on his shorts, and stepped onto a balcony that circled the upper floor of the power station.

There appeared to be no guards and no personnel at work. No lights gleamed through the slits of the shuttered windows or pierced the louvers in the metal doors. There was no watchman's booth beside the main entrance. The place seemed as deserted as the blank surface of the lake above. The nearest sign of life was the floodlight above the guardhouse, shining pale through the complexities of transformer and pylon from the gates a quarter of a mile down the valley.

He edged his way around the balcony and found a door on the far side of the building from the gates. There was no sound now from the lip of the dam above. Dean carried two pen-sized tubes clipped to the waistband of his shorts. One was a small but powerful flashlight; the other housed a selection of slender instruments in stainless steel. Feeling for the keyhole of the door, he slid out one of these and inserted it gently in the lock. Fifty seconds later, he tried another. And another. At the fourth attempt he uttered a small grunt of satisfaction. There was a slight click in the dark, followed by the sound of metal wards shifting. For a short while longer, he maneuvered the instrument, and then the door swung silently inward at his touch. Dean vanished into the blackness of the interior.

He felt at once that something was wrong. At first he was unable to pinpoint what it was that worried him. Then, over the muted, more muffled roar of the water, he had the answer: it was nothing positive; it was an absence that troubled him. There should have been a humming of generators, a whine from the giant turbines spun by the falling water, a whiff of ozone in the air.

But there wasn't.

Dean stood silent, listening. He was certain that he was alone in the vast building. He unclipped the flashlight and thumbed the button. As soon as the thin beam split the dark he saw why.

For whatever purpose the dam and the reservoir had been constructed, it wasn't that of supplying electricity to the problematical city of Getuliana. For, apart from ducts that led the seething water direct from the pipes out to the river that wound down the valley toward the gates and the bridge, the great power station was an empty shell. There were no turbines, no generators, no insulators, no glassed-in control rooms or gauge-and-dial regulating consoles. Apart from the railed iron gallery on which he stood, there weren't even any catwalks. Like the metaled but trafficless road that led to it, the place was nothing but a blind, a colossal sham.

9

Professor Rodrigo Manuel de Soares smiled. The gold teeth gleamed on a level with Dean's eyes. "Clearly, *senhor,* your time—and ours—has not been wasted," he said. "Even if your discoveries in fact deepen the mystery surrounding these extremists and their plans." He spread the ends of his bushy mustache with a finger and thumb. "It now becomes essential to find out precisely what those plans are. You have not changed your mind about the . . . methods to be used . . . in the second part of your assignment? On the terms that we agreed?"

Dean shook his head. "The way I see it, blasting our way in with a small, picked squad's the only answer, sir."

"Very well. Then I suggest it be done as speedily as possible. You have my permission to proceed, and I am sure that my friend Gonçalves, were he here today, would concur." De Soares sipped his schooner of Boal Madeira and leaned back in his chair. They were sitting in the parlor of Mendoza's CIA safe house on the outskirts of Rio, Dean, Mazzari, and the professor. Quinnel had flown down again from Venezuela, but he was taking no part in the conversation, standing by the window looking out at the rain that was falling from a sultry sky. Judging from the savory odors filtering through the door, Mendoza was in his kitchen cooking something in wine. "Lest there should be repercussions later," de Soares said, "I am bound to ask you formally, nevertheless, if you have considered all other means of entry—or possible entry—to this private property."

"Sure have," Dean said. "You can get to the lake, all right, from the forest side. We proved that. But even if you crossed it, there seems to be nothing to get to over the water. The second estancia looks like some kind of rest home—and this screwball power station doesn't exist! I'm one hundred percent convinced that the answer's through that tunnel. And it's guarded by a blockhouse: we drove by a second time to check."

"And that," Mazzari added, "is where this Candomblé center is—the place these johnnies seem to use to keep the natives quiet. Or rather to scare them into silence."

The Brazilian nodded. "It is just that I have to make sure," he said. "I am certain you understand. Matters of state, you know."

"Yeah," said Dean. "I know. In case of repercussions."

The gold teeth shone again. "How long would it take you to organize and mount this operation?"

"If you want arms that can't be traced to this country, or anyplace politically interested in it, I guess I'll have to fly to Europe and see a friend of mine. He'll probably be able to arrange delivery from someplace in the Caribbean. Direct. Then I have to contact a few guys and get them moving. Say, a week from now."

"Excellent. How many men do you think you will want?"

"For a fact-finding raid? Another four, I guess. There's Sean Hammer, an Irish-American sometimes acts as my number-two; a Pole named Novotny—very reliable guy; and a couple of heavies."

"The necessary money will be made available to you tomorrow," de Soares said. "May I tempt you to a glass of this admirable Madeira?"

"Thanks," Dean said. "It's a mite too sticky for me."

"True, true. I have what the British call a sweet tooth." De Soares chuckled. "Your friend Mendoza does not approve."

Silhouetted in the window, Quinnel's angular frame swung suddenly around to face them. "I suppose you know you were followed here?" he said accusingly to Dean.

"Followed . . . ?" Dean half-rose from his chair. "Are you serious? Are you sure?"

Quinnel plunged a bony hand and wrist into one of the baggy side pockets of his jacket. It emerged holding a scrap of paper. "Followed ever since you quit the airport, arriving from Brasilia, according to Captain Oliveira," he said. "Seems that she—"

"*She!* A woman? . . . My God, I'd clean forgotten! The mystery girl who rented the other Lada!" Mazzari burst out.

"—wears the uniform of this SISTERS group," Quinnel continued. "I just checked: she's in an auto across the street, and it has to be the same one. Oliveira's man described her. I quote"—he glanced at the paper—" 'A young curved American lady with short and golden hairs.' "

To begin with, it was too simple. Dean and Quinnel left together. The blond followed. And Mazzari followed the blond in a small Fiat belonging to Mendoza that had been parked in a lane behind the villa.

When Dean parked outside the small hotel they had chosen in back of the port, the girl slid her car into a vacant space on the far side of the road and stayed at the wheel. "She must have checked out that the place is built against the rock and both entrances are on this street," Mazzari said when he had arrived by the service stairway sometime later.

"Okay," Dean said. "Now, listen, Edmond. I'm going on out and fix me a ticket for Brussels first thing tomorrow. I've got to see Jammot in Belgium in the next twenty-four hours if we're going to get these weapons on schedule."

"Wouldn't they do that for you in Reception?" Mazzari said.

"Maybe. But the lobby's full of drunks for some reason. Perhaps there's a convention in town. In any case, I guess there's a better chance of a seat if I go direct to the airline office: it's only a block away. I'm going to walk there, and then I'll lead this dame someplace else. You tail her . . . and then we'll play it by ear."

Mazzari nodded and grinned. He figured his chief's professional pride was smarting because he'd failed to notice that they were being followed.

If that was so, Dean found that the wound was salved once he was on foot and aware that he was tailed. For the girl was an expert. She never hurried, she never dawdled, she never did anything obvious like staying too long staring into a store window displaying goods that wouldn't interest a woman. Yet she was always there: she was never close enough to be noticed, but she was always near enough to catch up and follow an unexpected move. She was hot on anticipation, too, often being already on the far side of the street before Dean himself crossed over.

He walked to the next intersection and turned into a broad avenue that was congested with traffic. The rain had stopped, and late-afternoon sunlight was drying out the crowded sidewalk between the big stores and the acacia trees lining the street. To Dean's surprise, the PanAir do Brasil offices were closed. And so, he saw as he looked around, were the neighboring stores and kiosks.

Frowning, he hurried toward the center. The girl followed, varying her distance skillfully and making such magisterial use of other people as cover that Dean found it difficult to keep his eye on her long enough to get a complete picture of her appearance. Since he was anxious that she shouldn't realize he was wised up to the tail, he contented himself with an occasional sideways glance at the plate-glass window of a store, the odd reflection provided by a cupped hand over one of the lenses of his sunglasses. From what he could see, the girl was slender, in her mid-twenties, with a lean, sweeping jawline and chiseled features thrown into dramatic relief by an orange bandeau confining her short blond hair. As Captain Oliveira's man had noted, the dark green, subtly retailored SISTERS uniform did nothing to hide the fact that she was indeed "curved."

Fifteen minutes later—steam had stopped rising from the street and the sun was setting—Dean discovered that both the TWA and the Pan Am offices were also shut. That was odd. In Latin countries, he knew, siesta-hour closing could be prolonged, but it was almost dusk, it was a Tuesday . . .

"Pardon me," he inquired, stopping a passerby, "would you know if these stores—the airline offices especially—will be open again later?"

White teeth flashed in a dark face. "Open later?" A mellifluous chuckle. "Tonight? Man, you have to be joking!"

"But I thought . . . Usually they're open at least until . . . ? Surely?"

"Usually is other days. You must be out of your mind! Don't you know what day it *is*?" the man demanded—and without enlightening Dean, passed on with a wave of his hand.

Dean frowned, shrugged, saw a modern hotel across the street, threaded his way through the snarled-up traffic, and went into the lobby. A crowd of noisy tourists milled around the elevators. Some of the women were wearing paper hats. Dean pushed his way to the reception desk. "Pardon me," he said to the clerk. "I wonder, could you help me? I want to book a plane ticket—"

"Booking? *Booking!* Plane tickets? But these are not for *tonight!*" the clerk exploded. He reached under his counter and came up with a half-full bottle of champagne. "Tonight is for drinking, senhor. Be my guest and drink with me. Tomorrow we can think about tickets!"

A chorus of giggles cut short his oratory. Teenage girls with linked arms infiltrated his cubbyhole and carried him away, shouting and splashing froth from the bottle. Dean was astonished. He went out into the street. From behind him a burst of laughter and the sound of breaking glass were cut short by the closing of the doors.

On the avenue, now that he noticed it, there was an air of subdued excitement; a purpose and a direction united the groups of people hurrying past. They were all heading for the ocean. And from somewhere down there floated a noise, distant, imprecise, but compelling, that he suddenly realized had been in the background ever since he left the hotel.

It was a composite, complex sound, rising, falling, altering in pitch but never in measure, sometimes drowned by the throbbing of motors or the laughter of the crowd, but always hammering away at the threshold of his hearing. And gradually, as he concentrated on it, he was able to separate the different components. There were more voices—many, many voices; there was the faint sound of musical instruments; there was clapping, cheering, shouting, and the stomp of multitudes of feet. But over and above everything else pulsed the persistent muttering and thumping of hundreds of drums.

It hit him then. If he hadn't been so preoccupied with the news that he was being tailed, he must have realized before. It was Tuesday, all right, but not just any Tuesday. This was Shrove Tuesday, the Mardi Gras, and it was the season of carnival in Rio! In a city where carnival is something close to a religion, it was no wonder that folks thought him crazy, asking if the stores were open! No wonder, too, that the streets were crowded and the hotel lobbies full of drunks.

Dean allowed himself to be carried along with the main body of the crowd. Night was falling and strange illuminations flared over the rooftops to the east. Here was an opportunity to lose his tail if he wished. But she knew where he was staying, and anyway, he preferred to lead her on in the hope that maybe he could maneuver her into a position where he could find out why she was following him and for whom. Was this another of the fake SISTERS employed by the fascist organization out at San Felipe? If so, had she been a party to the attempt on his life in Goiás? Not if it was the same girl who had rented his Lada, for that had been *after* the attempt was made. Could she nevertheless be some kind of hit woman, a female killer who had accepted a contract on him? He doubted it—and in any case, Mazzari should be backing him up somewhere in the crowd.

The street they were following led now into an open space. A dense throng jammed the roadway, stalling all traffic. And on the far side of the palm-fringed square stretched the vast expanse of Copacabana beach.

Dean stopped, amazed at the sight. The esplanade was crammed with revelers, weaving and dancing, bouncing to the music of at least half a dozen different bands. He could see guitars, mandolins, accordions, flutes, an occasional trumpet or trombone, and everywhere among them the insistent pounding of percussion—hand-hit conga drums, timbales thrashed with sticks, tom-toms, snares, maracas, claves, guiros, and above all, bongos, beaten by professionals and amateurs, by bandsmen and individuals, in a complexity of rhythms so intoxicating as to be irresistible.

Into the surging mass of dancers flooding the spaces between the bands wound a parade bright with huge papier-mâché masks, banners, and outsize balloons shaped like mythical animals. Farther away, a stream of floats bearing gigantic effigies strewn with flowers was spearheaded by its own group of buglers. Fifty-foot monsters, garish with crepe paper, floated in the air from wires, breasting a tide of ornate lanterns on sticks. Beyond, the immense strand was black with people against the lines of phosphorescence rolled shoreward by the incoming tide.

The noise was deafening. As Dean watched, the sky at the far end of the esplanade was split by fireworks jetting red, gold, and green stars into the dark. A cheer went up from the great crowd, most of whom were either garlanded or in some kind of colorful costume. The air was full of paper streamers and confetti. Spun around by a rush of dancers, he was just in time to see the girl following him taking delivery of a headdress from one of the stalls selling favors and elaborate carnival masks. He couldn't make out exactly what it was: she had the thing folded over her arm. And then, before he could move nearer, she had ducked out of sight behind a truck whose sides were opened up to make a shooting-gallery sideshow.

Dean hesitated. It was a smart move on the girl's part. She would reemerge in disguise, indistinguishable from the rest of the crowd, and he wouldn't know if she was still following or not. On the other hand, if *he* followed *her* around to the other side of the truck, he could identify the headdress, but it would tip her off that he had tumbled . . .

Abruptly he changed his plans. He had, after all, promised himself that he would play it by ear. Instead of leading the girl to some place where he could turn the tables, he would simply vanish—and then start following her. For carnival disguise, he thought with an inward smile, was a game with room for more than one player. He hurried to the nearest stall and bought a headdress himself.

It was a giant Chinese coolie head, with bucolic oriental features surmounted by a three-tiered pagoda hat. From within the hollow sphere of this mask he peered around the corner of the shooting-gallery truck. The girl was at the edge of the crowd, turning this way and that. She was wearing a costume shaped a little like a North American Indian totem pole: a tall, beaked animal with huge round eyes. The wearer's own viewpoint was a second pair of eyes pierced in the neck, below which a cascade of paper feathers fell almost to the ground.

Clearly she was trying to locate Dean. But the crowd pressed densely around her. The drums thudded deafeningly on either side. Isolated snatches of conversation broke the surface of sound like bubbles in a glass of champagne.

"Fantastic, darling! The whole thing's just fantastic!"

"Hey, lookit them star shells over the sea!"

". . . never been kissed by a man with a *beard*?"

"Charlie! Over here, for Chrissake! . . . *Charlie!*"

"Perhaps, *senhor*, perhaps not. The night is young."

"No fuckin' wop bartender's gonna tell *me* . . ."

". . . so beautiful I wanna cry. Oh, Hal, *look!* I'd like . . ."

"Room for a little one on that muscular arm, handsome?"

"*Charleeeee!* . . ."

Suddenly the mask with the bird's beak and the paper feathers was moving away. Dean watched it forge through the merrymakers ahead of him now. It looked as though the girl had given up the chase. Blue and green meteors thundered overhead. Scarlet rain showered above the apartment blocks behind the esplanade. But the beaked mask, bobbing now near, now farther away, was heading for the fringes of the crowd. He shouldered people aside, struggling to close the gap between them. "What's your hurry, honey lamb?" A fat woman in a jockey cap laughed. A girl twined an arm around his neck and kissed his cheek. Several times Dean was in danger of being separated from his quarry by phalanxes of laughing, singing dancers with linked arms. Once he did lose sight of her altogether when a circle of howling admirers surrounded an amazon in tight blue jeans who decided to give an exhibition of frenzied acrobatics just in front of him. Then he caught sight of the beak and the feathers once more, farther to the left then he had expected, hurrying up a side street away from the waterfront.

Dean plunged in pursuit. The girl crossed two wide avenues and threaded her way up a narrow street toward one of the heights that lay behind the old town. On all sides the yowl of electric guitars and the rattle of tambourines filled the air. The roadway was disgorging a stream of plastic mandarins, Popeyes, and mythical beasts, all pressing down toward the sea. The population here was predominantly black, the laughter more boisterous, the dancing less inhibited.

The beaked mask traversed a cobbled square and started up a grade, climbing the side of a bluff dotted with wooden shacks among the trees. More than once Dean was forced to dodge into a doorway or hide behind a parked automobile when the grotesque head turned in a questing way—almost, he thought with a frown, as though she knew she was being followed and wanted to make sure *I* was still there! He quickened his pace as the girl in the carnival disguise sprang across a gap in a ruined wall and began toiling up a path steep enough to be buttressed every few yards with risers of planking pegged into the hard earth. Again the beak swung his way as he closed the gap between them.

The shanties clinging to the cliffside were ablaze with lights and shaking with music. *Now*, Dean thought, before she contacts her confederates . . .

As he panted up the steps, his eyes drew level with the girl's hurrying heels. It was odd that she should be wearing rope-soled espadrilles with a uniform suit. And hadn't he heard the click of *high* heels behind him? Suddenly suspicious, he spurted, caught up with her—and halted. She had stopped outside the door of one of the huts. A dim light burned behind a window that looked onto a tiny porch.

Before Dean could speak, she turned toward him, raised slender arms, and lifted the beaked mask from her head and shoulders. "Man," she said, "I thought you was *never* goin' to make the strike!"

Aghast, he stared at a tight black skirt, the deep cleft separating breasts sheathed in red sequins. Above the girl's plump cheeks, violet eyes shone in a twenty-year-old face that was the color of mahogany.

Dean was cursing himself for not realizing that the vendors of carnival masks would sell many of the same design, when the girl said, "It's fifty bucks for a short time, but you can have the whole night for a century and a half . . . and at least you saved cab fare, walking all this way."

Mazzari lost sight of Dean when the girl disappeared behind the truck. He didn't see his chief put on the coolie mask, but he did see the girl disguise herself, and since Dean had vanished, he followed her. But before long he lost her too. They got separated by some religious procession, and when it had passed, there was no sign of her.

For a while he stood scanning the crowds. But he saw no more totem poles, and eventually made his way back to the hotel in disgust. It was a hot night and he was sweating. He had loused up his assignment and there was nothing he could do about it. Better to write the whole thing off, have a nice, refreshing bath, and get up early to make amends to Dean any way he could tomorrow.

He unlocked his door, switched on the lights in his room, and checked his personal "signposts" to make sure it had not been searched in his absence. Then he dragged off his jacket and strode through to the bathroom to turn on the faucets.

"This absurdly large perforated thing is a silencer," the girl, the right girl, said. She was sitting on the edge of the tub. "The gun behind it is very small. It's a .22 Beretta, and unless you shoot terribly accurately, you haven't a hope in hell of stopping a big man like you. The only thing is, I'm afraid I do shoot terribly accurately."

She rose swiftly to her feet. "Now," she said, "in the other room, if you please. There are one or two questions I want to ask you."

10

Edmond Mazzari slumped into an easy chair in his bedroom, sighed, and broke open a pack of cigarettes. "Look, sweetheart, I haven't the faintest who you are—" he began.

"Put that down!" the girl rapped. "I've seen that one before—the first cigarette to come out of that pack is a bolt of metal, painted white. It comes out fast, because there is a powerful spring inside the pack, and it hits me right between the eyes. By the time I recover consciousness, you have the gun."

Mazzari's liquid chuckle filled the room. "You watched too many episodes of *The Man from UNCLE* when you were a baby," he said. "Or do you have a kid yourself who buys all those James Bond gadgets?"

"Put it down. On the bed."

The big Congolese shrugged and tossed the innocent pack onto the covers. There were honey-colored glints in the girl's close-cropped pale hair, he saw in the bright light of the hotel room, and the body beneath that rakish, thoroughbred face was even more voluptuous than he had thought.

"All right," she said. "We'll have your hands lying along the arms of your chair, please. That's it. And now perhaps you'll tell me just exactly who you are, what you are doing here, and why you were following me."

"I think you're reading the wrong lines, old thing," Mazzari murmured. "Surely those are questions *I* should be asking."

The blond tossed her head impatiently. "I lose my temper easily," she warned, "and a slug even from the smallest Beretta can hurt like hell—through the ear or a wrist, for example."

"Oh, come on, ducky," he said easily, leaning forward to rise from the chair. "You know very well you wouldn't use that thing, even if it is silenced."

He dropped abruptly back into his seat, seeing the almost imperceptible whitening of a knuckle as the girl took up the first pressure on the trigger. "So-ho!" he said softly. "We really would have played with our toy, would we? Or else we're smart enough to show that we are taking up first pressure as a bluff, knowing also that a professional couldn't afford to take a chance on it."

"All right, all right," the girl said. "So you read the sign—which told me what *I* wanted to know, too. So let's just assume that we are both professionals, shall we, and take it from there? . . . I repeat, who are you? And what are you doing here?"

"My dear old darling, there's no secret about that," he said casually. "I mean to say, you could have found out simply by coming up to me and asking. There was no need for all the melodrama."

"I'm waiting."

"My name is Mazzari. I was staying in Kingston, Jamaica. And I came to Rio to look for a friend who seemed to have disappeared."

"What was his name? And what was *he* doing here?"

"His name *is* Forster, I hope. You should know the rest: you were following him."

"I asked you what he was doing here."

"He was investigating something for some friends of ours."

"Investigating what?"

"I'm frightfully sorry, but I don't think that's any of your business."

"That's where you're wrong," the girl said. "It is just that which makes it my business. For these friends of yours on whose behalf the so-called Mr. Forster was investigating are in fact friends of *mine* . . . and they have never heard of Mr. Forster!"

"Friends of yours!" Mazzari echoed. "You mean you do actually belong to the SISTERS organization? But this is ludicrous!"

"I didn't say I was working for Sanders International. Your Mr. Forster affected to be doing that. So did another Mr. Forster—the tall, thin, gawky one I saw you with today. Each of them went all over, asking questions and ferreting about, each claiming to be a lawyer briefed by the organization. This was not true; nor is there any qualified New York lawyer named Forster with the dossier and description of either of them. Naturally enough, therefore, there are a number of interested parties wanting to find out what gives."

"I see. Forgetting the uniform for a moment, which of them do you represent?"

"So, to begin with," the girl said, ignoring his question, "I ask you once more: who sent you here? And who sent Forster?"

"The same people."

"Thank you very much," she said sarcastically. "And it's no use pretending that you are a member of the CIA, the Brazilian counterintelligence service, or any special branch of the Rio police. I have friends in many places and I've checked all the—"

"I wouldn't presume," Mazzari interrupted. "I wasn't aware that any of this had anything to do with espionage. . . . Look, simply, a man disappeared. I was sent here to try to find him. I found him—alive and well, as you have seen. That's all."

"Are you working for any American group?"

"No."

"Any Brazilian organization?"

Mazzari shook his head.

"Any underworld organization? Any international syndicate?"

"I told you," he said patiently. "I was hired. To find a man. The hirers are clients and their identity is privileged information. You know that."

"I'm not a policewoman. I have a gun on you. I don't have to observe the niceties of legal protocol. . . . You're a private detective?"

Mazzari glanced over the girl's shoulder and raised an eyebrow. "All right, Mendoza," he said. "Don't hurt her. Just take the gun."

The weapon itself remained steady as she said evenly, "The French windows are locked. The catch makes quite a noise when it's operated. This balcony is nine floors up. There is no stackpipe, no fire escape connecting with it, and no way of reaching it from the neighboring rooms. . . . Do you think I'd sit here with my back to the windows if I hadn't checked out all that, for God's sake? I thought we'd at least agreed to consider each other professionals. You let yourself down, trying to pull a chestnut like that!"

"My apologies for underestimating both your training and your intelligence," Mazzari said. "What is your name?"

"Coralie Willys, if it matters. Don't you ever smile?"

"Only when something amuses me. Don't you?"

"I'm too busy to notice. Now, if you were sent simply to

find a man, why were you following me once you'd located him and your job was finished?"

"We wanted to find out why *you* were tailing *him*."

"You and who else? Once again: who hired you?"

"An organization calling itself the BBW," Mazzari said blandly.

"I never heard of it." For the first time Coralie Willys looked bewildered. "Who the hell are they?"

"A group of fascists and ex-Nazis with a lot of pull somewhere; a gang of international cranks planning some dirty work."

"I don't believe you."

"Don't believe what? That there is such an organization? Or that they hired me?"

"I don't believe either of them."

"By Jove, you're a difficult girl to please," Mazzari said. "However pretty you are—and I must say you're a knockout—I have to say that I'm rather glad you're not my particular armful. . . ."

The affair of the windows hadn't fooled the girl for a moment. He hadn't thought it would. But the subsequent exchange had sufficiently diverted and held her attention for him to do what he wanted to do. He was sitting fairly well forward in the chair, his forearms lying along its padded arms. The chair, he knew, ran easily on its casters across the tiled floor. Imperceptibly, as he talked and stalled and held her eyes with his own, he had drawn his feet back under him and edged his hands forward so that the fingers now grasped the front ends of the chair arms. His center of gravity should now be such that, if the chair was suddenly removed, he could remain in the same squatting position and not fall over. He flexed his muscles experimentally. . . . Yes, he could make it: the time had come to end the interview. He was by no means sure that Coralie Willys was employed by the SISTERS. If she was, surely they would have liaised with this man Mackenzie in New York, and Dean would have been informed. On the other hand, he could hardly believe that she was associated with the fascists. In an adventurous life that had brought him into contact with many villains, male and female, Mazzari had formed the opinion that the baddies almost invariably looked bad in some way or another . . . or, in the case of con men, too good. There was also that old saw concerning the female of the species. Mazzari didn't think she was deadlier but simply that lack of principles showed more clearly on the smoother contours of a female face. In his Oxford-modeled estimation, the feminine associates of evil men never looked like *ladies*. Coralie Willys did. And even the most accomplished of actresses could scarcely have feigned that puzzled innocence when he had slipped in the Big Bad Wolf reference.

In any case, the riddle of her allegiance must wait until another time: right now, he was tired of being questioned himself.

". . .essential that you tell me their names," she was saying.

Once more Mazzari held her eye. "Very well," he began, "if it's really so important . . ."

Tensing the muscles of calf, back, and thigh, he raised himself minutely from the chair . . . and then sent it rocketing backward across the floor with a flick of his powerful wrists.

The girl's eyes left his face as the chair skated away behind him with a rumble and a screech. Involuntarily she watched it speed away from the still apparently seated man. At the same time, like a *trepak* dancer in a cossack ballet, he kicked out one leg horizontally from his squatting position.

The toe of his shoe slammed against the underneath of the automatic's butt as it nestled in her hand, sending the gun spinning upward. Before she had switched her gaze back from the errant chair, he had leaped to his feet, stretched out a large hand, and snatched the Beretta from the air.

"Frightfully sorry, dear lady," he said quietly. "Forgive the bloody liberty and all that. But my friend has to leave early in the morning and I really do need some sleep, you know."

Coralie Willys was scarlet with mortification. Her eyes flashed angrily as she nursed her hand and watched him slide the clip from the gun butt and then shake out the tiny shells. He crossed the room to the bed, picked up a purse on a shoulder strap that she had left there, and dropped them inside. Then he bowed, handed her the purse and the unloaded automatic, and turned to open the door for her. He was smiling.

"Until the next time, Miss Willys," he said gently.

"If there is one," the girl said with suppressed fury. "I do not like people opening my handbag without my permission. It is rude. Also, I have a rooted objection to being followed by men. Still, you were kind enough to say that I was a knockout. So, if *you'll* forgive *me* . . ."

She reversed the Beretta in her hand and slashed the butt

expertly down to the side of Mazzari's head while he was bent over the lock.

He was still out when Dean returned to the hotel soon after midnight.

IV

The Arena

The credit belongs to the man who is actually in the arena, whose face is marred by dirt and sweat and blood ... who at least knows in the end the triumph of high achievement [or] fails daring greatly, so that his place shall never be with those cold, timid souls who know neither victory nor defeat.

—John F. Kennedy

11

Sean Hammer arrived in Europe from New York via a prepaid PanAir do Brasil ticket that landed him in Lisbon at five o'clock on a rainy Portuguese morning. He had just time to sink two shots of Fundador before an air hostess whose makeup was wearing a little thin shepherded him to the transit lounge where Sabena was about to expedite 346 trusting passengers to Brussels in a Boeing 747. Two hours later he was in a Mercedes cab taking him to the Central Station in the Belgian capital. And it was still five minutes short of ten A.M. when Dean ordered him a coffee at the Excelsior café in Mons, only a dozen miles north of the French border.

"Jet lag?" Hammer said. "I only just got used to Idlewild being called Kennedy!"

He was a short, wiry, forty-year-old Irish-American whose father had been a Protestant pastor in Ulster, immigrating in disgust to the United States when the Catholic south achieved independence in the 1920's. He had a seamed walnut face, piercing brown eyes, and a wide, rectangular mouth that resembled nothing so much as a mailbox slit. He was also the toughest, calmest, most reliable fighter Dean had ever met and, with Mazzari, the man he liked best to have by his side when the smoke of battle was thickest.

The coffee was served on a scalloped silver tray, along with a miniature beaker of cream, a cellophane-wrapped cookie, two sugar loaves in silver paper, and a matching chocolate pastille. "I hate to say this," Hammer observed, staring at the neatly arranged assortment, "but would the management die of shock and outrage if I asked for a brandy—preferably not Portuguese?"

"They'd bring you a beer if you wanted," Dean said.

The white-jacketed waiter didn't even raise an eyebrow when the order was given, though he tucked the pay slip discreetly beneath the tray. "In a country where they take ale instead of orange juice when they wake up," Dean explained, "you won't hurt anyone's feelings ordering liquor before ten!"

"Dandy!" the little Ulsterman exclaimed. "Then I'll take another right away!" And soon afterward, sipping at the small cup, he enthused, "Hey, this is great coffee!"

"After Colombia, they make the world's best," Dean assured him.

Hammer wiped his mouth with the back of his hand. "As the Russian said, enough of this love talk. What gives, Marc? Why am I here?"

"Coffee again." Dean smiled. "Number three on my personal world-cup list. And they say there's an awful lot of it."

"Brazil?"

"Right. Fascists planning some villainy south of the Mato Grosso. It seems there's a nuclear angle, a team of B-girls posing as SISTERS, a powerless power station, an artificial lake, and a dame tailing me who zapped Mazzari last night. Was it just *last* night?"

"You got the material there for a Broadway musical," Hammer said. "So where do we come in?"

"Whatever they're doing, it goes on inside some kind of a fortress they built in the center of a mountain. They want us to bust in, take a look-see, and tell them the score."

"They?"

"High-powered Brazilians who oppose the military junta running the country, but dare not use official Brazilian forces to make the hit."

Hammer nodded. "Okay. How's the money?"

"Usual rates. Half down, half when it's over."

"Suits me. How long?"

"Not long. A few days to collect the hardware and make it to the area. Couple of days' preparation. The raid itself should be short. Mazzari and I already cased the stronghold. I reckon two or three hours should cover it: shoot our way in, persuade someone to talk, take photos of the installations, whatever they are, lay a few charges if necessary . . . then back to Rio to make a report."

Hammer was unwrapping a stick of gum. He made a Special Delivery in the mailbox mouth. "Sounds okay. How many men?"

"I guess half a dozen would do. You, me, Mazzari. Could you contact Novotny?"

Chewing, Hammer said, "Sure. He's shacked up in Queens with some broad looks like she was in the back line of the original cast of *West Side Story*. Maybe the downtown angle appeals to him."

"Okay. So all we need is a couple of anchormen. Can do?"

"Yeah. I know a pair of ex-family boys from Staten Island who are looking for a foreign vacation. They'd be thanking you for the opportunity, sure."

"I'll leave that to you, then," Dean said. "Rendezvous at the Hotel Estoril in Rio in . . . let's see: today's Thursday . . . in forty-eight hours. Saturday P.M., okay? I can fix the tickets and you get paid as of yesterday."

"Bejasus, I'll be back at bloody Kennedy before I even knew it was there, but!" The little Ulsterman shifted his wad of gum. "One thing: you said the clients was the Brazilian opposition. Does that mean we'd be ranged against the government? Are they supportin' your fascist boyos?"

"No, no. The guys paying us are members of the administration themselves, though not of the government. They oppose the junta's *policies*—and they try to modify them from like inside. There's no suggestion that the rulers know about the fascist setup, just that they might not take positive enough action if they did."

Before Hammer could reply, the glass doors of the café burst open and a little old man with gray hair and gold-rimmed spectacles hurried across to their table. "My boy!" he exclaimed. "I am keeping you waiting! Please excuse. An African client; one of those difficult men. You understand."

Dean was on his feet, his large hand held out. "Gaston! A real pleasure. Good to see you. Meet my friend Sean Hammer . . ."

Gaston Jammot's wizened face with the laugh lines surrounding twinkling eyes had been likened to that of a Swiss watchmaker in a Disney movie. He had in fact once worked as a watchmaker in Zurich—though not for Walt Disney—but it was as a gunsmith that he had become internationally known ever since the end of World War II. He had emigrated to the Congo in 1950. Homeless after the Belgian withdrawal from the country, he had been acting as an adviser in Biafra when Dean first met him during his Peace Corps tour. Despite their difference in age, the two men had become close friends: Jammot had taught the young American all he knew about firearms, and it was through Dean's influence when he was an arms salesman himself that Jammot had been able to set up his business back in Belgium. It was hard to define exactly what the business was. On the one hand, he carried out ballistics tests for police investigators and acted as armorer and consultant to a number of specialized government agencies in Europe; on the other hand, he was an agent and supplier of clandestine arms to private security forces and most of the world's mercenaries.

"What is it this time?" he asked when the formalities were over and he was sitting with a tall glass of Stella Artois before him. "You have a little shopping list for the old man, perhaps?"

"Yeah." Dean looked around him. The Excelsior was filling up with beer drinkers and housewives chattering over their morning coffee, but the three men were sitting in a glassed-in extension built out over the sidewalk and the adjacent tables were still untenanted. "A little assignment in Latin America. Kind of a break-in deal. An underground setup guarded by a blockhouse."

Jammot took a gold pencil and a small notebook from his inside pocket. "What had you in mind?"

"There's no problem about the hardware itself," Dean said. "Any difficulties will be over delivery and the provenance of the stuff."

Jammot's seamed forehead wrinkled even more. "Provenance?"

"Where it comes from. For political reasons, the operation mustn't on any account have connections with either of the big blocs. So that means no ex-WD gear from Britain, no U.S. Army rejects, no Soviet specialties, and no guns from Omnipol in Czechoslovakia. Okay?"

The old man was writing busily. "The Israelis. And of course there is our own FN arsenal near Liège," he suggested. "Or at a pinch, Chatellerault, in France."

"At a pinch. I'd prefer FN: they sell all over the world and they carry less of an aligned tag."

"Very well. What kind of quantities?"

Dean cleared his throat. "Very few, Gaston, I'm afraid. It's a six-man job."

Jammot looked over his spectacles. "*Half a dozen!* That is such a small order that . . . No matter. For an old friend, maybe."

"I know, I know. Why not go to an ordinary black-market dealer in Paris or Brussels. But this is pretty specialized stuff," Dean said helpfully.

The old man sighed. "Just what did you want, my boy?"

"Plastic, grenades, Primacord—the usual explosive gear. Half a dozen FAL Model 49 automatic rifles from your FN factory—equipped with Trilux night sights. Six Uzi submachine guns from Israel. A couple of bazookas."

"Mortars?"

Dean shook his head. "Uh-uh. It's all quick, short-range action. Kind of like a bank raid, you know? That's why we'll also require two MICV's."

"Armored *vehicles?* Now you are talking!" The little man's face visibly brightened. "All these things I can supply from friends of mine in the West Indies: for such an amount it is not worth a consignment from Europe. But you said there might be delivery problems?"

"Yeah. This is not an operation where you can crate the stuff up, label it 'machine tools,' and bribe customs officials to allow you to land it through the docks at Rio or Bahia. The place is hundreds of miles from the coast, in pretty wild country, and although I was tipped off that the law can look the other way some, we can't just drive through half a dozen different states like a package tour. Aside from that, there's the question of time. It's like urgent."

Jammot drained his glass of beer and plucked at his lower lip. "The nearest rivers are the Araguaia and the Tocantins, but neither is navigable that far, especially for boats big enough to carry vehicles. Besides, it would take days. If you want the merchandise delivered near the area of operations, the only answer, I am afraid, is a drop—and that would be expensive."

"It doesn't matter. The money is available."

"In that case . . ." Jammot started writing again. "I would suggest a Chinook helicopter: she can carry the men and the weapons, with the vehicles slung beneath. Can your clients arrange free passage over Brazilian air space?"

"Perhaps. But you got more than five hundred miles of country there; a thousand if you cross the coast coming south from the West Indies. Double that for the return journey, and where's your fuel coming from?"

"In such a case," Jammot said smoothly, "I would arrange that delivery was made from the west or south—from Bolivia or Paraguay—where the distances involved would be less."

Hammer had been chewing furiously. "Holy God!" he said now, half in admiration, half in awe. "Your man has it all sorted out, does he not?"

The gold pencil was still poised over the page. "A small suggestion," Jammot said. "On such an expedition, could you not use half a dozen Gyrojet pistols? The weapon weighs only one pound, and it fires miniature rockets, no bigger than a magnum automatic round."

Dean laughed. "I know. Four-ounce rockets, 13mm caliber, and a muzzle velocity of twelve hundred feet per second. But the velocity drops to zero once the rocket fuel is burned, and the damned things are so inaccurate that you can't better a twelve-inch group at *ten yards*! Aside from that, they were made by Mainhardt and Biehl—and despite the name, that's an American firm." He punched Jammot playfully on the shoulder. "You old bastard! You been trying to sell me those six Gyrojet dogs for more than two years now!"

The Belgian was in no way put out. "No hard feelings. A salesman is a salesman; you should know that," he said equably.

"Now, about the ammunition . . ." Dean began.

Jammot picked up the tabs and signaled the waiter. "There is Gewurztraminer in the icebox," he said. "And Dagmar has prepared a cassoulet of duck. May I suggest that we discuss that over lunch?"

"With pleasure," Dean said. Jammot's comfortably built blond wife was revered throughout the mercenary world for her cooking. "We can arrange about payment for the merchandise at the same time."

They went out into the Grand' Place. It was raining, but a slant of anomalous sunlight shone from behind a cloud mass to gild the great bell tower on its hilltop behind the city hall. "Damned nearly holiday weather, that is," Hammer said as they crossed the wet street to the parking lot in the center of the square. "Do you know how deep the fuckin' snow was when I left New York?"

"Don't be too sure," said Dean, who kept a one-room *pied-à-terre* in a Brussels apartment block and knew the Belgian weather. "That may be our sunshine ration for the whole goddamn winter! And, talking of vacations, what about these two Staten Island guys you plan to hire? You figure they'll suit the outfit okay?"

"Oh, they will that," Hammer said. "Yes, you may be sure they'll fit, all right. Weber used to be a hit man for Annunzio, but he went straight when the family broke up. A good man with a shooter, Weber: doesn't talk much, but he aims real good. The other's a Sicilian. Ratted on the team when they started pushing dope, and he's been kind of a low-profile man ever since. A Catholic with a bleedin' conscience, that's Poinsettia."

"*Poinsettia*! That's an exotic tropical flower!" Dean said.

The Irishman shook his bullet head. "Not this one," he said firmly.

12

The body of Salvatore Poinsettia was almost completely covered in black hair, a discreet triangle of which curled over the open neck of his bush shirt. He was less tall than Mazzari, shorter than Dean, but nearly as wide as the two of them put together, with a barrel chest and long muscular arms. "Sal don't approve of violence," Sean Hammer said to Dean when he introduced the two men, "but he's always prepared to *protect* a man—especially if that man would happen to be his meal ticket."

Dean grinned. "And he'd . . . withhold his disapproval . . . if it became necessary to take action in a good cause? Against racism, for example, or pushing dope?"

"Yeah," Poinsettia said hoarsely. "Them bums need their teeth pushed in; rottin' folks' bodies, rottin' their minds. It gives guys runnin' a regular racket a bad name."

"The organization we're leaning on here," Dean said, "we don't know yet exactly what they're planning, but it sure smells to high heaven, so there must be something rotten in there." He turned to Hammer's other recruit and added, "I guess you don't have any scruples, pulling a trigger a few times . . . in a good cause?"

"The best cause I can think of is me gettin' paid," Manfred Weber said. Apart from a slight blueness of chin that they shared, he was as unlike Poinsettia as could be—a medium-height, middleweight man with nondescript features and mousy hair whose toughness only showed in the width of his shoulders and the flinty stare of his eyes. Novotny, the third man to arrive, was a weathered Polish veteran who looked like Moshe Dayan without the eyepatch. Or Peter Lorre on an off day. He liked and respected both Dean and his lieutenants, with whom he had often worked before.

At the hotel in Rio, Dean explained the complex BBW

story so far and sketched out the rough plan he had formed for storming the tunnel behind the estancia in San Felipe. The following day—Rio was still exhausted after the carnival, with paper streamers and confetti littering every corner—Mazzari, Hammer, and the three other mercs flew to Brasilia. They traveled on three separate flights, to minimize suspicion in case they should be seen together later, and to throw any watchers off the scent in case Dean was still under some kind of surveillance. Mazzari took the earliest plane because he had some advance scouting work to do. Dean was not leaving the city until the following day. There was a great deal of liaison and dovetailing to effect among Gaston Jammot, Quinnel, and the Brazilian representatives—whose go-between, he was pleased to discover, was none other than the obliging Captain Oliveira.

Once again Mazzari rented a Lada and made the long drive to San Felipe (the young rental-company dispatcher, he figured, must somehow have gotten hold of the complete works of P. G. Wodehouse). As Dean had done before him, he concealed the car near the estancia and climbed the sun-drenched hillside to make a preliminary reconnaissance through his field glasses. There seemed to be little difference since his previous visit. The tracks of many tires still turned in through the open gates; there were still women in SISTERS uniform mixing with off-duty technicians in the grounds; armed guards and their dogs were still on patrol.

Mazzari's plan, worked out in some detail by Dean, was to use his color as an entry card and visit the place openly in the guise of an anthropologist seeking information on the Candomblé rituals. He scrambled down the slope, threaded his way through a birch wood, and found the Lada below. He put his key in the door lock and twisted.

The key refused to turn.

Puzzled, he tried again. Once more he was unable to unlock the door. He stood back and stared at the vehicle . . . and realized suddenly that it was not his own. It was the same color, the same model, the same year—but the license number was one integer different. And inside, tossed carelessly on the back seat behind a valise, was the cockaded hat of a member of the SISTERS.

On the leather side of the valise, gilt initials in the form of a C and a W had been attached. The initials C.W. could stand for Charles Wilford or Clancy Wladyslaw. They could stand for Cable & Wireless Ltd. But they were much more likely here to stand for Coralie Willys.

Was she following him again, or had she gotten here before him? Mazzari would very much have liked to know which of the two Ladas (now that he was wised up, he could see the top of his own glinting through the thicket some way to the north) had been rented first. Before he could think any further, any doubts he might have had were resolved by the voice of the girl herself.

It seemed to come from only a few yards away: a smothered exclamation followed by a gasp of pain.

Mazzari pushed his way through the thicket and parted the branches of a wild oleander growing beside the road. Between scarlet and white flowers he could see the fence and the strip of cleared ground on the far side. Beyond the fence was Coralie Willys. She was struggling with one of the guards, who had bent one of her arms up behind her back and held a palm under her chin. "Come on, sweetheart," the man was saying in English. "You know as well as I fuckin' do that you ain't allowed this side of the fence. Now, how'd you get over and what the hell are you doin'?"

"You're hurting my arm," the girl said. "*Oh!* . . . I . . . I walked around from the gates. Down by the powerhouse."

"Don't give me that!" the guard rasped. "Them gates are as near as dammit five miles from here an' your shoes are still polished—there ain't even a scratch on 'em."

"I can't help that. . . . *Will* you let go my arm!"

"You come across from the estancia, that's what, am I right? Now, you know you chicks got no business this side of the wire. That's why Findley'd never have let you through the gates down there. Either you go through the mountain or you stay outside at the estancia, right? So I'm gonna take you right on back to the guardroom an' we'll see what . . . *Wait* a minute, though," he reflected as Coralie Willys began to struggle again. "Wait a minute! Maybe we could come to some kind of an arrangement, huh? I go for a broad she has spirit. And anyway, that's what you're here for, ain't it? Keep the goddamn wooden-faces quiet, and . . . uh . . . comfort for the boys?" He laughed coarsely.

Then suddenly he was lying on the ground. Mazzari failed to see exactly how it was done—a slender ankle placed to one side, a hip outthrust, and something expert done with the arm held behind her back—but the guard, momentarily inattentive as his thoughts ran ahead, found himself flying through the air over Coralie's shoulder.

He landed flat on his back in the grass. There were lumps of limestone among the tussocks, and the force of the impact would have knocked many men out. But this one was a hard nut. He was on his feet almost at once, lips snarled back from discolored teeth, approaching the girl like a wrestler, with outstretched hands.

His mistake was to go on thinking, after the initial surprise, that he could handle the thing himself. Had he blasted the whistle hanging around his neck on a chain, the end would have come quickly: a squad of men would have been down on them within minutes and the girl would have been taken prisoner. But with the arrogance of the true bully, the guard was confident that he could overpower a mere woman.

From behind the oleander, Mazzari watched the two of them circling one another over the rough ground. He wasn't sure what to do. He had been instructed at all costs to keep his nose clean—and in any case, for the girl's sake he must avoid any alarm. As it happened, the decision was taken from his hands. Having three attempts at grappling with his adversary foiled by judo grips, the guard began to lose his temper. He leaped at the girl with flailing fists.

Coralie Willys sprang agilely away, but as she went, one heel caught in a rock among the grasses and she stumbled backward. With a growl of triumph, the man was on her, pinning her arms to her sides in a bear hug and forcing her to the ground. The girl brought one sharp knee up into his belly as she tried desperately to free her arms. She twisted her head and sank her teeth into the rough material of his uniform sleeve, attempting to bite through the cloth to the muscles of the biceps beneath. She jerked her forehead back and forth trying to butt him in the face.

The man chuckled and spun her around as easily as if her body had been a bale of cotton. As she lay facedown in the tall grass, he knelt on the backs of her thighs and seized the collar of her jacket in both hands. The green stuff ripped up the back seam as he yanked with all his strength, and the garment came away from her in two pieces.

Again he grunted in triumph and amusement as he flung it aside and reached for her. Pink flesh writhed beneath him. The waistband of her skirt tore. Fingers with black-rimmed nails hooked under the elasticized strap of her brassiere and burst it.

Mazzari had no option now: he had to get in there and help the girl before she was raped or killed. In front of the oleander, several dozen of the youngest saplings had been cut down, trimmed, and stacked beside the road. The staves were around eight feet long, shorter, less springy, and a little thicker than the specialized equipment that had made him pole-vault champion at Oxford, but they would have to do. He selected the slimmest and burst out from behind the bushes.

The guard was hunched over the struggling girl, his hands burrowing beneath her half-naked figure. He didn't see the big Congolese sergeant sprint across the roadway and plant the tip of the pole in the soft ground before the fence.

Mazzari sailed up into the air. But although the fence was lower than the athletics crossbars he had once vaulted, there was far less whip in the pole and he caught his heels on the wire as he went over, sprawling to the ground beside the couple with an impact that jarred the breath from his body.

The guard looked up with a curse. "Where the fuck did you come from? You know you niggers ain't got no right this side of the fence."

Mazzari scrambled to his feet. "Get up," he said.

Still kneeling on the prostrate girl, the guard grinned. "What's eatin' you, black boy?" he sneered. "You want to horn in on a nice piece of ofay tail, is that it? Ain't there enough dark meat in this neck of the woods to keep your motherfuckin' pricks busy, you an' the other munts around here?"

Mazzari reached forward, grasped the man's collar, and jerked him bodily upright with one hand. "Why, you dirty goddam nigger—" the guard began. Mazzari hit him on the mouth.

He staggered back and then rushed in with big fists swinging, his pig eyes glittering evilly. "I can see there's some smart-ass houseboys around here need taught a lesson," he snarled.

Mazzari stood solid as a rock, taking a heavy body punch and a right cross to the head without moving a muscle. He hit the guard once, a short, stiff-arm blow that thudded home over the man's heart. The guard's heavy body shuddered. For half a second he stood swaying; then a left hook that felt like a steel door slamming inside his head exploded against his cheekbone and he went down.

Mazzari turned his back. The girl was sitting up, holding together the fragments of her vandalized clothes. She was trembling. *"You!"* she said. "What . . . what are you doing here? I guess I ought to thank you, though in fact I could have handled him perfectly well myself."

"Sure." Mazzari smiled. "In time. Of course you could."

She got shakily to her feet. "If you touched the fence . . . there are alarm wires . . . we must go before—"

"I know. I'm only thankful the bally thing doesn't seem to be electrified this far out. So far as thanks go, I think I deserve some, considering that I still have a headache from our last date!"

Coralie Willys blushed. "I'm sorry about that, really. But I had to make sure you didn't follow me here."

"You could have saved your energy, as you see. But why not?"

"Because I have an investigation to carry out and I don't like snoopers. You wouldn't say who you were."

"So have I, and nor would you, old thing. But before we start exchanging compliments, I think we should push off, you know. It won't be long before our charming host's chums arrive." He tilted his head to one side and listened. From the direction of the estancia they could hear whistles blowing and the faint shrilling of a bell.

"But . . . how do we get out of here? And what about him?" She gestured at the unconscious guard. "He'll tell them—"

"He won't wake up for some time. And while he's out, we can contrive that he gives them a bit of bogus information." Mazzari picked up the guard as if he were weightless, carried him thirty yards up the hill, and left him facedown on a rock outcrop with his feet toward the fence below. He threw the man's gun a little way off among the brushwood. "They'll think he was zapped chasing intruders who escaped penetrating *farther into the property*—so they'll spread out away from the road, toward the ridge." Mazzari strode back to the man and dropped an expert rabbit punch to the limp neck. "Just to make sure he can't tell them anything different for the next couple of hours," he explained.

"Meanwhile . . . ?"

"Meanwhile we make ourselves scarce—and it doesn't matter too much if we do set off the beastly alarms again." He hoisted her up until she was standing on his wide shoulders. "Now, drape that torn jacket over the top of the wire," he instructed her, "grab hold of the fence, and vault over. It's about a ten-foot drop, but the ground's soft."

"Thank you. I imagine I'll survive," the girl said tartly.

From the far side, she tossed Mazzari's makeshift pole over the fence to him, and he left the BBW grounds the way he had come in—this time without touching the wire. "Do you have a change of clothes in your bag?" he asked.

"Of course." She was still trying to cover herself with the remains of her savaged garments. "Why?"

"Because while the soldier boys are out looking for the dastardly intruders, I want to take a shufti at that estancia—openly, as a chap interested in the Candomblé affair. Obviously, I want to be away before the guards get back and our friend can tell the tale"—his lips twisted into an ironic smile—"of the naughty girl and the prancing nigger. And if you can tog up in mufti, you can help by posing as my secretary or assistant or something. Are you game?"

She stared at him. "You're quite serious?"

"Absolutely. Dash it, the last place they'd look for an intruder would be in their own backyard. We'll be safer there than anywhere—until they get a description circulating."

She shook her head. "I suppose so," she said.

Mazzari was staring at the torn halves of her jacket, which he had carried across to the Lada for her. "Oho!" he said softly.

"What is it, Sherlock Holmes?"

He held up a portion of the jacket lining. Below the ripped collar, a name tape, shiny with continued use, slightly soiled from contact with other clothes, hung from the material. On the pale ribbon, faint red letters spelled out "C. Willys." "Unless your bosses specialize in detail work more perfect than any used by the world's intelligence services," Mazzari said, "this is an old jacket that's been worn a lot. It really is your own garment—not a cover disguise. You do actually work for the SISTERS."

"Of course I do," she said impatiently. "I work for the Special Investigation section. Many of our girls come from very . . . particular . . . families and we have to take special care about conditions when we send teams abroad. We are always having to make inquiries about one thing or another. And of course when we find people *pretending* to be SISTERS, when in fact they are not, then naturally the foundation steering committee wants to find out why."

"But, dear girl, why not say so? It would have saved—"

"Why should I tell *you*? Who are you, anyway?"

"If you must know, I'm part of a team that's been hired to find out the same thing—plus what the devil's going on here."

"Why don't the Brazilians do it themselves? Why hire foreigners?"

"Political reasons," Mazzari said.

The girl unzipped her valise and went around to the other side of the automobile to change her clothes. "I can't think,"

Mazzari said, "why your people didn't brief the . . . didn't let the people who are hiring us know that they had a representative down here."

"Political reasons," she said acidly. "It seems there's a man called Mackenzie. Mrs. Bowling, our commandant, said that as he couldn't be bothered to be cooperative, she didn't see why he should."

"That's the way wars start," Mazzari said.

"What did you say?" she called over the roof of the Lada.

"Nothing. Forget it."

A few minutes later she asked casually, "Your friend—the man calling himself Forster that I was tailing: he's part of your team too, I mean the investigating team?"

"That's right."

"He's very good-looking, isn't he?"

Mazzari grinned. "If you like the type."

"You know, he reminds me a bit of that movie actor . . ."

"I know. James Coburn. But younger. And tougher."

"I was going to say Nick Nolte, actually," Coralie Willys said.

Soon afterward, as they drove toward the estancia, she asked, "I keep hearing this word Candomblé. I've spoken to some of the local blacks, Indians too, but all of them seem scared to talk about the dam or the company building it . . . because of the Candomblé. Even the ones who lost their homes under the lake won't talk. What *is* this thing—a secret society?"

"Not exactly. More like a religion. There are several different cults here in Brazil, all of them a mixture of African and Indian worship with Christianity and spiritualism. People who don't know say they're something like voodoo in Haiti, but voodoo's harmful, like black magic, and these cults are helpful. White magic, if you like. The two most affecting your actual peasants—and a hell of a lot of them belong—are Candomblé and Umbanda."

"What's the difference?" she asked with a show of interest.

Mazzari cleared his throat. "In both cases, their gods are a mixture of Christian and pagan ones. But while spiritualists believe you can communicate with dead *people,* these cults believe you can actually contact the gods themselves through mediums. The difference is that Candomblé initiates, or so they say, can be visited or contacted by these gods personally, whereas the *umbandistas'* mediums have to have the gods' wishes interpreted through a guide. A bit like a séance with jolly old Madame Arcati, in fact."

"How fascinating," the girl said. "How come the difference?"

"I don't know too much about it," Mazzari said truthfully, trying to remember the rest of the lecture Dean had given him. "It all seems to go back to the days of slavery. The most advanced people brought over from my country as slaves were the Yoruba. They had the most complex religions and gods, and the mixture of these with missionary Catholicism produced Candomblé—the cult with the strongest African influence, which took off in Bahia. The less-developed Bantu from Angola, centered more on Rio, were that much more influenced by the great spiritualist movement that shook the good burghers of Brazil rigid in the last century. Their cult is the one called Umbanda today."

"Thank you, Professor," the girl said gravely. "Now perhaps you can tell me why a religion or cult devoted to helping folks should bar local inhabitants from talking—"

"We'll ask," Mazzari interrupted swiftly, "when we get there."

But the tall, white-haired black with the Harvard accent and the lined face who met them in the Candomblé *tenda*—a wooden building like a mission hut that stood among trees to one side of the estancia—was uncooperative. They had left the Lada outside and walked through the gates—to their surprise, unchallenged. But there were guards in the now familiar black-and-khaki uniform everywhere, and Mazzari was sure that if they had left the signposted path leading to the *tenda* they would have been stopped within yards. A black woman in a white robe had left them in a waiting room while she went to fetch Pai Hernando.

"If, as you claim, you are an anthropology graduate from the University of Southern California," the priest said in his well-modulated voice, "I cannot understand why you and your assistant should have chosen to come all the way here to this very modest, uninspiring *tenda*, when there are so many others more interesting elsewhere." He sat at a simple desk. Through an uncurtained window behind him they could see technicians strolling toward the big house. The tunnel in the cliff was hidden behind a grove of trees at the foot of a slope.

"But that's just it!" Mazzari exclaimed. "*All* the way here. Since Candomblé is centered on Bahia state and the areas to the north and east of it, we find it intensely interesting, demographically, to find any *tenda* as far west as this. We had no idea the Yoruba had ever been transported as far as this."

"They probably migrated after abolition. In any case, the

boundary between former slave peoples and Indian aboriginals is hopelessly blurred now." Hernando flicked a speck of dust from his pale gray suit and drummed his fingers on the top of the desk.

"As the priest in charge of this place," Coralie asked suddenly, "can you explain why the *spirits*—or the gods—should frown on the local people talking about the dam back there? We wondered how the forced moves had affected them, sociologically, you know, but we couldn't get a soul to talk about it at all. They said the gods forbade them to."

"I am only Pai Hernando, the horse on which the spirits ride," the black said. "It is not for me to question the wisdom of the Orixás, the great ones. Indeed, I had no idea such messages had been transmitted through me. And now," he added pointedly, "if you could tell me how I could help you . . . ?"

"We should like very much to see some ceremonies—perhaps an *ôrunkó*—to compare with those performed in the Candomblés farther east," Mazzari said.

"I am afraid that is quite impossible. This is a simple country place. No such rituals take place here."

"But I thought . . . ?"

"Definitely not, sir. Apart from which, the local folk are—as you have seen—superstitious and *sus*picious. They would resent any outside participation, any hint of an *audience*, at their devotions, as I am sure you will understand."

Mazzari rose from his chair and paced up and down. "But surely," he cried in simulated agitation, "there must be something in a cult that can impose so strong a taboo on discussion—"

"I regret extremely," Pai Hernando said, rising to his feet also, "that I cannot help you at all. It is a pity that you should have traveled so far and so fruitlessly. Had you had the prudence to inquire first . . ."

"Are those soldiers out there?" Coralie asked innocently as he showed them to the door.

"Certainly not. They are members of the construction company's security guard."

"There are an awful lot of them."

"There is valuable property in here, madam."

"Your *tenda* is financed by Intacon, then?"

"By no means. The directors have been very generous, allowing us to continue operating on their land after they acquired it; granting us, indeed, certain facilities."

"That aspect of paternalism in a foreign concern is very interesting," Mazzari said. "Perhaps we could ask you a few—"

"Good day to you," Pai Hernando said firmly. He closed the door.

"Well, I've heard of people who discourage visitors," Coralie said as they walked out the gates, "but this is ridiculous!" She laughed. "That private army—I'm sure they would have fired on us if we'd turned right instead of left when we left the hut; I mean toward the cliff and the tunnel."

"They probably would," Mazzari said soberly. "Clearly the whole Candomblé bit is a cheap device to blackmail the locals into silence about the whole project: the thing's bogus from beginning to end."

"Why are you so sure?" She was turning the Lada, about to take him back to his own vehicle.

"Several reasons." Dean's religious instruction had stuck, Mazzari realized with a certain smug satisfaction. "In the first place, Pai Hernando, Father Hernando, is a form of address used in Umbanda associations, not in Candomblé. If there *is* a priest in a Candomblé *tenda*—it's usually a priestess, as it happens—he is called a Babalorixá, or Father-of-Saint. *Caboclo*, the term for an Indian spiritualist guide, is from the Umbanda vocabulary too. Apart from that, to say that they hold no ceremonies such as an ôrunkó is absurd—like a Catholic curé saying they don't hold masses in his church. The ôrunkó is the be-all and end-all of Candomblé—the climax of months of preparation, the ceremony at which initiates are 'visited' by their particular deities."

"You mean they go into a trance and throw themselves about and shriek, and all that? Something like a voodoo bean feast, as you say?"

"They are apparently possessed, yes. But it's supposed to be their particular gods who've temporarily taken possession. Finally," Mazzari said, "if that place was a genuine Candomblé *tenda*, it would have been surrounded by miniature shacks, supposed to be the dwelling place of specific gods, which have to be sited at special places—especially where two trails cross."

Coralie braked to a halt opposite Mazzari's Lada. Beyond the safety fence, they could see armed men and dogs spreading out over the rocky hillside below the ridge. Two women in SISTERS uniform stood guard over the unconscious sentry. "Why is it so important, this crossroads thing?" Coralie asked. "I've heard about it before, in Rio and other places."

"Because that's where the god Exú and his attendant spirits

are supposed to be placated—and they seem to control half the bloody country! You won't find many Brazilians who'll cross over an intersection when there's one of those *despacho* offerings in the middle! Did *you* see any offerings, any shrines, any trees hung with ribbons back there?"

She shook her head. "I didn't see any long-distance trucks either. Did you?"

He smiled. "There were none to see. I had a good look when I did my pacing-up-and-down bit. Couldn't even see the blasted tunnel: they'd planted trees to cover the entrance, down at the foot of the slope. But I did see the corner of a blockhouse, and that means the tunnel is pretty well guarded, I imagine. Maybe Intacon doesn't have as much faith in the gods' protection as the locals!"

"I suppose it's because you are African yourself that you know so much about these cults and customs?" Coralie offered as he climbed into his own Lada.

Mazzari glanced over his shoulder. "No doubt about it," he said dryly.

13

They waited in silence while a half-moon sank behind the Serra do Roncador. A complicated system of relays with infrared signal lamps had tipped off Dean via Mazzari, Hammer, and the girl, Coralie Willys, that a convoy was approaching the estancia and Gaston Jammot's helicopter could safely lower itself over the pass at the head of the valley without being heard. Dean figured that the sinister inhabitants of the estancia were unlikely to go far along the atrocious road leading to Aguacalinda, especially after dark, and he had decided therefore to make his approach from that direction.

The two FV1611 Humber Pig armored cars were winched down and released from the grapples in less than three minutes. Dean himself, with Novotny and the two Americans, swarmed down a rope ladder at the same time and checked the arms and equipment inside the vehicles. As the big chopper lifted off and flew away toward the south, the two armored cars started coasting down the grade with dead motors.

Dean was at the wheel of one Pig, Novotny drove the other. All the members of his miniature assault team could in fact have been transported in a single FV1611, as they were designed to take a commander, a driver, and six men in back. But Dean had reckoned, first, that a backup vehicle would be invaluable, and second, that their attack would be far more flexible if it was two-pronged. This plus the psychological advantage of an apparently stronger force.

Halting on the way to pick up the signalers, the two Humbers rolled down the last two miles with only an occasional squeak of disk brakes to announce their passing. Dean was carrying Poinsettia and Weber in the leading vehicle: Hammer and Mazzari swung aboard Novotny's as he slowed at the two prearranged rendezvous. The girl, whom Dean had been reluctant to accept on the operation at all, had instructions to regain her own Lada and wait for them in San Felipe.

Now the two armored carriers waited side by side on the pitted roadway less than three hundred yards from the estancia entrance. As the moon reddened and vanished, darkness dissolved the outlines of building and tree, brimming the valley with shadow. Dean unhooked a hand microphone from the fascia and thumbed a switch. A red pilot light glowed ten feet away on Novotny's dash. "Listening," the Pole whispered into his own handset.

"Switch on and down shutters," Dean breathed.

Powerful infrared lamps mounted above the windshield of each Humber shone beams of invisible light down the roadway toward the gates. Through special glass mounted in the center of each windshield the two drivers saw the outlines of their target spring to life like the components of some fantastic snowscape. There was a faint whine of electrical gear as twin armored shutters folded down over the glass on each vehicle, leaving only a narrow viewing slit behind the treated section. "Five minutes," Dean's voice murmured in Novotny's earpiece.

The entrance to the estancia was at the apex of a curve in the road. From where the two Humber Pigs were halted, therefore, it was almost a straight run down the remainder of the grade, through the gateway, and on down, swerving past the trees, to the tunnel mouth. Except of course that the gates were closed.

Dean had examined them carefully each time he passed. They were double gates of steel mesh stretched over tubular iron frames, locking in the center with bolts that located in a metal plate set in the ground. At night they would almost certainly be electrified, which ruled out any attempt to ram them with an armored vehicle, unless its occupants were protected by the most sophisticated insulation. Dean preferred to burst them open with explosive, which would at the same time cut the current. For this purpose, Jammot had supplied him with two German World War II RP54 Panzerfausten. The hollow-charge warheads fired by these bazooka-type antitank guns were capable of penetrating nearly eight inches of armor at a range of one hundred yards, and the old Belgian had assured Dean that so far as steel gates were concerned, it would be almost as easy as having a key.

No sentries were visible in the ghostly infrared light on the far side of the gates, but there was a small building that acted as a guardhouse just off the driveway, and Dean was sure from his experience before that the entire perimeter would in some way or other be patrolled throughout the night, even if the number of men involved was less than in the daylight hours. No lights showed in the big house, but a faint radiance now discernible above the trees indicated that lights still burned in the tunnel. It was just 0500 hours.

"Action stations!" Dean whispered into the mike.

Weber climbed silently out from under the canvas in back, and dropped to the road. He stole up to the flat top of the offside front fender and lay prone along the armorplate, aiming one of the bazookas at the center of the gates. Beside him, Mazzari took up position along the nearside fender of the other Pig. "This'll show the sons of bitches!" Weber murmured.

Through the side window just behind him, Poinsettia hissed, "You ain't got no call to say that, Mannie. Callin' someone an SOB you ain't even met—that's not Christian, son."

"Anyone I'm paid to shoot at, he's a son of a bitch," Weber said, squinting through the Trilux night sight on his weapon.

"Quit talking!" Dean ordered. "Okay . . . let's go!"

He released the handbrake. With a sibilant rustle of heavy-duty tires, the two Humbers started to move. Side by side, slowly gathering momentum, they rolled down toward the gates. When they were fifty yards away, there was a shout from the guardhouse. Somewhere ahead, a whistle blew.

Dean yelled, *"Fire!"*

The cracking twin detonations sounded as one. Flame belched from the bazookas; the two bombs streaked for the gates and burst with a shattering roar. The livid glare of the double explosion was instantly eclipsed by a blinding flash of blue light that momentarily illuminated the whole bleak valley as the electrical circuits shorted.

Weber and Mazzari dropped to the roadway and leaped aboard over the open tailgates to reload. At the same time the 120HP Rolls-Royce motors throbbed to life and the armored cars accelerated toward the estancia.

One of the gates, buckled and distorted, sagged drunkenly on its hinges; the other, mangled as though it had been crumpled in a giant fist, lay some yards away against the guardhouse wall. Novotny braked to allow Dean to take the lead, and the two 5½-ton carriers sped through the gap. Around the irregular crater torn by the bombs, the macadam was fiercely burning.

The Humbers had been chosen rather than Bren-carriers or MICV's because of the noise factor: it would have been impossible with tracked or half-tracked vehicles to approach as close to the gates without the threshing of caterpillars alerting the guards. But once the bazookas had been fired and the element of surprise no longer existed, this advantage was counterbalanced by certain faults inseparable from the lighter vehicles. They were already being shot at from the guardhouse and—to Dean's surprise—from behind the cypress hedge surrounding the gardens of the big house. The defenders must, he thought, have been in a state of fairly constant alert to have reacted so quickly. And because of the canvas top covering the back of the Pigs, Mazzari and Weber were severely restricted in their field of fire, being forced to lie flat behind the shallow armored sides and fire bazooka or machine pistol rearward over the tailgates. Additionally, lacking any fixed armament, Dean's only forward firepower was an occasional burst loosed off through the side window by Poinsettia's Uzi.

Slugs flattened themselves against the armorplate and tore through the canvas behind the cabs as they approached the wood masking the entrance to the tunnel. From both sides of the driveway a murderous crossfire from automatic weapons hosed the two carriers. Over the appalling clamor from these guns and the roar of Poinsettia's machine pistol, Dean heard the thump of Panzerfausten each time Weber and Mazzari launched bombs at the guardhouse behind them or the points of fire stabbing out at them from among the trees.

Then they rounded a bend and found themselves at the top of the final downgrade approaching the bluff. To the naked eye, the cliff face was just visible as a darker blur against the night sky, blackened still further by the imprecise lozenge of the tunnel mouth. It was possible too, as they came closer, dimly to make out the double row of low-power ceiling bulbs that marked the course of the subterranean passage curving away into the heart of the hill. But to Dean and Novotny, gunning the motors now up to their 45mph maximum, the tunnel mouth and the blockhouse beside it showed clearly and exactly in the beams of their infrared spotlights.

Dean stormed past the reinforced concrete bunker, swerving to allow Poinsettia and then Weber to spray the entrance with lead, and at last raced the Humber straight for the tunnel.

Poinsettia scrutinized the strange lunar landscape thrown into relief by the magic spotlight beam, staring at the shadowed interstices of the cliff face, the trees standing proud like cardboard cutouts against the rock, the arched brickwork of the tunnel mouth...

"*Boss!*" he screamed. "*Watch out there! The tunnel! Stop!*"

Tires screeched as Dean stamped on the pedal to lock the Humber's wheels. The great steel shutter that Poinsettia had seen rumbling down to seal off the entrance slammed home in its metal guides; the carrier, slowing but not able to stop entirely, slid into it with a nosie like a hundred thunderclaps, throwing them violently against the fascia. "Must have crossed a photoelectric guard cell," Dean shouted as he restarted the stalled motor, crashed the lever into reverse, and backed the buckled Humber away from the blanked-off tunnel mouth. "If that thing wasn't automatically operated, I..."

A burst of shooting drowned his words. Heavy-caliber bullets thumped against the armor and tore the canvas back to ribbons as he wrenched the vehicle around in a half-circle, thumped a tree bole, and then shoved the lever back into first. At the same time some kind of missile, probably an antitank grenade, exploded beneath their rear quarter, blowing off one of the wheels and tipping the Humber over onto its side.

Dean's head was still singing from the blast as he crawled dazedly from the wrecked cab over shards of broken glass.

Suddenly the darkness seemed absurdly intense. He had seen none of the guards, though the firing was still as heavy as ever. Above the explosions he could still hear an insistent, thin shrilling, an alarm bell ringing and ringing. Painfully he dragged himself into the shelter of the trees.

A second missile burst against the overturned Humber... and at once, as the gasoline tank ruptured, the entire vehicle became a blazing fireball. Beneath a mushroom of black smoke veined with flame, Dean saw the second Pig. Novotny had been able to brake in time, but then, looking for a lead from Dean, he had slowed fatally turning around. Now a third missile erupted beneath his motor, and the carrier nose-dived into the ground like a kneeling camel.

"Jesus!" a voice said hoarsely near to Dean. He turned and saw in the light of the flames the huge bulk of Poinsettia by his side.

"Did you get your gun out?" Dean murmured.

"Yeah. But only the one goddamn magazine. The rest was—"

"Did Weber get out?"

"Naw. He was right over that rear wheel when they blasted it. He's a goner. His guts was spilled all over the fuckin' floor."

Dean bit his lip. He could see shadows flitting from the wrecked cab of the second Humber. "This way!" he shouted. "Over by the wood!"

Instantly there was a furious volley of machine-gun fire from the far side of the driveway. He could hear the shells ripping through the leaves above his head as he dropped to the ground. "Shit!" he breathed. "They must have sensors posted all over. Those guns have to be computerized: they could never fire so accurately in the dark otherwise."

"Yeah. Like that son-of-a-bitch shutter on the tunnel. That's how they were able to take out the carriers so easy," Poinsettia replied. "Look, you can see the bastards over there beyond them flames!"

Dean saw a group of muzzles belching fire from a steel screen behind a clump of bushes. "In among the trees," he ordered. "Maybe the trunks'll slow down their radar responses some."

"You want I should give them a squirt?"

"Not now. Wait until we're further in." Figures materialized from the smoke and flame and cast themselves down beside the two men. Hammer and Novotny, each with a submachine gun. "Where's Mazzari?" Dean panted.

"Other side of the wreck," Hammer said. "He's goin' to—"

His words were cut off by the whiplash detonation of a bazooka. The livid flash from the weapon was drowned in a brighter orange burst as the missile exploded against the steel gun screen. For an instant the air shook with the echoes of the detonation . . . and then there was a sudden silence. For the moment, the shooting seemed to have stopped. Above the shrilling bell, they heard the distant shouts of orders, a door opening and slamming as men filed through. Somewhere through the trees, a searchlight dazzled on and outlined the branches in golden light. "They've halted the automatic fire to let their men move in," Dean whispered. "Why the hell doesn't Mazzari . . . ?"

He stopped in mid-sentence as a giant figure appeared in silhouette against the glare of the still-blazing Humber. It ran ten yards up the driveway toward the guardhouse and then dropped to a kneeling position, the long tube of the bazooka balanced on one big shoulder. Once more the weapon spat flame. But there were guards running from the bushes behind him now. A knot of men converged on the solitary marksman. Grotesque shadows lengthened and shortened along the macadam as a frantic and obscure struggle took place. Then something that glinted in the pulsating light of the burning vehicle rose and fell twice. Gradually some order returned to the group. Dean saw the unconscious figure of Mazzari being dragged away from the illumination cast by the blaze.

"You want us to go get him out?" Novotny asked.

"You're joking," Dean said. "Three Uzis and my Webley automatic against batteries of computerized machine guns? They'd home in on the heat of our bodies as soon as we left the wood." He sighed. "No. I know when I'm beaten . . . for the moment. All we have to do now is get *us* the hell out if we can—and think again. They took Edmond prisoner: all we can hope is that he stays alive long enough for us to rescue him when we come back."

"Get out, he says!" Hammer sounded pessimistic. "And just how would a man be after—?"

"Shutting his mouth for a start!" Dean said savagely. "Come on, this way! And move your asses, all of you!" Dodging between the trees, he led the way back by a circuitous route toward the fence. They heard a tractor grinding along the roadway in the direction of the thicket. There was a flurry of commands, and then a second searchlight lanced the dark behind them. Tiger-striped with bars of light, the wood seemed suddenly a bare and empty place, the black shadows the only hints of comfort within it. Once more there was a volley of gunshots; once more they threw themselves flat as slugs ripped through the foliage above them.

"All right," Dean snapped. "Cover me. I'll settle that bastard and then we'll split!"

Taking Poinsettia's Uzi, he crouched low and ran back in the direction of the tractor. Loosing off the remainder of their magazines in the general direction of the shouting voices, Hammer and Novotny watched him flit from shadow to shadow, from trunk to trunk, until he was only forty to fifty yards from the machine. He dropped to one knee and cradled the weapon, with the butt extended, against his right shoulder. Flame stabbed the dark as the submachine gun leaped and juddered in his hands. The blinding white eye of the searchlight on the tractor dimmed abruptly to yellow, to orange, and then vanished.

Seconds later he was back beside them. "On our way," he ordered breathlessly. "If they run true to form, it'll be grenades after this. Then dogs."

There was a dull plop behind them while they threaded their way through thickening undergrowth as quietly as they could. It was followed by a second, a third, a fourth. Among the tatters of mist that the approaching dawn limned white against the trees, another and more pungent vapor eddied and swirled. For a fraction of a second the wood sprang vividly to life in the green glare of an explosion. Simultaneously they heard the flat crump of the detonation. Metal rasped, glass tinkled, and shrapnel tore through the leaves. "Tear gas and mortar fire," Dean said hoarsely, suppressing a cough and trying not to dab his streaming eyes. "Sounds like they're making sure none of us are left in the Pigs!"

"Aye. And thank the dear Lord they are," Hammer said. "At least we are far enough gone to miss the full effect. Next thing, they will start quartering the wood and sending in the bloody dogs!"

"Let them," Novotny said. "That's the fence just ahead there."

"So fine." This was Poinsettia. "Any of you bums got ideas how we get ourselves over the motherfucker?"

In fact their escape was not as difficult as it might have been. Ground clearance had been effected with the aim of keeping the curious *out*, but the BBW planners had given less thought to the possibility that those already in might wish to cross the fence. So although there was a ten-yard zone bare of any vegetation on the outside, several trees on the fringe of the wood grew closer than that on the inside. One big chestnut in particular thrust out a bough as thick as a man's thigh to within five feet of the top of the wire.

Dean slipped off his jacket and flung it up and over the barbed lip of the fence. "Drape your jackets on top of mine," he instructed. "Then work your way to the end of the bough, swing out until you can touch the jackets with your feet, and launch yourself out and over, using the wire as a springboard. You don't need to concern yourselves with electrification: we cut the current when we blew the gates."

"Just so long as Poinsettia goes last," Hammer said. "The dear knows whether that bough will still be in working order after it has taken that man's weight!"

Five minutes later, as the baying of dogs grew louder behind them through the wood, they were all on the roadway, running silently toward the head of the valley.

Three hundred yards further on, they saw a tall, square shape silhouetted against the paling sky. It was a Lada Niva utility parked on the grass shoulder. "It's just as well that I waited," Coralie Willys's voice said from the dark interior. "Trust men to lose their transport in a simple guerrilla assault!"

"I take full responsibility," Dean said two days later in Rio. "I guess I completely underestimated the strength—and especially the sophistication—of the opposition."

"You must not blame yourself, Senhor Dean," said Rodrigo Manuel de Soares. "You were not to know; we were not to know. And the very fact that you underestimated itself tells us a great deal about this evil organization."

"Oh, sure," Dean said bitterly. "At the cost of one man's life, one of my most trusted associates taken prisoner, and the loss of thousands of dollars in valuable equipment."

De Soares rose to his feet (they were in a private room at a Copacabana businessmen's club) and laid his hand on Dean's shoulder. "Gonçalves and the other members of our group," he said, "are in total agreement with me. This . . . this vipers' nest must be wiped out. Whatever they are doing there—and it must be something terrible to warrant such protection—whatever they are doing must be stopped."

"The whole deal will have to be rethought," said Dean. "Clearly it'll have to be something on a far bigger scale, with a lot more men and a heap more equipment."

"You can have as much money as you want. Exactly what kind of approach did you contemplate this time?"

"That's the hell of it," Dean said. "I'm damned if I know. If only we had some idea of what's going on, of what lies on the far side of that tunnel . . ." He shook his head. "All I know is that I'm going to blast the place wide open, rescue my man if it's humanly possible, and smash those fascist bastards into the ground!"

There was a knock on the door. Oliveira, the police captain, came into the room. He was in plain clothes, shorter than Dean, dwarfed by the lean height of de Soares. "Forgive me, gentlemen, for intruding," he said. And then, to Dean: "Your friend Mendoza telephoned me. It seems that he has received a mysterious radio message from a man named Mazzaro or Massati or something like that."

V

Hearse Underwater

From the flaming and flashing of certain igneous mixtures, and the terror inspired by their noise, wonderful consequences ensue which no one can guard against or endure.
—Roger Bacon (A.D. 1266)

14

Although the walls were damp to the touch, there seemed to be a current of dry air blowing through the cell.

Edmond Mazzari had no idea how long he had been there. A bright light was always burning, and the only means he had of marking the passage of time was the doctor's visit—if indeed he was a doctor. At least he wore a white coat and he was always attended by two women in nurses' uniform. On the other hand, the visits might be sporadic and not regular at all. Certainly it seemed to Mazzari that there was more time now between the hypodermic injections than there had been before when he was strapped to the bed.

The bed was made of iron and enameled white. It was high and narrow, with a thin, hard mattress and no covers, and its legs were cemented into the floor of the cell.

For a long time this had been Mazzari's world. Although he was not particularly uncomfortable with his wrists and ankles buckled into the leather bracelets at the four corners of the bed, and his middle restrained by a broad webbing strap passing under its frame, it nevertheless afforded him only a limited horizon. The walls of the cell were of smooth green concrete; the ceiling, with its four powerful bulbs behind armored glass, was stone-colored; and what little he could see of the floor looked like slate. The door was a single sheet of steel without even a Judas window. And that was all: there was no furniture of any kind, no decoration to break the monotony, only a single small grille through which he imagined the warm, dry air was extracted. The faint hum of air conditioning was the only sound to break the silence.

In the circumstances it was only natural that he should take an abnormal interest in the bed. He knew by heart every chip and scratch and imperfection in the shiny surface of its headrail. With eyes closed, he could have mapped accurately the graining on the leather handcuffs attaching his wrists to the frame. He was an authority on the disparate personalities of three flies and a daddy longlegs in the cell whose existence was dedicated to the avoidance of webs spun by a spider that lived in one corner of the grille.

Every now and then the door would swing noiselessly open and in would come the doctor with his crisp white women. The women varied, but the doctor was always the same: a pudding-faced man, rather plump, with staring brown eyes behind thick spectacles. Once Mazzari's more intimate needs had been attended to, one of the women would open a small valise and hand things to the doctor while the other put the heel of her hand under Mazzari's chin and forced his head back on to the mattress so that he couldn't raise himself. Then the doctor would pinch up a fold of skin and the needle would go in. After that, Mazzari went to sleep.

This routine was not invariable. There were different treatments involving tubes and clips and something like a dentist's gag. It was to do with food or feeding, Mazzari thought. Sometimes too there was a clip biting into his arm with a tube attached to it, and sometimes something went into his throat. In either case, it left him with an ache—and in each case he went to sleep afterward. The man and the two women always worked in complete silence, which he found unnerving at first, but his throat was too dry and too raw to allow him to talk or ask questions, and he soon got used to it.

And yet there *was* talking, somewhere. Or there had been. And one of the voices, he could almost have sworn, was his own. But he could in no way remember speaking or even think of anything to talk about. Perhaps he dreamed while he slept, but he retained definite impressions of voices and movement, the words surging and receding like bees on a summer afternoon. Sometime or other, also, there had been a person shouting. Perhaps it was him.

It was all very puzzling.

And then suddenly, one day—one night? one morning? one afternoon? there was no way of telling—one day the doctor had come in with his two assistants and they had unbuckled the straps and taken them away. He was left alone in the cell, free to get up, sit down, move around, just as he liked. Mazzari thought that was very kind of them. He was so grateful that he offered no resistance when they came back a little later to give him another injection.

It was odd about the injections. Sometimes afterward he felt quite dizzy. Everything seemed to spin around, and he could never tell if he really had been to sleep or whether perhaps he had in fact only just awakened from the time before. Sometimes he thought he had been in the cell for weeks, perhaps months; sometimes he was convinced he had been there only a few hours and would soon begin to feel hungry. On the whole, he was inclined to favor the former view, mainly because one of the nurses, a pretty one he had noticed on several visits, had styled her hair a different way on different occasions.

He remembered who he was—and what he had been doing—in a single moment of awareness. The doctor and the nurses were just coming in; the cell door had opened . . . and there was a second's delay: a man outside had called a question to the doctor. And in the instant that he replied, somewhere in the distance a door slammed sharply.

As it shut, Mazzari's mind opened. Every detail of his life up to the moment he had fired the bazooka at the guardhouse in the San Felipe estancia returned to him. It was exactly as though the preceding period really had been a confused and disturbing dream from which now suddenly he was wide-awake.

"Just how long have I been held here under sedation with an artificially induced amnesia?" he asked quietly as the doctor approached.

"Ah! So! The moment of breakthrough has arrived!"—the voice was not the doctor's; it came in a curiously disembodied way from the grille that extracted breathed air from the cell. *"So Sergeant Mazzari knows once more who he is! Never mind: maybe we have been fortunate, having him as our . . . guest . . . for so long."*

"You haven't answered my question," Mazzari said, still facing the doctor.

"Dr. Brenner is not permitted to speak with you, Sergeant," the voice continued. *"You may talk to me. After all, we could almost be considered intimates!"*

"I'm afraid you have the advantage of me," Mazzari said, turning to face the grille and feeling a little foolish as he did so. "Or have we held . . . er . . . conversations that I don't recall?"

A deep chuckle floated from the grating. *"'Have the advantage' is good!"* the voice said. *"Through the closed-circuit video cameras mounted behind two of the lighting panels in your ceiling, you have been under constant surveillance since the moment you joined us. And thanks to the good doctor's persuasionary methods, you have indeed proved most cooperative in the matter of conversation."*

"You have been questioning me under the influence of Pentothal?"

"A refined version of a drug discovered centuries ago by the Mato Grosso Indians—a drug that makes Pentothal seem as mild and innocuous as a seltzer. So far as information goes, Sergeant Mazzari, you have been sucked as dry as a lemon. Now it remains only to decide whether or not that lemon might add zest to a cocktail if the rind was shaved and then twisted."

"Let's hope you ferreted out the gen you wanted," Mazzari said politely. "Though I have my doubts. You're out-of-date, you know."

"What do you mean?" There was an edge of irritation to the voice.

"Well, for one thing, I certainly *was* a sergeant—but that was in the Congolese Army. And that's a devil of a time ago!"

"A trivial detail," the voice snapped. *"Despite your remarkable—your really remarkable—powers of resistance, we have been able to find out all we wish to know. All. We have every single detail on your mission; on the CIA agent Quinnel; on the man Dean, alias Forster, whom you picked up on the road to Goiás; on the planning of your futile little raid."*

"Tell me another! I don't believe a word of it," Mazzari said.

"What do you mean, you don't believe it?"

"Just that. You could have found out those things from many sources. You couldn't possibly have gotten them from me: we're subliminally conditioned," Mazzari lied. "You know: deep hypnosis. We can only give away what is already known; it's subconsciously impossible to do more."

"We could have found out from other sources, possibly. But we didn't. You came across with the whole works."

"Rubbish!" Mazzari needled. "I don't believe a word of it!"

"I tell you, you told us everything." There was a definite edge to the voice now. *"You are not an imbecile, Mazzari, despite your origins. You can believe me when I tell you—"*

"And *I* tell *you* I don't believe you," the African maintained. "It's just a trick—and a very old, threadbare, and shabby trick, too, like telling a man his confederate has confessed all—to make me talk."

"You have *talked, man. So much that there's no need—no*

point, for God's sake!—asking anything more. We have it all."

"Balls!" said Mazzari. He turned away from the grille and sat on the bed. The pretty nurse flashed him a knowing smile as she left the cell with her colleague and the doctor. The door slammed.

"Do you want me to prove it to you, for Christ's sake?" the voice cried.

"Prove it? You couldn't! Not in a million years!" Mazzari gibed.

"No? Not if I was to tell you that we knew Dean was sent to Brazil because of the fingerprints of those women in the auto wreck? Because the CIA dare not investigate here openly? Not if I furnished the details of your briefing from Quinnel and the conversations you had with the obliging Captain Oliveira? Not even if I quoted the extraordinary phrases used by the boy at the car-rental company in Brasilia? If I had more time, I'd play you the tapes!" There was a hint of laughter and triumph in the voice now.

Mazzari allowed his shoulders to droop. In a contrary direction, he had brought off the trick he had accused the voice of playing on him: by stubbornly refusing to accept a few facts, he had provoked his captor into revealing all the facts; and it was clear that he did know virtually everything. Mazzari's own strategy now was to feign total defeat while he planned how to deal with the situation, insofar as he was in a position to act at all.

"You look crestfallen, Mazzari," the voice was saying jubilantly. *"I told you I could prove it. Never mind: there has to be a loser in every game, has there not? For the moment, while we decide what is to be done with you, and how to dispose of Dean, you can take a little rest . . . on our laurels!"* There was a dry chuckle and the sound of a switch snapping off.

Mazzari lay back on the bed and stared moodily at the ceiling. After a while he turned over and lay facedownward with his chin pillowed on crossed arms. It was then that he felt something beneath the tightly drawn mattress covering that had certainly not been there before—a foreign body or bodies, irregular in shape, sharp at the edges, and extremely hard.

And suddenly he remembered that last glance thrown at him by the prettier of the nurses. Hadn't she been swiveling her eyes in a meaningful way at this corner of the room? Now that he came to think of it, wasn't that parting gaze the last of several? Had she not been staring continually at the bed today after she had straightened the cover?

If they were in fact leaving him alone for a while, if they felt there was no more information to be gained from him, there was a chance that the video cameras had been switched off as well as the two-way radio grille. Especially if he appeared as despondent as possible. Carefully, slowly, in case he was still under surveillance, he slid one hand beneath the cover. In a few moments he had it back under his chin with something small and metallic clenched in his fist. There were several separate objects under the cover, and not until he had withdrawn all of them did he lower his eyes to see what lay beneath the protective wall of his cupped palms.

Four small stainless-steel instruments: a nail file, a scalpel, an implement like a crochet hook with a sharp point, and a thin, flexible spatula.

Mazzari stared at the collection unbelievingly. With these he could probably pick the lock of the cell door. If the spatula was strong enough and bendy enough, he might even be able to slip the tongues without picking it. Could she have known this? And, if so, why had she left the things? Why should she wish to help him?

He would puzzle that out later, he thought. For the moment, the important question to answer was whether or not he was still being watched—and therefore whether or not he could safely make use of the gift he had received. After a few minutes he decided that the simplest way to find out would be to sit up on the bed holding the instruments in full view of the cameras. If they were still operating, someone would come through the door soon enough to take them away from him! If not, he could get to work.

In fact, after sitting for some time with the shining steel implements in his hands, he decided his luck must have changed. No sound filtered through the grille; no footsteps clattered in the passage outside; no guard burst into the cell.

In three strides Mazzari was at the door, his big fingers delicately twisting, probing, manipulating. He slid the spatula between the edge of the door and the jamb, testing the tongues and the resilience of their springs. It couldn't be opened with the spatula alone, that was for sure. Perhaps the slender point of the scalpel, aided with a little extra leverage from the file *here* . . . Ah! He heard and felt the slight rolling movement of a tumbler that was beginning to fall.

He paused with the two instruments inserted, one supporting the other, in the keyhole. No matter how he turned, the wretched thing would not quite overcome its inertia and drop.

But of course! That was what the crochet hook was for! He fed the shaft in, questing sensitively with the curved point. It was tricky, feeling about blind with this while he maintained a complementary pressure on the other two instruments with his left hand. But eventually he sensed the satisfying *chuck!* of the wards as they fell home. The door should now be unlocked and ready to open.

He pulled with his fingertips at the edge. The steel panel remained immovable. There was no movement to the door at all.

Puzzled, Mazzari squinted into the crack by the lock, trying to recall the long-ago instructions he had received from a safecracker in Lagos during the Biafran war. Of course! This was the Mark III model of this particular lock! He had moved back the retaining bars but the tongues were still grooved into their vanadium nests in the jamb. A gentle pressure was needed to push them aside—and *that*, naturally, was what the spatula was for!

He eased the flat blade into the crack and worked at it with his wrist. One after the other, the greased metal bars slid silently back into the body of the lock.

The door swung slowly open.

Outside, he saw a dimly lit passage stretching away for fifteen or twenty yards in each direction. On either side there were closed doors like the one he had just opened, with countersunk armored-glass lamps in the low ceiling outside each door. Somewhere beyond a corner in the corridor to his right, machinery hummed quietly. Feeling faintly ridiculous—he had been stripped to his undershirt and shorts—Mazzari tiptoed on stocking feet toward the sound.

The girl was waiting around the bend in the passage. She had removed the white nurse's uniform and now she was dressed in the SISTERS green. For a moment he hesitated . . . and then he saw the welcoming smile on her face and breathed a long sigh of relief.

"I thought you were never coming!" she whispered. "What happened?"

Mazzari stared at her. Through the material of her uniform, the contours of her body curved invitingly. Her lips were still parted in a smile, but the brown eyes, shadowed by a bang of dark hair, were troubled. He said, "I had to wait to make sure the bloody TV had been switched off before I moved. But I don't understand. Frightfully kind of you, and all that. But why did you leave those tools? Why are you helping me? And how the deuce did you know that those particular instruments were right for that particular lock?"

"I hated my foster parents," the girl murmured. "They kept birds in cages. When I was eight, I set most of them free. The old man half-killed me ... and ever since then, I've always hated to see anything in captivity. Setting things free, unlocking anything that's locked, is my way of getting even, I guess. I suppose that's why I married Ricky."

"Ricky?"

"Ricky Rinaldo. Greatest safe man on the Coast. There wasn't a lock made that he couldn't master."

"Wasn't?"

"He got knocked off on some government job in East Asia, but not before he'd taught me most everything he knew. Come to think of it, you're a little like him. Ricky was a black guy too. And big! Maybe that's why I kinda took a shine to you when I saw you on the bed in there."

"Well, thanks. So it was no accident the tools were right?"

"Uh-uh. I just hoped you'd know enough to be able to use them. No, but honest, I'd of fancied you anyway. Even without you looking like Ricky, truly."

Mazzari grinned. "I think you're pretty too," he said. "But before we continue the mutal-admiration bit, suppose you tell me where I am and what the hell goes on here. Also, I feel I'm not really dressed for the occasion."

"Gee, I'm sorry! Of course. Here ... put these on." She produced a rolled-up dungaree suit from under her arm. "It ain't much, but it's all I could lay hands on at the time. I'll talk while you dress."

"Shouldn't we go somewhere ... quieter?" Mazzari glanced over her shoulder at the long, empty corridor.

"What for? We're on C Level down here. Just the cells, the stores, some of the minor offices, and the reactor."

Mazzari paused with one foot in the coverall. "You did say reactor?"

"Why, sure. It's only a little one, though. But since the power station's a blind, we have to get energy someplace, don't we?"

"Er ... yes. I suppose so. What about the offices, though? Isn't somebody likely to come out of one of them?"

"At three-thirty in the morning?"

"Oh. I imagined ..." Mazzari smiled again. "For some reason, I thought it was the middle of the afternoon!"

The girl laughed. "I guess you'd hardly know down here, at that. Not that it's too much different on B and A."

"And what does one find on B and A?"

"Well, living quarters on B, of course. And catering. And the big shots' offices and the council chamber. Plus the radio room, the barracks, and the armory. You know. A Level is mostly the pen, of course."

"The . . . pen?"

"Yeah, the pen. For the ship. It has to go someplace, doesn't it?"

"There's a boat connected with this place . . . and it docks on the *top* story? Presumably A Level *is* the upper one?"

"Well, of course. For the depth. They dare not risk her grounding, you know."

"I *don't* know!" Mazzari said irritably. "Look, dolly, just to please me, tell me what's going on here. Obviously it has to do with the dam, right? . . . Well, I know about the dam; I know about the bogus power station; I know Getuliana's as much of a sham as the rest of it. But that's all I know. I don't know what's going *on*!"

"Well, the pen has to be on the top floor because, with the whole dump underwater—"

"Under*water!*"

"You didn't even know that? Jesus, you do need filling in! Well, yeah, while they were constructing the dam, they also built this place—against the bluff, on the floor of the valley. They made it completely watertight, and then, when the valley was flooded and the water rose, it was completely covered over, see."

Mazzari nodded. "And you get in and out . . . ?"

"Through the tunnel from the estancia. The surface of the lake's much higher than the ground the estancia's built on. And of course you can get in and out through the dock. But that don't do you much good: the ship doesn't go anyplace. It always comes back here."

"I see." Mazzari's expression showed that this was far from the truth. "Where do you girls come in, then?"

"We helped resettle the natives from the valley, and—"

"Yes, I know that. But why not real SISTERS?"

She stared at him. "Well, it ain't exactly legal, what they do here! I guess they felt they'd be safer if we all had records. We do, you know. And then I figure they thought it would look better if any Brazilian officials looked in on us— having members of an okay welfare group around, I mean. They preferred West Coast girls because of the swimming."

"The swimming?" Mazzari felt himself looking more and more foolish, repeating almost everything the girl said.

"They only recruited first-rate swimmers and divers," she explained patiently. "Divers especially, to help with the ship in the pen."

"Are you telling me"—the coin finally dropped—"that the pen, the dock, is underwater too? The ship is in fact a submarine?"

She flashed him an amused glance. "You hadn't tumbled?"

"They go to all this trouble to . . . to find spurious reasons to construct an artificial lake, just so they can build an underwater dock and play submarines with it?" He shook his head. "But *why?*"

The girl told him why.

Mazzari gave a long, low whistle of astonishment. "Christ!" he said. "Look, I don't know how you think we can get out—"

"I don't expect we can. It's just that I don't like to see guys locked up. I told you."

"So you did. The point is, in or out, I've got to make contact with my chief now. I've got to. I gather you . . . I imagine you don't feel any particular loyalty to these people?"

"I couldn't care less. They pay me. Period. And then, when it comes to keeping people in cells . . ."

"You have a thing about it. I know. Lucky for jolly old me."

She was smiling again. "You do talk funny!"

"Blame it on the imperialist powers."

"How was that?"

"Never mind," Mazzari said. "Look, you did say there was a radio room here? Well, it seems to me the wisest thing would be for me to try to crash that and send a message from here, rather than to escape and do it from outside. Especially as you say we probably can't escape. Are you with me?"

"Sure," the girl said. "I think there's only one operator left on duty, nights. And I guess he wouldn't be one hundred percent alert at this hour. But you watch out. You don't have too much reserve of strength, you know. You been under heavy sedation for days."

"Just lead me to the bloody radio room," Mazzari said, "and I'll worry about my strength when we get there. All right?"

She took his arm and led him through a maze of passages, past louvered doors shaking with the vibrations of unseen machinery, past control boards winking with red and green and blue pilot lights, and then up a flight of stairs winding around a shaft housing three elevators. On the level above, the humming of the plant was less obtrusive, though he still found the subterranean atmosphere, with its dry and hygienic air, oppressive in the extreme. Somewhere below them, beneath the massive foundations of the fortress, lay the inundated earth which had until so recently echoed to the footsteps of simple farmers, produced their crops, and perhaps even buoyed up lovers in the spring; somewhere around and above, millions of tons of water now pressed remorselessly in upon the walls.

And somewhere not far away must be the heads within whose crania lay the warped brains that had conceived the monstrous plot he had just heard about and which now only he could thwart.

If he was lucky and could get in touch with Dean.

The doors on this higher level were mostly glass-paned, and Mazzari saw, as they stole past, offices with rows of desks, a library lined with filing cabinets, a computer room bright with levers and dials and lights. There was even a small lecture theater where seats in a semicircle surrounded a vast wall map whose rash of bulbs and flags concentrated around the newly filled-in outline of the lake. "It could almost be a conducted tour in Langley, Virginia!" he murmured.

Finally the girl drew him against the corridor wall and put her lips to his ear. "First door around the next corner is the radio room," she breathed. "Like I told you, there's probably only one guy there right now. But the council chamber is immediately beyond, and the main control room leads off that. So there may be other folks within call, is all I mean."

"I don't know why you should do all this for me, Mrs. Rinaldo—"

"You can call me Glory."

"Glory be!" Mazzari chuckled. "But I don't know why you'd want to risk your life like this for me; I only know that I'll do every bally thing I can to make it up to you if ever we get out of here. . . . Listen, are you actually on duty tonight? Could you have a valid reason for walking past the radio-room door?"

"Sure I could. You want me to check out who's there?"

"It would help, Glory."

"Okay," the brunette said. "You want me to try to get the guy to come outside?"

He shook his head. "I don't think so. Could be there's other people who might overhear. If you could just go past and signal to me afterward . . ."

"Will do," Glory said. She walked on around the corner in the passageway, with Mazzari sidling after her like a disembodied shadow. Beyond the right angle the corridor was wider, with rubber floor tiles in marled gray. Halfway along, a shaft of bright light barred the gloom by an open door. Glory Rinaldo walked up and paused, looking into the room.

"Hi, there!" she said. "You all on your lonesome?"

"Like usual on this trick," a man's voice replied over the faint burble of automatic Morse. "I'm waitin' for some bastard call to come through from some guy he has a report to make from Zurich, Switzerland. You wanna come in an' share the solitude?"

"I don't mind. Watcha got there?" The girl stepped across the threshold, trailing behind her one arm with which she gave Mazzari first the thumbs-up sign, then a single finger pointing inward.

Taking this to mean that the man was indeed alone and that it would be safe to approach, Mazzari crept stealthily up and peered around the door. The room was small, but it was packed with chassis after chassis, console upon console of the most advanced electronic equipment he had ever seen. On the far side, bent over the dials of a shortwave receiver, the brunette and the operator had their backs to him. "Now, this filter slope here," the man was saying, "with this . . . See! You can tune out—"

He cut the dialogue in mid-sentence. There was a small monitor speaker above the set from which static occasionally sputtered. Mazzari had hoped to use this noise to cover his shoeless approach into the room, but some small current of movement that he made in the dry air, perhaps some inadvertent telltale sign from the girl, alerted the operator. He moved fast. He was out of his chair before the African was within striking distance—a brawny blue-jowled man in an undershirt and uniform pants.

He had time to shoot an accusing glance at Glory Rinaldo before Mazzari's fist caught him in the solar plexus. It was essential that the man should not cry out or call for help, that any struggle should be as silent as possible. Once anyone else's attention was attracted, Mazzari's plan, such as it was, was finished.

The radio operator doubled forward with a grunt of astonishment and pain. His lips drew back from his teeth as he straightened, tugging at a blackjack in his waistband. Before he could draw enough breath back into his savaged lungs to yell, Mazzari had first to disarm and then to silence him.

Wheezing, his eyes streaming, the man lurched forward. Mazzari chopped viciously down, flat-handed, at his wrist, and the cosh clattered to the floor. At the same time, he raked a stinging blow across the bridge of the big operator's nose with the back of his other hand and thudded one stockinged heel to his kneecap. In his weakened state, the one card Mazzari held was surprise, and he had to play it for all it was worth before his opponent could recover his breath and move in to close quarters.

He dodged back from a roundhouse left but was unable to avoid the follow-up—a short, pounding right that carried all the man's weight and slammed into his body just below the heart.

Mazzari heard his own grunt of pain as his legs abruptly turned to rubber and he collapsed backward onto a wooden chair. Still groaning for breath, the operator pounced. Grabbing a handful of dungarees, knuckling himself a firm hold, and dragging Mazzari to his feet, he smashed a fist to the African's jaw.

Through the blackness that threatened to engulf him, Mazzari dimly saw the big fist draw back once more, the evil grin on the hoodlum face poised menacingly over him. With his remaining strength he reached up desperately and grabbed the man's ears. Then he went suddenly limp and drew his adversary's head down after him. Caught momentarily off balance, the radio operator pitched forward, both hands flying out instinctively to break his fall before his forehead crashed into a bank of equipment behind the chair.

Using the seat for leverage, Mazzari executed a kind of half back-somersault and brought his knee jarringly up to connect with the man's chin as he hauled down on the ears. There was a sudden cessation of movement and then he was smothered in the deadweight of the operator's unconscious body.

Panting, with sweat streaming into his eyes, Mazzari laboriously extricated himself from underneath. The girl helped him to his feet. Brief though it had been, the fight had totally exhausted him. She had been right: it would be some time before he had regained his normal ferocious strength.

There could be no question of any more action, he realized bitterly as he stumbled across the room to a transmitter. He must do what he had to do and worry about any subsequent activity when the need arose. He slumped into another chair and began methodically testing switches and revolving dials. Quinnel had told him that a twenty-four-hour watch was kept on the warning lights above the receiver in Mendoza's attic in Rio. He hoped it was true, for this was almost certainly the only opportunity he would have of putting Dean wise to the BBW conspiracy. Behind the chair, the girl watched wide-eyed as he tuned in to the correct frequency, repeated a call sign, and began to transmit.

It must have been around twenty minutes later, by which time Mazzari's labored breathing had settled down to a steadier and quieter rhythm as he concentrated on his task, that a section of wall behind them swung aside to reveal three men standing there.

"All right, you—away from that transmitter! *Move!*" The words cracked out from the thin-lipped mouth of the man in the center. Mazzari whirled away from the radio. The man had slender, almost feminine hands with grimed nails and fingers stained saffron by nicotine. There was a half-smoked cigarette drooping from a corner of his mouth now. And a short-barreled Walther P.38 hung negligently from his right hand.

Beside him were the tall white-haired black whom Mazzari knew as Pai Hernando, and a bulky, well-dressed man whom Dean would have recognized as the Intacon president, Menezes. The man who had chiseled the concession to build Getuliana and the dam said quietly, "Do not do anything foolish, my good fellow. McCaffery may appear a trifle lackadaisical—but it is deceptive, I assure you. The two girls in the automobile accident, a truck driver, and an old peasant on a mule could have confirmed what I say, were they still alive. The fact that your confederate Dean—or should I say Forster?—is still living was due to an accident of nature and was in no way McCaffery's fault. Doubtless he will rectify the error shortly."

Mazzari stood perfectly still, his hands at his sides. A few feet away, the girl crouched above the unconscious radio operator in a pose that was almost a caricature of guilty surprise. Apart from a sharp intake of breath when McCaffery had spoken, she had remained completely silent.

"I am most surprised to find you abusing our hospitality, Mazzari," the Negro said. "And disappointed. As . . . ah . . . a researcher from the . . . um . . . University of Southern California, I should have thought you would welcome the fact that we had finally acceded to your request to see more of the workings of this establishment! I had hoped, too, that you were one of our more cooperative guests." The voice, of course, Mazzari realized now, was that of his interlocutor in the cell: Pai Hernando, so-called. That was why there had been something familiar about it: he had met the man before.

"Unfortunately," Menezes added, "we were not attending to our monitor speakers in the control room, otherwise we should have noticed sooner that clandestine signals were being transmitted."

"Too bad, old chap," Mazzari murmured. "Actually, I'd said all I wanted to say anyway."

"So we gathered. Far too much for your own good. Fortunately our plans are sufficiently far advanced for that indiscretion not to matter. Fortunately for us, that is; for you personally, it will prove to be unfortunate."

Two more men had appeared in the opening behind the other three—a tall, thin man with a skull-like face, and a shorter, meatier individual whose eyes peered myopically through thick-lensed shell glasses beneath a thatch of pig-bristle hair. "Nothing your confederate Dean can do could in any way affect or alter these plans," the thin man drawled. "They can even be advanced if need be. In any case, they will have been put into action long before he could drum up another band of hired thugs large enough to embarrass us."

"It would not matter even if he could," said Hernando. "We have—shall we say?—friends at court: the Brazilian authorities would never permit terrorists in such numbers to roam the country or move against us."

Mazzari said nothing. He was thankful that his radio message, which had necessarily been in clear, had confined itself to the alarming facts he had learned from the girl, and had made no mention of Gonçalves, de Soares, and their colleagues. Neither, it seemed, had he revealed any details of their own "friends at court" under the influence of the truth drug. Perhaps Hernando had not put the right questions. It was the first piece of luck he had had.

"So far as you yourself are concerned," Hernando continued, "you have transgressed the laws of hospitality, and now you have become merely an embarrassment. You must be got rid of."

"Didn't they teach you not to end sentences with a preposition, brother, when you 'left the kraal and took your postal course in English?" Mazzari asked.

Hernando smiled. "I am immune to insults, Mazzari. As I

was saying, you must now die. You have until darkness tomorrow night. Tonight, I should say, for it must be almost dawn now."

"A break with tradition, surely?" Mazzari said. "I thought it was always *at* dawn."

"It is a question of method and efficacy," Menezes explained. "We like to be tidy; we do not like to arouse too much curiosity on the part of our Brazilian hosts. So any deaths that are necessary are customarily arranged to look like accidents—a hit-and-run driver, a heart attack, a robbery with violence. You know the kind of thing. It saves a great deal of unnecessary trouble."

"And the girls in the Alfa Romeo?"

"One of the troubles about employing members of the criminal classes," the tall, thin man said, "is that they will not obey rules. Despite clearly expressed orders, individual members of our company persisted in a foolish desire to drive all the way to Rio de Janeiro or Bahia—to, as they put it, amuse themselves in their spare time. This particular pair drove carelessly, that is all. Then they had to be silenced to ward off the prying questions of your confederates."

The man named McCaffery spoke for the first time. "It was a pleasure," he said. "A guy always likes to do a neat, professional job."

"Neatness. Efficiency. Obeying the rules. *Order!*" the short-sighted man announced. "This is what the world lacks today. This is what we shall impose when Phase One is completed." Magnified eyes gleamed behind the thick, curved lenses. "You already have some small demonstration of this. The elimination of witnesses. The defeat of your puny attack on the estancia. The precautions against unauthorized surveys of the lake. The fact that we have been fully informed, through agents in the United States and Rio, of every move made since the man Mackenzie interested himself in this absurd accident."

"All right, Doctor, save it for the lecture theater," Menezes said. "In the case of your own death, Mazzari, this will be arranged to look like an accidental drowning. A foolhardy and overinquisitive trespasser who missed his footing and fell into the lake."

"Why does it have to be in the dark?" Mazzari was stalling for time, hoping to learn more from the conspirators' boasting while he regained some of his lost strength.

"Better to stage it that way, simply to avoid possible witnesses," Menezes said. "Don't you agree, Fleischman?"

"Certainly," the thin man replied. "The way Dr. Glaser has designed this complex—"

"Based on the simple air-lock system," Glaser interrupted. His thick lips stretched into a self-congratulatory smile. "The submarine pen has two sets of watertight doors, so that the craft can enter submerged, wait until the water has been extracted, and then disgorge its crew in safety. In your case the process is reversed. You will be left in the pen when it is air-filled. The inner doors will close. The outer doors will open . . . and water will fill the pen."

"Later," Fleischman resumed, "your body will float to the surface in the normal way, once it has become bloated with gases from the decomposing tissue. And some worthy peasant will discover it, no doubt, at a future date. The method has the additional advantage that there will be no marks on the body."

"Bodies—not body," Menezes put in. "Disloyalty cannot be tolerated." He walked across the room to Glory Rinaldo. "You treacherous slut," he snapped, "you could seriously have compromised our plans if you had helped this man earlier. As it is, you will have to pay for your stupidity with your life." He raised his arm and slapped her repeatedly, forehand and backhand, across the face. The girl's head rocked on her shoulders with the force of the blows. The marks of his fingers stood out lividly against her pallor as a thread of blood crawled slowly down her chin from a corner of her split mouth.

"All right, Umberto, that's enough," said Fleischman, who seemed to be the leader of the group. "*No*, Mazzari, I wouldn't! I really wouldn't if I were you. . . . McCaffery, you'd better . . . ah . . . calm this fellow down before we take him back to his cell with his fellow prisoner to await the night."

"Okay," McCaffery said. He handed his gun to Menezes and shambled forward across the room, his pale, baggy suit flapping on his bony frame. "Only thing is," he said as he approached the African, "my hands is kinda delicate and I hate to bruise them. You know?"

Mazzari automatically raised his arms to defend himself as the gunman came near. But McCaffery took him by surprise. Moving with the speed of a striking snake, his left hand streaked out and grasped Mazzari's shoulder, spinning him deftly around so that he was facing the wall. Then, almost in the same movement, he whipped a cosh from the waistband of his pants and struck. The weapon consisted of a leather-covered lead weight the size and shape of an egg, which was connected to the handle by a short plastic-covered coil spring. The heavy lead thudded into Mazzari's back, immediately over the left kidney, with paralyzing force.

Mazzari's fingers scrabbled at the wall as he sank to the ground, a strangled cry forcing itself from his lips. Dimly, through waves of nausea, he heard the girl call out—though whether it was in pain or in horror at what was happening to him he never knew.

Behind him, McCaffery poised birdlike, polishing the toecap of one tan-and-white steel-tipped shoe against the trousering that covered the calf of his other leg. Then, measuring his distance carefully, he drew back his foot.

15

"The whole deal has to be entirely rethought," Dean said. "Urgently. With a different approach and a far bigger force available. But if I cannot get the go-ahead from you gentlemen within the next half-hour, the consequences—I don't want to sound melodramatic—but the consequences could be literally disastrous." He looked around at the five Brazilians gathered in the small room—Gonçalves, de Soares, two high-ranking army officers, and the police captain, Oliveira. Sean Hammer stood beside him, chewing rapidly, ready with a pointer by a large wall map. This time, for security reasons, they had once more changed the meeting place and were assembled in the interrogation room of a suburban precinct house officered by a colleague of Oliveira's.

Gonçalves smoothed a fat hand over his hair. "Perhaps if you were to summarize what we know already for the benefit of our military friends . . . Before you come to this new discovery, that is."

"I'll give you a straight recap, a rundown from the top," Dean said crisply. He moved across to the map. "First, this BBW neo-Nazi syndicate used the ostensible building of a new city and a bogus hydroelectric scheme as a blind to move a large force of contractors into this area." He turned to Sean Hammer, whose pointer touched the map in the San Felipe region.

"Secondly, this force built in fact a sophisticated fortress powered with atomic fuel on the floor of the valley some way behind the dam." There were murmurs of astonishment as the pointer circled the valley on the fringe of the Serra do Roncador.

"Yes," Dean said. "It appears that there is a small nuclear reactor within the complex. When the valley was flooded to make the artificial lake slated to power the hydroelectric station, the fortress was submerged. It can now be entered only through a tunnel bored under the ridge separating the reservoir from the adjoining valley." He paused. "Or via a special underwater entrance I'll come back to in a minute.

"Third, the fake SISTERS are a collection of women with criminal records recruited from the West Coast of the U.S. to help the conspirators in three ways: with certain underwater aspects of the plan, as companions for the work force, and to aid in resettlement of the peasants dispossessed by the flooding of the valley. Most fortunately for us, their . . . individuality . . . has proved more a liability to the plotters than an asset.

"Fourth, these peasants and other locals likely to see a cause for gossip in the BBW activities have been scared off by the head of an equally spurious Candomblé *terreiro*, a man named Hernando who plays upon their superstitions and invokes their gods to blackmail them into silence—which is why no stories of these activities in such a remote part of the country seem to have reached Rio or Salvador or even Brasilia. Apparently Hernando is one of the leading fascists, despite the fact that he is himself a man of color."

Dean paused again to regard his audience. Oliveira and the two army men—a colonel and a full general—were staring fixedly at the map. Gonçalves was nodding his sleek egg head: I told you! That's what I told you! Professor de Soares, sitting a good six inches taller than the others, was looking down his nose at the twin curves of his mustache. Every few minutes, as trucks on the way into town from the mines in Belo Horizonte roared past, the wooden walls of the room shook.

"Number five," Dean resumed. "The purpose of all this crookery. I can put it in a few words. The lake was created as a safe base for tests of a new atomic-powered submarine developed in the fortress by right-wing scientists belonging to the BBW conspiracy."

"*What!*" exploded the general. "How dare these people!"

"In a landlocked stretch of water far from civilization in the Mato Grosso, they can experiment on a scale impossible in the crowded seas of the world," Dean said. "Not, of course, from the space point of view, but from that of detection. The craft is completing a series of proving runs right now, but the plan is about to move into its next phase: intermediate-range ballistic missiles with nuclear warheads are to be fired at selected targets."

This announcement was greeted with stunned silence—and then suddenly everybody was on his feet, shouting.

"The whole operation"—Dean's calm voice rode over the outburst—"is only in the nature of a pilot scheme to give them information to be used later in projects destined to start beneath the oceans of the world. Even so, it involves warheads of one or more kilotons, each being launched at six cities in Argentina and Chile—Bahía Blanca, Buenos Aires, Concepción, Córdoba, Santiago, and Valparaíso, according to the message I received." He cleared his throat. "With the Pan-American Conference coming up, you can readily imagine, gentlemen, what such a series of attacks could do to the OAS!"

"But . . . Good Christ! . . . Surely you can't be . . . ?"

"I never heard such an outrageous . . ."

"It's unbelievable! Unbelievable!"

"Why? Why? What possible purpose could be served . . . ?"

"Power, General," said Dean. "These are crazy men. It's not just ordinary madness. They are power-crazy. They want to hold the world to ransom: this is what we can do if we want; now, play it our warped and wicked way if you don't want the same thing to happen to you."

"But . . . surely, with modern early warning systems . . . with all the sophisticated detection apparatus . . . ? Surely the base from which these things were fired could be . . . would be pinpointed?" The general was almost incoherent.

"Certainly it would. But that wouldn't save those six towns." Dean paused. "Or Brazil's reputation, once it *was* pinpointed."

After a short silence the general said, "You are quite, quite sure—one hundred percent sure—of the accuracy of your information?"

"It was radioed to me by a colleague from inside the fortress," Dean said. "As the message was interrupted, he was presumably caught and will now be in great danger. If, indeed, he hasn't been murdered already. To tell you the truth, getting him out is the main reason I want to go back in there. You gentlemen may have other priorities..."

The thin walls vibrated as another truck thundered past. "This ... bigger force you spoke of," the colonel said. "You could assemble such a unit in time?"

Dean looked at Sean Hammer. The Ulsterman mailed a fresh stick of gum and nodded. "The most of them would still be around."

"We just completed a ... er ... delivery to one of the islands," Dean said. "Thirty, thirty-five of the guys should still be contactable in the Caribbean, here at a few hours' notice. Right?" He looked again at Hammer.

"Surely," Hammer said, chewing busily. "Maybe more."

"And how much time is there?"

"None that we can afford to lose. My message said 'imminent'—but I can't quote you hours and minutes," Dean said.

The general looked at the colonel, and then both of them turned to Gonçalves. Gonçalves' brows rose to corrugate his bland forehead as he glanced at de Soares. The professor's gold teeth gleamed. "I think Senhor Dean should be given immediate overseas telephone and telex facilities," he said. "Are you confident, sir, that even with thirty or forty men you can force this steel shutter that seals off your tunnel? If artillery help could be arranged ..."

Dean shook his head. "For my money, that armorplate could be anything up to eight-inch warship stuff. Nothing short of 105mm AP shells would make an impression, and even then ..." He shrugged. "You might just buckle it, or block the tunnel. And give them enough warning to launch at least one missile."

The colonel shivered. "Then how ...?"

"I'd aim to neutralize their main control and operations center," Dean replied, "and open the doors mechanically ... from inside the fortress."

All three of the uniformed men stared at him. Oliveira, who seemed to have been awed into silence by the presence of two such senior officers, was startled into saying, "But how the devil ...?"

"I have a plan," Dean said. "The underwater entrance I was telling you about. I may need—undercover, of course— the help of the U.S. Navy."

"Doubtless—in the circumstances—that can be arranged," Gonçalves said dryly. "Even so ...?"

"Once we are inside," said Dean, "it seems that there's a lady who can act as a guide."

"Why the hell didn't you tell me before," he had said angrily to Coralie Willys, "that you knew the goddamn place?"

"I don't know it. I was there while it was being built."

"Well, that you were familiar with the layout of the part on the far side of the tunnel. Why didn't you say?"

"You didn't ask me."

"For God's sake . . ." Dean spread his hands in exasperation. "Why would I ask you? Why should I think for one moment that you'd know? You knew how important it was: you could have spoken up without being asked." He shook his head. "Why not?"

"I'll give you the same answer I gave your friend," she said. "Your people refused to cooperate with us; why should we help you?"

"To try to avoid what might turn into the biggest world crisis since the Berlin airlift," Dean snapped. "In any case, I don't have any 'people'; I'm being hired to find out what goes on there. You could have told me some of it. How come you do know, anyway?"

She lit a cigarette and shifted her position on the padded leather stool. They were in the tiny bar in back of Dean's hotel. "We heard about these girls pretending to be us long before your . . . before the people hiring you did," she said. "It's like I said—only I left out the fact that I'd been here before. The Sanderson Trust council asked our commandant to investigate, and I was sent down here. Before the valley was flooded, the site was in chaos: there were construction workers and guards and women wearing our uniform everywhere. It wasn't too difficult to mingle one time with a detail going on duty. And while I was there, I was lucky enough to get a look at the architect's plans—though of course I had no idea what the place was for, or why they were faking SISTERS personnel. The council was trying to decide what to do about it—I mean, we have no representation here, and we couldn't expect help from the Brazilian authorities—they were trying to decide, when there was this auto accident and, well, you and your friend were hired."

"Can you remember those plans?" Dean asked urgently.

"Pretty well. So far as the general layout is concerned, anyway."

"Tell me everything you can remember, every damned

thing," Dean said. "Then I'll tell you what I plan to do . . . and why *you* have to come with me. If you're game, that is."

"I'm game, but not fair game," Coralie said two Campari-sodas later, when the exchange was completed. Over the rim of her glass she glanced appreciatively at the rakish lines of his jaw. "As I told your friend Mazzari when we were out at the dam together . . . Oh, well, never mind." She sighed. "I think sometimes it's a shame I wasn't born a redhead."

Dean's pale brows rose. "A redhead? But why?"

"The original feminists," she said obscurely. "Hadn't you noticed in your philandering days—if you ever found time to philander, that is—hadn't you noticed the way redheads went after their men, any men that attracted them? I mean, it's always the same: they just go up—brazenly, my mother would say—and tell the guy so. Or make it so obvious that even the thickest jerk couldn't fail to get the message. They're all like that, redheads." Coralie shook her own blond head. "Sometimes I envy them. I guess it must be something to do with upbringing or family background, but even as a libber I can't bring myself to go right up to a man and say: Brother, I think you're a dish! Maybe I'm just old-fashioned, but I have to be told I'm beautiful and intelligent and fun before I can even show interest."

Dean studied her through the layers of cigarette smoke weaving above the bar. She certainly didn't look the stereotype women's libber. She had narrow feet and beautiful calves. Above a slender but soft waist, the graceful curves of her breasts contoured the top of a white dress covered with huge printed flowers. Below a burnished cap of hair, Samantha's eyes when they were first married stared at him. Why the hell did he always have to pick blonds that reminded him of her? he thought fiercely. Or was it that all blonds reminded him of Samantha? "I think you're beautiful and intelligent and fun," he said.

Coralie grinned impishly. "Let me buy you a drink," she said.

Fifteen minutes passed. And then—it was almost automatic, no questions and answers were exchanged—they left the bar and went up to his room. They didn't look at each other in the elevator.

He locked the door on the inside and left the key on the night table. It was a very hot evening, and the sounds from the street outside were dissolved and swept away by the whirring of a fan spinning above the bed. Dean turned and looked at her. She was standing with her back to him in front of the unshuttered window, staring at the gathering dusk over the sharp spines of a phoenix palm. He approached without switching on the light. Her face was shadowed beneath the pale cap of hair, her body firm-fleshed and alien as he closed his fingers around her upper arms.

He felt her tremble through the thin stuff of the dress. "Is the door locked?" she whispered.

Dean's lips were on the nape of her neck. He murmured an affirmative without moving his mouth, and she shivered again. "Take off my clothes," she ordered, still staring out into the night.

There was a zipper that ran from the neckline to the base of her spine. The noise was lost in the creak of the fan, and the lightweight garment dropped to pool around her feet.

In the gloom, her body appeared to be dark against a white lace brassière. He unsnapped the fasteners, feeling her shudder from head to toe now as he palmed the soft, stiff-nippled weight of her breasts and spun her around to face him, sensing himself harden against her, peeling the cool nylon panties down over her buttocks, stripping them down the length of her legs, and carrying her across to the bed.

Lying with her then on the stretched white covers, the cool, smooth swell of her belly against his cheek, he thought wildly: No, it's too good, too fine, too soon! Kissing the triangle of stiffly curling musk-scented hair, he reflected as she writhed and arched her back: Coralie . . . Samantha . . . Dagmar . . . a girl he had picked up once at the central station in Brussels—why was it always the same? How come it was always utterly different?

He went into her and made love in time with the creaking fan, until the sounds of the city were lost in her sighs and moans, and a last, long cry escaped through the open window into the dark.

Dean lay limp and giddy, aware only after some time that her fingernails were grinding into his shoulders, wondering if he had the right to ask her to risk her life with him in one of the craziest operations he had ever planned. "Do I have? Maybe I shouldn't—after all, on my side, it's only for money," he muttered indistinctly, forgetting that the original thought had remained unvoiced. She whispered some words that he couldn't catch, still gripping him with her thighs, reluctant to allow him to escape out of her. When he did, she gave another anguished cry and turned away from him, sitting up on the bed with her weight resting on one elbow.

Sometime afterward, when the glowing ends of their cigarettes burned holes in the dark ceiling, he shook his head and said, "Darling, you're a strange one; an adventurer, a brave one—but a strange one."

"Yes," Coralie said. "I'm a strange one. I like to fuck with a man who isn't afraid—but I can't bring myself to say so until it's over." She laughed softly beside him. "Maybe I should go to a beautician and get me a red rinse."

Hearing her use the coarse word, Dean felt desire rise in him again. "Now that you *have* said it," he chided, his fingers teasing and probing, "there'd be one way I could still tell you weren't a genuine redhead!"

Coralie's hand wrapped around him. She leaned over his chest and kissed him, wide-lipped, her hot tongue rolling lasciviously around his mouth. "Kiss and don't tell," she said at last, letting him breathe once more, "that's the safest bet!"

He pulled her onto him, cramming the lean, tender breasts against the hair on his chest, his fingers sliding down the long back, over the mounds of her buttocks to feel her warm and wet between the thighs. "I don't bet," he said breathlessly; "I only back winners!"

They were lying quiet again, his hand around her shoulders and one hand between her legs, when the phone on the night table rang. "Did you get the men you wanted?" she whispered when he had finished talking.

"Yes," Dean said. "I got the men I wanted. They'll be here before noon tomorrow, more than thirty of them."

"And your friend Hammer will be able to use them to attack the outside while you and I go inside?"

"Sure. After we go inside, to be exact. When we're ready to open the tunnel doors."

"You're certain this man in Florida will let you have the ... the craft we need to *get* inside?"

"He's a friend," Dean said simply.

"That's fine. That's just fine. Especially if the Brazilians will let us ... if we can get to San Felipe without any trouble."

"They will. We will. This guy Quinnel's handling all that. It'll be all right."

"Well, I'm glad you got the men you wanted," Coralie said. "Did you get the girl you wanted?"

Dean reached for her. "What do *you* think?" he said.

16

The Forrest Ward Underwater Research Center was north of Cape Romano and the Ten Thousand Islands, between Naples and Pine Island Sound. Except for the two Wurzburg bowls and the revolving radar antennae, it could have been a holiday camp or a Spartan health farm—a collection of single-story prefabs clustered around the far end of a low-lying spit that ran out into the clear waters of the Gulf. But there were two uniformed guards at the red-and-white-striped barrier pole barring the roadway at the landward end of the spit, and direction indicators at the first intersection inside the perimeter pointed to "Subaqueous Topographical Studies," to "Marine Biology," to "Sonar Research," and to "Oceanographic Laboratory." Fifty yards before the signs, white lettering on a red enameled board warned: *No Unauthorized Entry Beyond This Point*.

Ward took the fifty-foot Magnum Flybridge cruiser past the new marina north of the point at a steady thirty knots, the creamy wake on his lee side washing out to rock the floating gin palaces and Riva Boats and blinding white Kris Kraft at their moorings. A storm was blowing up and more dressed-to-kill vacation yachtsmen and their ladies were strolling the glassed-in shopping center and the plazas between the unfinished condominium towers than were visible along the slips or on the sundecks of the pleasure boats. There was still one fifty-acre undeveloped lot between two of the high-rise apartment blocks, and beyond the flatland palmettos, where the turnpike arrowed eastward across Big Cypress Swamp toward Fort Lauderdale and Miami, Ward could see the angry cloud front low on the horizon.

He throttled back the twin turbo-charged diesels and coasted into the basin at the far end of the spit, a tall, florid, heavily built man in his mid-thirties with an all-weather tan and features accustomed to hot towels. The cruiser spun neatly around and backed up skillfully to a mooring between two flat-bottomed research barges. Ward cast a line ashore, where it was caught and hitched around a bollard by a grizzled ex-mariner standing at the edge of the quay. Like Ward himself, the seaman was wearing a navy-blue T-shirt with the letters FWURC embroidered in white across the chest. He was barefoot below faded denims. "Person-to-person call for you, Mr. Ward," he said as the big man stepped ashore. "Somebody name of Dean wants you to call him back at once. Says it's kind of urgent."

"Oh, Christ," Ward said good-naturedly. "What does he want now?"

"He didn't say, sir. He was calling from Rio de Janeiro."

Ward sighed, shook his head, and said, "Where else!"

At college, he had rowed with Marc Dean and played football with him and tennis against him. He had beaten Dean, often, on the courts; on the other hand, Dean had saved Ward's life twice during the Tet offensive in Vietnam. Whether this left him one up or one down, Ward was never sure. He preferred to think of the game so far as Even Steven. There remained now just the one difference separating them: Forrest Ward happened to be a millionaire because his old man had once had the foresight to acquire land and construct a railroad that ran near some oilfields in Venezuela.

The research center was still a new toy so far as he was concerned. In his student days he had sailed with Dean on the Delaware River and in Chesapeake Bay. After the war, he had graduated to the throat-tightening, fast-running cruiser thrill, hunting the big ones on the blue waters of the Gulf. In between, to fill in an idle three years, he had taken a master's degree in marine genetics. A friend in some hush-hush section of the Navy Department's biological-warfare executive had then offered interest-free capital and guaranteed research contracts if Ward would set up the center. The project still held a certain fascination for him: the ocean floor was, after all, the only place left where there was still exploring to do. But Ward's number-one priority in the matter of research was establishing the highest speed at which machinery on four wheels could be hurled around corners on a racetrack. He was a regular competitor at Indianapolis and his personal automobile stable included such foreign exotica as the products of Lamborghini, Maserati, and Monteverdi. Ward, Dean had once said, handled sports cars the way trainers handle lions—or the way Spanish men think they handle women. What was the cussed son of a bitch going to say now? Ward wondered as he crossed to the administration building that housed his small but luxurious office. Whatever it was, it was sure to be something difficult, probably dangerous, and liable to get him in a whole heap of trouble!

In fact it was none of those things. It was just impossible. "You're crazy!" Ward said when the connection had been made and Dean had phrased his curt request. "For God's sake, we don't run some kind of a jumbo-size mail-order service!"

"I only want one." Dean's calm voice, spiced with faint amusement, came clearly across the 4,200 miles separating them.

"You only want . . . ? What the hell d'you expect me to do, feller? Paste postage stamps over the rudder and airmail it to you, General Delivery, Rio? Call up Western Union? Do you know how long those things are?"

"Yeah, I've a pretty good idea, Forrest. I guess the size will suit me just fine."

"Twenty-three feet," Ward said, as though Dean had not spoken. "Do you know how much they weigh? How much they *cost*, for Pete's sake? Do you want it gift-wrapped, or will the economy-size Jiffy bag do?" he added sarcastically.

Dean was unruffled. "The important thing is: you do have one?"

"Sure I have one. I have three, if it matters. But I'm damned if I see why—"

"How long would it take you to get one to Key West?"

"Three hours, if I slung it aboard the cruiser. Maybe three and a half. It's all of a hundred miles."

"That'll be fine. Know Macdonald's yacht basin? It's kind of a run-down dump to look at, but they repair—"

"I know Macdonald's."

"Great. Be there in three and a half hours, and we'll arrange to have the merchandise collected."

"We?"

"In this case a Navy chopper."

"The U.S. Navy?" Ward sounded scandalized. "But why don't they use one of their own—?"

"It mustn't be identifiable as American, especially American forces. Reasons of state."

"Jesus, Marc, the things you get into! I sure hope the hell you know what you're doing. You're not going to blow up the Sugarloaf?"

"It's not for offensive purposes. Call it, you know, research." Dean paused. "You'll do it?"

His friend exhaled a theatrical sigh. "I suppose so. If it's really urgent."

"It's urgent, all right."

"And really important."

"Just about the most important deal I ever got involved in," Dean said. "It could even be important for you too—if I don't make it."

"But what the *hell* is all this—?"

"I'll tell you next time we sink a highball together," Dean interrupted. "If we ever do. Naturally you'll be reimbursed if there's any damage; we'll pay for the rental of the ship." And with that, Forrest Ward had to be content.

Out on the quay, the wind was gusting now, grinding and tilting the pleasure boats in the marina, whipping the waves into occasional whitecaps. Across the water, Ward could hear expensive hulls creaking against fenders, the clank of wire rigging against aluminum masts. "Maybe I should have quoted him four hours," he said, looking up into the darkening sky.

"What was that, Mr. Ward?" the old seaman asked, falling in step as they headed toward the research buildings.

Ward didn't answer directly. "There was a Broadway musical, Diego, years ago," he said, "and one of the hit songs was called 'Whatever Lola Wants, Lola Gets.'"

Diego glanced up at him uncomprehendingly, padding along the bleached boards in his bare feet.

"It seems we're working for Mr. Lola," Ward explained. He led the way into a study building, where girls in white lab coats sat with clipboards, noting down the social habits of creatures living in slab-sided green glass tanks. Beyond was a laboratory bright with comparison microscopes and specimen slides racked beneath low-hung lamps. The sound of water gurgling in one of the sinks was drowned by the buffeting of the wind when Ward pulled open a door and strode out into what looked something like a marine patio.

A six-foot boardwalk surrounded the area, which was completely enclosed by the research buildings. In the center, water heaved and slapped a dozen feet below the boardwalk. And here, clustered around a tunnel that led to the open sea, a collection of odd craft rocked at their moorings: a pint-size dredger, inspection barges with transparent perspex bottoms, a power boat fitted with trawls, several cigar-shaped vessels with blisters resembling airplane cockpit covers. There was even a small bathysphere lashed to the wooden piers.

"I'm going on out and back up the cruiser," Ward said. "I

want to load one of the MSM-6's. You better get her out and ready the tackle, okay?"

Diego was already halfway down a ladder. "Which one, Mr. Ward?" he asked.

"The best," Ward replied. "Mr. Lola's a friend. More than that: he sounded damn well like a friend in need!"

17

The sun had sunk beneath the bleached rim of rock formed by the higher ridges of the Serra do Roncador a quarter of an hour before the giant Chinook helicopter whirred in from the east. It had been touch and go whether or not they could swing a Navy troop carrier to assist the first phase of Dean's crazy plan, but Quinnel had been pulling strings in certain military quarters all afternoon, Mackenzie had been on a hot wire to Washington since early morning, and eventually they had made it. Even so, the nearest chopper with a suitably modified bomb bay had been aboard a ship somewhere off Central America, and they had spent an anxious hour and a half wondering if the pilot was going to reach them in time—during the time, that is, that certain Brazilian blind eyes were in strategic positions, and certain flight-control officers briefed. Eventually, however, the Chinook had zigzagged in beneath the radar screen and lowered itself to a perimeter track in the farthest corner of the Brasilia field, and the operation was at last under way.

Now H-hour was at hand. Quinnel was standing by with Mendoza in the Rio safe house; Mackenzie was still at his desk in New York; Hammer, Novotny, and the thirty-odd mercenaries they had been able to collect in the Caribbean had set off for San Felipe some time ago in a hired truck. Dean and Coralie Willys, in skintight black rubber scuba suits, sat just behind the double doors of the chopper's bomb bay, staring through the ports at the fading gleam of the San

Felipe reservoir a thousand feet below and some miles to the west.

In front of them, the MSM-6 midget submarine lay sleekly in specially rigged davits. The cigar-shaped craft, with its two perspex blisters, looked as frail and crushable as the fabric of the aircraft itself in the faint light escaping from the instrument panel through the half-open door of the cockpit. Soon the second pilot emerged from the greenhouse and shut the door. Although he was there "unofficially," wearing a turtleneck sweater and jeans, the crew cut and the Bostonian accent spelled Navy as clearly as if he had been wearing a badge. He sat down beside Dean and began to speak, raising his voice to make himself heard over the jets.

"Just to check out the details with you people," he said. "I'd like to repeat, one, that you take your places and we screw you down before we lose height at twenty-seventeen." He glanced at the luminous dial of an outsize chronometer strapped to his wrist. "That's in exactly seven-minutes-twelve. You've already been briefed and done a dry run on the quick release mechanism opening the hatches from inside. Two, we shall set her down to within twenty feet of the surface and lower away. You'll have to be prepared for a certain amount of bumping if there's anything of a breeze down there, anything enough to raise waves on that water. Three, in her present trim, it would be unwise to go lower than forty fathoms. Just how deep down is this underwater pen, d'you know?"

Dean shook his head. "Search me. Deep enough, clearly, for the fortress to escape detection from the air."

The navy man caressed his immaculately barbered chin. "H'mm. If the water's clean, even with almost vertical sides and first-class camouflage, I'd say that you'd still need a good twenty to thirty fathoms to the *top* of the pen. To make quite sure, I mean."

"I know. And these are the kind of guys who *would* make quite sure. I guess we just have to hope that the entry to this pen is on the topmost floor!" He turned to the girl. "You don't have any information on that, do you?"

"No," she said. "Planning and construction of the control complex—that was what they were working on the first time I was there. I didn't hear anything about a pen. But the fortress itself is sandwiched between the side of the valley and a rock outlier: maybe they used that to support the pen?"

"Let's hope so," Dean said somberly.

"Right." The navy man was eager to complete his rundown. "Now. Radar. RDF, sonar, and all that. The equipment you'll find is the usual rig; directional gear handled by the back-marker. There's not much room in there, as you see, but there's a miniature aqualung each, in case you do have to bail out. Remember, though: you only have thirty minutes' oxygen in them. Any questions?"

Dean shook his head.

"Okay. Here's one from us, in that case. Number One wants to know: do they have any AI at all? Can they spot any kind of unscheduled UFO . . . and if they did, would they open up? It's a question of being, you know, prepared to take evasive action," the second pilot said apologetically.

"We don't *know*," Dean said. "The whole damned plan, of course, is predicated on the assumption that they don't. Since they took all this trouble to build a secret place, to make one hundred percent certain that nobody could overlook them, we're backing a hunch that they'll feel secure enough not to have gone that one step further. No scheduled air corridors cross the region, and we can see no reason for them to have guarded against air or water invasion—in the first place, there's nothing for a plane to see; in the second, there couldn't be any other craft on the goddamn lake because it's just been made and their own two places—the pen and the second estancia—are the only docks on it. Just the same, these are thorough bastards: there's always a chance, and if they have the equipment, they'll find us on it."

"Better keep our fingers crossed for each other, in that case." The Bostonian smiled. "Right. In you go, now."

Coralie smoothed her tight cap of pale hair and dragged on the rubber helmet. Highlights slid along the surface of the polished latex suit, sculpturing the soft outlines of her body as she reached up to set the oval mask in place. A moment later she was lowering herself into the tiny rear compartment of the submarine.

Dean climbed into the forward cockpit, turned to give her thumbs-up, and allowed the perspex nacelle to drop over his head and shoulders. The navy man screwed down both the transparent hatches, and soon afterward they felt the chopper sinking toward the lake, invisible now in the darkness below.

The MSM-6 with its twin blisters, despite its aerodynamic form, lurched sickeningly and swayed from side to side on its guide ropes when the bomb-bay doors of the Chinook opened and the crew winched them slowly down toward the water. Through the perspex now they could dimly make out the drowned valley curving away to the southwest—fifteen or twenty miles of smooth lead foil wrapped around the black swell of the hills. Lights pricked the darkness to the south and northeast, but they were very far off. Immediately below, there was not a sign of life. Were Fleischman, Menezes, and their power-mad colleagues even now preparing the first underwater blast-off that could plunge the world into a final holocaust?

They hit the water stern-first with a ringing slap that echoed thunderously in the tiny submarine. Half a minute later they were pitching uneasily in the choppy waves agitating the surface of the lake. The helicopter, actuating the automatic release grapples on the guides, rose into the night and clattered away toward Brasilia. Dean and the girl were left alone to face their monumental task.

The mercenary leader immediately switched on the motors and took the midget beneath the surface. Coralie Willys had a fleeting impression of waves splashing toward her up the shallow incline of the screen that was so close to her eyes ... and then they were in a blackness so intense that it almost hurt. She was aware of a complex hum from the electric propulsion system and its auxiliaries—and of a dark and heavy chill that pervaded the air in the minute cockpit and numbed her senses.

"No time to lose." Dean's amplified voice split the silence from the intercom by her ear. "The air's very limited in this buggy, and we dare not use the oxygen cylinders in case we have to get the hell out underwater. Can you actuate the equipment right away?"

"Of course," Coralie said, and she willed her hands to the chores they had learned that afternoon. There were two systems aboard: the normal echo-sound device for revealing undersea topography, other shapes traversing the ocean, and so on; and more modern sensor equipment, analogous to the techniques used by air-to-air missiles, which homed on the heat energy released by the motors of a quarry. "Will they have the same equipment on their nuclear sub, do you think?" she asked as she busied herself with dials and indicators.

"I'd guess not," Dean's voice replied. "We hope not. Even if it was fitted, they'd hardly be using it. I mean, they'd make use of the normal navigational aids, of course—but why would they watch a screen for possible ships when it's their tank and they know they're the only fish in it?"

"I expect you're right. But if they did have it . . . and used it?"

"Then we'd be finished," Dean said shortly. "Are you getting anything interesting yet?"

"It's kind of difficult at first. I mean, I'm not a trained operator, am I? And there are still so many things on the valley floor—the remains of houses, I guess, and trees and walls—that it's almost impossible to distinguish . . . Wait a minute! Here's something now! It's something big . . . very big!"

She began reading off figures, and Dean concentrated on his dials and controls. "It'll be the nuclear sub, won't it, if it proves to be moving?" Coralie asked.

"Sure thing. According to Mazzari, they only test at night—to avoid any possible witnesses again. What are you seeing?"

"It *is* moving. The blip's increasing in size faster than others representing static obstructions we're passing over! . . . My God, it must be *enormous!*"

Dean switched on his monitors. "Yeah, you're right," he said. "Generously built! Seems to be on a cross-course some way above us."

"How deep are we?" the girl asked.

"About ten fathoms. From the disturbance, I'd judge that their sub's actually on the surface, or at most only half-submerged. We'll go on up and see how near we can get."

Now gaining, now falling behind, the midget submarine stalked the nuclear vessel in the black waters of the lake. The skipper of the larger craft was adopting an erratic course, zig-zagging from side to side of the valley, accelerating and slowing every few minutes. "He's testing the surface maneuverability," Dean said. "Must be. At least that should mean they're not ready to blast off. I wish to hell we could surface too: it'd be a damned sight easier to keep track of him. But we dare not: there might be a phosphorescent wake, a too-smart lookout, anything. We'll just have to hope he goes in soon."

Once, concentrating too closely on the livid radiance of the screens, they almost rammed the tiny craft straight into a massive wall of rock that rose sheer from the valley floor. Another time, the nuclear submarine took them by surprise, making a tight U-turn and passing directly overhead in the opposite direction. Staring up through the perspex domes at the faint hint of light drifting down from the surface, they watched the great hull—only inches above their eyes, it seemed—draw smoothly past. It was shark-shaped, sinister, and efficient, blotting out the light.

Shortly afterward, there was a commotion in the water around them and the midget rocked violently. They realized that the big submarine was submerging.

"Jesus!" Dean exclaimed sometime later—it had taken them a few minutes to locate the craft on their screens again. "It must have crash-dived around fifty fathoms! And now it's scooting along the floor of the old valley like a bat out of hell!"

They followed the nuclear craft right up to the shallows at the far end of the lake, and then back to the dam, where they froze near the rock face to minimize the risk of detection as the bigger vessel turned. "And off she goes again!" Dean exclaimed in exasperation. "But the power of that thing! Do you realize the *speed* they're getting out of her on those straight runs? Shit, on that last one, she was hitting—"

"Honey!" Coralie's voice was urgent over the intercom. "Quit talking for a moment, would you? She's altered course through ninety degrees; she's turned away to port, toward the side of the lake. I think she may be going in."

"Right. We'll do our best to catch up and tail her. In the final stages, I shall have to rely on direct vision: the only thing we can do is follow her into this pen and hope to hell nobody spots us before they exhaust the water!"

It was a strange journey, the last part of that underwater voyage. Deeper and deeper they plunged in pursuit of the big sub. Black water streamed past the two inclined screens, the fragile craft vibrating with the thrust of its screws as the man and the girl bent over their cathode tubes to concentrate on the luminous blob that represented their quarry. "Forty-three fathoms," Coralie warned anxiously. "The man said—"

"*I can see her!*" Dean interrupted. "Look! Full ahead!"

In front of them and a little below, the faintest hint of luminescence marbled the black. The radiance became discernible, stained the dark depths, wavered, spread, and finally revealed the tapering nose of their own craft, on which it then cast a direct highlight. And in front of them, silhouetted against the underwater beam, the huge bulk of the nuclear submarine hung like a resting fish.

"Strap on your lung and harness"—Dean's voice was no more than a whisper—"and be ready to bail out at any time. No more talking now."

As he himself shrugged into the shoulder webbing and snapped the clasps about his hips, a series of rectangular planes assembled themselves in the faint illumination into the outline of some man-made structure. Monolithic and immense, it jutted from the drowned rock face like a legendary castle keep seen through a dream, its functional lines distorted and imprecise through the movement of the water. Somewhere near the top, a great opening yawned—and it was from this gap in the facade that the light came streaming.

The submarine was moving again, the huge hull sliding smoothly into the opening, the green light that washed outward contouring the sophisticated curves of its steel sides.

Dean maneuvered the midget adroitly so that—like a traffic cop trying to catch out a speeding motorist—he was positioned just behind and to one side of the nuclear vessel's rear quarter. Together, the two craft, a whale with an enemy pilot fish, sank into the gigantic subaqueous pen through the opening in the fortress wall. A moment later (Dean saw, glancing over his shoulder) colossal double doors rolled across and sealed off the entry. And then slowly, as air was pumped in at the top, the water level began to sink in the chamber.

Ten minutes later, the nuclear submarine was bobbing against a dock on the left-hand side of the pen. There was about fifteen feet of water left in the chamber, and it was still just afloat. The midget was submerged on its offside; Dean and the girl, breathless from the aqualungs on their backs, were below the surface astern of the huge craft, hoping that no guard would think of walking to the aft rail and look directly down into the water.

Later Dean raised a cautious head. Grotesquely distorted by the acoustics of the chamber, he heard the sounds of feet and of voices as the crew trooped ashore and waited their turn to pass through hydraulically controlled doors that led through an airlock to the interior of the fortress. There seemed to be no personnel on duty in the pen itself—and indeed why should there be, Dean thought, since it was itself little more than a second airlock between the subterranean complex and the lake.

When the last footstep had died away, he led the girl on a submerged exploration of the chamber. Basically, it was just an enormous box, one end of which was formed by the watertight gates. Ceiling, floor, end wall, and one side wall were unbroken by any recess or projection; the remaining side wall carried along its whole length the platform against which the sub was moored. The surface of this quay was a couple of feet above the level of the water slapping and sucking at the vessel's sides. Above it, armored-glass slits let out the green light that flooded the chamber. Coralie must have been right, Dean thought, making mental calculations: with fifteen feet of water over that area, the place had to be supported on some kind of rocky prominence projecting through the lower parts of the fortress; no stories immediately below could have been robustly enough constructed to withstand such a weight.

Before they had quit the pen through the airlock at the far end of the quay, crew members had rolled ashore a quantity of steel drums which now lay stacked near the sub's massive stern. Sheltered by these—perhaps they were some kind of ballast?—Dean reached up and gripped the edge of the platform to drag himself laboriously from the water. Flopping facedown across the wet concrete, he lay for a moment regaining his breath before he rose to his feet and held out his hands to the girl.

They unhitched their aqualungs and propped them against the drums, turning to survey the great pen now from above water level. The submarine filled exactly half the space available. Everywhere around them, above and on all sides, reminders of how recently the place had been no more than an oversize tank obtruded on eye and ear. Moisture streamed down the blank walls, dropped hollowly from the roof to the curved decks of the ship, trickled into the water, and dripped from every ledge and cranny and beam and angle to be seen. Dean had stripped off his helmet and was halfway out of his scuba suit when Coralie laid a hand on his arm. "It'll take an age to get back into these if they're still wet," she whispered. "Shouldn't we maybe keep them on—in case we have to leave this way in a hurry?"

He shook his head. "It's true, what you say. But look . . ." He pointed to her legs.

From the tight curves of her hips, down gleaming thighs and over her shapely calves, the black rubber suit was beaded and pearled with drops of water that slid further down with every muscle she moved. "For ten minutes at least," Dean said, "we'd be leaving enough wet footprints to make Man Friday look like a beginner! And since the only cards we have are speed and surprise . . . well, I guess we'd better play them as quickly as possible."

They rolled off the frogman suits and dropped them in two damply quivering heaps beside the aqualungs. Dean was wearing a lightweight two-piece combat suit with sneakers; the girl was in stretch nylon jeans and a black turtleneck sweater that revealed the greyhound lines of her supple body to perfection. "We'll leave it all here," Dean said. "It's hidden from anything but the closest inspection by these drums—and the midget's near, but out of sight around the stern of this nuclear monster."

From a waterproofed satchel attached to his aqualung, he produced Coralie's Beretta, his own Walther PPK, and several plastic-cased concussion grenades, which he stowed in the knee pockets of his battledress. Then, moving swiftly but on tiptoe, he led her toward the double doors at the far end of the quay. "It's here, most of all, that we need to keep our fingers crossed," he murmured. "If there's no way to open these except through some master switch inside, we're..."

He stopped in mid-sentence. As they passed into the embrasure housing the exit from the chamber, the first pair of doors swung open before them with a muffled hiss of compressed air. "A magic-eye beam," Coralie exclaimed. "Just like they have in the supermarkets!"

"There must be an automatic cutout overriding it once they actuate the machinery that raises the water level in the chamber," Dean commented. "Otherwise the beam would be broken as the water rose, the doors would open, and the whole place could be flooded!"

They walked into the airlock. As the padded doors closed behind them, a crimson bulb winked on and off, on and off, above a notice warning in five languages:

> **Important! Do NOT attempt to operate handle opening inner doors until red light has stopped flashing.**

When the intermittent pulse had glowed and died, Dean opened the doors and they saw a short length of empty passageway ending in a T-junction with an indicator board on the wall.

By the corner, the mercenary leader flattened himself against the wall of the corridor and listened. Barely above the threshold of hearing, machines hummed someplace. Louder, although still not very near, a confused murmur of voices surged. In the immediate neighborhood, all seemed to be silent.

He peered cautiously around the corner.

The two arms of the crossway curved symmetrically away from him—as though they were circling some central feature: a giant ventilation shaft? the reactor? On each one, a line of doors began about forty feet from the junction. The doors were featureless, flat, fitting flush with the stone-colored wall. To the left, the indicators read: "Briefing" . . . "Operations Control" . . . "Communications" . . . "Welfare" . . . "Library." Those pointing to the right were labeled: "Maintenance" . . . "Armory" . . . "Catering" . . . "Personnel" . . . "Elevators to Levels B and C, Administration, and Reactor." There was nobody in sight along either passage.

"The right looks more interesting," Dean whispered. "But that's the direction those voices are coming from. Maybe they have a commissary in Personnel—and there are about sixty crew members of that sub to think of, besides Christ knows how many soldiers in their private army! We'll play it safe and take the left, huh?"

With guns at the ready, they stole noiselessly into the interior of the fortress.

18

It wasn't just a coincidence that Sean Hammer went to the same auto-rental company in Brasilia that Dean, Mazzari, and Coralie Willys had already used. "It's kind of a crummy joint," Dean had said. "But the merchandise is okay, there's not too many guys around to ask awkward questions, and you'll run up against less formality there."

"An *artic*?" the boy behind his scarred desk repeated when Hammer and Novotny had made their request. "You want to rent an artic?"

"That's what we said."

"But . . . by Jove, one sees some odd chaps in this trade! What do you want to carry in it? I mean, what kind of freight?"

"Men," said Hammer.

The boy—his name, they discovered, was Rafael—stared at them. "Of course, old fruit, I *can* get you one. But I mean to say, that's a jolly funny cargo for haulers. How many men? I could get you an old Greyhound bus, you know. Or what about a smaller truck? A ten-tonner or even your actual two-tonner . . ."

Novotny shook his head. "It has to be an artic."

"Well, I'm blessed if I know . . ." Rafael patted the edges of a pile of application forms on the desk with his fingertips. "How many fellows are there? Why do you want to carry them in an artic? And what the devil are you going to *do*? Smuggle fifty tons of heroin in from Paraguay? Hold up a bank?"

"We're going to storm the radio station in Rio and proclaim an independent Irish republic in Copacabana," Hammer said.

"Now you're pulling my leg! I don't suppose you'd want the bloody thing any special color?" the boy asked with heavy sarcasm.

"Actually, yes," the Irishman mimicked. "As Henry Ford said: any color you like, so long as it's black."

"Or dark blue," Novotny added. "Something that would pass for black at night."

"With no lettering on the sides."

Rafael picked up the phone. "There's a chum of mine who can probably oblige. It'll be a thirty-ton Volvo, 1977 vintage."

"That's just fine."

"Dash it all, you chaps will have to cool your heels for a bit, though. Can't always cope with this kind of caper instanter, you know. It may take an hour or so."

"We'll have a beer," Hammer said.

Later, when all the papers had been signed, the money paid, and the giant diesel truck fueled, he said, "That's quare and dated, that English you use, boyo. Where d'you get the comic-opera dialog?"

"But it's absolutely the latest," Rafael protested. "Mr. Forster and Mr. Mazzari told me so. I mean to say, you jolly well have to be into the in thing, what!"

"Mr. Forster and Mr. Mazzari are too busy to go to the movies often," Hammer said gravely. "Okay, the British style *is* in, but not that stiff-upper-lip David Niven drawing-room stuff. That's but *dead*; you need a refresher course. Did you never see *Sunday, Bloody Sunday*? What you want to get into, it's what they call the kitchen-sink drama. You know— the uneducated, working-class, meritocrat loudmouth. He's the man in the hero spot now . . . old fruit."

"Whyn't you keep your flamin' lip buttoned, mate?" the

boy said. "Talk about takin' a fuckin' liberty! Straight up, you bleedin' know-alls fair turn me stomach, you do!"

The plan that Dean had worked out with Hammer, Novotny, and the Dane, Neilsen, who had collaborated in the Caribbean assault, was simple. It was also dangerous because it depended on split-second timing. The dark-colored artic, adorned with a facsimile of the Intacon monogram, was to wait a little way up the San Felipe road until a BBW convoy passed on its way from the Getuliana airstrip to the estancia. The last truck in the convoy was to be ambushed just before a sharp bend a couple of hundred yards from the intersection, and run off the road with its crew silenced. Hammer and Novotny, already dressed in a reasonable copy of the security guards' uniform, would then roar the Volvo out from its hiding place and tag along at the tail of the convoy, taking the hijacked vehicle's place. In this way, even if their truck lacked some electronic identification pulse, they hoped at least to get inside the estancia grounds, maybe as far as the tunnel mouth, before the sensors tipped off the defenders that there were strangers in town.

At first, the plan worked smoothly. The mercenaries, arriving in Brasilia in small groups by bus, car, and commercial airplane, mustered in a small wood fringing a park on the outskirts of the city. The Volvo, once they were concealed inside its huge trailer, then drove to a Brazilian military airfield some thirty miles distant on the road to Goiás, where a number of heavy crates were transferred to it by forklift truck from an unmarked transport ship parked in a distant dispersal pan. On the way to San Felipe, the mercs pried open the crates, donned the lightweight combat gear inside one of them, and then unpacked and assembled the Belgian and Israeli rifles, mortars, SMG's, and 40mm cannon that Gaston Jammot had supplied in the others. Bazookas, grenades, and a quantity of ammunition had also been crated.

It was when they reached the San Felipe intersection that things began to go wrong. The Volvo was concealed behind a cane thicket at the foot of the grade. A detail of two sharpshooters and three heavies was dispatched to a small clearing that Hammer considered ideal for the kind of ambush they planned. Hammer himself then climbed into the cab with Novotny and tested the walkie-talkie contact with his outpost. Reception was five on five.

A rattletrap Ford pickup loaded with vegetables groaned up the grade toward the village. Two large sedans and a small panel truck passed along the highway in the direction of Getuliana. But no convoy of artics appeared in the other direction.

The sun sank below the forest roof. Light beneath the trees thickened as the whine and buzz of insects invaded the silence. Night fell.

And still there was no sign of any trucks shuttling between the airstrip and the fortress.

"Shit!" Hammer muttered. "What the fuck goes on? Dean said they ran damned near continuously, especially after dark."

"You think maybe we should risk going on down this construction site and check out what happened?" Novotny asked.

Hammer bit his lip. "Damned if I know." He looked at his watch. "Give them another fifteen minutes, huh?"

"Even if we did pass a convoy going the other way . . . hell, all they'd see would be a pair of headlamps in the dark," Novotny offered a little later.

"Yeah. But we'd louse up the hijack deal: by the time we'd turned this buggy around, it'd be too late to catch up and tag along as part of that convoy. . . . Oh, shit! The hell with it. Let's go take a look, but!"

Novotny eased the big articulated truck out on to the highway, gunning the motor as they turned right for Getuliana. They passed no other vehicle in either direction. When they got there, they found the entire vast site in darkness. Novotny switched off the motor. A profound silence brimmed the wide valley, broken only by the ticking of contracted metal as the Volvo's muffler cooled. They coasted down to the dirt road that led to the airstrip, and Hammer flicked the switch that put the lights on high beam. The strip was deserted. No artics, no transport planes, no merchandise stacked.

Whatever the reason, there would clearly be no convoys heading for the estancia tonight.

"Son of a bitch!" Novotny growled. "What do we do now?"

The little Ulsterman sighed. He unwrapped a stick of gum and slid it past the mailbox mouth. "The dear knows," he said, chewing. "I guess we drive as close as we can, stash this crate someplace, make a recce in depth—and then play it by ear. Okay?"

He called up the ambush detail as Novotny swung the truck around, telling them the plan was changed and instructing them to be ready to jump aboard as the Volvo passed.

But the second plan—such as it was—had to be abandoned

before it even got off the ground. There was no question of driving close and hiding the truck, because when they were still more than a quarter of a mile away from the estancia, the dipped lights showed a double line of automobiles, parked on either side of the roadway, that stretched as far as they could see. Novotny pulled up sharply, drawing a volley of curses from the mercs in back of the truck as they were pitched against the bulkhead or shot from their temporary seats. "What the *hell* . . . ?" he breathed, cutting the motor again.

Most of the cars were old, many had rusted fenders and door sills, a lot of the coachwork was crumpled and dented. And now that the Volvo's diesel was silent, the sound of distant music was audible. From time to time, a hint of singing drifted on the breeze that was blowing down the valley.

"Jesus!" Hammer burst out. "Don't tell me the fuckers are having a *party*!"

Novotny backed up the artic and pulled in under the trees, and the two of them walked slowly up toward the estancia in the shelter of the vehicles parked on the far side from the perimeter fence. As they neared the gates, the singing grew louder and the music—mostly flutes and percussion—accelerated in tempo. A thin radiance brightened and then faded somewhere behind the big house. It did indeed sound as though some kind of barbecue was under way.

Hammer and Novotny walked around the bamboo thicket opposite the gates and climbed a little way up the hillside so that they could look down into the property over the tops of the spear-blade leaves. The wavering light, they saw at once, was produced by a procession of white-robed figures carrying flaming torches. There were about forty of them, weaving in and out of the trees at one side of the tunnel entrance. They seemed to be heading for a narrow creek—evidently a tributary of the river running down the center of the valley—around which a crowd was gathered. The roof of the big house cut off Hammer's view, but so far as he could see through his night-vision binoculars, there was an irregular outer ring of spectators, inside which three concentric circles of girls in some kind of ceremonial dress surrounded a natural rock basin in the creek.

The torchbearers were singing. The voices rose sweetly through the branches, modulating into an insistent chant in counterpoint to the drums as they approached the pool. The flames from the torches reflected dully in the massive steel shutter sealing off the tunnel, and then scattered to rain downward like falling stars as the singers jumped over the rock shelves on either side of the basin and formed up around the cascade splashing into the pool.

The singing and the sound of the drums died away. For an instant there was complete silence. Between the torches and the starless sky leaves rose and fell, rustling in a sudden flutter of hot wind. A spectator coughed nervously, and somewhere nearer to the two watching mercs a bough rubbed against another, squeaking. Very quietly at first, the drums began again—and over their insistent muttering, a man's voice rose in incantation.

"Holy God!" Hammer breathed. "You know what this is?"

Novotny shook his head, and then, remembering that Hammer could not see him, he muttered, "Search me!"

"It's one of them bastard voodoo things," Hammer said. "The Colonel told me about it. Kind of a mix-up between religion and magic and that spiritualist crap. You know: ghosts and spirit writing and such. It's called Candomblé. They have a sort of temple down there."

"Sounds spooky."

"You're damn right it's spooky. These dames get what they called possessed and chuck themselves about." Hammer snorted in derision. "Do their fuckin' nut!"

"You don't say!"

"My guess is that we're watchin' one of them ritual routines. You know, the kids get like an initiation."

"Yeah? You mean like the Elks or some kind of a sorority?"

"Kind of. All those parked autos. Old heaps, most of 'em. That's the country folk, driven in to watch their daughters received into the sect, if you ask me."

"I wouldn't let *my* daughter within a mile," Novotny said.

"Only thing is, the Colonel said the boss man down there told him they *never* held these initiation parties in that place. Know what that means?"

"Uh-uh."

"It means, boyo, that this shindig is being held for a special purpose: to attract the attention of the hillbillies and the Indians around here, and keep them occupied so they won't notice some shit that the guys we're after will be handing out."

"What kind of shit, you figure?" Novotny asked.

"You tell me," said Hammer. "But it'll be tough, you may be sure, whatever it is. Plus of course there's a special angle affecting us."

"How come?"

"A man could be forgiven, Novotny, takin' you for a fuckin' nitwit," the Ulsterman said angrily. "Use your head, man! Take a look down there."

Novotny looked. The priest pronouncing the incantation was a tall, thin black man in a multicolored robe. Two female assistants stood beside him on the bank above the pool. He was shouting now, raising his arms toward the sky. And behind his voice, softly, insistently, the syncopated cross-rhythms of the drums commanded the attention, exciting the blood, compelling the muscles to twitch. As the beat, too, grew louder, the tempo swifter, an electric tension formed in the air between the spectators and those taking part in the ritual. It was as though the drums were daring them not to dance, to fling out their arms, to wheel and stomp in the velvet, vibrating dark. Around the reflected torches in the water, the curve of novices, the innermost of the three circles, shivered like corn in a breeze. They were dressed in gaudy robes of satin and silk and taffeta, their bodies loaded with the bizarre regalia said to be special to their chosen spirits. And all at once their voices rose in a shrill chant above the thudding percussion. Breaking through the outer circles, they stamped their way to the space in front of the tunnel and began to dance.

"All those innocent country folks," Hammer said savagely. "You think we could mount an assault on that son-of-a-bitch tunnel through that?"

"You mean . . . ?"

"I mean someone's been damned smart, or the arm of bloody coincidence is a lot longer nor I thought. Can you see the boys bustin' in there with guns blazin'? Oh, sure, the crowd'd scatter. But they got sensors controlling automatic fire in there; the moment we opened up, those folks would be cut down in dozens. We dare not risk it, man."

"What are we going to do?"

"There's only one thing to do: call up the Colonel and tell him we can't go through with it as planned. No convoy, an' you can see bloody why! Kind of a country fair in front of the target. Oh, somebody's been smart, all right!"

"You figure they were wise to our whole plan?"

"Not necessarily. Might be normal precautions, just in case. Whatever the reason, we have to wait till it's over before we can act, and I got to tip him off." Hammer unclipped a device not unlike his walkie-talkie from his belt. It was in fact a kind of bleeper, a pair to one in Dean's breast pocket, more powerful than those used by hospitals and government departments, drawing attention not aurally but by a heavy and silent vibration. Hammer crouched down behind the bamboo and began to revolve a tiny dial on the face of the transmitter.

Below, the novices were back in the center of the circles now, dancing toward the priest—swirls of black and yellow, green and chestnut, violet and white, dressed in the colors of their familiars, stomping and shaking their way around the pool. Focusing Hammer's glasses, Novotny saw with astonishment that their heads were shaven, the polished skulls gleaming in the light of the flares.

The assistant priestesses swooped on flasks of palm oil and sugarcane brandy, on flat bowls of toasted manioc flour, that stood on the edge of the rock basin, and capered off among the trees, bursting through the ring of torch-bearers to scatter the flour and sprinkle the liquids. The massed voices of the novices altered in pitch and gained in intensity as they began to repeat the special incantations for each *Orixá*—each familiar spirit—seven, fourteen, or twenty-one times. Xango, Oxossi, Omulu, Oxun, Nanaburucu, Elegbara, Pomba-Gira . . . the Candomblé gods were summoned in turn to earth, each to take possession of his or her initiate. Clearly, the ceremony was about to reach some climax.

Hammer was bent over his bleeper, now listening, now talking. When he finally stood up, Novotny asked, "What did he say?"

"He said 'Shit!' " Hammer reported grimly. "And then he said to wait until this hooly is over, like I thought. To tip him off the minute we were ready to go."

"The only thing," Novotny said. "If this party has been put on specially to hide something . . . if it's to stop folks getting to whatever it is *we* have to stop . . . well, I mean, you know—if it's well organized, by the time it's over it may be too late to do whatever we have to do."

Hammer sighed. "Yeah," he said. "It may be too late."

19

The second door on the left of the curving passageway stood ajar. Through it, Dean and Coralie Willys could see a large room equipped with a blackboard and benches rather like a schoolroom. In the corner nearest the corridor a desk littered with papers stood by a green baize board to which were pinned charts, graphs, and schedules. The door of the room, which was empty, bore a small plaque carrying the engraved word "Briefing."

"This must be where the boss men pass on the orders," Dean began. He stopped. Approaching them around the curve of the passage, voices echoed.

Seizing the girl's arm, he thrust her through the half-open doorway. "Let's hope they're not on the way to get their orders now!" he whispered, thumbing back the safety catch on his gun. He pushed the door almost shut and squinted through the crack as two burly men in khaki-and-black uniform passed down the passage and continued on around the bend, conversing animatedly in a language that Coralie could not place. "Serbo-Croat," Dean murmured. "They were on their way to the canteen. It'd be great to think that the majority of the BBW personnel were there. At least it's dinnertime: we could strike it lucky."

Among the wall charts behind the desk, Coralie had found what appeared to be an exploded diagram of the fortress, showing the relationship of the three levels to the lake and to the tunnel. "This we have to memorize," Dean said. "With what you know already, it could save us a hell of a lot of time ... maybe our lives even."

She had explained to him before they left that the basic design of the place when she had last seen it could have been represented by three oval pans, one above the other. From the diagram they could now see that Dean's hunch had been right: the topmost pan had a short handle—the submarine pen—and as he had thought, this projection was supported on a column of rock standing away from the valley wall. The rest of the complex was fitted in between wall and column. "Damned near impregnable," he muttered. "Sandwiched in between two rock masses with forty fathoms of water above—nothing short of an explosion in their own reactor could touch them!"

"Maybe they never heard of the Trojan horse," Coralie said.

The remainder of the fortress, in plan anyway, was much as she had remembered it. The circular passageway to which the corridor from the pen had led was repeated on all three floors of the redoubt. Outside it, on the floor they were on, were the services they had seen labeled by the wall indicator. Living quarters, offices, laboratories, and a radio room lay outside it on the floor below. And on the lowest level were stores, more offices, and—Dean saw with a quickening pulse—a cellblock. Was there a chance that Mazzari might still be there and alive?

Within the area enclosed by the circular passage, the bottom floor housed the reactor and the next some kind of council chamber. This was two stories high and reached to the top of the complex, with a gallery accessible from the passageway they had been traversing. The gallery led to what seemed on the diagram to be some kind of control center.

"What I hadn't allowed for," Dean said, "was the size of this maintenance unit they have. Look, we'd have gone past it if we'd chosen the other branch of the corridor. It must connect with the pen—probably sliding doors we didn't notice on the far side from the quay. After all, even if they didn't *build* their sub here, the bits they shipped in by air and in those trucks had to be assembled someplace. And that would need kind of a comprehensive shop."

"Yes," the girl said. "And here's where the stuff did—and still does—come in." She pointed to the floor plan of the fortress' lowest level. A large area to one side of the reactor was marked "Truck Park," and from it an arrow indicated a break in the periphery of the diagram and a label, "Double Steel Doors." "What d'you bet they blank off the tunnel leading to the estancia?" Coralie said.

Dean nodded. "What we have to do is find out how they operate. First, though, I want to locate Mazzari, if he's still here. We could sure do with a third pair of hands. And if there's a cellblock, I guess he'd be in it."

On the far side of the fortress from the passage leading to

the pen, a bank of elevators and a stairway were indicated on the plan. "We'll go down the stairs," Dean decided. "They're probably used only in an emergency . . . and this *is* an emergency—for us!"

Cautiously they eased open the door and crept out of the briefing room. The passageway was empty. Nor did they see anybody as they sped past closed doors and gained the open space where the elevators were. Voices were approaching, nevertheless, from the direction of the commissary along the other branch of the corridor. Swiftly Dean pulled the girl after him down the concrete stairway that twisted away around the shaft housing the three cages.

The rough, curving walls glistened with moisture, though the air current surging up from the depths at the command of some extractor plant behind them was dry and acrid. Increasingly, as they stole down, the two of them were aware of the relentless cold pressure of those countless thousands of tons of water leaning, day in and day out, on the masonry of the redoubt. And as though to underline the point, the string of low-power electric lamps set in the slanting ceiling of the stairway dimmed abruptly and then slowly flared again— though not quite, the girl thought with a shiver, to their former brightness. It was probably some minor fluctuation in the output of the reactor below.

The sound of voices above swelled, the echoes expanded, then dwindled as the people talking passed the entrance to the shaft and continued on around the passageway. There was a light dew of sweat on Dean's forehead when they crept into the reflected light from the hallway on B Level. Coralie's upper lip was similarly beaded. She was very pale.

Footsteps and voices echoed here too, advancing and receding in some numbers. Elevator doors opened and closed. They heard the cages whining away upward beyond the wall of their stairway.

It was some minutes before Dean was satisfied that it would be safe to peer around the last corner and prospect the landing. He drew back suddenly. A solitary guard was waiting for an elevator to return.

Two minutes later, after the doors had hissed shut and the cage had ascended once more, he ventured to look again. The hallway was empty.

Beckoning to the girl to follow him, he raced across and plunged down the farther flight of stairs toward the lowest level. Here it was quieter, the lights were even dimmer, and there were no signs of any BBW personnel or any guards.

There was no sign, either, of Edmond Mazzari. Six featureless cells led off the cul-de-sac at one side of the circular corridor. All of them were empty.

"What now?" Coralie asked, seeing something that she took for a flicker of near-despair twist Dean's features. "Is there anywhere else we could look?"

He shook his head slowly, his blue eyes somber. "Anywhere," he said. "He could be anywhere . . . here or at the estancia . . . alive or dead . . . on this side of the lake or the other. We shall just have to proceed as though—"

"But I thought your friend—?"

"The mission," Dean said savagely. "The mission comes first. That's the way it's always been. He knows that. . . . We'll try to get back to that control center on the top story and see what we can do there."

They completed the circuit of the corridor. Through a half-open door hedged with red notices warning off unauthorized personnel and those with no protective clothing, they glimpsed behind coils of tubing a segment of the reactor's silver sphere. Farther on, an arch led to a huge open space where a dozen artics drawn up in two rows faced twenty-foot steel doors running on rails. To Dean's amazement, there seemed to be no guard, no sentry box, only a series of metal housings that flanked the doors with inset magic-eye disks— and an old-fashioned set of stop-go lights.

"The whole damned thing's electronically controlled!" he breathed. "No personnel staffing the exit! If only we could get to that control room and somehow take it over . . ."

"You mean that your man Hammer could walk straight in?"

"No," Dean said. "The defenses outside the tunnel would be a separate system. He'd still have to overcome them by force. But if, as I'd always hoped, I could open both sets of tunnel doors from inside . . ." He shook his head. "Well, that's what we came for, baby, isn't it?"

They skirted the empty trucks and made for the staircase again. And it was at that moment that the miniature transceiver in his breast pocket vibrated against Dean's chest. Seconds later they had received Hammer's fateful message.

"My God! What are we going to do?" Coralie was paler than ever.

"Wait," Dean said shortly. "The moves have got to be coordinated. Useless my opening the goddamn doors if he isn't there to come in."

"But . . . It's all very well to say: Wait. Where shall we wait . . . and what shall we do while we're waiting?"

He eyed the swell of her breasts beneath the tight sweater. A mischievous smile twisted the corners of his mouth. It was the kind of explosive and unexpected situation he delighted in; the challenge that submerged the calculating professional soldier in him and brought out that devil-may-care, bet-the-whole-wad-on-one-card quality which had ruled so much of his life—and brought him so many successes. "There are beds in those cells," he said.

She stared at him. "You can't mean . . . ? You're *crazy!* Marc, you're out of your mind! . . . We can't! Darling, we simply *can't!*"

But they did.

On the far side of the ridge, the throbbing of the drums grew louder, faster; the chanting became hoarse with expectancy. Beads, charms, shells, fetishes, sewn on or hung around the bright robes, dipped and glittered. Sweat streamed down the novices' faces as they danced. The flaming torches scythed about their heads. The hot wind leaned against the trees.

Stepping into the center of the circle, the robed priest grasped the arm of one of the girls and handed her to the taller of his two assistants, who was wearing a yellow cloak. The initiate—or Iao, in the Candomblé jargon—was about to be possessed by the god Oxossi, the god of hunting. She was wearing a green satin shift garlanded with rows of white beads, for these were the colors of her *Orixá*, and there were large white spots daubed over her bare shoulders, across her cheeks, and around the gleaming ebony ball of her skull.

The priestess rose up onto a flat rock at the side of the pool, handing the girl over and down, so that she was standing up to her knees in the water. She stood there twitching compulsively, her eyes rolled up so that only the whites were showing, as the woman produced a knife and severed the shoulder straps of the dress. The green garment fell away, to float like a water lily around the girl's bare legs, and her naked breasts swung free to quiver in the torchlight.

"Shit!" Novotny breathed in the hillside clearing above the bamboos. He reached over and took the glasses from Hammer.

Below, the sound of the drums had died away to a whisper. The chanting was no more than a moan on the wind. The priestess bent down and scooped water over the Iao's trembling body. A concerted intake of breath from the onlookers that was audible on the far side of the roadway. The circle of votaries crowded in closer, bending like reeds while the drumbeats quickened and the singing swelled and then broke into a shout of triumph. The priestess had made an incision in the novice's shaven skull with the point of her knife.

She spun around, grasping a live black rooster handed to her by the priest, held it for a moment over the girl's head, and then raised the knife. With a deft movement of her wrist, she drew the blade across its throat and allowed the blood from the slaughtered bird to mingle with the novice's own and form a fine tracery of scarlet over her head and shoulders. There was a roar of acclaim from the crowd.

Tossing the carcass aside, the priestess raised the girl up onto the rock beside her. Together they shouted some ritual phrase that was answered by the torchbearers. A sudden flurry of drums, and the girl was stepping down to make way for the next Iao.

"Holy God," Hammer muttered, "if we have to wait while herself goes through the bloody lot, we'll be here till Christmas! Here, give me those glasses. . . . Bejasus, I wouldn't mind getting me hands on them lady preachers, the both of them. Would you look at the tits of the one in red!"

The warm, dry wind had died down. Now it redoubled its force, carrying with it a hint of thunder far away in the interior.

"The trouble," said Hammer, "is that after the little dears have all been done in the pool, the whole damned lot of 'em get tanked up an' go through this possession routine. At least that's what the Colonel told me."

"Oh, fuck! How long will that take?"

"Christ knows," Hammer said. "Maybe till the end of the world."

Lying on the narrow prison bed, Dean was lost in a world of sensation. Coralie's warm thigh lay across his hip. Her hand was between his legs, massaging, guiding. "You *know* we're crazy, doing this," she said. "But do you have to be offbeat the whole way through? It's too cute, the way you keep wearing that garment, but . . ."

He looked down at the long, pale, naked length of her beneath him and grinned. "Hammer's signal," he explained. "The bleeper's got to stay next to my flesh: it doesn't bleep, it vibrates, remember?"

"It's not the only thing," Coralie said. "And next to *my* flesh—"

Dean choked off the words in her mouth, kissing her fiercely, his tongue forcing itself between her wet lips. His hand swept across the shallow curve of her belly, fingers tangling in the springy curls of hair, and there too she opened and melted at his touch.

Bending low to kiss the hard, dark nipples, he felt himself taut as a drawn bowstring against her. She moved slowly, gently, easing her hips farther beneath him. The pulse in her throat was beating wildly. And then suddenly he was inside, the clasp of her scalding flesh tight as a glove, his two hands cupping the cool weight of her buttocks. "Now," Coralie whispered. "Yes, now!"

But as he arched back his loins, she said, "No, no. Don't move. I want to hold you close. I want it to be like this: all the violence in the mind."

Breathing heavily mouth to mouth, their arms wrapped tightly around each other, they lay sweating in the warm, dry air of the cell. Her belly was sliding beneath him. With almost imperceptible undulations of pelvis and hip, the delicate friction of their two skins generated a thin, high, thrilling tension as charged as the unseen humming of the reactor in the dark heart of the redoubt. For Dean, time and place blurred in this ecstasy of controlled excitement. Patrick was playing in the corridor. The blond girl took off her . . . Samantha's mouth opened and . . . The sand was hot under their feet below the boardwalk in Atlantic . . . The one with the ripe thighs leaned over Patrick's baby carriage . . . And Coralie's breath, then her whole body, began to shudder. The coiled ridges of muscle that were gripping him began a series of repeated, accelerating contractions, and Dean came.

The orgasm seemed to him to go on for a long time, exploding into her with all the force they had been denying themselves; with a savagery that he, like so many men of action, found ultimately calming and relaxing on the eve of battle. From this content welled the strength that gave them the impetus to advance.

He lay with his head between her breasts, listening to the fast flutter of her heart. It was some time before he realized that the pulsations he could feel came not from her but from the tiny plastic-sheathed receiver in the pocket of his damp combat suit.

Above the steep, wooded sides of the valley, distant lightning flickered now and the roll of thunder competed with the hammering of the drums. The two priestesses had gone into trance. They stood, the yellow and the red, each straight as a spear, the fingertips of their crossed hands touching their shoulders. In front of them the pool was bright with floating robes. On either side the initiates weaved in ever more complex patterns beneath the impassive figure of the priest on his rock. Swirled around on a frenzied tide of percussion, they lurched and swayed faster and faster as the rhythm increased in volume. Their eyes were closed. Their mouths hung open. Their heads threshed from side to side like dahlias in a storm.

As the real storm approached across the angry sky, the torchbearers moved outward to allow the frantic dancers more space. Tension had communicated itself to the spectators also. A restless movement stirred their ranks; some huddled together in breathless groups, wavering between awe and dread. The moment of possession was very near.

A black girl staggered out of the line of initiates. The first to receive "the call," she was shivering uncontrollably, the dark flesh quaking, red and white beads bouncing on her bare chest. She slewed around toward the pool, and the priest raised his hand.

Appositely enough, the first *Orixá* to "descend" was to be Xango, the god of thunder and lightning, rain and the rocks. *"Xango-Agajul"* boomed the priest—and the massed voices of the torchbearers cried back: *"Vem trabalhar! Vem trabalhar!"* as the drumbeats rose to a shattering climax.

As though she herself was an instrument actuated by the complexities of percussion, the girl's glistening body shook more furiously still. And then, as the spirit entity supposedly summoned by the mediums took possession of her, she fell prostrate to the ground, crying in a great voice the name of her *Orixá*: "Xangooooooo!"

There was a roar of applause from torchbearers and onlookers. The singing and the drums faded down, only to swell again a few minutes later when another Iao broke ranks and reeled toward the priest. And soon, in a second triumphant crescendo of sound, she too was dropping like a puppet whose strings have been cut, screaming: "Elegbaraaaaaaa!"

With blood and sweat streaking their trembling torsos, the remaining novices danced on beneath the lividly flashing sky.

"Fucking hysterics!" Sean Hammer growled on the hillside above the thicket. "All this possession mularkey. Hypnotize their bloody selves, if you ask me!" His men had been summoned from the Volvo with their arms and equipment. They were staked out behind the thicket and among clumps of bushes studding the slope.

"Even if it was true, it wouldn't do them no good here," Novotny said. "This whole Candomblé's fake from top to bottom—the phony ritual too."

Hammer stared at him. "How the fuck do you know?"

"Colonel talked to me too; you ain't the only one, Mick!" Novotny grinned.

"All right . . . polack! Lay it on me," Hammer said. "Pour it on."

"Well, it seems like this whole scene down there—an *Orûnkó* I think they call it—the whole thing is screwball, not the real McCoy at all, just a setup to fool the natives. You know?"

"Jesus, you mean every one of them folks is in on it? They're all part of the act?"

"I guess not. From what the Colonel said, the kids being initiated and the fond mums and dads are on the level. They really believe they're 'At Home' to the spirits! Auto-suggestion, I think they call it."

"That's just what I said."

"Yeah. But the guys and gals with the torches, and the reverend and his dames, they're all part of the team from in there. What you see is any old crap, so long as it looks impressive. They added bits from the other cults and left out stuff that oughta be in. Also, if it was a regular *Orûnkó*, those kids would have been in special quarters here for weeks, bein' schooled for the great day and stuff."

"Well, whaddya know! Meet Wladyslaw Doe: the I-told-ya soldier and culture vulture!" Hammer kidded. He might have done better the second time around, but nature intervened. A white-hot flash that seared the eyeballs flamed out of the sky and went to earth somewhere behind the estancia. At the same time, a colossal thunderclap cracked out immediately overhead. Before the reverberating echoes of that terrifying noise had rumbled away among the surrounding hills, rain fell from the dark with tropical force.

"Boy!" said Novotny. "Like you say, they sure lay on a good show!"

The rain pelted down in solid sheets, bouncing knee-high off the ground, soaking through garments in seconds, transforming every slope into rivers of mud. The spectators screamed, then scattered and broke, making a run for their automobiles. The Iaos, heedless of the furiously shouting priest and his assistants, turned and raced for the wooden Candomblé shack behind the house, bedraggled mannequin dolls, pathetically streaked with their own blood and paint that had run. Before the downpour extinguished the torches, the space in front of the tunnel was deserted; the valley was a chaos of gunned motors, grinding gears, and headlamps probing the deluge while the thunder and lightning crashed and flared overhead.

Hammer was dancing up and down like a maniac. His hair was plastered to his skull. His sodden battle fatigues clung to his body. "Get on down there and tell those schmucks to move their asses!" he shouted over the fury of the storm. "I'm goin' on and call up the Colonel, tell him we aim to move in there in ten minutes!"

20

"Now we've *got* to get to that control room: Sean will be starting his assault before we reach the top floor," Dean said as they crept from the empty cell. They skirted the truck park and gained the emergency stairs. By the time they had reached A Level, Coralie was out of breath: Dean had sprinted up like an Olympic runner. But they were in luck. They had seen nobody. "Which way?" Dean asked.

She was taking deep breaths to steady her racing pulse. "Straight on . . . if you can call this passage straight. It's the only door on the inside wall. I saw it when we left the briefing room."

Bullets splatted against the concave surface of the outer wall. Simultaneously, from behind them the sharp crack of an automatic rang out three times, reverberating in the narrow corridor.

"Run!" Dean yelled, grabbing her hand, pelting farther, farther around the curve of the convex inner wall. The uniformed officer he had seen out of the corner of his eye as he

glanced over his shoulder fired again and again, trying to wing them with ricochets off the outer wall now that they were invisible to him.

As they ran, voices shouted. Footsteps started in pursuit. A door in the outer wall opened and two women in SISTERS uniform emerged just in front of them, one carrying a black frogman suit over her arm. "Sorry, sister," Dean panted, snatching the heavy rubber garment from her hands and twisting it around her head. He shoved her, reeling, to the far side of the passage. The second woman swore and began to tug something from the pocket of her jacket. Without breaking her stride, Coralie Willys slashed across a backhanded blow and caught her, karate-style, on the side of the neck. She dropped to the floor, rolled against the calves of the woman struggling to free herself from the folds of the diving suit, and brought her down too.

Dean and the girl sprinted on. The shooting from behind had stopped once the marksman had come in sight of the two women. He was shouting at them to get the hell out of the way. But now there were heavy footsteps pounding *toward* the intruders from around the curved passageway ahead. A deeper report thundered in the confined space, and a slug chiseled a groove in the wall beside Coralie's head.

"I was afraid of that," Dean gasped, dragging her to a halt. "Sent a buddy around the other way to cut us off." He dropped to one knee. Along the surface of the outer wall, where it curved out of sight ahead of them, a grotesquely distorted shadow was approaching. Raising the barrel of the PPK, he aimed at this and fired.

A puff of plaster dust marked the channel gouged by the bullet. Before the screech of the richochet had died away, both footsteps and shadow had stopped dead. Suddenly there was silence.

"Let's go," Dean whispered, his lips close to the girl's ear, "before they think of sidling up to us along the inner wall. If the control-room door's near enough, we'll reach it before we come in sight of the man ahead."

"Suppose it's locked?" Coralie murmured as they began to move.

He flashed her a reassuring grin, the reckless, daredevil expression in his eyes lending his features a look that was almost boyish. "Suppose it isn't?"

Now they could hear more footsteps in the distance, and then a susurrus of low voices asking questions somewhere in the circle of corridor behind them. Backs to the inner wall, they edged toward the elusive door. Slowly, inexorably, the corridor uncoiled before their advance; as relentlessly, the inner wall remained blank. Suddenly Dean leaped to the far side of the passage and ripped off a shot, left, right, in each direction. There was a distant scrambling of feet as he jumped back again, a single shot from the left, from the heavier-caliber gun with the deeper tone, and then a shout of protest and of warning from the other side as the slug screamed to the right.

"They're too close to shoot at us now," Dean said. "Every time they fire, they risk the round bouncing on and hitting their own people around the bend. . . . The door's very close: I could see it from over there." He jerked his head and they began to move once more.

Sure enough, the heavy, flush-fitting steel door, looking so much like the entrance to a warship cabin, was soon sliding around the curve toward them. Once it was fully in view, Dean sprang ahead and seized the handle. It turned easily and the door swung inward. With a sigh of relief he shoved her through, closed the door, and dropped two steel struts in place across it. The pursuers' bullets thwacking against the other side were scarcely audible.

Dean's eyebrows rose. "Close fit!" He smiled. "And close shave!"

The door opened directly onto a narrow gallery that ran all the way around the walls of a lofty circular room whose floor, just as Coralie had said, was on the level below. Halfway around, to their left, a staircase spiraled down to link the two. Opposite this, to their right, a glassed-in projection resembling the control room of a television or recording studio was cantilevered out from the gallery. Through the huge panes they could see colored lights winking, the glint of stainless-steel levers, and banks of terminals spined with electrical leads. On the floor below, desks with telephones stood around the wall, but most of the enormous room was occupied by a circular table so vast that the dozen or so people grouped along one sector of it were dwarfed by its size.

A woman in the now-familiar green uniform stood talking to the thin man with the skull-like face whom Dean remembered as Fleischman. On either side of him sat Menezes and the shortsighted scientist, Glaser. The rest of them were all men in late middle age, with identical sleek, groomed, manicured exteriors. "The central council of this BBW deal," Dean breathed. "Multinational kings, most of them. You'll know some of the faces. Oil, newspapers, electronics, automobiles, you name it."

". . . took the prisoners through and left them on the quay as you ordered," the woman in green was saying. Dean caught his breath. Prisoners? In the plural? Could one of them . . . could one of them possibly be Mazzari?

"The girl was a little difficult and I had to have her subdued. But the man was still . . . quiet. Mr. McCaffery's shoes do their job well."

A bony man lost in a voluminous pale suit smiled thinly. "After that," the woman continued, "I locked the double doors and put the controls on Security. The chamber can be flooded anytime you want."

"Excellent," said Fleischman. "Well, gentlemen, I think we can claim at last that Phase One can be—shall we say?—launched." A ripple of amusement ran through the men seated at the table. The air of expectancy hanging over the group was an almost tangible thing. "There have been delays," Fleischman said. "There have been annoyances and intrusions. They have been attended to. At any time in the next two or three hours, while Hernando's . . . festivities . . . continue, the master can take out the ship and start the countdown."

There was a murmur of approval. Dean had to keep telling himself that he wasn't dreaming. These smooth tycoons were about to embark on an insane adventure that could start a third, and final, world war and would in any case result in the deaths of several million innocent people. Yet they were as calm as directors at a board meeting. "Phase One," said Glaser, the thickset man with thick lenses, "will be both a lesson and a warning. That those who know how to establish order also know their business. And that an unpleasant fate awaits the rabble who refuse to come to heel."

The oldest man there, a frail white-haired figure with a high color, rose to his feet. He spoke with a strong German accent. "Such a plan to rationalize the chaos in the world was formulated fifty years ago!" he cried. "The Führer was a visionary as well as a leader. He was betrayed by fools and opportunists and cowards before his New Order was consolidated, before he was even allowed to win the war. In the name of those who are still proud to carry his standard, I felicitate you, Herr Fleischman and your colleagues, for the wisdom and foresight and enthusiasm your generation has shown, projecting these bright ideals into a new era."

Before Fleischman could reply, a door beneath the control

room banged open and Hernando staggered into the room. He was drenched from head to foot. His hair was plastered to his head. His multicolored robe was ripped and stained with mud, and there was a gash bleeding above his left eye.

Fleischman half-rose to his feet. "What the devil . . . ?"

"An attack," Hernando choked. "Armed men are assaulting the estancia and the tunnel blockhouse. We couldn't—"

"But the *Orûnkó*, man," Menezes shouted over the sudden hubbub. "Surely nobody would attack through all that . . . That was the whole idea of staging it tonight . . . a diversion in case—"

"A freak storm . . . the forecasters didn't . . . I never saw such rain." Hernando was almost incoherent. "I couldn't stop them . . . they just ran."

"But, for Christ's sake," Fleischman raged, "couldn't you—?"

"I did what I could. It was impossible. Even our own people . . . fools and traitors . . . they ran for the *tenda*. The place was drowned and deserted within minutes. And then this volley . . ." He stopped speaking, staring up at the gallery openmouthed.

Every member of the group reacted differently to the sight of Dean and the girl . . . and to the sound of muffled hammering that had broken out on the barred steel door behind them.

Fleischman gaped in astonishment without moving. Two bulky, muscular men pushed their chairs back from the table and sat tensely watchful. The woman's hard face creased into an expression of derision. Glaser cowered and seemed to shrink into his chair. And the man named McCaffery sprang backward, tipping over his seat as a gun blossomed in his right hand, spitting fire. Quick as he was, though, Fleischman was even more rapid. After that first tenth of a second when he was bemused with surprise, only his hand moved, diving into the space between his lapels while the rest of him remained as motionless as a statue. But the gun with which it reappeared had fired twice while McCaffery was still in midair.

Dean had already pulled the girl down below the solid steel balustrade of the gallery. Bent double, they were moving toward the control room as fast as they could. The first of Fleischman's shots had passed so close to Dean's head that he felt the scorching breath of its passage on his neck.

"McCaffery! Quick!" Fleischman shouted from below. "You too, Helmore! The spiral staircase. Enfilade them before they reach the control room! Wunsche, run underneath. You know what to do: Plan D . . ."

Feet pounded amid the uproar of voices, and then Fleischman called again: "For heaven's sake, Menezes, get a grip on yourself, man—or get under the table if you're so scared." The tone was full of contempt. "You up there—Moraes—stay where you are. We are relying on you."

Dean risked a quick glance over the balustrade. Fleischman's shot was only inches wide. In the brief moment that his head was above the rail, Dean saw McCaffery and one of the bulky men racing up the stairway on the far side of the gallery. The second bulky man was disappearing beneath the control room, presumably to put the mysterious Plan D—whatever that was—into operation. But Dean was more concerned with Moraes. Who was he? And where?

As luck favors the audacious, Dean's held good that night. In the heartbeat of time that he needed, his eye caught the flicker of movement behind the windows of the control room. It was a difficult shot to fire, across the curve of the gallery and through a sheet of glass angled away from him and obscured by reflections, but it had to be done, it had to be right . . . and it had to be quick. The Walther roared in the confined space between wall and balustrade.

The man Moraes, standing on a table with a Bergmann MP18 submachine gun ready to rake them from above, leaned forward out of the shining reflections and touched the glass. At the same time, the entire pane seemed to leap outward, hang for an instant in space, and then plunge to the floor below in gigantic shards. After it, lazily somersaulting, arched the body of the man with the gun. In the appalling clangor made by the plate glass shivering on the lower level, Dean and the girl gained the door of the control room and slipped inside. "Check out what happens down below," Dean panted. "Got to find out . . . try to cut off all troops and submarine crew in that canteen somehow. Must be something like a watertight-bulkhead system . . ."

While he scanned the banks of dials and screens, Coralie peered over the jagged remains of the big window into the conference room below. Glaser appeared to have been struck by a fragment of flying glass. He was sitting on the floor, staring at the blood that streamed from a gash in the sleeve of his jacket. The rest of them had retreated beneath the gallery—though they could not have left the room, for the only lower-level exit door was in full view on the far side. Of McCaffery and Helmore there was no sign. They must have gained the top of the spiral stairs and were now probably worming their way toward the control room, one on either side of the gallery.

Dean was intent on a great slanting console at the back of the room. It was covered with small levers that moved in labeled slots, flanked by a panel full of knobs and switches. Behind it were three illuminated screens. "Hey, what about this!" he exclaimed. "These screens are schematic diagrams of the three different levels here. Like the indicators in a trainmaster's office at a railroad depot. And the place damned well *is* divided into watertight compartments; there *are* bulkheads partitioning it in case of flooding. So here's our chance of immobilizing half the opposition—if we can block them off on the wrong side of the watertight doors."

He spun a small wheel on the panel until an arrow on its perimeter pointed to the words "Maximum power." Then, staring fixedly at the screens, he began repositioning the levers set in the console. As each one moved, a bar of red light appeared on the screen, blocking off some section of the diagram above.

"Now . . . A7 and A9," he muttered, his eyes roving the screens until they located the reference. "That will be the two top-floor entrances to the commissary. There—that should seal off quite a party among the food and drink! B12 and 14. That barricades the living quarters below. And this—B3, isn't it? Yeah, I thought it was—this will stop anyone getting at the armory or the maintenance stores."

Glass splintered to his left. A needle spun emptily around a black dial pierced by a small hole as the pieces tinkled to the floor. Coralie was firing her Beretta at a section of balustrade about a third of the way around the gallery. "McCaffery," she said. "They're not risking a straight attack from either side to enfilade us. He and his mate will just keep on popping up here and there from across the well, because they know one of us must concentrate on the controls and the other can't watch the whole . . . *Look out!*"

Dean flung himself to the floor as she loosed off two more shots, this time at the other side of the gallery. But the gunman—Helmore this time—had dropped behind the shelter of the steel balustrade. A torn fragment of paper fluttered down from a clipboard hooked to the wall where Dean had been standing. "Thanks," he said soberly. "That was just in time." He pushed himself to his feet. This time the two shots sounded as one, and both came from the same section of gallery. One of the screens starred, though the diagram behind it remained illuminated. "All right," Dean said. "Before they realize they can fuck up what we're trying to do . . ." He drew up the top of his combat suit. Around his waist was a lightweight, pocketed band, something like a cartridge belt. From one of its compartments he withdrew a small, square object with a sliding switch on one side. "Draw their fire," he said. "I'll kid them I'm making it at the console again. If I know the mentality of these boys, this'll be the time they'll shoot for the second time from exactly the same place."

Coralie deliberately turned away from the section of gallery where the last two shots had been fired and stared to her right. Dean had his back to the window. He was bending over the console—but one hand shielded a black-dialed pressure gauge in such a way that it acted as a mirror. A few seconds later he saw the reflected heads of the two killers rise cautiously above the balustrade exactly where he said they would. He whirled around. Instantly the heads dropped from sight. But it wasn't a gunshot target that he was looking for; he had needed to know the precise section of gallery they were in. He sprang to the glassless control-room window. His right arm straightened like a baseball pitcher's.

The small, square object sailed across the well and fell down between the balustrade and the wall. There was a subdued, flat detonation, a livid flash, and an upsurge of smoke. Something rose above the rail for an instant, threshing, and then flopped down out of sight, leaving a huge splash of blood on the wall. There were no more shots from the far side of the gallery.

"Small grenades are very useful in a confined space," Dean said conversationally. "Even if they are only made with plastic covers. Now, let's see: the watertight bulkheads are closed, all that can be of any use to us, anyway. That leaves us free in the central area with a woman and ten men below, plus any guards who happened to be on our side of the doors when I closed them."

"And the reactor? Those things give me the creeps."

He gestured toward the indicator boards. On that detailing the lowest floor, the central rondel was bracketed at all its entrances by illuminated red lines. "It's the only part of the center core that can be shut off," Dean said. "Now we have to move to this other panel and see if we can't open a few things. The shutters at each end of the tunnel, for instance."

Down below, the door to the conference room was flung violently open. The crash of the steel panels against the wall was drowned in the clamor of submachine guns held by two uniformed guards poised in the entrance. Once more Dean and the girl dropped to the floor—registering from the corners of their eyes a blur of movement from under the gallery toward the soldiers and their covering fire.

Dean crawled a few yards along the gallery as the staccato hail of slugs ripped into the walls and ceiling above them. He bobbed up, gun in hand, and blasted off a single shot. The clatter of the SMG's ceased. Something fell metallically to the floor. A moment later the door slammed again.

Dean rose to his feet. "Got one of them," he said, blowing a curl of smoke from the barrel of the automatic. "It was just a diversion—to make us keep our heads down while they got the big shots away. In any case, it's easier for us without them down there." He turned his back on the chamber below and began to study the mass of complex equipment stacked around the room. "Look at this," he said, opening what looked like an outsize Victrola cabinet. "There's a groundglass screen in the lid—complete with schematic diagram and pilot lights in a pattern I don't recognize—and there are knobs and levers on top of the chassis in the box itself. But the only identification is this plaque marked 'Section E.' Now, if E could stand for 'estancia...'"

He never knew what extra sense made him turn his head at that moment. A faint current of air, maybe; something that moved, reflecting on a bright surface in the tail of his eye; a sound too small to be registered by the conscious mind? Perhaps it was just that his luck was still running.

Whatever it was, he did turn—and saw the blackjack whistling down on its way to the back of his skull.

Sean Hammer's men were on the move before the last decrepit pickup truck had backed and filled, swinging around to lurch home to San Felipe through the downpour. They were inside the gates while taillights were still visible, fading mistily behind the sheets of rain.

On Dean's instructions, Hammer had divided the mercenary force into four sections. Before they left the shelter of the thicket, he whispered his orders. "Novotny, you take your squad through the wood. Neilsen, take the open space where tonight's entertainment just got washed out. The guards have been keeping a low profile—but there'll be plenty of 'em, stashed around the big house and looking after the chicks who ran for that wooden shack behind. See if you can pin them down on the far side of that hedge, Schneider, okay?" He paused, the torrential rain splashing from the hood of his combat jacket. "I'll take my guys straight down the middle, try to knock out the men in the guardhouse, and head for the bunker guarding the tunnel. We'll meet up there after the defenses have been silenced, right? Let's go before somebody thinks of swimming up to close the fuckin' gates!"

He led the way across the road, dropping flat on the far side and crawling through the gates on his belly. Orders were to stay flat until shooting began: if the sensors directing the automatic fire were simple magic-eye beams on posts, they might get away with a surprise attack. But if they were later, more sophisticated devices, homing like certain night-sighted weapons on the heat of the human body, they could expect the trip to be rugged. In any case, both Dean and Hammer had emphasized at the preliminary briefing that the chief danger came from the electronically controlled batteries.

Typically, Hammer had given himself and his squad the toughest job, the route with the least cover, the one with the most chance of coming under fire from both men and machines. Before he was halfway to the gatehouse, he and his men looked like survivors of an earthquake disaster in the rainy season. They were soaked to the skin, covered in mud, with the incessant downpour beating a tattoo on the sodden garments that clung to their limbs. But they had found out that at least the outer ring of defenses was indeed controlled by photoelectric cell beams . . . and that they had successfully passed beneath them: no alarm was sounded from the gatehouse; no guards ran out with submachine guns at the ready; most important, no batteries fired.

Hammer raised his head and stared at the dark bulk of the concrete building. He could scarcely make out its shape against the sky. Motioning his men to lie still, he waited, rain that was surprisingly cold battering his face with a thousand icy needles. He wanted to allow the other three sections time to outflank the gatehouse: what he was going to do would start the battle in earnest.

In fact Novotny's section ran up against sensors that were not simply magic-eye beams in the wood. Over the pelting of the rain, a sudden burst of automatic fire split the silence on their left flank. Hammer swore. He rose to his feet, unclipping a grenade from his belt. Light filtering through slatted shutters told him that the one wide slit window in the gatehouse wall was protected by a wire-mesh grille. He swore again, dodging around to the front of the building as a confused uproar from inside told him that the guard, clearly taken by surprise, were about to turn out. Three of his men, armed with Uzi SMG's, were on the far side of the driveway. There were three more behind the gatehouse, and one was standing by him.

The door opened. Light streamed out, transforming the rain into close-packed silver lances. The first guard appeared in the doorway, cradling an MP18 in his arms. The man beside Hammer fired a single short burst. The guard vanished into the night, almost cut in two by the hail of lead at point-blank range. Hammer stepped momentarily into the illumination and lobbed a grenade past a second man and into the interior.

After the flash of the explosion, brown smoke billowed out into the shaft of light and was then swallowed up by the dark. To mop up any survivors, Hammer leaped back to the doorway and hosed the guardroom with a short burst from his own Uzi. Alarm bells were shrilling when he rejoined his men at the side of the driveway, and rhythmic volleys of heavy machine-gun fire echoed from Novotny's sector of the wood. He could see the points of flame stabbing the dark beneath the trees.

There was gunfire too from bushes on the far side of the pool where the Candomblé ritual had taken place. Neilsen's squad, as well as Novotny's, had been located by the sensors and was being shot at by automatically directed weapons.

The primary aim of the operation was to draw the fire of these batteries, and then, once their positions were known, knock them out with cannon and with rocket grenades from the four RPG-7's brought from the truck. Two of these bazookalike weapons were being laboriously dragged through the mud by members of Novotny's squad; the remaining pair were with Schneider. If the automatic batteries could be silenced, Dean had figured, opposition from the human element of the BBW defenses might be less difficult to subdue. Hammer's mission was to eliminate both factors and then wait for Dean's key move: the opening of the tunnel gates from inside. Attempting to smash open the steel shutters with rocket grenades would be unwise, it was decided: the armorplate might be too thick . . . or, worse, it might buckle and get jammed in its own runners so that nobody could get in or out.

Livid, greenish explosions in the wood vied with the sound and fury of the storm as Hammer led his men farther into the property. Somewhere ahead, guards from the tunnel blockhouse were being deployed to meet the invaders. He could hear orders shouted over the drumming of the rain. Off to his right, two of Schneider's men were preparing to fire a bazooka. The merc carrying the weapon over his shoulder aimed through the Trilux night-sight as his companion fed the finned grenade into the open end of the tube. The flat crack and whoosh of the detonation was followed almost instantly by the heavier explosion of the grenade on the far side of the pool. And then all at once there were guns firing everywhere.

Hammer flung himself flat as bullets whistled over his head. Somewhere in the night a man screamed. Scrambling up to move forward with their cumbersome weapon, the bazooka crew were cut down where they stood. Hammer grabbed the bazooka and a satchel of grenades, then continued to crawl forward. A great deal of the shooting now came from guards on the far side of the hedge. But there were hand grenades bursting left and right—and over all stammered the incessant clamor of the automatic batteries.

A sudden flare of orange light and a shattering detonation on the edge of the wood showed that Novotny had put at least one of these out of action, but the other three sections were advancing under a murderous crossfire. Beside Hammer, the man who had shot the guard spun sideways and fell to the ground, groaning, with a smashed knee. On the other side of the driveway another merc died instantly as he rose momentarily upright to aim his Uzi.

Cursing, Hammer ordered the rest of his section into a shallow ditch running beside the road. He peered through the driving rain, waiting for each lightning flash to check the position of targets. Firing beneath the tangle of branches at the bottom of the hedge, Schneider's men were decimating guards as they ran from the big house, but Neilsen had been forced to take refuge behind a swell of ground on the nearer side of the pool. "All right," Hammer growled, "let's see if we can't knock the shit out of those fuckers." Sighting carefully through the Trilux, he aimed the bazooka at the bushes on the far side of the basin. "Pellini, feed in the last three grenades from that satchel, double quick!"

One after the other, the rockets streaked across the water. The triple explosion was eclipsed by a sudden burst of flame that stained the night with crimson, and then a thunderous blast that left their ears ringing. A single stream of tracer shot into the sky like a Fourth of July firework, and then ceased. "Got the bastard! Sent up the fuckin' magazine!" Hammer exulted. Rising, he ran toward the tunnel.

Dean's reactions were good. As the blackjack descended, he lurched to one side, an arm upraised to ward off the blow. Coralie, pivoting at the same time, gave a gasp of alarm as she registered in a single agonized glance the yawning trapdoor which had been silently opened behind a bank of teleprinters; the attacker—Wunsche, the remaining thickset man—with murderous expression and raised arm; the whistle of the descending cosh...

It was too late for Dean to escape the blow completely. The blackjack glanced off his wrist and thudded into the muscle between his collarbone and the point of his shoulder, forcing a shout of pain from his lips and paralyzing his arm.

As the Walther crashed to the floor from his numbed hand, Wunsche swung around in a smooth spiral of controlled energy, knocked the Beretta from the girl's grasp with the cosh, and before the gun had spun out of the window to drop below, swung back on the rebound and sent her sprawling to the far side of the room.

Dean reeled, his whole side seared with agony. Desperately, through half-blinded eyes, he fixed his gaze on the cosh and groped upward to fasten wiry fingers on the wrist that wielded it. Wunsche snarled, shaking Dean's whole 180 pounds from side to side as a mongoose shakes a snake. But eventually the crushing nerve grip forced his fingers apart and the weapon clattered down. Panting, he went limp and slumped suddenly to the floor, dragging the mercenary leader on top of him. Dean brought his knee up to the man's solar plexus and forced his sound forearm beneath the blue chin. But his attacker knew all the tricks in the wrestling trade, and he was formidably strong. At a distance, Dean could probably have taken him, but they were already too close for the odds to be in his favor.

The thug rolled over, holding Dean to him in a bear hug, caromed off the teleprinters, and sat up holding his adversary in a scissors grip. Three times his fist viciously jarred Dean's head, and then again they were locked together toe to toe, wrist to wrist, every muscle straining to sound out a weakness in the opponent's guard.

Abruptly Dean abandoned the trial of strength, and he in turn went limp. For a moment he was bent over the opening left by the trapdoor; then, wrapping his legs around Wunsche's hips, he dropped through, dragging the thug with him. From below came the sound of splintering wood and a strangled shout.

Coralie had already struggled to her feet. In the fight, the Walther had been kicked somewhere under a cabinet and she had been circling the two men, not knowing how to help. Her mascara had run and her nose was bleeding. Now she sprang to the edge of the trapdoor and looked down.

Amid the remains of a table, Wunsche had Dean bent backward in the excruciating grip known as the Boston Crab. In wrestling bouts this dangerous hold almost always results in a submission; if there is no referee and the pressure is continued, a spine snaps. Aghast, the girl watched the veins on the big man's temple and arms bulge as Dean's eyes turned up and his face broke out in a rash of sweat.

"*Marc!*" she screamed.

"Pen . . . pen . . ." Dean choked. "Quick! Floor!"

In anguish, her eyes swept the room below. In the exertion of the combat, most of the contents of Dean's belt had been spilled out onto the floor. Among them was a slim cylinder resembling a ball-point.

Without hesitation she dropped through the trapdoor, hit the floor with a numbing impact, staggered, recovered herself, and reached for the object. She found a button at one end. Before the thug could realize what was happening, she pointed the other end at his face and thumbed the button. There was a shrill hiss as gas escaped under pressure. Wunsche's eyes widened. His mouth split open in an expression of total astonishment. For an instant he swayed, clawing at his throat; then he pitched forward like a felled tree.

Dean collapsed with a groan of relief. "Good girl," he panted. "Thanks . . . Proprietary object . . . antiburglar . . . a harmless nerve gas that puts them out for a half-hour." He rolled over and sat up. "But we need this one out of the way longer than that." Neatly and expertly he raised the unconscious man's head by the hair and chopped the flat of his hand down to a spot just below the left ear. "That should be good for a couple of hours," he said.

Ten minutes later, after the girl had tidied herself and Dean had recovered sufficiently to climb the spiral stairway back to the control room, they were once more wondering whether the cabinet with the screen in the lid was a control for the outer gates of the tunnel. "We can only try," Dean said, grasping a lever. "What do you say we try E.1 for a start?"

"*I wouldn't, Mr Dean. I really wouldn't!*" The voice spoke behind them. Together they whirled around. Zigzag lines chased each other across one of three small monitor television screens set above the shattered window. The voice had undoubtedly come from there.

"*The levers may no longer control the equipment specified on the accompanying label, you see,*" the disembodied voice went on. "*Because although you have unfortunately incapacitated the man we left behind us, he had done his work first.*"

Above the central monitor was a fixed closed-circuit television camera. Dean looked directly into the lens. "I have no idea what you mean," he said. On the screen, white patches streamed from right to left, finally assembling with the darker zigzags into a picture of three men and a woman sitting at a console similar to the one behind him. The woman was the one who had been in the conference chamber; the men were Fleischman, Hernando, and Glaser. It was Fleischman whose level, slightly sneering tones they were hearing.

"*I will tell you what I mean,*" he drawled. "*Ah! . . . I see from your face that you can see us now. So much the better. We have been able to see you all the time. Now, when you burst in and disrupted our meeting, you may or may not have heard Senhora Mestoso here report that she had delivered two prisoners to a certain place. A man and a woman.*"

"Okay, so I heard. So what?"

"*The place she had taken them was the submarine pen.*"

"Yeah? I don't see what—"

"*Where she had left them and double-locked the exit doors. There is now no conceivable way in which they can reenter the fortress.*"

"So?"

"*The man is your confederate, Edmond Mazzari. A one-time sergeant, I believe. The woman is a foolish minor employee who for some reason attempted to help him.*"

Dean caught his breath. But all he said was, "Sorry. I still don't . . . ?"

"*We now come back to Wunsche.*" A smile spread across Fleischman's skeletal features. "*If you heard Senhora Mestoso, you will also have heard me instruct Wunsche to put into operation a certain Plan D.*"

"All right," Dean said. "I'll buy it. What *is* Plan D?"

"*An emergency device, a contingency plan evolved in case intruders should ever gain temporary possession of the control room. It is very simple. Wunsche merely disconnected some of the leads linking the console with the operating plant . . . and then replaced them in a different order.*"

"And that means?" Dean asked, dry-mouthed.

"That when you pull Lever A or twist Knob B, you may not now observe Reaction A or Reaction B on the indicator screens. Not necessarily. You may operate Lever A and set in train Reaction X."

Dean stared at the screen, his mind racing.

"You might find—to give a more concrete example—that you twisted a knob designed to open the gates of a tunnel . . . and succeeded only in flooding a submarine pen. Which would be awkward for your friend Mazzari."

There was a long silence.

Dean turned and walked to the open trapdoor, looking down into the room below. It resembled the "racks" beneath a television control room, a chaos of connectors and electronic gadgetry. All along the back wall, metal housings like giant fuse boxes hung open—and inside, festooned like fronds of weed and anemone in some fantastic undersea pool, he could see hundreds upon hundreds of strands of insulated wire in dozens of different colors.

"And not one of those leads is labeled," the voice went on. *"Nor are the wires for a given circuit necessarily the same color above and below the junction box. That would make it too easy to reposition them in the correct order."*

From where he stood, Dean could see that the man was not bluffing. Deliberately he kept his back turned to the camera and surveyed the console. According to the coded letters and numerals—repeated against sections of the diagram above—the function of the wheels and levers was to actuate fire extinguishers, switch magic-eye circuits in or out of operation, raise or lower screens, and control a number of other services as well as blocking off parts of the fortress with watertight doors. But now any of them might give the lie to its label and open sluices that could bring thousands of tons of water down on the defenseless Mazzari and his companion.

"You have been lucky so far," Fleischman said persuasively. *"You have contrived to seal off a good proportion of our forces, because the watertight bulkheads are excluded from Plan D. For reasons of security, they have to be. Obviously. But will you be so lucky next time?"*

For answer, Dean reached out and grasped a lever at random. "Marc!" the girl cried. "You can't! Surely—"

"Be quiet!" he snapped. "The mission comes first."

"To hell with the mission. You can't take the risk. You haven't the right to," she insisted.

"The lady is right. You are acting foolishly, my dear fellow." It was Hernando speaking now, his dark, lined face in

close-up on the monitor screen. *"We are in a small auxiliary control room here, next to the radio room. We cannot overrule any action you take, but each one is duplicated on our indicators. Think. You may bring death to your friend with that lever. You may cut off the oxygen supply to the whole fortress and bring death to all of us. You may dowse the room you are in with foam or overfuel the reactor . . ."*

Dean set his teeth and pulled resolutely on the lever.

"Watch the big screen in the corner," Hernando said. *"The pen is a rectangle, at the moment glowing green. The reactor is a red circle below it. If it is overfueled, the red glow becomes intermittent. When water is admitted to the pen, the rectangle goes blank and then slowly fills with blue."*

Dean's eyes were fixed on the small screen in the lid of the cabinet controlling Section E. He was staring at a red bar marking what he hoped was the closed exit to the tunnel, willing it to turn green. A sharp cry from the girl dragged his eyes back to the other indicator.

The rectangle symbolizing the submarine pen was no longer green. As he watched, horror-struck, a luminous blue line appeared at the bottom of the oblong, relentlessly thickening upward.

With a smothered exclamation he seized the lever and struggled to push it back up again. There was a chuckle from the monitor screen. *"Oh, no, Mr. Dean"*—it was the scientist, Glaser, this time—*"you cannot do that! The action is irreversible. Think it out. There must be a censor overriding all controls while the chamber is filling: we could not have water levels rising and falling like yo-yos, with expensive machinery like nuclear submarines in there, could we? I designed the system so that the 'Exhaust Pen' control remains inoperative for thirty minutes after the chamber is full. To ensure that it cannot mistakenly be emptied while the craft is maneuvering, you understand. However, in the case of your unhappy friend . . ."* He shrugged and turned away.

Fleischman: *"Why don't you give up, Dean? You played your card and you lost. You're alone in here. To get out, you will have to reopen the watertight bulkheads—and face several hundred angry men. You cannot win. Even if your hired thugs eliminate our entire exterior force, even if by some mischance you killed all of us. We have branches all over South America: the organization has power; nothing can stop its march toward victory."*

"Not even if I hit the right lever and open the tunnel?"

"Oh, come now: what are the odds?" Fleischman was

scornful. *"How many wheels and levers are there? Be realistic, man: surrender before it is too late."*

"Ah, go jump in the lake!" Dean shouted in a childish and uncharacterisitc burst of temper.

"Curiously, that is exactly what we are going to do—in a manner of speaking. You have gravely compromised our plans. For that presumption you will suffer. But for the moment we have more important things to do. We shall return to deal with you later."

There was a click and the sound went dead. The vision dwindled to a tiny white square, brightened for an instant, and then vanished.

"They're nuts," Dean said. "Crazy, the whole lot of them."

But Coralie had turned her back on him. Her face was stony.

He ran to the trapdoor, dropped to the floor below, and began frenziedly to search among the brightly colored leads. But the task was hopeless: there were hundreds of them; it would have taken an expert electronics man hours to trace them all back and check the altered connections through the fused junction boxes that married them. Dispiritedly, guilt over Mazzari's certain death weighing heavily on his shoulders, he dragged himself back to the control room. Coralie still refused to look at him. The rectangle on the indicator screen was now blue more than three-quarters of the way up.

On an impulse he examined the two monitors on either side of the one they had been watching. Each had a simple on/off switch. He flipped them to the "on" position. That on the right glowed at once with a sectionalized diagram of what must be the nuclear submarine. Dean recognized compartments for the turbines and heat exchangers, gyroscopic controls for the ailerons, governors controlling the dive angle, and what must be an atmospheric-regeneration plant. The cathode tube on the left took longer to warm up. When finally the picture coalesced, it looked to him like a film negative—and then suddenly he realized that it was shot with an infrared camera; he was in fact looking down on the estancia from a point above the tunnel mouth.

Miniature figures hurried to and fro across the pale ground, now provoking and now creating black shell-bursts that blossomed darkly over the infrared snowscape. Clearly, much more clearly than the protagonists, Dean could see Hammer's four sections converging on the bunker guarding the tunnel. The image was momentarily obscured by a rash of somber growths that must, he thought, be the explosion of rocket grenades. Then one of the squads advanced in open order toward the clearing in front of the bunker.

Dean dragged his eyes away from the screen. The rectangle on the big indicator was now glowing blue all over.

He sighed and began a haphazard experimentation with the levers on the cabinet devoted to Section E. Shortly after that the television screen came suddenly to life again. The picture was blurred and grainy, but the sound was fine. Fleischman appeared to be in a confined space: the walls were covered with pipes and dials. *"Just to thank you, Dean, for so conveniently filling the chamber and thus allowing us to leave the fortress by submarine,"* he said suavely. *"You blocked five of the missiles by sealing off the maintenance unit, but fortunately one is already in place aboard the ship. I am speaking from the conning tower, and we are on our way to the far end of the lake to prepare for firing. Buenos Aires, I think. It is not the full-scale effect we planned, but it will be better than nothing. It will show the weaklings who run the world that there are still men with foresight and power— power that they are not afraid to use. And just in case your friends prove stronger than we thought, it is as well—rather than risk failure after so much work—to actuate Phase One even if it is only partly—"*

The screen blacked out, losing both sound and vision in mid-sentence. Simultaneously the monitor showing the submarine diagram went blank. Fragments of glass lying shattered on the floor jingled as the control room trembled beneath their feet. The lights dimmed and then brightened; a long, rumbling roar, felt in the diaphragm rather than heard, shivered and reverberated through the fortress.

After the echoes had died away, Dean realized that there was still a vibration discernible at his diaphragm. Hammer was calling him from the other side of the ridge. He flashed a glance at the infrared monitor. No figures moved across the snowscape now: the foreground was filled with the angular mass of the Volvo artic. This was the final stage of Dean's plan: the truck was to move up, ready to convey the mercs through the tunnel, once the opposition had been silenced. "In the bag, boyo," Hammer's voice rasped from the small transceiver. "Behold, as your man said, I stand at the door and knock. And the quicker you can open the bugger, the better: it's still rainin' like fuck out here!"

Before Dean could voice his satisfaction that Hammer's men had won their tough battle, Coralie called out. "Look!" she cried, excited despite her anger at Dean's action. She pointed at the ground-glass screen in the lid of the cabinet. Somewhere in his idle manipulation of the controls, Dean had hit upon the right circuit.

Across the entrance and exit of the diagram tunnel, bars that had formerly been red now shone bright green.

Dean slumped into a chair and reached for the girl's hand. He raised the transceiver to his mouth and pressed the "Send" button. "Come on in," he said wearily. "The water's fine."

21

"By Jove," Mazzari said, "what a piece of luck that you two left those scuba suits and aqualungs behind the oil drums! If they hadn't been there, we'd have been in Davy Jones's locker for keeps! I thought we were done for anyway when I heard more water come bubbling in from the vent beneath the sub. Then, when it was washing over the quay, we climbed onto the drums ... and there the stuff was."

"I can't figure out why they didn't see you—when they came through the airlock in their own diving gear to board the vessel," said Dean.

"The drums, old chap. The drums again. They'd been filled with concrete to act as ballast—simulating the missile payload, I suppose—and so of course they didn't float. They just sat on the bloody quay and we sat out of sight behind them."

"And you saw our midget ... ?"

"As soon as the Big Bad Wolf pulled out. There she was, parked on the other side of the garage. Very with it, your actual neo-Nazis: a two-ship garage with every family."

"But how come you knew it was time to ... ?"

"Press the button? I guessed the midget might have the usual small HE torpedo underslung, and I knew from what I'd heard that there was dirty work afoot, so I thought it best to get the baddies out of the way. We hopped aboard and tailed them out into the lake. Then it was simply a matter of waiting until they were far enough away not to wreck the fortress when she went up."

"But the missile they were carrying—the nuclear warhead they threatened to launch—*that* didn't explode?" Coralie Willys said.

"Oh, no. It takes a small atom bomb to trigger off a thermonuclear blast; ordinary high explosive isn't hot enough to start the reaction." Mazzari grinned happily. "But she was carrying a fair amount of conventional armament in her magazine—and I happened to be lucky enough to hit it spot-on with our little tinfish. It was quite a big bang!"

They were sitting in the Brasilia airport departure lounge, Dean, Coralie, the big sergeant, Glory Rinaldo, and Hammer. Soon the flight would be called that was to take them to Rio and then New York. In the meantime there were gaps to fill in and confidences to be exchanged. Hammer opened his mailbox mouth and dropped in a stick of spearmint. "Them fellers must of left a skeleton crew aboard that sub," he said. "Else the big brass could never have—"

"But you're right, Sean!" Dean interrupted. "Of course. All the crewmen we saw coming ashore were locked in the commissary." He turned to the girl. "Thank God nobody came up to the conning tower while we were doing our striptease act!"

"Striptease, is it?" Hammer's battered face split open in a smile. "It'd be a con all right if . . ."

The joke was left unfinished. Captain Oliveira, impeccably groomed but looking more tired than ever, was standing over them. He clicked his heels and gave them a languid salute. "Senhor Dean, if you and your party would care to follow me," he began, "I will convey you past Immigration and—"

"Our flight hasn't been called," Coralie objected.

"If you would have the kindness to follow me nevertheless . . ."

Dean got to his feet. "You heard what the man said."

Oliveira led them through a door marked "Private" and then past a row of glass-fronted offices where uniformed officials seemed intent on keeping their backs turned toward the little procession. "There isn't going to be any trouble, is there?" Glory Rinaldo whispered to Mazzari. "I know my passport—"

"Not a chance, duckie. Just relax and leave it to Uncle Olly." Mazzari's face was still swollen from the savage kicking that had rendered him unconscious, but he managed to smile once more. He tucked the girl's hand under his massive arm.

Oliveira led them through another door and down a long passageway. Soon they walked out of the terminal and found themselves on a concrete apron on the far side of the complex from Departures. "What is this? Some kind of VIP treatment?" Coralie asked Dean.

He gave a short bark of laughter. "We should be so lucky! No, honey, it's just the reverse. They want to get rid of us as quickly and unobtrusively as possible."

"But why? You'd think those high-powered politicians who . . . well, who engaged you, would be grateful for what you did. They didn't even come to the airport to . . . I mean, they might at least thank you for—"

"Not on your life. Not in this business. They hired us. We did the job. They paid us. After that, but nobody wants to know you. They never met you. They never heard of you. It was two other guys."

"You mean the whole operation never happened?"

"Right. The BBW bosses went up with the submarine. The authorities will put out a story that Intacon went bankrupt. Some other corporation will take over Getuliana and the dam. Some other board of directors will be handling the kickbacks and the graft, organizing handouts to the officials who okay their government loans."

"Only this time they won't be crazy neo-Nazis as well?"

"Let's just hope not," Dean said.

"Talking of Nazis—what happened to all those men . . . ?"

"In the fortress? The dead will be quietly shoveled away. Once Sean rushed the tunnel with that truckful of mercs, the guys inside didn't offer too much resistance. Most of them were locked away behind watertight doors anyway."

"But what will they do with the . . . the survivors?"

"Good question. They'd be an embarrassment here. They can't very well indict them—not without blowing the whole deal. And there's about a hundred and fifty of them! My guess is, the army boys who took charge of them will wheel them to some remote part of the Paraguayan border, shove them across, and say, 'Don't come back!' "

Oliveira had stopped them fifty yards from a twin-jet Cessna with civilian markings that had apparently been registered in Mexico. A tall, thin figure dropped to the ground from the open cabin door and strode toward them. With astonishment, Dean recognized the flapping jacket, the bladelike nose, the unruly tuft of hair fanned out in the wind that had blown away the storm clouds. "Quinnel!" he exclaimed.

The CIA man nodded, but he spoke directly to Oliveira. "Good of you to cooperate. Obliged."

"It is nothing," the policeman said. "It was felt that perhaps these ladies and gentlemen would feel more comfortable..."

"Right. No need to fuss with Rio, either. This way," he said to Dean, "you fly direct to the United States. Refuel at Miami."

"We're an embarrassment to him too," Dean murmured to the girl. "American nationals, you see. Scared the U.S. could be tied in."

"Handle a Cessna, can't you?" Quinnel demanded, and when Dean nodded, he went on, "Papers in the cabin. Ten minutes to study the flight plan. After that the control tower will give you the green. Cross the coast at the nearest point—get the hell out, right?—then head north. I fixed clearance at Miami."

"Many thanks," Dean said dryly. "Very good of you."

"Pleasure." Quinnel looked swiftly over his shoulder, leaned forward, and said out of the side of his mouth, "Good work."

Dean grinned and turned toward Oliveira. But the police captain was already halfway back to the terminal buildings.

Hammer was still chewing as they sat waiting for Dean to familiarize himself with the ship's papers in their cellophane folders. He sighed, shifting the wad of gum. "So what now?" he asked.

Mazzari chuckled. "In view of past favors received," he said, "one plans to beard a certain West Coast parole officer in his den. Mrs. Rinaldo and I have a date with him to see if her life can't be put in order again. After that, I rather hope we may have a date with each other. What's on your agenda, old man?"

"Och, I think maybe I'll away to the ould country awhile," Hammer replied. "There's a coupla fellers I know back there in Belfast could do with a helping hand."

Dean was suddenly aware that the others were looking at him. "Me?" he said, seeing Samantha's eyes and Samantha's smile beneath Coralie's pale cap of hair. "Oh, I guess maybe I'll team up with . . . with a friend." He raised an eyebrow at her and added, "I figure it's time I did some exploring."

LOOKING FORWARD

The following is the opening section from the next novel in the exciting new Marc Dean MERCENARY series from Signet:

THE DEADLY BIRDMEN

Marc Dean was in bed when the two contact men arrived at his apartment high above the Rue Cavalotti in Paris. The magic-eye burglar alarm flashed its crimson telltale warning seconds before the doorbell shrilled in the hallway. Dean was on his feet, shrugging his lean, tough frame into a short terry-towel bathrobe in a single lithe movement. A washleather holster sewed to the inside of the robe concealed a six-inch Beretta Model 1935 automatic.

At the doorway he turned and held a finger to his lips. The girl in the bed was a redhead he had salvaged from Régine's nightclub in the early hours of the morning when her Swedish airline-pilot escort had passed out cold in the washroom. She still looked good to Dean—much too sleepy to pay doorbells any mind, or notice the fact that his bathrobe sagged at one side where the weight of the gun pulled it out of shape. He tiptoed into the hallway and peered through the spyhole set in the front door.

Two men in gray topcoats, gray fedoras, blue-and-gray-checkered pants, and gray suede shoes. Only their faces were black. They stood well back between the door and the elevator so that they were clearly visible. Dean saw from the indicator that the cage was still at street level—

and no buzzer had sounded from the talk-through grille at the entrance to the building. So they were professionals. But if they had been hit men or regular hoods, they would hardly have signaled their arrival, after a clandestine entry, by pressing his doorbell. He slid back the bars of the three Chubb locks and opened the door.

One of the men had thick lips and the other wore shell glasses, otherwise they were almost indistinguishable—nondescript international travelers, capable of fading into the background at any airport, in the lobby of any Hilton in the Western world. "Colonel Dean?" the man with the shell glasses inquired.

"What do you want? How the hell did you get in?" Dean said. His voice was not friendly.

"We have ways," said Thick Lips. "It is better to be discreet."

"There is a proposition we would like to discuss," his companion added.

Dean sighed. He had not reached the rank of colonel in the U.S. Army; the fact that they had addressed him in this way was a tip-off that they wished to see him in his capacity as organizer and leader of soldiers for hire, as a mercenary. "You'd better come in," he said shortly. He held open the door and jerked his head toward the far side of the tiny hallway.

The apartment was on the top floor of a narrow new block behind the Gaumont cinema in the Place Clichy. Rue Cavalotti twisted away between small-time groceries and delicatessen, a multi-story parking lot and neighborhood liquor stores, yet it was only a couple of blocks from the brawling nightlife center of Pigalle, where the sleazier side of Montmartre offered protective cover to anybody from anywhere among the pimps and whores and gangsters beneath the red neon of porn shops and live sex shows. Dean owned a similar apartment near the central railroad station in Brussels, for these were the two cities where the shadow men who contact and commission mercenaries were most likely to congregate. Nevertheless, although he organized and planned his operations in one or the other of these flats, meetings with his clients customarily took place in restaurants, bars or hotel rooms booked specially for the purpose. In his business it was best to keep the base location a secret, and

Excerpt From THE DEADLY BIRDMEN

he was anxious to find out how these two men had traced him here.

The layout of the apartment was simple: a living room on one side of the hallway, the bedroom on the other, and a kitchenette and bathroom facing the entrance. An additional advantage was that the bathroom window looked out on a complex of mansarded roofs across which an agile man could gain the shelter of the Montmartre cemetery without crossing a street or descending to ground level.

From the living room, a picture window afforded a panoramic view of the city center, down past the church of La Trinité and the huge dome of the opera toward the severe facades of the Louvre and the Palais Royal. Dean's visitors ignored the view. They stared speculatively around the room—wall-to-wall Axminster in sage green, black leather armchairs and divan, a Buffet canvas depicting a Normandy fishing port on the white wall above a liquor cabinet. It was tasteful but anonymous; the only personal touch lay in the selection of books ranged on shelves above a sophisticated stereo deck. Dylan Thomas and T.S. Eliot next to the metaphysical poets, Travis McGee and the 87th Precinct among the Faulkners and Dos Passos and Gertrude Stein. The two men scrutinized the titles carefully. It was as though they were trying to evaluate the worth of their owner against some preconceived standard of values. "The old and the new, Colonel." Thick Lips turned computer eyes toward Dean. "The classical and romantic, the good and the bad." He twisted the lips into a perfunctory smile. "The black and the white."

"How the hell did you know that I lived here?" Dean demanded.

"Our principals are very well informed," the man in shell glasses said. "You were born under the sign of Gemini, if I am not mistaken?"

"So what if I was?"

"June sixth, nineteen and forty-four. A date of some military significance: the biggest seaborne assault in history, the invasion that led to the end of World War II."

"Look," Dean said, "I have better things to do than—"

"Gemini, the twins," Thick Lips interrupted. "The resolution of opposites, a synthesis between opposing polarities. It shows in your selection of books, in the music, and even the view." He pointed at the stereo and then gestured out the window. "Soft Machine and Vivaldi in here; the Eiffel Tower and the Montparnasse skyscraper out there."

Dean's face was darkening angrily. "We wish your help," Shell Glasses said, "in an enterprise in some way analogous to such antitheses. We want to make a synthesis between the old and the new. Which means military suppression of the old."

"Specifically?"

The two men sat down side by side on the divan. They were still wearing their hats. "How well do you know the Caribbean, Colonel?" Thick Lips asked.

Of course, Dean thought. Their voices were accentless mid-Atlantic, but the suede shoes that were a trifle too pointed, the topcoats wrapping a little too tightly around their bodies, the checks a shade too loud should have tipped him off. "As you are so well informed, I guess you must know," he said evenly, "that before a certain Brazilian operation I ran an arms shipment and other merchandise into the island of—"

"Exactly. What we have in mind is in some way similar."

Dean folded his muscular length into one of the armchairs. "I'm listening."

Shell Glasses said: "What do you know of Haiti?"

"Haiti?" Dean's eyebrows rose. "Like it's a dangerous place for a start. The dictator Duvalier—Papa Doc, they called him—ran a reign of terror there for years. Those strongarm thugs of his—Tontons-Macoutes?—had the place sewn up tighter than the Gestapo, the KGB, and Attila the Hun rolled together."

The contact man nodded. "And since Papa Doc died, and his son, Jean-Claude Duvalier, took over, there's been no sign of relaxation. What else do you know, Colonel?"

Dean shrugged. "Coffee. Bananas. Voodoo rituals?"

"An anachronism surviving from the days of slavery, when the island served as a clearing house for black cargoes arriving from Africa. Its influence has been greatly exaggerated. What you may not know is that there exists a rival to Duvalier, who is a little more—shall we say?—libertarian. And that he is already on the island."

"I certainly didn't know." Dean sat up. "And you guys represent. . . ?"

"Let us say"—the voice was silk-smooth—"that certain parties would look favorably upon the establishment of a less fascist regime in Haiti."

"And your rival to Duvalier could use some help, is that it?"

Shell Glasses didn't answer the question directly. "The man in question," he said, "is Cristoforo Martinez, the great-nephew of a Haitian grandee who was exiled to New Orleans early in this century. He has set up something like a revolutionary headquarters in a remote part of the Cordillera Centrale, near the border of the Dominican Republic." The contact man paused. From the street ten floors below came the sound of voices raised in argument, followed by a chorus of blaring horns. Evidently a delivery truck unloading between the double line of parked cars was blocking the narrow roadway again.

Thick Lips took up the story. "Martinez is presently expecting an important paramilitary delegation, landed secretly from a submarine, to visit this mountain stronghold and discuss with him the possibility of undercover aid from the United States."

"Well, bully for him," Dean said. "But if he's up for a helping hand from Uncle Sam. . . ?"

"Why are we talking to you? A good question. But the aid is by no means certain. The situation is delicate. There are many things to be discussed . . . and Duvalier's secret police have gotten wind of the delegation's visit."

"Ah. So now we come to the bad news."

Shell Glasses said: "According to information we have received from Port-au-Prince, they plan to land a fake party, ahead of the genuine negotiators, with orders to—uh—louse up the deal. Since they are unable to contact Martinez any longer, our principals wish to retain your services; they want you to foil this scheme."

Dean smiled. "And just who is it that's unwilling to dirty his own hands? Are you guys acting as front men for the CIA? For one of those Cuban-Haitian refugee associations? Or do you represent some international business syndicate out to make a pile if only they can open up the island? I mean like property developers or people after mining concessions."

"Interested parties, Colonel." Thick Lips smiled in his

Excerpt From THE DEADLY BIRDMEN

turn. "Let us just say interested parties. You would not be required to take part in any military operations mounted against Duvalier by Cristoforo Martinez. Your mission would be strictly preliminary. The proposition is that you should pick a small band of men you can trust, land secretly on the island, link up with Martinez sympathizers and train them to ambush and eliminate the impostors before they can do any damage."

"You want me to train and lead an assassination squad?"

"If you want to put it that way."

Dean favored them with a wintry smile. "Can you think of a better way?"

Shell Glasses coughed. "I should perhaps add that a large sum of money—a very large sum—is available."

"How much?"

"That you will have to discuss with our treasurer. We will take you to him at once. If you are interested."

"Okay," Dean said. "So I'm interested."

"We have a table booked at the Tour d'Argent. Our automobile is waiting nearby."

Dean rose to his feet. "You'll have to give me a few minutes to freshen up and dress. If you'd care for a coffee or a drink while you wait. . . ?"

Thick Lips shook his head. "Thank you. We are used to waiting."

Dean showered and then shaved. Dabbing at a cut on his chin, he studied his reflection in the mirror. Beneath tousled, sandy hair, pouches of dissipation circled the piercing blue eyes, but the lines of his rugged face were taut and alert. There was no trace of sag to the muscles around his jawline, and the mouth was wide and firm. "Fearless Frazer strikes again!" he murmured. He wiped the dried lather from his cheeks, tossed the towel into a linen basket, and strode back into the bedroom.

The girl was crouched on the rumpled sheets manicuring the toenails of her left foot. Through a gap in the curtains the late morning sunlight kindled flames in her red-gold hair. She was still naked.

She raised her head as he closed the door. "Hallo, you," she said. "I thought maybe you'd been drafted or something. What happened?"

Dean brushed a pair of stockings and a torn brassiere from the seat of a chair and sat down. "Something's come up," he said. "I'm real sorry, honey, but I have to split."

"Split?" The redhead was indignant. "But you promised me—"

"I know. I'm sorry, but the guys who just called . . . I have a lunch date. It's important, and it's like business."

"Business? Lunch date?" She was sitting upright now, green eyes flashing, the nipples of her quivering breasts amber in the soft light. "You told me we could spend the whole day—"

"I know, honey. I meant it. But I told you, something's come up and—"

"Don't give me that," the girl interrupted angrily. "If you ask me, you're just making excuses. If you really had a business date, you'd have known about it last night, wouldn't you?"

"Darling, please . . . Trixie . . ."

"Trudi!"

"All right—Trudi. I got this sudden call. You heard the bell. They couldn't reach me before. Honest."

"How convenient!" She had rolled over on to her face and was clasping the pillow. "After all that big talk! If you want to know what I think . . ."

"I don't."

". . . I think all this is just a getout."

"Just what do you mean by that?" Dean asked quietly.

"Why do I always end up with the loudmouths who can't make good their little-boy boasts?" Trudi complained to the pillow.

"I said what do you mean by that?"

She tossed her hair and looked at him over her shoulder. "I mean all this about something coming up. If you ask me, something *won't* come up, and that's the truth."

Dean eyed the curve of her ass. The sunlight was burnishing the triangle of down at the base of her spine, shadowing the blue veins beneath the creases of flesh. "Go on," he said.

The girl smiled. " 'I'll give you a wonderful time,' " she quoted scornfully. " 'I want to fuck you all night and all day tomorrow' . . . and then he passes out after the first time and can't make it at all the next morning!"

"Fighting words," said Dean.

"I'm a fighting girl." She reached out one hand and

Excerpt From THE DEADLY BIRDMEN

tweaked the edges of his bathrobe apart. *"Oh!"* she said. "I didn't. . . !"

Dean was on his feet. "You move one inch from that bed and I'll destroy you!" he said.

He stalked to the door, jerked it open, and called across the hallway: "Gentlemen—I'll have to keep you waiting a little longer. There's a couple of things I have to attend to before I'm ready. I'll be with you in fifteen minutes."

She was lying on her back among the pillows now, with her arms above her head. "That's my boy!" she said.